ACCLAIM FOR JACK DRISCOLL

The stories "provide a privileged glimpse into the male heart confronted with loss. These are men grappling with a world whose cruelties have cornered them. And Ultimately Jack Driscoll's poetic language give them a stature that makes their struggle meaningful, tragic, and universal."
—*The New York Times Book Review*

"Driscoll's stories are elegant, chilly, and understated. His people, of course, want more than to be heard; they want to be with someone, they want their lives to mean something, they want to be warm."
—(London) *Times Literary Supplement*

"An impressive, gritty northern Michigan version of Andre Dubus"
—*Kirkus Reviews*

"I once believed, with good reason, that after reading Norman Maclean's *A River Runs Through It*, I'd never read anything that equaled its quiet power, its clear, classic, soft-spoken prose, as bracing as ice water. But now I've read *Wanting Only To Be Heard*, and now I feel differently. I read Jack Driscoll saying to myself, Yes! That's how it's done, that's how you tell a story, that's how you do it so we'll never forget these people and their voices and this place."
—Bob Shacochis

"Driscoll's frozen landscape is at once chilling and intoxicating, at once frighteningly sterile and alarmingly seductive. His characters are brave and honest and heartbreakingly bent on survival against all physical and emotional odds. This book is an act of courage and generosity from a wildly talented man."
—Pam Houston

"The Roman poet Horace once wrote, 'The art is to hide the art,' and Driscoll seamlessly manages to take the reader within his tales so that we are part of people's lives and not just fictional characters actions."
—*Shenandoah*

"Driscoll has written the Great American Fertility Novel . . . a miraculous accomplishment." —*San Francisco Chronicle*

"You'll savor every word as Driscoll sings the sad, sweet songs of rural America. These songs believe in heartaches and miracles. These miracles look up at the stars and see humanity in the constellations."
—Bonnie Jo Campbell

"A new book by Jack Driscoll is a cause for celebration. *The Goat Fish And The Lover's Knot* reminds me—not that I'd forgotten—exactly why Driscoll has long been one of my favorite American writers. The qualities that have made his work indelible—his deeply intimate relationship with the natural world, the natural lyricism, and the palpability of his language, the authentic way in which his always credible narratives earn their mystery—are here in abundance in this beautiful collection."
—Stuart Dybek

"Reading Jack Driscoll's *The World Of A Few Minutes Ago* feels like a trip through a museum of portraits, each story a finely observed and carefully rendered life as distilled in a telling moment. This writer knows not only what makes people tick but how to turn the reader's eye to the most salient and stirring instant of recognition." —Antonya Nelson

"Jack Driscoll's insight into 'the complex repertoire of human grief' and his empathy for characters confronted with 'the debris of human misery' is singular. We encounter many of his characters—skittish and sometimes feeling forsaken—looking back over the trail of their lives and trying to plan a workable future in the wake of some kind of bad accident. Strung out as they are between desire and despair, they have in Driscoll their deft and savvy guardian." —Barry Lopez

"The writer in me delights in the stylistic innovation of this collection. But the reader in me is moved by the book's moral ambiguity, gritty drama, and startling humor. I wouldn't be surprised if *The World Of A Few Minutes Ago* were nominated for a National Book Award. Driscoll deserves nothing less. He is a master of the short story . . ."
—*The Nervous Breakdown*

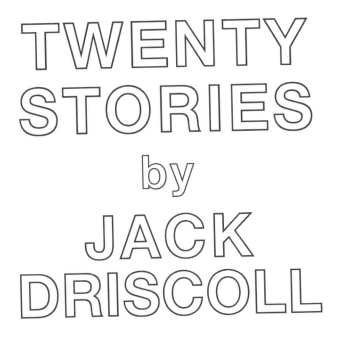

TWENTY STORIES by JACK DRISCOLL

NEW AND SELECTED

ISBN 979-8-9854697-1-4

Cover designed by Mary Kornblum

Published by Pushcart Press
P.O. Box 380
Wainscott, NY 11975

Distributed by W.W. Norton & Company, Inc
500 Fifth Avenue
New York, NY 10110

For Lois,
From first story to last.

There are days we live
as if death were nowhere
in the background; from joy
to joy to joy, from wing to wing,
from blossom to blossom to
impossible blossom, to sweet impossible blossom.

—Li Young Lee

And
For Cate, Amelia, John, and Robert Hotchkiss.

CONTENTS

ACKNOWLEDGMENTS

These stories, sometimes in a slightly different form, appeared in the following publications:

"The Season of Families" in *Epoch;* "Wanting Only to be Heard," "Prowlers," "The Goat Fish and the Lover's Knot," "All the Time in the World," "A Woman Gone Missing," "On This Day You are All Your Ages," "That Story," "At Any Given Time," and "Gracie and Devere" in *The Georgia Review*; "St. Ours," and "After Everyone Else Has Left" in *Idaho Review*; "Squalls" in *Mid-American Review*; "Death Parts" in *Missouri Review*; "Pigs and Lobsters" in *Pennsylvania Review*; "The New World Merging" in *River Styx*; "From Here to There," "Wonder," and "The World of a Few Minutes Ago" in *Southern Review*.

"Prowlers" was reprinted in the 2009 *Pushcart Prize Anthology*.

"That Story" was reprinted in the 2012 *Pushcart Prize Anthology*.

"All the Time in the World" was reprinted in the 2015 *New Stories from the Midwest*.

"Wanting Only to be Heard," "Wonder," and "On This Day You are All Your Ages," were named *Distinguished Stories—Best American Short Stories*.

My deep and abiding gratitude to those friends, editors, and fellow writers whose unwavering support and feedback over the years has made all the difference in the creation of these stories: Nick Bozanic, Mike Delp, Stephen Dunn, William Meissner, and Bonnie Jo Campbell.

Pete Fromm and Rich Chiappone. Doug Stanton, Chris Dombrowski, Claire Davis, Cate Kennedy, and Sheryl Johnston.

Shelley Washburn, director extraordinaire, and my Pacific University colleagues, as well as those from my three plus decades of teaching at Interlochen Center for the Arts.

A loud shout-out to Stephen Corey for his eagle-eyed editorial brilliance, and which dates back to 1987 when he first published a story of mine.

To Annie Martin and staff at Wayne State University Press.

And finally, to all my students, present and former: "I have nothing but affection for those who sailed with me."

—Bob Dylan

FROM

FROM
WANTING ONLY TO BE HEARD

WANTING ONLY TO BE HEARD

Ashelby Judge was an odd name for a kid growing up in northern Michigan, so we just called him by his last name, Judge. Everyone did. In a way he always was holding court, pronouncing sentence: Kevin Moriarty was a first-class cockroach, Jake Reardon a homo from the word "go." He had once called me a dicksqueeze, but later he took it back, gladly, he said, having indicted me prematurely. I was okay, he said, I really was, that being the final verdict.

Judge was not easy sometimes, but I liked him. I liked his impatience with boredom and the way he gathered all the pertinent information in the end, the evidence to prove or discredit a story. He always proceeded step-by-step, building an airtight case for whatever he was defending or attacking, whatever he was attempting to pin down. It wouldn't have surprised me, forty years later, to read he'd been appointed to the Supreme Court. Judge Ashelby Judge. Or, for the sake of a joke, Judge Judge. I liked famous names that repeated or almost did, names like Robin Roberts or Ricky Ricardo, or even slant combos like Jack Johnson. The duplication had a friendly ring, a sense of conviction and rectitude, the feeling that they really knew who they were and liked it and would never entirely grow up, grow old.

It was a Friday night, no wind for a change, and we were fishing smelt, three of us inside my father's shanty, when Judge told me and Timmy Murphy about the claustrophobic Irish setter who, after being locked all afternoon in a fishing hut on Torch Lake, jumped right through the spearing hole just after dark and, ten or twelve feet under the ice, swam toward the faint, opalescent glow of another shanty almost fifty yards away (someone later measured it) and came bursting up there from the muck like some monster awakened, the water swelling, convulsing up over the wooden floor. That one simile, "like some monster," was the only embellishment, Judge's single artistic touch.

He was not a natural storyteller who tested his listeners by saying, "imagine this," or "pretend that," or "just think if," and on and on, suspending their willingness to imprint the local tales into myth. He despised the "what then, what next" demands made on every story. Which was exactly what Timmy was doing, all excited and ahead of himself as usual: "What'd the guy do? Holy shit, I bet he croaked right there. I can't believe it, a dog under the ice. That's great!"

Judge, calculatedly slow and flat, said the guy was plenty scared, who wouldn't be, but not berserk scared the way you might expect. "He was old," Judge said—a simple observation of fact, like what day it was or how cold. He never speculated that age buffered the body's reaction to shock or trauma, but I translated it that way anyhow, without thinking.

"Who cares?" Timmy asked. "Twenty, fifty-seven, a hundred-and-two years old. It doesn't matter."

But it did, the way it mattered that the dog was an Irish setter and male and was abandoned by his owner who loved him but hadn't gotten any fish, and instead of a quick trip to the 7-Eleven for a six-pack of Stroh's, he drank away the afternoon, alone in a bar that said just that in red neon, *BAR*, just outside Bellaire, forgetting the dog, and playing, over and over on the free juke box, Patsy Cline's "Walking After Midnight." Which was about the time he left the bar, broke and drunk, and halfway home remembered the dog and right there, on 137, opened his window full for the few seconds it took him to slow down and power slide into the other lane, the pickup fishtailing back up the gradual incline beneath the stars, the hook of the moon. And it mattered that he honked his horn a couple of times from the lake's edge, his shanty invisible somewhere beyond the white perimeter of his high beams. That was the real story, that sadness, and the way the guy, on both knees, fiddled with the combination lock until his fingers went numb, the whole time talking to the dog who wasn't even there. When he finally opened the door and lit the lantern, the white flame hissing in the mantle, he stepped back outside and screamed the dog's name a single time across the emptiness.

Judge said you could measure a story by its private disclosures, by how far a person came forward to confess a part of himself, asking forgiveness. The dramatics meant nothing, those exaggerations that served only to engage our obvious and temporary fascinations. And he continued, refining the art of meticulous detachment from such a rare and bizarre event by saying he didn't care what the Irish setter looked like emerging—a giant muskie or sturgeon or a red freshwater seal. "The fact is," he repeated, "it was a hundred-pound dog. That's it, cut and dried!"

I thought maybe the "cut and dried" part was a pun, and I smiled until Timmy, really miffed, said, "You take away all the magic. You make everything too real, too damn ordinary."

But Timmy was at least partly wrong. There *was* something principled about facts, something stark and real that required nothing but themselves to survive. Maybe that's why I liked "Dragnet" so much, the claim that it was a true story, and that the sentence handed down after the last TV commercial was really being served. I thought of that while leaving the shanty to pee and to check the tip-ups set for browns behind us in the dark. My father let me and my buddies use the shanty on weeknights while he worked at the Fisk. Usually he'd drop us off at the state park and we'd take turns dragging the sled with the minnow bucket and spud and the gallon can of stove gas straight toward the village of fifty or sixty tiny structures in a cluster set over the deep water. It was easy to find my father's shanty because it was separated a little ways from the others, and because of the spoked hubcap from a Cadillac Eldorado he'd nailed to the door. His house sign, he called it. Other guys had other things, and it was fun to traipse around at night out there, just looking around, the world glaciated, frozen so tight you could feel your breath clinging to the fine hairs on your face.

The name of each owner and town he was from was painted on every shanty—that was the law—some from as far south as Clare, though those were the ones that were not used very much. Sometimes as you passed you could hear talking from inside, or good laughter, or country music on the radio, and when you returned to the heat of your own hut, maybe you'd be humming a certain song, surprised by how happy you were, how peaceful, knowing that you belonged. I figured that was why my father decided to fish again after all these years, why he spent most of every weekend out here, calm and without worries.

That wasn't the feeling, however, when I stepped back inside and Judge and Timmy were both just staring into the rectangular hole, staring at the blue rubber-band bobbers and saying nothing. The smelt pail was still empty and half the minnows in the other bucket had turned belly up. My father would have said no big deal, that smelt would go for the dead bait just as good if they were feeding, but either Judge or

Timmy, having already given up, had entered a big 0, a goose egg, in the calendar square for February 12th. On good nights you loaded up fast, constant action, and on the homemade speed reels you could bring in two or three smelt at a time, every few minutes without a break. Just three nights earlier my father had recorded 268, and that was by himself. That's how it happened, streaky and unpredictable, and you simply had to like being out there, maybe sharing a Pall Mall around or talking girls if that's what mystery happened to be biting. But on this night of the Irish setter story, everything had gone closemouthed.

"No flags," I said, latching the door and hanging the gaff on a hook above the stove. This was Judge's first time ice fishing, and I knew he was bored—knew it even better when he said to Timmy, "Why not?" Responding to whether a person (forget the dog) could survive the 33 degree water long enough to swim from this shanty to the one closest by, the one that said M. KULANDA, KALKASKA, MI, the largest one on the ice. I'd never seen anybody there, not once.

"Houdini stayed under twenty minutes," Judge said, "under the Detroit River. No wetsuit. Nothing but a pair of pants."

"What was he doing there? A trick?" Timmy asked.

"An escape," Judge corrected, and although Timmy argued, "Trick, escape, whatever he did . . ." I understood the difference, the dangerous mishandling of a single word so that a story softened, collapsed like a fragile set of lungs.

"Houdini said later he sucked the air pockets, bubbles trapped between the water and ice, and with the current, followed his dead mother's voice until he emerged, a quarter mile downriver." Judge was still staring into the thick, dark water while he talked, until Timmy, excited, just like at first with the Irish setter story, said, "You're shitting me!" Judge, looking up finally, straight-faced and serious, said, "I shit you not," as if under oath, and they both went silent as if the naked truth of Houdini and the Irish setter were tempting them to find out.

It started simple as that, and next thing I knew we were pacing off the distance between the shanties. About thirty yards. I had once stayed underwater in the bathtub for as long as I could, just sliding back and holding my nose. I counted a minute and forty-four seconds, long seconds—one, one thousand, two, one thousand, three, the facecloth kind of floating back and forth across my stomach. And sneaking into the Camp Ketch-A-Tonk swim-grounds one night last summer, I breast stroked real close to the sandy bottom, from the Great Raft all the way up to shore. My father did it too, swimming behind me, and without coming up for air he turned and swam half-way back. I was scared, the way you get when someone's been down a long time, maybe just monkeying around, but scaring you just the same. I remembered whispering, "Come up, please come up, " and he did, beyond the blue lifeline, gracefully rolling onto his back in a single motion and kicking, eyes closed I imagined, straight out toward whatever secret had surfaced in his memory. That's how it is with the mind, always buoyant, bobbing up and down on the complex sea of recollection.

Judge knocked on Kulanda's door, but nobody was there. "Nobody has been," Timmy said, trying to take charge. "Look around. No footprints anywhere."

And I noticed there were no bloodstains from trout or pike tossed into the snow, no frozen minnows. Nothing. The shanty was unlocked, a lousy idea my father always lectured, every time he'd see a door blown open, slapping backwards hard against its hinges. He said that only invited trouble, people snooping around, poking their heads in where they didn't belong, which was exactly what we were doing and I didn't like it and said, "Come on you guys, let's go. Let's get out of here."

But when Timmy stepped inside with the lantern, the hut was nearly empty, unused, the kind that just got left sitting there until the ice softened toward spring, and one morning it would be gone forever. Who knows, maybe the owner died or got sick or one Sunday started watching the Pistons on TV with his son-in-law and thought *screw the fishing* and that was that for the whole season.

Timmy said, "The guy's got a couch in here," and when he sat down he was staring at a calendar hanging on the opposite wall. It was the kind of calendar I first saw in a gas station in Germfask when my father's station wagon broke down. We were there a good part of the afternoon while the garage owner phoned around until he finally located a water pump at a junkyard in Greighton. The owner's kid drove over to pick it up, and while our fathers small talked engines and horsepower and cubic inches, I snuck into the men's room three or four times to examine, close-up, this woman who was showing me everything, her lips parted just enough to show the pink edge of her tongue. The last time I stepped out my father was waiting by the door and he told me, "Pee out back. I don't want you in there anymore." And that was the feeling I had again in Kulanda's abandoned shanty, of wanting to be there and not, both at the same time. Timmy lowered the lantern to the ice, right under the calendar where the fishing hole should have been, really lighting up the glossy nude, and he said, acting the big shot for this lucky find, "I'd swim anywhere if I could surface between legs like that!"

But it was Judge who decided to really do it, and when my father dropped us off again the next night, we brought, along with the fishing gear, a book on Houdini and a *National Geographic* that showed people in swimsuits running toward the Atlantic Ocean from a snowy beach, in Rhode Island, I think. And Judge talked on and on about some Mr. Maslowski who chipped a large round hole in the ice of his man-made pond, and letting the same red towel drop behind him, he'd hold his hands flat to the sides of his thighs, and each morning, without hesitation, he'd step right through over his head. "For his rheumatism," Judge said. "He worshiped what he called 'certitude,' the ancient and natural cure taking place under the world."

Judge had done his homework, covering the Polar Bear Club and U.S. Navy ice divers, the whole time spouting off dates and temperatures and distances, building his case until I believed there was hardly any danger after the initial shock of entering, and he said, staring at me, "You'll be my key witness." And to Timmy, "Who knows what you'll see."

Of course we wanted to see everything: the entry, the look of his eyes behind the mask the instant he surfaced in Kulanda's shanty. But most of all we wanted desperately to watch him moving under the ice, so later that week Judge waterproofed a flashlight with candle wax and electrician's tape, and tested it by lowering the light about twenty feet under the ice. Then Timmy turned off the Coleman lantern and we just stared, all three of us in complete darkness, at that dim glimmer wavering back and forth below us, slow motion, soporific.

Judge was the first to speak, his unquestionable right now, presiding and authoritative, factitious as always, but Timmy was making no objections anymore. Judge said, "It works," and we just nodded, accomplices who had learned to listen closely, to rehearse every detail at night in our dreams. "We'll fasten the light to my back," Judge said, "and you guys can walk right above me."

Although we didn't actually fish anymore that week, we'd make up numbers and jot them down each night on my father's calendar, keeping the records current: 114, 226, and—a slow night, Timmy's entry—27. "Just to keep things honest," he said, and we laughed, sitting and clowning around and smoking Pall Malls in what now seemed more like a fort, a refuge—not from the gusting wind, but from the predictable, ordinary things we might have done late after school, like playing Ping-Pong in Timmy's basement, or being home alone tinkering with science projects, or making up a story for English—something sensational and dangerous and totally unbelievable. And whenever my father asked about the fishing I'd tell him Judge and Timmy were splitting up the smelt, taking them home. "Good," he said, as though it were the proper courtesy, the way to make and keep good friends.

If Judge had moments of panic, he never let on, not even on the night of his dive, the Saturday my father decided to work OT. He dropped us at the state park as usual and asked, "You got a ride back?" and Timmy said, "Yep, my father's picking us up," which was true, but he was coming later than usual. He wouldn't be here until eleven. I don't know why we wanted the extra time, I really don't. Maybe to change our minds, or to deny, as Judge would have been the first to point out, that redemption had anything to do with danger, with the spectacular moments in a life.

But that didn't happen. We felt transformed, faithful to the careful preparation of an entire week, and when we started across the ice toward the village, we believed those two shanties were ours, and ours to swim between if we wanted, the way you might swim deep under a cliff in order to come up in a secret cave. After the first time, it would be easy.

We felt all set, having already stashed an extra heater and lantern, an army blanket, and towels in Kulanda's, and we'd hung a thermometer on the same nail that held what Judge was calling Timmy's porno queen, but I'd seen him peeking from the couch at those hard nipples, too, or at the red mercury rising slowly between her breasts after we'd fired the heater up. Chips of ice were bouncing off her paper flesh as Timmy started to spud the hole, Judge's exit, and Judge and I left him there and headed for the other hut. But Judge stopped halfway and said, "No hurry," and we stood there, watching the lights of houses blink on the far side of the lake. I felt calm as the lights vanished and appeared again, floating, I thought, behind a cold vapor of darkness. And I could hear Timmy in Kulanda's shanty, a strange thud, thud, as though coming from a great distance, and already we'd begun walking even farther away.

By the time Timmy got to my father's hut he was breathing heavily, but he laughed real hard at Judge just sitting there in his white boxers, the flashlight already taped to his back like a dorsal fin.

"All you need now are scales," Timmy said, taking off his gloves and coat, and Judge, reaching into his knapsack, said, "This will have to do," and pulled out a tub of ball bearing grease and said, "Cover me real good," scooping the first brown gob himself with his fingers and sculpting it up and down one arm. Then he stood there, arms out, and me and Timmy did the rest, each a skinny side, and Judge, still joking around said, "Save a little for my dick," and Timmy said back, "A little is all you'll need," as I knelt and reached my greasy hand into the freezing water to see if this translucent coating really helped, and for that second I was terrified of falling in, the rectangular hole seeming so much like a grave, calm and so carefully ladled out. And without them seeing me, I crossed myself, as my father had taught me to do every, every time before entering strange water.

When I stood up, Timmy, having taken charge of things in Kulanda's shanty, had left again, and Judge was wiping his hands clean on a rag. Then he knotted the white clothesline around his waist—knotted it a couple of times, nothing fancy, but I knew by the way he tugged it wasn't coming free. Still, I wanted something thicker, stronger, a new length of rope, a boat line maybe. Judge said he just needed something to follow back if he got lost or in trouble. It didn't need to be strong. The other end was already tied off around the single roof brace, the rest of the clothesline coiled in wide loops on the floor. Nobody needed to be there to watch or feed it out. It would uncoil smoothly, trailing behind him like a long umbilical cord. Judge, the literalist, would have hated the metaphor, as he would have hated me telling him he looked a little like the creature in *The Creature from the Black Lagoon*, standing there. But he did, primordial and weedy-green in the bright light of the lantern, breathing hard now, and hyperventilating for whatever extra oxygen he could squeeze into his lungs.

I thought there would be some talk, a final go-over of the details, maybe even a last-minute pardon from this craziness if my father would unexpectedly burst in. But it was Timmy, back again and out of breath, who said, "All set," and Judge simply reached back without hesitation, snapped on the flashlight, then pushed the mask with both hands to his face for better suction and stepped under. I wasn't even sure it happened—he disappeared that fast, without a single word or even a human splash, as though all that body grease had dissolved his bones, his skull, the entire weight of him so that only a ghost drifted under the ice, a vague iridescence.

When we got outside Judge was moving in the right direction. All winter the winds had blown the snow from the ice, so we could see the blurry light down there, and Timmy had one of his own which he kept blinking on and off to let Judge know we were there, right above him, ready to guide him home. The moon was up too, and suddenly the distance to Kulanda's shanty did not seem so far, not with Judge already

24

halfway there and Timmy, all wound up and hooting, "He's got it made, he's got it now!"

It was right then that Judge's light conked out, and we both stopped, as if Judge would surface there. Neither of us wanted to move, afraid, I think, that we would step on him in the dark and send him deeper, and when we started running for Kulanda's, I circled wide, way behind where Judge would be, hoping he wouldn't hear the slapping panic of our boots, the fear inside us struggling desperately to break free.

Timmy pumped and pumped the lantern until I thought the glass globe would explode. Then he held it just inches above the black water, and he seemed to be staring at the nude, staring all the way through her as if counting each vertebra, the soft curves of her back, and I knew Judge was not coming up. I didn't have to tell Timmy to stay. He was crying now. He was all done, and I think if Judge had surfaced right then, Timmy would have just dropped the lantern and walked away and would never have spoken of this again.

I slipped and fell hard, almost knocking myself out, and in that moment of dizziness, face down on the ice, I imagined Judge staring back, just ten inches away, his black hair wavering in the moonlight, his eyes wide-open behind his mask. And I imagined him pointing and pointing and I got up and ran, sweating now, into my father's shanty. I believed the rope twitched or pulsed when I picked it up, something like a nibble, but when I yanked back there was nothing there, just the loose arc of slack, and I remembered my father always shouting from the stern of the boat, "Reel hard, keep reeling," when I thought I'd lost a big one, and this time the weight was there, solid and unforgiving. It was the same heavy feeling of a snag that begins to move just when you're sure it will bust your line, and I knew that bulk dragged backwards was enough to snap any line with a nick or fray, and to hurry was to lose it all.

I kept it coming, hand over hand, Judge's body drifting sideways, then back again, always rising slowly from the deep water. I shouted for Timmy four or five times, tilting my head backwards and toward the door, but he did not come. And it was during one of those shouts that the flashlight on Judge's back appeared in the center of the hole, then the whole back hunched in a deadman's float. I could not get him up, my arms weak and shaking, and I hauled back one last time and dropped the rope and grabbed, all in the same motion, his thick hair with both my hands, his face finally lifting out of the water.

His mask was gone and I just held him like that for a long time, one arm under his chin, the lantern dimming. I was stretched on my belly, our cheeks touching, and I had never felt anything so cold, so silent. I knew mouth-to-mouth resuscitation would do Judge no good in this position, his lungs full of water, so maybe I was really kissing him, not trying to reclaim a heartbeat, but rather to confess, as Judge said, a part of myself, and to ask forgiveness. I did not know how long I could hold him there, though I promised over and over I would never let him slide back to that bottom, alone among those tentacles of weeds. I closed my eyes, and in what must have been a kind of shock or sleep, I drifted into a strange current of emptiness, a white vaporous light, the absolute and lovely beginning of nothing.

I did not see the two ice fishermen hoist Judge from the hole, and I did not remember being carried to Kulanda's shanty or being wrapped in the army blanket on the couch. I awakened alone there, still dizzy but very warm. I was wearing Judge's sweatshirt, the one we had waiting for him for when he came up. I did not take it off or even move very much, and I could hear my father's voice just outside the door, though it sounded distant, too, and dull, the blunt echo of a voice approaching. I thought if he entered, the flood of his words would drown me for good. But only silence followed him in. I did not look up and I did not cry when he touched my head, or when he turned away to face the wall. There would be no sermonizing, no interrogation from him or from anyone else. Not that night anyway.

And I noticed eye-level across from me, that the nude was gone, removed like evidence we didn't want found. The cigarette butts on the floor had disappeared too. And it sounded strange to hear someone knock on the door. My father did not say, "Come in," but a man did, an ambulance driver, and he bent down on one knee and said, "How do you feel now?" I didn't know, but I said, "Good," and I wanted to stay there, maybe all night, making sure the hole did not freeze over.

Next morning, as we walked together toward the shanties, my father said, "Tell them everything exactly like it happened. There's only one story." What he meant was that the options narrowed and narrowed when the ending was already known. "They won't keep us long," he said. "We'll get back home." I thought he might add, "For the Pistons-Celtics game," but he didn't.

It was Sunday morning and sunny, and up ahead, off to the left, I saw a red flag go up from the ice, then someone running toward the tip-up, shaking his gloves off. I watched him set the hook and after a few seconds, with his left hand, move the gaff a little bit away from the hole. "Probably a pike," my father said, and I was glad he did, so natural, and without the conviction of disguise.

There were not all that many people gathered at the shanties, not the way I thought it would be with a lot of photographers and sheriff's department deputies. Timmy was already there. I could see his green hat and his arms flailing like an exhausted swimmer, and for that split second I imagined he was yelling, "Help, help me," and I started to run, not toward him, but the other way, back toward the car. My father caught me from behind, caught me first by the collar, then wrapped both his arms around me and turned me back slowly to face Timmy and whatever version he was carving of the story. My father just held me there and released the pressure gradually and then, after a couple minutes, let me go.

His shanty had been moved back and two divers were adjusting their masks at the side of the hole. I did not know what they were searching for, what more they could possibly find. But they jumped through, one after the other as Judge had, but with black wetsuits and yellow tanks and searchlights sealed with more than candle wax and electrician's tape. The sheriff met us and shook my hand and my father's hand and said Judge's parents were not there and wouldn't be. Then he said, "We've called Marv Kulanda," as though he knew him personally. "He's on his way."

I was okay after that. They kept me and Timmy separated, though we caught each other's eye a couple times. The two fishermen who had pulled Judge out kept nodding a lot, and once they pointed at me, both of them did, then shrugged, and they finally left, to fish and talk, I guess, since they walked that way into the village of shanties. I knew the stories wouldn't be the same, but not the same in a way that didn't matter to the law.

The sheriff asked me about approximate times: how long before Timmy ran for help, how long I held Judge partially out of the water—all questions I couldn't answer, and that seemed to be all right. But before he let me go he said, "Whose idea was this?" It was the first time he spoke without detachment, accusatory now, and I did not deny that it was me though it wasn't, and my father the whole time shaking his head, shaking it back and forth, no, no, insisting that could never be.

Before the first diver was helped out of the hole, he tossed Judge's mask a few feet onto the ice, and then, behind it—crumpled into a pulpy ball—what I knew was the calendar nude. I didn't know why that frightened me so much, except that it was a detail I had consciously left out, perhaps to protect Timmy's secret need to destroy the crime of her nakedness, one of the reasons we stayed there and smoked cigarettes and talked big in front of her, already outlining the plans of our story. When the sheriff unwadded the nude she fell apart, and he just shook the wet pieces from his hands. In his investigation for details, she meant nothing—a piece of newspaper, a bag, anything that might have floated up.

We left and my father said, "It's over," and I knew he'd protect me from whatever came next. Behind us I could hear them nailing my father's shanty closed, and I could see, angling beyond us from the shore, a single man, half stepping and half sliding across the ice. I knew that it was Kulanda, who should have locked his hut, and who was wishing at that very moment that we had broken in. And beyond him, running between the avenues of shanties, a single dog, tall and thin and red like an Irish setter. But maybe not. Maybe he was something else, barking like that, wanting only to be heard.

FROM HERE TO THERE

Nelson Pelky said to my father, "Personally, I don't give a rat's ass. If it were up to me, I'd deliver the mail." But it wasn't, so he passed our house and waved to my father, who was watching out the kitchen window and did not wave back.

The town was growing, and Luis Darby was replaced by a new postmaster from downstate who announced that his carriers would abide by U.S. Postal regulations or be fired, rural route delivery included. At first my father said, "Screw that noise." He'd lived at this same address for over twenty years, and Nelson Pelky knew him well, and he knew me, too, and my mother, who had recently left us, but he said it meant his job, and if he couldn't see the numbers marked clearly on the box or on the house or on the garage, then he couldn't leave the mail. "I know, I know, goddamn it," Nelson had said when my father argued common sense. "I know all that, Tommy, and I'm on your side, but I can't stop here."

I was eating lunch, and my father saw me peeking at him and he stood suddenly, and, with his back to me, he said, "Finish up and come on outside and help me," and he put his coffee mug on the table and lit a cigarette and nodded to me to make sure I'd heard him, and I said, "Yes." I said, "I'm all done," and I wiped my mouth and got up and put my dish and glass in the sink and followed him down the back stairs and out into the garage. That's where he stored the paint, the gallon cans dusty and dented, and you could tell the different colors by what had dripped across the labels.

"Here," he said, and handed me a can of bright red. Then he picked up a brush that was very stiff, and bent the bristles back and forth until

29

they softened some, and then he turned the brush handle down and slid it into his back pocket. "Stirrer," he said, and reached for one higher up, but it was stuck to the wooden shelf. I started to shake the can but he said, "No, don't do that," as though the cover might fly off. But it wouldn't have. It took him going almost all the way around the lid with a screwdriver, and when the lid did come off, there was this skin he had to puncture, a rubbery red skin, but the paint underneath was fine, and I liked the smell.

Mostly my father didn't give two hoots about the mail, but he was waiting now for a letter from my mother, so he gave in and painted those numbers, 335, across the two white doors. It took him a good half hour, and when he stood back I joked, "A blind man could see those from the road."

"From Lansing," he said, but I didn't get what he meant and I said, "That's a long way," and he just walked off after turning and heaving the empty can across the dirt road and into the ditch. I moved up closer to the numbers, and they were much taller than me, and I was tall for twelve years old.

"Yeah," I yelled, "for sure they'll see these in Lansing," but my father let it drop, saying nothing. Then I heard him say, "Bastards," as he dabbed the metal flag on the mailbox with what little paint he had left on his brush. He left the flag up so it would dry by the time Nelson Pelky stopped the next morning, which he did, but only to ease the flag down. I could tell it was still sticky by the way he rubbed his thumb and fingers together. He waved to me, sitting on the porch stairs, and I yelled, "Hi Mr. Pelky," and after he drove off my father stepped outside and touched my head, and I looked up at him and said, "No mail."

"You sure?" he said, and I said, "Maybe tomorrow," but I knew what he was waiting for wouldn't arrive, not this time, most likely not ever. My mother didn't want him finding her, which is why she left so late at night the way she did, my father working the graveyard shift at the sheet metal plant. She sat on the edge of my bed for a long time, explaining nothing but saying over and over how she loved me very much, and that someday I'd understand. Then she kissed me and rubbed my back real gently and I didn't cry, not right then I didn't. And she said for me not to let anyone in except my father, and she locked the door behind her when a car drove into the driveway, killing its lights. "I'll be back for you," she shouted from outside. "I promise I'll be back." And then I heard her say, "Oh, God," and then the trunk slam, and then the two car doors, and she was gone.

That happened over three weeks ago, and I missed her something terrible, but I was awful mad at her, too. My father had lots of sick days coming, and he started taking them, plus his vacation time so he had over a month to stay home, and he spent most of it near the phone, which almost never rang. Once a wrong number, and once my Grandpa Eby called, and all that my father said was, "Lynette's not here. No." He said "no" again, and a third time, and then he hung up. When it rang a few seconds later, he didn't answer it.

And Nelson Pelky left only bills, which went unpaid. And my father started drinking more, and he didn't shave often or go to the laundromat. All the towels were dirty, and it got so I'd have to dry off with a T-shirt after getting out of the shower. When his good friend Paul Tremblay stopped by late one night he told my father, "You look like shit."

"Get out," my father said. "Get the hell out, unless you know where she is."

"I don't," Paul said, "nobody in town does," and he said he didn't know who the guy was either. Then he said, "Listen to me, Tommy, I'm no goddamn private eye," and my father grabbed him by the shirtfront and backed him hard against the refrigerator, my father's elbow wedged under Paul's chin, all this right in front of me, and I shouted, "Stop, stop it," and this time I *was* crying, bawling my eyes out, and I sat down on the floor in the corner of the kitchen, my face in my hands, and when I looked up a few minutes later my father was crying, too, and Paul was gone. My father tried to talk, but he could not. Then finally he said, "She'll write to us, and we'll go pick her up, wherever she is. She'll come home."

But I knew if she did, it wouldn't be to stay. She'd left before, I don't know how many times, but always for only one day and always to the Cottage Motel. My father even learned to joke about it, saying, "Your mother's at the Cottage," like it was a vacation spot or something, like she'd gone off to the lake or the mountains for a rest. But the motel was just down Route 28, right outside of town, and it was cheap and real dingy. Paul Tremblay once told me, "A woman who issues a man his walking papers don't just go to the Cottage. She ups and leaves town." Which my mother never did. Until now. Now it was all different. Now there was another man involved.

If my father found him, he'd beat him up bad, maybe even kill him. The guy most likely didn't know my father could dead-lift over

500 pounds. He proved it one year at the state fair, coming right out of the crowd, and he won fifty bucks. People clapped, and when he stepped down from the platform he was counting his money. Then he put it in his wallet and smiled and rubbed his fingers through my hair. My mother was holding his shirt, which he put on and buttoned, and she held his arm when we walked off across the fairgrounds because that's when we were all happy.

Maybe I was five then, small enough to still ride on his shoulders. I ate cotton candy and hardly made a peep up there, watching all the different colored lights on the amusement rides and the people passing and smiling up at me. My mother would nod to them and reach up and pat my bare leg. She'd say, "Having fun?" And I'd say, "Yes," but of course that was before they hurt each other.

My father was first. He hit her one evening right before supper, I don't even know what for, and then he stared for a long time at his hand, stared like it wasn't a part of him, and when my mother finally turned from the cupboard, her nose was bleeding from one nostril. She wiped the blood away with the back of her hand. "It's okay," she said to me, and she sounded very calm. "Your father didn't mean it."

"No," he said, "I didn't, I didn't mean it," and if he meant to say something else, it did not come. She spoke first. She said to him, "Turn down the burners," and he did, all the way to off, and all with his left hand, the one that hadn't struck her, and she left to go lie down on the couch in the living room, pulling the white afghan over her, snug to her chin.

"I love your mother," he said. He said, "I'm sorry," loud enough for her to hear, but he did not go to her. Instead he walked outside, and I stayed seated at the table. I turned my head and I could see my mother, and she was shaking.

"Mom?" I said, and she got real quiet, so I called her again, and she said, "He didn't mean it, Sweetheart," which I knew was true, and that he really was sorry, but that nothing in the world could ever change what had happened.

My mother slept finally, and I cleared the unused dishes from the table, then the silverware, knowing we wouldn't sit together as a family, not that night we wouldn't. I drank a glass of cold water, and ate peach halves right from the can, and then, without saying goodnight to anyone, I went to bed. My window was open halfway, and I could hear my father singing *Jamaica Farewell*, his favorite Harry Belafonte song. I wondered if my mom was listening. She loved when my father sang, and so did I. He had a beautiful, sad voice, and I hummed along with the words, my cheek kind of vibrating on the pillow:

> I'm sad to say I'm on my way,
> I won't be back for many a day,
> My heart is down, my head is turning around,
> I have to leave a little girl in Kingston Town.

Now she was gone to Texas. That was the postmark on the certified letter the lawyer sent. It came the day my father returned to work, this time on the day shift, so I wouldn't have to be alone at night. Nelson Pelky let me sign for the letter—he said he owed my father that much, but he seemed nervous, so I said to him, "I'll be sure he gets it." Mr. Pelky nodded and drove off. I knew he could get into trouble if I opened it, but I did anyway. My mother was filing for divorce and asking for custody—my full name was right there in black and white among all those legal terms. I slid the letter back in the envelope and folded it into my back pocket. Then I walked around back of the house and lined up a bunch of empty beer bottles at the edge of the lawn and got the .22 out of my father's closet and racked the first round into the chamber. Then I filled the clip and, outside, I steadied the rifle on the porch railing and sighted down that long barrel and popped one bottle after the other without a miss. A crow flew overhead, and I took aim on it, too, but it was already way out of range, gliding downwind with the heavy clouds.

It was feeling a lot like fall, and I spun around and, from the hip, I fired into the metal drum my father sometimes used for burning papers and boxes. And I went around front to the road, and although I did not squeeze the trigger, I pretended to pepper the mailbox with a million holes, blow it right off its post, and then shoot it some more on the ground like it was a wounded and dangerous animal. But all I did was walk up slowly and lower the shiny red flag with the barrel tip, as though there had been no mail. "It sure ain't the goddamn numbers we painted," my father would most likely say when he got home, and I'd say back, "Nope, they can read those from the state capitol," and he'd smile and nod to me and say, "Yep," and I'd wish, more than anything in the world, that my mother had written a letter of forgiveness, saying that she was sorry, too, and that she'd come home now to talk it all through.

My father did not want to grow even one more day older without her, but he knew what was what. In his heart he did. Twice this last week he'd said to me, "You're all I've got now," but I knew if they got him into court, he'd lose me, too. If the judge asked me who I'd rather live with I'd say, " Both of them." I'd tell the truth and say I didn't like my mother running away all the time and that my father sometimes scared me with his temper, but that he cooked all my meals and played catch with me in the backyard and, at night, over an open fire, we'd roast marshmallows, and he'd tell some funny jokes and stories and name the constellations. And if they asked, I'd say my mother had some nerve saying my father wasn't fit to raise me.

He'd promised to take me to see *Ben Hur* when it came to Munising, about a half-hour away, and when he got home from work one day he said, "Let's go." He said, "Step on it, Buster Brown, we're on our way to the movies."

On the drive over he talked to me a little about my mother. He said life was too short to fritter away, waiting for a woman, even your own wife, if she couldn't make up her mind. It's not like he'd adjusted to being without her, but he did seem to be doing better. Until halfway through the show he did, right after Ben Hur won the chariot race. I could tell that my father loved that scene and, I guess not thinking about where he was, he lit a cigarette. Nobody was close to us in the front row, and nobody shouted down for him to put the cigarette out. And he didn't, not even when the usher told him to. Instead, my father took a long, slow drag, tilted his head back and exhaled, the smoke blue and floating through the beam of the projector light. I said to him, "It's okay to smoke in the lobby," but he got mad and flicked the butt up at the big screen, and it was as though he'd spooked those six white horses that reared and whinnied, Ben Hur straining against them, heavy on the reins.

"Let's go," I said. "Come on, Dad," and when I turned my head I could see the manager coming, his flashlight on. He shouldn't have shined it in our eyes because when he did my father grabbed it and stood up and threw *it* at the screen, too, and the light made a loud clunk when it bounced off and hit the floor. He said to the manager, "In Rome they'd hang scum like you up by the balls. They'd feed you to the swine."

Right then the theater lights along both walls came on, and the projector stopped, and the manager said, "Please, just leave." The usher was bigger than me, but I was ready to fight him if I had to, the two of us duking it out in the aisle. But he made no move when my father shoved the manager, first with one hand and then much harder with both hands,

34

knocking him on his can on the worn, red carpet. My father reached for the ticket stubs in his shirt pocket and threw them in the manager's face, and crouched down and whispered something I couldn't hear, and then we left quickly through the EXIT door. I thought sure the cops would be waiting, but they were not. It was still partly light out, but the moon up already and almost full, and my father a few steps ahead of me.

"Drop that box of popcorn," he said, "and come on," and he started to run, and by the time we got to the car he was out of breath, but he said, "Get on the floor in back and stay down." And which I did until we hit Route 28 and he said, "It's all clear," and I climbed into the front seat.

It was dark now and the dash lights glowed green. My father pushed in the lighter and reached for his pack of Chesterfields between us on the seat.

"I wish I could undo a lot that I've done in my life," he said, "but I've drifted too far downstream to paddle back now."

The lighter popped and he lit his cigarette, and I stared straight ahead and imagined the car was a boat, and that there were fish below us in the dark water where we'd lower our lines or nets. Maybe there was a lantern on the stern and behind us a village and the women waving, the way my mother used to do from the porch each morning when my father drove off to work. He'd reappear, what seemed like days later, his head-lights on, and she'd have a late supper ready for him, sometimes fresh walleye or perch or a batch of bluegill fillets that Paul Tremblay would drop off on his way home from the lake. Paul Tremblay always caught fish, and he said he'd take me when I got older, but he never did, not once. We had never owned a boat, but here we were, drifting at night, and my father said, "It's easy, really," and I asked, "What is?" and he said, "This, just this," and he motioned to the fields flooded with moon-light. And to the moon itself, and the stars which were very bright and then to the two of us, and he yawned because the days had already grown shorter, and all he was doing was pointing out the obvious land-scape of our lives, how we traveled from here to there, growing older, even during those few seconds it took us to cross Black Creek, which meant we were only a few minutes from home. And only one week until school started again, and maybe two months until the heavy snow, and I knew if my mother hadn't come by then, I wouldn't see her until spring. Or never, depending on what the court decided.

"We made it," my father said, same as he always did, turning into the driveway, and when he hit the high beams those red numbers seemed to waver back and forth like a buoy. He stopped and I got out to open the garage doors, and my knees were a little shaky, as though I'd stepped ashore after being out all day on a rough lake. My father did not seem to notice. He walked right past me and up the stairs and yelled for me to close the garage doors. I did, and I leaned my back against them, and I stayed like that, repeating the posture I'd seen him take that first night he realized for certain that my mother was gone for good. And then those numbers, as though we'd had no real address all these years, no way for her to contact us if she changed her mind about Texas and whoever it was she was with there.

I wished Nelson Pelky had sent the lawyer's letter back—"Insufficient Address" or "Undeliverable" or "Deceased"—whatever lie was necessary to keep the mail away so that I wouldn't have to hide it and get blamed when my father found out, which he would, and he'd ask, "Why, why?" and I'd just shake my head like I didn't know what was wrong or right anymore, only that this was home, and I didn't want anyone, not even my mother, ruining that from somewhere else. Let her come here, I thought, and say what it was she wanted. I was exhausted from imagining what that was, and I closed my eyes and listened to the three Harry Belafonte albums my father stacked on the hi fi.

He must have thought I'd gone to bed because he never called to me and when I went in after midnight, I could hear him snoring on the couch. I peeked in and he was asleep on his stomach, one hand almost touching the floor. I could see the orange of the alarm clock dial and the phone pulled up close. I knew, by morning, only the alarm would ring. He'd hit the snooze, and then again, and then he'd have to rush so as not to be late for work. As soon as he left, I'd take the receiver off the hook in case my mother called me.

And before Nelson Pelky arrived I'd grab the .22 and hide in the cellar hole across the road. Not in ambush, exactly, but if he spotted me and started toward me with another certified letter, I'd say, "You stop right there, Mr. Pelky," and I'd click off the safety so he knew I meant business, so he knew that I was nobody to mess with. He'd probably call me my father's boy. Grownups did, especially teachers, whenever I'd fistfight at school. "That's a fact," I'd say, "I am," and I'd tell my father, and he'd say, "Let 'em make something of it. Let 'em say it to me."

But the only one who ever did was my mother. She'd say, "I suppose you want him to raise a hand to me, too?" which I'd never do, and my father had only done it the one time, which, like I said, had ruined everything. After that my mother seemed to dare him to do it again. She'd lift her chin and step close and say mean stuff, but he'd just slide his hands into his pockets and stand there and take it. He said to me once, "I won't forever, I won't," but I knew he would. It was him who loved her, not the other way around. When I got older and got married my wife would have to love me back. That's what I hated about my mother. Not that she ran off to Texas, but that she made it seem like my father's fault. He was no angel, that's for sure, but he could be awful kind. I'd say that to the judge, too, if they really did subpoena my father, and I'd say how he left me fresh cut slices of pumpernickel on the bread-board each morning so I could have toast with my cereal. But I figured that wouldn't matter to the law. They'd talk on and on about how I had no friends and how I was always real quiet and shy and showed no emotion, like it was some crime to be alone and keep your thoughts to yourself. But like my father said about me to the counselor at school one day, "He don't look punched or bored, now does he?" And I never was bored, and I was never hit at home. I read a lot and stayed to myself, fishing and hunting and building forts. My father would say to the court, "Is there something wrong with that?" He'd say, "Goddamn it, answer me," but nobody would, and I knew that's what they'd all want to see, my father's sudden temper, so they'd have grounds to snatch me as far away from him as they could. That's what Paul Tremblay told me one night when we were outside by ourselves. He said, "If you're the man, then poof, in your face. In this state the woman reigns."

So it was probably best the hearing went on without my dad. He knew nothing about it and dropped me off at school on his way to work, same as always. He small-talked about the weather and how we needed to put up another five cords of wood for the stove, and about how there was a good fight on TV that night—lightweights. "About your size," he said, and flicked out a soft jab to my shoulder, and then another before he covered up, both arms hugging the steering wheel, forehead wedged between his fists. "Never make an easy target," he said. "Give them as little as possible to hit." But I knew he'd left himself wide open this time, and that I was to blame. My mother and her lawyer would throw shot after shot—they'd give him a real pounding. And the decision? Custody of me to my mother, just like Paul Tremblay had predicted.

All day in the back row I wondered if she'd be there when I got home, waiting on the verdict. There was no car in the driveway, but I stood in the road awhile, watching the dust kicked up by the school bus tires, and I could see Kevin St. Germain and Carl Thunstrom flipping me the bird out the back window. Usually I'd yell something at those dopes, but not today. Today I nodded, like you win, you're right.

My mother was seated at the kitchen table, her hands folded on top, folded like she'd been praying or listening to someone talk at her for a long time. Her hair had grown past her shoulders and she was wearing a new dress, and lipstick, and from where I was standing I could see her feet under the table, her high heels.

"It's just like your father not to show up, to tell his side," she said. "It's just like him." Then she opened her pocketbook and pulled out a folded paper and asked, "Do you know what this is?"

"Yes." I said. "It says that you can take me away."

"It's all wrong," she said, "the whole thing, me sitting here. There's a limit," she said, "and after that it's all wrong, everything's wrong, wrong. But I'm never coming back here to live, and after the divorce is final, I'll marry again, right away."

And then she told me about Texas and about a man named Will Roop who she loved enough to be happy, and who would adopt me and give me his name. She said I could meet him when he came to pick her up, but I said no, and I asked if he'd been in this house.

"Yes," she said. "Here in the kitchen, right where your father hit me that time."

And I wanted to hit her, too, just walk over and slap her good and tell her, get out, get out of here. But I just stood there and she said, "Those numbers on the garage, is that where we lived?"

"Yes," I said, "335. It's how you have to address everything now, or it doesn't arrive."

"All those years," she said, "and I never knew where I lived. On a county road in northern Michigan."

"I want to stay here," I said, and I paused, and I don't know why, but I said to her, "They can see those numbers all the way to Lansing."

"Yes," she said, "you're officially listed; you exist on the map." Then she said, "Put down your books," and I did. And she said, "Now come sit next to me," and I crossed the kitchen and sat down and thought, when I looked at her close up, that if my father were to appear right now, my mother would stay forever. She would. But it was Will Roop who stood in the doorway, older than my father and not a big man, and wearing cowboy boots. I hadn't heard the car pull in, but I could hear it idling now.

"Will Roop," my mother said, "this is my son, and he does not want to come with us."

38

"Correction," Will Roop said. "There's nothing in those papers about 'want to.' He can want to or not when he's eighteen. Or he can want to, but don't you listen. Don't give in, or you'll never see him again."

I gave Will Roop a hate stare, and he looked down at the floor, and my mother said to him, "I'll be right out," and he didn't argue. He turned and shut the door quietly, then the screen door behind him.

"Here's my phone number," she said, and wrote it on a napkin. "You call me. You call when you decide to come live with us." I thought, by the way her lips opened and stayed that way a minute, that she was going to describe Texas, but she didn't.

"Okay," I said, "I will," and I was glad that she didn't start crying when she hugged me, and without saying anything else she got up and left, quick as that.

From the kitchen window I watched the car back onto the road, then drive down the wrong side to the mailbox. Will Roop reached into it and raised the metal flag and drove away. I knew my father would be home soon, but I waited a good fifteen minutes before going out there.

My father's name was on the envelope, and under it, in red lipstick, 335, and nothing else. I opened it and read the letter, which asked my father not to contest the divorce, and if he needed to contact her it had to be through the courts. Never by phone, never face to face. She said she loved Will Roop, though she didn't mention his name, and I knew that was a lie, which seemed okay in a way. And she said that she had never really loved my father, which I hoped wasn't true. She was still angry, writing that letter right here on our kitchen table, probably. I figured the end of something like this needed an honest distance, a real stamp and postmark and return address, the kind of letter Nelson Pelky could deliver without risking a thing. I could smell the perfume in the lipstick when I crumpled the letter up and stuck it in my pocket. And I could see when my father's car was in sight that he had Paul Tremblay with him, as he often did on Friday nights.

"You been with a lady," Paul said, putting his arm around my shoulder. "Hey, Tommy," he said, "your kid's got himself a dame."

"Probably Janet Knoble," I said, "sometimes she stinks up the whole bus."

"Women do that when they're away from home," Paul joked. "They leave their scent for you to remember them by, ain't that right, Tommy?"

My father didn't answer, and Paul laughed again and reached for the football on the lawn and said, "Slant pattern," and I cut just a few yards in front of him, and when I caught the wobbly pass he yelled, "Yes, yes, yes," while my father walked away, not to check the mail, but to kind of stare off down the road.

"He'll get over it," Paul said, when I came back to hand him the ball, "and you will, too," and I nodded to show I understood. We both watched my father for a few seconds more before Paul barked out another play, and this time I ran the deep route, as fast and far from the two of them as I could.

DEATH PARTS

I do not advertise as a taxidermist, but each year I take a little work, mostly local. Occasionally, a downstater will get lucky and shoot a trophy whitetail on the opener, and for the right price I will mount the buck's head, usually a ten-point or better. My reputation has spread these past few years, and so I can choose and charge what I want. Plus I always agree to work on an animal I've never held, dead or alive, or a freak of nature, like the pure white skunk that was caught in a neighbor's trap, the eyes oversized and deep blue.

A black bear is the only animal I refuse to touch with the knife, no matter how much money I am offered. They are not rare in these parts, and if you have connections there are private dumps in the U.P. where the bears are easily killed. Most evenings they wade out from the dark woods and move slowly through the avenues of junked cars in the high grass. Although my father never shot a bear with a rifle, he often watched them close up through the scope. Five straight years he arranged to hunt at the same dump, and for a few days before he arrived the owner would empty pails of rotten fish and meat by the blind. "Smells something awful," the guy would boast over the phone, his guarantee that the bears would be there in the half-light, and they always were, my father confirmed, they always were, repeating it as though he were ashamed by such certainty, by the bears' intractable greed for garbage. He never explained more than that why he passed the easy shots every single time.

And I figured he'd pass again the first time he invited me to go with him. He was given a loner, a VW Beetle while the station wagon was in the shop, and right before pulling out of the yard he said, "What the hell. Let's at least give them a chance," and he went back into the house for his compound bow and quiver of arrows, and left the rifle right there on the kitchen table.

I was fourteen and I remember how we drove down a long dirt road to its dead end, a cloud of dust continuing past into the tall weeds. Already in camouflage we both got out of the car, and I watched my father stop and lean close up to the side mirror, uncap his small tin of cream and began to smear black streaks across his cheeks and forehead. "You won't be with me in the blind," he explained. "I've got a spot for you to watch from. You'll see fine from there, and it's safer." He paused, then he said, "Take these," and swung me the binoculars by the cracked leather strap. I hung them around my neck while he strapped on his holster and pistol, and we started walking in.

I was surprised how close the dump was from where we'd parked. It looked like a dried-up swamp, the low land curving in a half circle around the perimeter of trees, the maples deep orange and yellow at the far edge, the sumac blood red. The clearing was not large, an acre at most. I expected the ground to be soft, but it wasn't when we stepped down and circled the pile of old refrigerators and washing machines and electric stoves, the white enamel rusted in small circles wherever a bullet had passed through.

The odor of fish hung thick in the air. "That's ripe," my father said, as he might while checking tomatoes in the garden. But it was more than ripe, here in the late fall, the nights already cold and heavy with frost. I thought about dump pickers who scavenged for a harvest of old bottles and inkwells and the porcelain heads of dolls in places just like this. But I couldn't imagine anyone digging in this stink for treasures, as I couldn't imagine why my father hunted every year over piles of entrails and fish heads. It was illegal to bait an area, and because he'd never in his life poached anything, I figured that explained why he could never bring himself to squeeze the trigger. Or maybe just breathing this awful air made him sick of the woods after a few hours, crouched and staring, and one time in so sudden and dense a snow that the bears came in and were gone without him ever seeing them, like ghosts. He'd come close, he said, but in the end he never fired, as he did at every other prey he'd ever hunted.

Halfway across he stopped and pointed toward a stand of birch trees about fifty yards distant. "The blind's in there," he said. "You'll see it better from the junkers."

42

And I did, the sun setting behind me as I looked out the windshield of a 1949 Studebaker after my father slammed down the hood. "Look at that," he said smiling, showing me the dipstick through the open window. "She didn't die from lack of oil."

And the seats too were still in decent shape, no broken springs poking through the gray upholstery. I imagined driving the car, the knee-high grass folding under the flaking chrome bumper on the zigzag of a final ride. But when I tried the steering wheel, it wouldn't budge, the tires buried to the hubcaps.

"Keep both doors locked and don't get out. If you have to pee, go right on the floor. I'll come get you just after dark when it's time to leave." Then he took the pistol from his holster, and, handle first, gave me the gun. A .32 caliber, too small to ever kill a bear, but it was loaded, and I took careful aim with the safety on as my father walked away, covering him until he reached the blind, believing at that moment no shot was out of range.

But accuracy is at least half luck as the light changes and your eyes strain too hard to make out shapes that aren't even there. Vision, as my dad said, it'll always adjust some, but still plays tricks enough to turn the mind toward other things. He's right, like jumping back to that first evening I plowed the garden under by myself, and stopped on the last row by the fence-line to place a few rotten pumpkins on the flat tops of the posts. Then, from the seat of the tractor, I reached out and fired point blank on my way back to the barn, the orange seeds and pulp exploding in a halo under the full moon.

And that's what I was thinking when that single bear, lumbering on all fours, angled in front of me, the momentum of her hind end carrying her whole body sideways toward the blind. I rolled down the window to listen, but hearing nothing after a few minutes, I opened the door and got slowly out. And, both elbows steadied on the hood, I focused, not on the path of the bear, but to the left where my father was standing at full draw, the satellite razor head catching a shred of light the instant he released. I shifted the binoculars as though I could follow the flight of the arrow, the landscape made crazy through the tinted blue lenses by the sudden leap.

Out of the high cover the bear charged into view, heading directly towards me, her enormous bulk low to the ground, and her head in a kind of slow motion lolling from side to side. My father told me later that he heard the door slam, the noise he speculated might have brought

43

the bear stumbling to the driver's side where she lifted on her hind feet, her undersides moist and shiny with blood. The bright yellow fletching of the arrow stuck out above her breastbone like a star, dead center at the base of the throat, the jugular and windpipe severed.

Unlike a 30.30 or .06, it's the cutting of the razor tip that kills, not the impact. What I know now is that she would have died right there from loss of blood and no air, but when she stared in, narrow-eyed, her hot breath rising, I fired six times at her face until she turned away into the open space of the field and collapsed for good.

The aluminum arrow shaft pointed straight up, and it seemed only seconds passed before the sky pulsed alive with millions of stars, and my father at full draw as he straddled the steamy hulk.

"Good Christ Almighty," he said. "What have we done? Tell me that you're okay?"

"Yes," I said. "I am," and when he aimed heavenward and drove a second arrow deep into the belly of the sky, I pointed at the constellation of the bears glowing brighter and brighter above us. "Ursus," I said, but he just put down his bow, and, without looking up, said, "Well this one's dead."

What I believe now is that each night establishes its own trajectory, and gazing north above the hills, I offered my father no help, nor did he ask until he stood up, stiff-legged, his forearms covered in blood. "Get the towel from my bag," he said. I did, but instead of wiping his hands he wrapped it around the arrow, and, using the full force of his legs and back, he wrenched it out, the bear's head lifting momentarily off the ground, as if she were attempting to sit up, and for that second or two I imagined this entire escapade was nothing more than some wild-weird dream I'd suddenly awakened from.

It took a long time to drag her back to the car, my father wheezing, always forcing himself a few steps too far before a rest, his palms rope-burned and blistered. I stayed a ways in front, carrying the bow and binoculars and empty pistol. But after about a half hour he yelled, "Get rid of that stuff and bring back the gloves from the trunk. And a can of beer from the cooler."

He lit a cigarette, and as I left I could hear him coughing real bad, coughing and spitting. I stopped and looked back from the edge of the dump. The night was bright and quiet, and although it had turned cold, I could feel the sweat on my back. I reached under the layers of clothes and pulled my T-shirt a couple of times away from my skin.

"Good," he said after I got back, and before putting on his gloves he squeezed the ice-cold can between his hands, and then took only a few quick sips before launching it like a grenade into the dump. "Now, let's get her out," he said.

And together we did, the rope lengthened and tied around his waist, hands on his hips, almost casual except for the strain on those thick legs, farmer's legs for dragging a wagon load of hay a few inches in the field to the trailer hitch of the tractor. While my legs were thin and long like a sprinter's, like my mother's he had once said. To run ahead in the night for cans of beer and gloves, I thought, and for the quick distance my father sometimes needed from me to think things through and make sure what he was teaching me was exactly what I needed to learn.

Getting her up and lashed on top of the VW was easier than I'd expected. She seemed to slide backwards up the smooth roundness of the hood. I pushed on the shoulders, and my father, stretching from the rear bumper, locked her huge back paws under his armpits and, leaning back, he hauled her over the windshield to the roof, a filmy streak of blood coating the glass. The Volkswagen was yellow and she seemed big enough to crush it in a bear hug. We stood back and watched a minute, then cut four lengths of rope and tied her down in that ridiculous pose. I was exhausted and needed sleep, and drifting off I imagined I was inside her belly as my father started driving toward the main road, craving a hamburger, he said, someplace well lighted where the bear would be safe in the parking lot while we chowed down. He was attracted, he said, to the scent of a particular all-night diner, and where the waitresses always asked if he'd had any luck, and him spinning halfway around this time on the counter stool to point out the window, and me nodding beside him, nodding real slow over the spread menu like someone pleased with our spoils, like someone with an appetite after a full day of hunting.

The car broke down on the long deserted stretch through the Hiawatha National Forest, the radio mostly static. I woke up hot in the sleeping bag draped around me, the red cotton lining patterned with deer. I asked my father the time and he said, "About 2:00 AM." He had just come from the rear of the car.

"What's the matter?"

"We started losing pressure a few miles back. There's no power, no traction. Must have labored too hard under this load."

He knew engines, but hated the foreign jobs. "Piece of crap," he said, "but what do you expect with the motor in the ass end?" I was back there with him this time as he reached in without a light, the way he had reached into the entrails of the bear, and when he pulled his hands out they were covered in oil. "Can't drive it," he said. "We're stuck here until someone comes by."

But nobody did, and every now and then he would pump up the Coleman lantern until the mantle glowed bright white inside the glass. Then he'd place it on the side of the road like a flare and walk off into the blackness. The lantern threw a lot of light into the pines, and it made the blood smear on the windshield seem even darker. I got out once and noticed for the first time that the bear's eyes were wide open, glassy from the bite of the wind.

"I'll close them," my father said, and, startled from behind, I just nodded as he dragged both thumbs slowly downward before the two of us climbed without another word back into the car.

"You bait or get him with dogs?" the wrecker driver asked. "Hell, he's bigger than the damn car!"

In the daylight I could see that the entire front of the VW was smeared slick with blood. "Didn't clean him out too good though," the guy continued. "We got a hose you can use at the station. Shove the nozzle right down his throat and rinse him out good before the meat goes bad."

"It's a her," I said. "A female." He was missing half of his middle finger on the right hand, the stub stained dark with nicotine.

"That a fact? Then we'll do her from the other end," he said, and flicked his unfinished cigarette at the bear and began manhandling the chains and harness and yanked back a lever that released the main cable from the spool on the wrecker. Then, grunting some, he took off his greasy baseball cap and crawled part way under the VW, his pants low under his fat stomach, and his legs spread wide enough on the gravel for an easy kick to the balls. I might even have taken a step closer, but probably not. "Ain't much to hook onto," the guy yelled back, but he came right out and the car went up easy on its rear wheels, the bear sliding back a bit on the roof.

The three of us rode together in the cab, with me squeezed in the middle. There was one of those sleazy crime magazines on the floor, a half-naked woman gagged and tied by her wrists and ankles to the bedposts. Seeing it, my father wedged the magazine under the seat with the heel of his boot, and the guy, shifting into third and staring into the side and rearview mirrors, smiled and shook his head as if in disbelief, and then pulled out with the emergency flashers pulsing down those miles of empty road.

"It's your lucky day," the guy started up. "We've got a VW wreck at the station. Had to tow it back on a flatbed. A disaster right to the rear seat, but the engine's untouched. Two people killed. Take it from me you can't hardly sell parts from a car like that. Superstition about robbing the dead. The dead!" He laughed and shook his head again, and paused to let that sink in. "You don't believe in that shit, do you?"

"I don't," I said too quickly, but my father, eyes closed and head tilted back against the rear window, asked, "How does anyone know one way or another?"

"I know," the guy snapped. "Sure as shit I know," and for several minutes after that he went dead silent.

My father said later that the guy was full of it, a big talker, and a blowhard, the worst kind of coward. But there was something frightening about the way he punched the radio buttons with that half finger and talked on and on about how he got people's attention "right now" when he flipped them the stubby bird.

At the station we helped him push the VW, the bear still on top, into the service bay. The customer bell rang as a car pulled away from the gas pumps out front, and the young gas attendant waving a five-dollar bill stepped from the sunlight and asked my father, "How much you want for the claws?"

"They're not for sale," my father answered. But I knew they were a good five hours later when the tow guy handed us the bill. He had written **DEATH PARTS** for everything he had stripped from the wreck. And knowing we couldn't pay, he sent the car back up on the lift as if to keep it out of reach, the bear on top rising in grotesque ascension into the darkness bunched under the roof.

"Now, let's talk turkey," the guy said, followed by his sermon of harsh facts. He looked mean now. "I'll take a hundred-fifty bucks and the bear."

While they dickered I walked outside and sat down on the concrete abutment at the base of the Texaco sign. Toward what there was of a town hung a blinking yellow light, suspended and swinging a little from a wire across the road. Just that single color, and beyond, the huge white numbers on the water tower: Pop. 412. I could hear the air brakes of a transport trailer slowing for the light, and then shifting through his

47

gears and moving at a pretty good clip by the time he passed me. I ducked my head from the sudden draft and noise, and I could smell the dirty cattle for a long time after the truck was out of sight.

When I started back my father was at the pumps, washing blood from the windshield of the VW, and behind him, the silhouette of the bear hanging by her neck, the rope fastened to one runner of the lift. The guy and the attendant were already spreading her claws, spreading them and laughing as she swayed, her toes no more than a few inches off the ground.

"Maybe they'd take the binoculars," I suggested. "Or the bow."

My father exhausted from no sleep, said, "Maybe," but climbed into the VW instead and said, "Let's go home," and tested the car's top end down that long straightaway, as if he were driving a hotrod. But he slowed after maybe half a mile, sensing, I guess, the danger of traveling at high speeds in such a small car. "Death parts," he whispered to himself, then put the headlights on at mid-afternoon, and pulled close to the right shoulder of the road whenever another vehicle passed, heading the other way.

PIG AND LOBSTERS

The only book I ever saw my father read was *Fear Strikes Out,* the autobiography of Jimmy Piersall. Even cooking breakfast my father held it open with one hand as though he were a teacher or a priest, his free hand turning down the blue flame flattening under a skillet of home fries on the back burner of the range. Sometimes, slamming the book face down on the table, he would stalk to the kitchen window, enraged, glancing back over one shoulder like a batter heading toward the dugout after arguing a strike three call. "The game ruined him," my father snapped. "Sent him straight to the asylum."

Maybe that's the reason we turned to other things, the reason my father began to stay inside and browse through fat catalogs from Sears and J.C. Penney, always lifting the pages real slow like they were sample squares of wallpaper. Whenever he came to *Hunting & Fishing* he would stare at the aluminum boats, small horsepower outboards, and nets and bait buckets, tackle boxes with fancy folding trays. Then he would drift to the bottom of the page for the corresponding code, H-4, and locate the price across the line of dots, lick his left thumb and move on dreaming through this warehouse of unaffordable glossy merchandise. When a new Wish Book arrived in the mail, he immediately opened it and ripped out the order forms in back, ripped them in half and then again, those shredded paper clouds disappearing into the wastebasket under the sink.

Only once did he make a purchase, a stopwatch to time the distractions of each day. When he wrote a check the first month the rent was raised, he held the sealed envelope just below his eyes, stared over the straight edge and announced, "Fifty-four seconds." Before long he knew

49

the length of every red light on his route home from work, how long it would take to walk to the IGA on Appleton to cash in his six-pack of empties, how much time it took for the bathtub to fill and drain, for the one-legged chickadee to land on the roof of the feeder after my father scattered his fistful of sunflower seeds. He said he wished he could press the stop button on the watch the moment he entered sleep, or time the distance of each dream. He'd heard somewhere that dreams lasted only a few seconds, brief sprints through the tortured unconscious. He did not believe this any more than he believed in the brevity of love. "Takes awhile," he said. "If you can, always measure love in decades."

But a few years after my mother died he did fall hard and fast for a woman I never met, whose name I never heard. I saw him stationed nights by the phone, trancelike, inhaling the smoke from his cigarette, containing it a long time, as if in those moments the world came to him calm, and clear, and quiet. I think he was listening then to the melody of some inner voice. The first sharp ring would always make him grimace, a shock like a man who sleepwalks only to reach out for the numbing pulse of an electric fence. Weekend nights he would sometimes leave the house after he thought I was asleep, the headlights of the pickup blinking on only after he hit the main road a quarter mile away.

It was October, cold I remember, a Sunday and we were leaning on the railing of the sow's sty, my father's eyes like scales weighing this pig for slaughter. "Next week," he mumbled. But it didn't happen. Instead he invited a guest for dinner and spent the days fussing inside, vacuuming both sides of the cushions on the couch and chairs, moving a glass figurine of a deer a few inches on the dark field of a table, then back again the next day. All week after school I was afraid she would be there waiting, not a guest, but my new mother invading with her woman's touch.

That Saturday he did not wake me early, though I heard him downstairs arguing with a man from the bank, here, the man emphasized, on a non-business day. This was the second time, the same identical conversation: bad money and good, loans and risks, foreclosures, preferred customers.

But that morning my father felt rich enough to drive two towns over and return with three live lobsters in a box of crushed ice. He hefted it onto the counter, nodded with exaggeration and boasted, "You're damn right." Then he opened the top, but the lobsters hardly moved until he lifted them out, claws pegged, tails snapping and snapping as if they might swim backwards from my father's hands, their eyes hard and round as B.B.'s, black and hostile looking as they focused on this bright and hungry world. He dropped them into the empty drawer of the refrigerator, a bubbly film enclosing each of their oval mouths.

By eight that night she still had not arrived. On the stove a huge pot of water boiled, oblong bubbles slow-rolling to the surface like waves. Outside the spotlight high on the barn flooded the ground, and inside on the dinner table the flame from a single candle wavered above the emptiness of our three white plates.

We said nothing to each other, and finally my father went outside, and an hour later when he started back toward the house, it was not to dine, but rather to watch the sow devour the main course live, those lobsters flown a thousand miles from Maine to the Midwest, an emblem of the distance *he* might have traveled to offer this invitation, his first in fifteen years. And she had stood him up, and now he had the sow around her neck by a rope, straining to manhandle 600 pounds of live pork up the back stairs.

Winded, he hollered, "Throw the lobsters on the floor and get out of the way. Get clear!" I could hear the pig grunting, and my father grunting back some primal response, promising perhaps, a feast, the language raspy, and guttural, and completely insane.

In panic I felt a sudden need to fold open a clean, wet towel for the lobsters and place them gently side by side, hard-shelled, tentacles wavering, testing the warm and sudden light as if it were an invisible ocean. But instead, I grabbed the largest lobster and yanked out both wooden pegs, yanked them out like thick slivers, and the lobster came struggling back to life, raising both fists above its head.

I half dropped, half slid him across a few feet of dull linoleum into the corner by the sink where the lobster wedged itself as if between two rocks. I reached for the others, and when I spun around, the sow was banging through the open door, heaving forward, her enormous body shaking the jambs, her narrow eyes fixed on the spot where I was standing. Terrified, I lobbed both lobsters simultaneously into the air toward her, as I might a hunk of meat to a wild dog to keep it away. They landed with a thud, with the unexpected heaviness only something live makes with its impact. And then the pig was on them, not biting as much as squashing and sucking them in, shells and all, her front legs spread and braced as if against some shallow, but powerful incoming tide.

I do not remember climbing up, but when the pig attacked the corner under my feet I realized I was standing on the countertop, my body shielded behind the half-opened cabinet door. I did not see my father angling for a shot with his .22, but looking down I watched the pig go suddenly to her knees, that horrible collapse of the body that means the brain's darkness has swallowed this tiny slug. I felt the whole house shake and thought then of passionate killing, my father's phrase for the quick and merciful execution of what we had raised in the sties and coops of the farm. But he did not slit her throat as he said you must until after he dragged her with a long rope tied to the tractor outside to the porch. All night she stayed there, bleeding, her head between her legs like a dog asleep, its snout just over the edge of the first step.

The biggest lobster was untouched, but dry and slow to defend itself, though my father would pick it up only with a glove. He never looked at me the whole time and just walked slowly back outside, and, standing a few feet from the barn, side-armed the lobster as hard as he could against the unpainted boards. It's that sound that is still so clear, clearer than the sound of the rifle fired inside the house, or the pig's awful single sharp squeal at the pain between its eyes. All this food and slaughter, and in the other room an uncorked bottled of wine my father would offer no woman so cruel as to leave him alone.

THE SEASON OF FAMILIES

Jack O'Conner is a pharmacist who is right now on his way to upstate New York to visit his father for the holidays. He has brought some sample packs of vitamins for him to try, a whole bagful, and small silver tubes of ointments for his father's persistent neck rash. And for himself, a sample pack of condoms. Red, white, and blue ones, which might be comical to someone with a more fluid sense of humor. His wife, Eartha, is forty-four, five years older than Jack, and he has just recently stopped supplying her with birth control pills. They're for younger women, as Jack says, and Eartha thinks, *Yes, for the sixteen-year-olds he hires to work Saturdays for minimum wage.* Until last year, Eartha worked three afternoons a week at Dove Song, a local flower shop. Since the recession, she has been unemployed. They have no children and want none and Jack's father has begun to refer to this as their selfishness. Which it is. But unlike most of their married friends, they are companionable enough and spend freely and, as Jack points out, without worry. They travel during his vacations, often by plane to exotic places, he always in an aisle seat in nonsmoking, she way in the back by the bathrooms.

Eartha has carefully wrapped the Christmas presents in shiny silver paper and blue stick-on bows from the drugstore. The presents are stacked on the back seat of their Saab turbo, which is parked again on the icy shoulder of Highway 23, this time between two long white fields. Eartha is sitting cross-legged on the front bumper, the wind gusting in miniature tornadoes of new snow through the barbed-wire fence to her right. That's why she's holding her coat collar up higher on that side of her face, and smoking faster than normal.

Jack, who is not impatient, believes that these are sugar beet fields, a major crop of mid-Michigan, where Eartha was born and raised and attended a community college, majoring in pre-med. Those dreams are long vanished. Jack uses sugar beets to bait the deer he hunts every fall in the woods behind their house. As well as the two suitcases in the trunk, he has packed a Styrofoam cooler with a dozen venison steaks which Eartha, a vegetarian, refuses to eat.

But Jack's father, a retired stockbroker, will, and has asked for some prime cuts, calling it deer meat. It's leaner, he claims, than anything he can buy in the supermarkets, and which is not, as he puts it, small potatoes to a man who has survived a second heart attack and now pays close attention to his cholesterol. Jack knows that twenty-two percent of Michigan residents can tell you their cholesterol level, the most informed state in the country. Wisconsin has the highest binge-drinking rate, by far the worst obesity. New York the most sedentary lifestyle. He bores Eartha with facts like these—this man who stands all day behind a glass partition in his long white coat, surrounded by plastic pull-out bins of pills he believes can cure most people's ills.

Jack knows nothing of Eartha's addiction to Valium, a prescription she gets filled in Mancelona, a twenty-minute drive from where they live. For this trip she has hidden the Valium in a metal Sucrets box, spread under the top layer of lozenges. She wishes her doctor would prescribe something stronger, especially for family visits. But, as he's explained, she's already at maximum dosage, already, as she knows, fading in and out of most days.

She dislikes Jack's father who referred to her once, trying to talk his only son out of the marriage, as "either incredibly dense or catatonic." She heard this while eavesdropping on the portable telephone in the basement. And which is what she did again a few nights ago, listening this time to her father-in-law read Jack the riot act about her smoking in his "home." He'd consented finally to this much: she can do it only on the new screened-in porch out back. "Any place," she said later to Jack. "Whatever."

On their only other visit since their marriage six years ago, the temperature outside near zero, she had gotten quietly out of bed that first night, Jack snoring lightly, and opened the window in the upstairs guest room just an inch, and pressed her lips right tight to the crack each time she exhaled through the screen. She remembers, in the cold hazy moonlight of the backyard, how the neighbor's black-and-white Great Dane had stared up at her, and how much it had resembled a zebra, her all-time favorite animal, standing knee-deep in the snow. *Mercy*, she had thought, a zebra, but she did not wake Jack, certain that he would understand this scene exactly for what it was—her sneaking cigarettes and watching a large dog let out to go to the bathroom. The bathroom she and Jack shared was right down the carpeted hallway, and she tiptoed there, carrying her shoe, the one she had used as an ashtray. She emptied the ashes, and the butts snubbed out just above the filters, into the toilet and flushed.

And she could not imagine the next morning how Jack's father knew. But he did. He was in his bathrobe and slippers, sitting alone at the kitchen table when she walked in, still headachy from the long drive and the late cocktails and way too little sleep. He did not offer her coffee, which is what she had craved, strong black coffee. That and a cigarette. When she said, "Good morning," and smiled at him, he stood slowly and pointed at her and said back, "Eartha, my wife died from lung cancer and, goddamn it all, I'll rent you a room at the Ramada if that's what it takes to keep you from lighting up in here, in my house. "Yes," he said, "mine, and I make the rules, like it or not." He paused, and then he added, "And I'll tell you something, just between you and me. You're trouble," and he started to say something else, but clenched his teeth instead and walked away.

She'd felt nabbed, as though he'd been waiting there for her since before sunup, his lips taut with that same kind of anger she had known other men to have. Her own father for one who slapped her hard across the face that first time he discovered a pack of Kents in her bedroom. He made her open her mouth and breathe her tobacco breath at him. "Tramp," he had called her. "Little tart-whore." She was thirteen and had just gotten out of the shower, rosy-skinned and nothing but a bath towel wrapped around her, her hair dripping wet. Because of her lankiness, the frayed edge of the towel hung only a little ways down her thighs. He did not even allow her to get dressed, though she had cried and then shivered badly. For almost an hour she stood there, chain-smoking the entire pack in front of him, and her mother walking meekly in afterward and sitting at the foot of the bed, her hands composing themselves as if in prayer on her lap.

"Sweetheart," her mother had said once they were alone. "Sweetheart, please. Please obey your father. He knows what's best for you. He does." And followed a few days later by her mother's secret inducements if Eartha would only give up the smoking—a new baton, private cello lessons—all kid's stuff. So she remained unrepentant, the nicotine stains darkening her fingers. She always hated her father after that—hated the single-minded wrath of any man laying down the law for her.

Jack was different—soft-spoken, encouraging rather than condemning her. She can't remember how many quick-fix gimmicks he has brought home over the years to help her quit—over-the-counter gums, then Nicorette, and finally long-filtered cigarettes that tasted like air. She knows what she lacks is will power, which is why one night while Jack was in Chicago at a pharmaceutical convention she had slept with his best friend, a man named Lyman Clark. It had not been her intention to do so, nor his, when he knocked on the wooden frame of the screen door. It was summer then and she undid the hook latch and stepped back, wearing a thin nightgown and, except for her panties, nothing underneath. A fan whirred at high speed from the corner of the kitchen, and Lyman was holding a cold beer to his forehead and inquiring as to Jack's whereabouts, and then only nodding and staring. She does not remember it being good or bad, but only that it happened. And again a few months later, what Lyman described as a relapse. But he phoned the next day saying that he was sick about it, nauseous. The three of them are not often together anymore, but whenever they are, Lyman seems jumpy and afraid. Jack, of course, does not notice.

At this moment he is consumed by the details of automobile navigation, the road map spread across the steering wheel. As long as Eartha has known him, he has never once gotten them lost. So it seems strange to her when a car stops to ask if they are all right. No, she wants to tell the woman on the passenger side. *For the love of Christ, no.* But it is Jack who answers and thanks them and waves by saluting with his left hand.

Jack, having figured in the cigarette breaks, one every fifty-five miles, exactly like the speed limit, says, "We're making good time." Eartha nods and snaps a Kleenex from the cellophane pack on the dashboard. She wipes her nose then presses her fingers between her knees. Jack turns up the heater a notch and adjusts the Lumbar knob to tighten the back of his seat, the solution to his achy vertebrae. Even after a morning's worth of driving and stopping there are no grievances to air. Over the years, routines have taken hold, and Jack simply says, "Onward," and shifts into first gear, and Eartha, the cold still deep inside her clothes, says, "Yes."

She blanks out often, not knowing if Jack has talked, or if she has answered. She can will these trances, and does so often, but this one is broken when Jack says, "Good God, look at that," and he points ahead and to his left. When Eartha leans forward she has to shade her eyes in order to see through the windshield a colossal blue silo with a Christmas tree on top. She wonders immediately from how far away on this flat land at night a person could see those blinking white lights if she were lost, that single star.

"Forever," Jack says, as if reading her mind, but of course he's talking about something else, about how long a man stays dead if he's not careful, decorating a tree that high up in the sky. Jack calculates, from the height of the house and the barn roof, that the silo must rise at least a hundred feet.

But what interests Eartha is the angle at which a man, his arms outspread like a swan, would hit the frozen ground. She gives the man a face she recognizes—it is Jack's face, his light blue eyes, and now she cannot dispel the image from her mind. He is wearing only one glove and no hat, and she is bending down to touch him, suddenly surrounded by all those cows. She thinks, maybe this is how it happens: a wife goes outside, calling and calling her husband back until she finds him dead. Eartha rarely feels the urge to touch Jack anymore, but she does that now, her fingertips soft on the back of his neck and, sorry for this vision she's created, she says, "Let's stop," says it as though she's asking for a motel room where they can draw the blinds against the late morning glare of the sun and make desperate and dangerous love.

Jack says, "Soon, there's a restaurant just up ahead." He says, "Hang on," and increases his speed by maybe five miles per hour. For a minute Eartha believes she is going to cry, and tears do come, but they do not leave her eyes, so that when she sees the giant inflatable reindeer staked and wavering above the parking lot, the day appears even more unreal, blurry now, distorted. She has lost her appetite for anything except a cigarette and another pill, her usual highway diet. Jack teases her at times like this, saying she should eat better and outlive him and collect on his net worth. It's a standing joke. Which is exactly what they are doing, standing. Both of them are, together in front of the car and staring up at the reindeer that smiles back down on them. Eartha is truly frightened. It strikes her that she is a small girl again and that she does not want to walk beneath this monstrous thing.

When she takes Jack's hand, it could be her father's, and what surges through her body is the adrenaline feeling that she is about to be yelled at, scolded, and hit again. She stands transfixed, unable to speak, her lips parted and heart-shaped as Jack—and yes, it is him—leans down to kiss her on the cheek. And does, puts his arm around her shoulder and leads her safely to the door, which he opens for her, and then she feels his hand on the small of her back, guiding her into the vestibule. The inner door is glass and, as it closes behind her, she glances back. Jack is fumbling in his pockets for the right change to buy a newspaper from the yellow vending machine against the wall.

The restaurant is warm, the walls dark knotty pine, and empty of any customers. And hanging from the scattered light fixtures, red-and-green crepe paper bells, the kind you can close-up and flatten and put away in a box until next Christmas. Although Eartha does not see a jukebox, she hears Willie Nelson's nasally version of *O, Holy Night*. There are thousands of silver sparkles in the swirled, textured ceiling, because it is that kind of place, the waitress just this moment noticing Eartha and cracking a roll of quarters on the corner of the cash register drawer. She pushes the last few out with her thumb, and says, "Smoking, hon?" as though there is no doubt. Eartha follows her and slides, without taking off her coat or scarf, into the corner of the booth bench. The waitress points out the Christmas week specials on the blackboard on the wall and says she'll be right back to take the order.

Eartha reads as far as the liver and onions, turning away again from the whole idea of food, turning instead to the window where she pulls open the wooden shutters. There is frost on the panes, and beyond, dwarfing the Saab in shadow, that awful reindeer. She stares and stares and is startled by the glass of ice water the waitress sets down in front of her in the thin rectangle of light.

"No," Eartha says, she is not quite ready to order. She's sorry, but she still needs a couple of minutes. She spends them, and more, locked in the stall in the ladies room. And this time she weeps openly, so hard she can taste the warm salt. For how long, she isn't sure. All she knows is that the cold tap water splashed on her face feels good. Then she brushes her hair and stares at her reflection in the mirror and decides she looks okay. It's not that she'll show no signs of this sadness, but she knows from experience, that from where Jack sits on the other side of the room, he will not see that her eyes are red and puffy. Perhaps he'll not even look up from the sports page.

But he does this time, just as she sits back down, calmed already by another Valium and a cigarette she has lit with the very last match in the book. Jack keeps pointing outside, pointing beyond her, and she realizes at what when he cocks his right arm back and curls three fingers around an imaginary bow string, his thumb anchored on his ear lobe.

58

He is taking aim at that reindeer floating there as big as a house. In his way, she thinks, he really has tried to destroy those beasts who possess her—the reason that she has stayed with him and, at moments like this, might even call it love.

The waitress has seen it differently, and she bends down on one knee, her chin resting on her fist at the edge of the table, and she asks Eartha in a whisper if that guy over there is bothering her.

Sometimes, Eartha wants to say, and she almost tells the woman how often her fingers go numb by the roadsides, how many times she has eaten alone. Like now, she wants to say. Like this. She says instead, "No. No, he's not."

"Yuck," the waitress says, glancing back at Jack in his perfectly creased suntans and burgundy turtleneck and shiny new loafers. "Double yuck," she says, which sounds to Eartha like double yolk, Jack's standard late morning order: two eggs sunny-side up.

"Coffee," Eartha says, "please. Black."

When it comes she presses both her hands around the heavy mug. The restaurant is drafty, especially when a young couple comes in, each smiling, the woman carrying a blond-headed child. Nothing unusual in that. Just a few other holiday travelers, Eartha suspects, in this the season of families.

FROM
THE WORLD OF
A FEW MINUTES AGO

THE WORLD OF A FEW MINUTES AGO

After a line by Gregory Djanikian

My name is Clyde Frysinger and my wife, Mary-Helen, is asleep upstairs in the spare bedroom down the hall. A recent and unexpected move, for which no explanation has been offered, and I haven't, nor will I, inquire as to why. We are—the two of us—and for a long time now, childless, and separated in age by only a few months, and suddenly pushing deep into our seventies. After fifty-three years of marriage, our days only vaguely intersect, and maybe *this* is the reason I am still awake and standing in the backyard, the stars at predictable intervals exploding across the sky.

Were she to look down she might mistake me for that prowler she insisted used to visit during my extended absences before I retired, though as far as I know there has never been a single confirmed sighting reported elsewhere in this neighborhood of vintage Victorian homes. No sudden run on deadbolts and not a single vigilante crime fighter rallying the troops for a community watch. And for sure no intermittent crisscross of searchlights sweeping the premises, though I have spent much of my life in places steeped deep in the madness of human misery and violence. As Buffalo Bill Cody put it: "If there is no God, then I am his prophet." I say, amen for owning up.

"Clyde, please. Don't go." Mary-Helen's anthem, and rubbing her temples, she'd say, "Not so soon." But there I'd be, boarding a plane again, and putting down so far distant of dreamland I'd sometimes forget where I was from. I'm a lifelong Wolverine, born and raised, and our son's bedroom, now the spare room where Mary-Helen sleeps, is still decorated in blue and maize. I might even have cast back on that while camped outside the compound of the Branch Davidians in Waco, Texas, April 1993, nineteenth day of the month. On assignment, where late morning I photographed hellfire so fierce I had to duck and quick pivot away. And on the blind run shoot backward over my shoulder, camera aimed into the roar of flames that consumed, nationwide, the covers of magazines such as *Newsweek* and *Time* and *U.S. News & World Report*.

Whenever I returned from assignment, Mary-Helen's insistence that she had seen the prowler was a barometer of my extended absence. "He's real. He's there outside the house in plain view. Sometimes he looks right at me," she would say, almost in a whisper, and certain nights to calm her down I would sit at the window seat waiting in darkness for him to arrive—figment or phantom or Peeping Tom. "Other times he's merely a glimpse in the occluded moonlight. Here and gone, Clyde. Silent and ghostlike." And later, while undressing for bed, I would not only imagine him out there, but imagine that I *was* him. This presence occupied my thoughts in a way that I now understand to be characteristic of men who have been betrayed by great loss and hopelessness, and by the desperate and simultaneous onset of wild and unrestrained desire.

The patio is directly to my left and illuminated by the full moon's blue penumbra. Perhaps I will make my slow way over there to finish this nightcap of bourbon I am holding, and stare out toward the garden where just this morning Mary-Helen pruned her lush and carefully tended hybrid roses, the fresh-cut redolence of them already long vanished. Right now, nothing seems so improbable as the world of a few minutes ago.

Remember Sergeant Joe Friday? "The facts ma'am, only the facts." Here's one: I am no stranger to sin, no model of moral reckoning. As a former AP photographer I am still prone to night terrors and torrential sweats seconds before the onset of first light. I come wide-awake, imagining my right eye pressed to the viewfinder, my night-vision camera turning the surrounding darkness an eerie green. I think of war that way, by the colors mostly, and by the chemical smells. Vietnam first. Later Nicaragua, and, tending toward the end of my career, Bosnia and Rwanda. One evening, a flak jacket saved my life, but I have never once strapped on a sidearm or carried a weapon of any kind for self-defense. Had I been drafted I would have fled this country in a heartbeat.

. Domestically I have covered a dozen executions, men and women both, at least two of the condemned wrongly convicted, as we now know, the death chambers as stark and blighted and bright white as butcher paper. Conrad had it right: the horror, the horror, and in the aftermath of mass suicides I have tiptoed among the corpses. I was there at Jonestown. Hale-Bopp is a late credit of mine, shot *not* in the comet's tail but rather in a nondescript house packed with bunk beds, the bodies neatly laid out, each face covered by a shroud of purple cloth. Black shirts and sweatpants, identical black Nikes. I touched nothing. I later read that seven of these men had voluntarily been castrated somewhere in Mexico. They wore triangular patches that said "Heaven's Gate Away Team," and died with a five-dollar bill and three shiny quarters in their pockets. Vodka and phenobarbital. It's true—too much of anything will kill you dead. I repeat: it will kill you dead.

It is likely that you have seen me during TV news clips over the years, that guy in the background on one knee, leaning in, focusing? Yes, that is me, the same figure who, when he moves, moves slowly and says nothing, but refuses to turn away. Maybe it's for the sake of the paycheck or the coverage itself, the need to expose, but either way, as Jesus is my witness, I manipulate not a single detail of what I've recorded.

Fact: in Mary-Helen's mind there is no difference between the downy breast feathers of songbirds that visit our feeders, and those dried rose petals that occasionally spiral down from the inside covers of our books.

For years she taught British literature at the university, and, like me, she continues to read. *Middlemarch* currently. This is a positive sign, and she is in all ways still beautiful. Stately, even, though nowadays much more easily confused and disoriented. And so the reminder notes that she leaves herself read like poems, like the tiny, crooked script of pure metaphor, but the following is not one: the top joint of her every finger is crabbed and canted out in a different direction. It is a wonder that she can write at all, this woman who no longer has enough hair to gather in her hand, the shiny auburn heft of it gone fine and white and brittle. Stick around long enough and you'll see what I mean.

I have endured two knee replacements that allow me to mow and rake the lawn without anxiety or undue pain, and, at my best, to forgo the support bar by the downstairs toilet. Minor miracles, of course, compared with the flight my legs used to take above a pommel horse, hips rotating like ball bearings and my toes pointed heavenward. Now I get around. I sort the mail. I check the weekly grocery receipt to be sure that the supermarket scanner has not taken advantage. Plus I do all the cooking, and weigh fifty pounds more than in my college days when

I attended the University of Michigan on a gymnastics scholarship. A full ride and trophies and plaques to prove it. To dismount in any approximation of those old ways would incite the fracture of every surviving bone in my body. Yes, I believe and accept that gravity has finally seized from me all sensation of grace and weightlessness.

Even my breathing sits like rock salt in my chest, which is why my cardiologist has scheduled another stress test for next week. "A reality check," he says. "A wake-up call, Mr. Frysinger." As if the scar connecting my clavicle to my navel isn't reminder enough, how it glows bright purple under the buzz of those fluorescent tubes, telltale of the emergency triple bypass I underwent on a Christmas Eve not so long past. I listen carefully and follow his instructions to exercise with caution, and geezer-like I swim my easy laps at the community pool. I swallow an aspirin first thing each morning, and carry at all times a tiny round tin of nitroglycerin pills like a final act of contrition. If I were suddenly stricken, I believe my final thoughts would be about how the arc of the hill behind our house rises and disappears in proportion to the various nighttime shades of light and dark.

This, however, is not yet that moment. It is 1963, and I am floating side by side in the Great Salt Lake with a woman who is slender and young and not my wife, her legs long and shapely and sunlit—hazy golden, her hair the color of fiery cinnamon. We are holding hands, our hipbones touching. We have detoured here from the barren and godforsaken salt flats, where yesterday a man avowing a lifelong death wish set the world land speed record at 407.45 mph.

Light-years removed from my usual beat, and bored by the spectacle and the unrelenting heat, this woman and I caught each other's eye and spent the night in a town too unremarkable to recall by name. But hers is Jeannine Van Manen, journalist. She is thirty-two and the first of my three infidelities. Divorced, no kids, and she asks me about my son, who, when I call, is still too young to come to the phone on his own. Mary-Helen holds the receiver to his ear, and he smiles and kicks his feet when I speak. That's what she tells me. She says, "Clyde." She says, "We miss you something awful. How much longer before you can come home?"

"What's his name?" Jeannine asks. "Your son."

"Eric," I say, which it is not. His name is Tucker, but I have known this woman for less than seventy-two hours, and my son is a sacred continent.

66

She lifts her free hand and lets the water run off her fingertips onto her throat and stomach and breasts, which are large and dark nippled. Then she does it to me, and I imagine I am seeing the two of us small, as if from an aerial view, the camera lens zooming in. The stretch of seconds it takes, the slowdown, the stop-time, and that image of us as a couple forever indelible in my mind. I will flash on it—though I don't know this yet—while Mary-Helen hammers brightly colored croquet stakes into the thick green turf our backyard will, by next Fourth of July, become. And intermittently, and without warning, I will key on this other, perpetually young woman, whose splayed legs glint in the sun, and whose eyes reflect the inexact blue distance of the Utah sky. The rental car is cherry red and the rumble strips loud as I swerve onto the highway's shoulder, where I brake hard and we lick the residue of salt from each other's lips and neck. A motorist passing—never mind how slow or fast—double honks. Followed by someone else. We are their momentary fantasy, a stay against the steady drone of traffic, the shimmering blacktop of late afternoon, and the treeless space pressing in all around us. We have earlier undressed in their honor. It is exactly what I would have daydreamed, too.

At the airport I promise Jeannine that I will keep in touch. We promise each other, but I have already lied to her about my son, my motives, and lastly, my address. "Badger," I said, instead of Wolverine, and jotted down for her invented numbers on an invented street in an actual town named Baraboo, where my first serious girlfriend led me into a pasture of sun-bleached skulls, the attached, tipped-up steer horns at dusk nearly incandescent. From behind I slid my index fingers through the belt loops of her jeans and pulled her tightly against me, the scent of her, I remember, akin to honeysuckle.

The day after she dumped me I referred to her to my buddies as a first-class, dumb-ass ball-buster of a bitch, notwithstanding that she had driven across three state lines to break the news to me face-to-face. If I could I would take back every ardent, angry, wrong word I have ever uttered about her or about anyone I have ever loved.

There is a grainy black-and-white self-portrait of me sitting cross-legged in the opening of a Mongol tent, the flaps pulled back to let in the moonlight. It is Mary-Helen's all-time favorite photograph of mine. A young and content Jimmy Cagney, she used to say, lifting the silver frame off the bureau top for a closer look. I am lucky now if some mornings she calls me by my rightful and time-honored Christian name.

But perhaps tonight I resemble the prowler more than the man in the photograph as I walk a few steps farther away from the house and stop and peer back. A single living-room lamp casts its low-wattage halo partway across the arm of the overstuffed easy chair, where our diabetic cat George is curled, his blindness a sorrow, I believe, only to me. Neither Mary-Helen nor I ever mention anymore how his eyes at night shine a brilliant, opaque bluish white when he stands and stares as if uncertain of what direction to go, or where he wants to be. Like me he is a creature of deep concentration, and in this way we are mirror images, parallel beings to the phantom prowler. And this drink I've poured is no doubt a toast to our collective and insatiable loneliness.

Would it surprise—possibly even shock you—to discover that I am nonetheless an optimist at heart? Or that I was present at the original sighting of the angel Gabriel minutes before a malarial fever that should have killed me broke? Consider this: stars exist that our night has never seen, but here it is again, a Friday night, and there is a breeze, and that scratchy music of crickets, like everything that rises and sets, has already begun to quiet.

If you listen closely you can hear the steady, low hum of our state-of-the-art air conditioning system. Before its installation Mary-Helen and I would drive to the abandoned quarry a few miles outside the town limits, a cooler of ice-cold beer in the back seat. Radio cranked up, and the two of us harmonizing to Perry Como's "Round and Round," the crook of her bare arm sweaty and burning on the nape of my neck.

Even in late July the temperature above the bottomless spring-fed water would plummet by as much as twenty-five degrees between twilight and dawn. We always brought a blanket, and it was there that Mary-Helen conceived. As few as five or six years ago she could have told you at precisely what instant, at what angle of rotation the dashboard clock's glowing green second hand might have paused for a tick or two. Now she becomes impatient and rattled by how to set an alarm. I schedule all her doctor's appointments, and I line up, in small paper cups each morning on the table, the pills we swallow to ease our lives along.

On cool, early summer mornings the screen door is sometimes so thick with mayflies that she mistakes their translucent, almost invisible wings for snow. She will pull on boots, a coat over her nightgown. I do not attempt to stop or correct her as she makes her worried trek outside toward the garden with an armload of sheets to cover and save however many roses she can, the organdy of some so dark they appear bruised and swollen faced. But the season, mercifully, has not been foreshortened. The stems are still prickly and shiny green, and I am standing on the porch, speaking her name, saying it over and over: "Mary-Helen. Mary-Helen," like some far-off echo she eventually hears, and, hearing, she turns, her body motionless and backlit so her face is all a shadow, her uncombed hair a delicate arc of rising mist. She is standing exactly where the clothesline used to be, and where the sheets used to billow like sails, the boat of a wicker basket afloat directly below on the grass.

It is as if I have asked her to hold the pose for the purpose of capturing this moment before it forever drifts away. But what if she were to stoop instead and pick up a single wooden clothespin and hold it out to me? Anybody care to take a guess as to how I might react? Yes. I would bury my face in my hands and begin to weep like some oddly familiar stranger she is nonetheless sure she has never before in her life seen.

For starters, the woman lets down her hair. It is damp and tangled. Late evening and there is a thunderstorm, the power out but the flashbulbs of lightning through the window illuminate the room. Not so much a slow-motion strobe effect as a series of stills, each frame exposing a little more of her nakedness. If this were for art's sake, I would not be sitting so close to her on the bed, the covers pulled back, and the unlatched shutters slapping like wings. No matter how often I shoot and reshoot the scene in my mind's eye, every detail remains identical.

This is the second of my three flings, each short-lived—but then again, what doesn't seem so anymore? And to what do we owe our days, to what new urgency or allotment, to whose skewed version of events? After all, everything is verb, the years advancing while we eat and sleep and make love, sometimes half a world and half a millennium away. Barcelona this time, though any attempt to map or diagram my life leads nowhere that I can either justify or condemn. I exist in that middle space, and haven't a clue to this day whether or not Mary-Helen, prior to her distant and recalcitrant haze, ever suspected a thing. Or, in the end, if she could have mustered need enough to even care. If so she will take that silence to her grave.

The closest she ever came to inquiring was the evening she glanced up at me at the dining room table and said, absent any distinguishable tone or context, "Tell me, Clyde, something inconsolable about you that I could never guess. Some murky reach inside you that you have never allowed me to see."

I had just recently arrived home, exhausted and jet-lagged, my eyes still stinging and red rimmed. And no wonder, given how I had been blindsided by homesickness. And just plain sick to death of the grind and the mayhem, and mourning virtually every second that I had been away, craving, of all things, familiar ceilings and walls, a king-size bed instead of an air mattress or army cot. A neighborhood where nobody has ever been fire-hosed or handcuffed or forced facedown onto the ground.

In answer to Mary-Helen's question, I might simply have overridden her curiosity with a shrug. Feigned disinterest, as if I hadn't a single dark-cellar haunt or secret to confess or confide, and nonchalantly returned to my crossword. Tucker was sound asleep upstairs, and the Greater Dog had already ambled through his nightly rounds to settle at the eastern edge of the Milky Way. We were a family all together again, and safe from whatever unforeseen wrongs or uprisings lurked out there. No backstory needed, and certainly no conscious will to impose or liberate. No sudden urge to piece together for her a single thing.

So why did I say, "Put down your book"? And when she did, I quietly unleashed in lurid detail how, while flat on my back—an Angolan soldier's camouflaged combat boot pressing down heavily on my chest— I offered up not my passport or press credentials but rather a single wallet-sized snapshot. "My wife," I said to him. "And my young son."

He smiled and nodded. "Do not make of her a widow," he said. "Do not father-orphan your child. Go home." And after ripping the film from my camera, he hauled back and slammed it full force into the ground, inches from my head. "Go now," he said. "The jails here, they afford— how do I say—few American luxuries. Leave while you still can, or you will remain here far longer than you wish."

There was a small group of nuns being detained at the same checkpoint. One of them walked over and bent down and blessed me and kissed my hand, and on the interminable flight home I dreamed of her being dragged away and tortured for refusing to admit to trumped-up political crimes.

These are conditions common to my vocation, but way more than Mary-Helen needed to hear in order to forgive me for whoever I was, whatever I might have done, there or elsewhere. The high-stake risks

70

I had run for half a lifetime, and without any serious consideration of ever giving that life up.

"*Which* hand did she kiss?" Mary-Helen asked, and I said, "The left one." And she said, "No, show me," and when I reached into that empty space between us, our fingers interlocked, our grips tightening. Above the table, a garish, low-hanging light fixture that we hadn't yet replaced. I could feel its radiant heat and I noticed for the first time the stencil of lines so fine in Mary-Helen's face that they vanished, as if airbrushed away, the instant she let go and leaned back slowly in her chair.

"Okay. Your turn to tell me something," I said, and without a second's pause she said, "The prowler. He was here again. Earlier, while you were napping."

But it was winter, an inch or two of fresh snow on the ground, and when I went outside to investigate, there were, of course, no footprints other than mine. And behind the glass slider, not ten yards away, Mary-Helen stood hugging herself, though I was the one in shirtsleeves and house slippers, frigid and shivering. A sudden full-body tremor I imagined coursing through the prowler whenever *he* spied her, in whatever weather, irrespective of the season. This woman with the top two buttons of her nightgown undone, standing stock-still, like a sleepwalker or a prisoner in the semi-dark solitude of her own house. Eyes wide open and the room dimly lit behind her.

I have outlived my two brothers, one older, one younger. My mother, naturally. And my father, who worked hard and long during certain evenings after hours as a machinist, multiplying his paycheck times two or three and bottom-lining for us in a scribble of bold red numerals what he needed—"Good Christ Almighty"—in order to raise three kids. "Impossible in this day and age. All these mouths to feed," he would say, that same identical script played out for a week straight. At which point, lips compressed, he would push back his chair and eyeball each one of us before storming out again. Nobody dared leave the table until we heard the heavy door of the station wagon slam shut. Followed by that brief screech of tires and the rear bumper banging hard onto the street at the tail end of our driveway.

Most often he would stay gone for only a day or two before circum-navigating his way back, from where or with whom I never knew. Whenever I asked, my mother would only slow-shake her head and shy away, as if unable to formulate even one hopeful, encouraging response

71

to our current sad state of affairs. To our "reduced circumstances," as I once overheard her tell my older brother, before she tucked, one by one, her three children into bed. "Go to sleep," she would say to me. "Go to sleep, Clyde, tomorrow's another day." Instead I would force myself to stay awake for as long as I could, whispering aloud, as if in my dad's ear, how the entire household lived in dread of his next outburst and disappearance. How we believed that one of these times he would vanish forever from our lives, never to be heard from again.

And so I understood the accuracy behind the words when Mary-Helen said, "You know full well that you can't be away like this and be a devoted father, too," and opening the bedside bureau drawer, she handed me a condom. "It's up to you. It's not as if you haven't been offered other jobs. Safe, high-paying jobs right here in town. A scaled-down version of what you already do, and where you'd be home with us every single night. You know how much I want another child, but not this way. Not living half my life as a widow or a single parent. No marriage over the long term can possibly endure this. Or don't those commitments apply anymore? When, for God's sake, Clyde, is enough, enough?"

In the complex mathematics of departures and arrivals, I concur that Mary-Helen and I existed apart and alone for much of our lives. It is true, even here on this late Indian summer night. Where, in the year 2009, I am standing directly below her window, the vast and endless sprawl of constellations casting loose such brilliance that for a split second I imagine the automatic sprinklers soaking the lawn with starlight.

Is this why my throat keeps burning, my eyes squeezed shut even though someone nearby is crying for help? And someone else is playing a tambourine on the narrow side street behind the hotel where this dark-haired woman and I have shared the cost of a room until just before daybreak. This woman, the final and longest lasting of my affairs, and we have made a lover's pact *not* to fall in love, though I have already folded her brightly embroidered blouse and pressed it to my face. And there is a train close enough to make out its ragged clatter of boxcars, its bulk of iron wheels sparking and pealing back across two and half decades. Do not ask if the muffled weeping that I hear is my own. No one else is around, least of all my son, whom I have also outlived. Unless, of course, you consider how memory thrusts up the dead on nights like this when the ground begins to swell and rupture underfoot. Like right now, and I have to sit down quickly in a chair on the patio before I collapse.

I can almost hear Mary-Helen's fitful breathing through the screen. If I were in bed next to her I would reach over, as I always do, and touch her back gently enough to quiet the house around us. But I have never once, in the ongoing wake of Tucker's sudden death, entered his room. He, a spitting image of me in all those early snapshots I took of him, albums worth, which I refuse to open and page through. His father's son who, on nights identical to this when I deferred to the stars his normal bedtime, would sit patiently on my lap. Motionless, and head tilted back, he would inquire about the twins of Gemini, why they always split apart only to reunite. "Depends on your interpretation," I would tell him. "It's all part of the ongoing story," all those celestial loops and knots, the receding, out-streaming ribbons of orange and blue firelight.

With every next conversion of day into night he would say, "Dad, tell me again, okay? Tell me more." Always more, and I would point in the direction of the brightest arcs and meridians. "Avis Ficarius," I would say. "The Fig Bird. And look, over there's the Bird of the Satyrs, the Raven of Rome, the Rump of the Ancient Lion." Visible or not, they always gathered to stare down on us from those millions and millions of light-years away. The Camel's Hump, the Ram's Horn. Lastly, and right before I would lift and carry him inside and upstairs to bed, I would always pause, the night suddenly incomplete, and ask him, "And?"

"Yup," he would say. "For Mom." And following his lead I would reach palms up into the sky with both hands and then make-believe drape— as if fresh from Mary-Helen's garden—a rose wreath around each of their luminous necks.

I have calculated the nearest mini-mart to be four point two miles distant of us, the highway bypass well out of earshot, on the far side of Memorial Gardens cemetery. And although the parochial elementary school that Tucker attended far exceeds my comfortable walking range, I have found myself more than once standing there by the front gate, waiting weekday afternoons for him. Like the ghost of some little kid's great grandfather, white-haired and slightly stooped, though without any apparent impairment of either speech or cognition.

Mary-Helen used to say that certain flowers only bloom in the dark, and as contrary as that seemed to me, it is nevertheless an image by which I am able to more easily summon our son back.

His dying, the emergency room doctor insisted, was as easy and natural as sleep. As painless as leaning forward over the steering wheel and watching for the stoplight to turn green, the radio tuned to NPR and his foot still pressed on the brake. "Whoever opened the car door," the doctor assured me, "might likely have tried to nudge him awake. No struggle or pain whatsoever. Think of him in an easier world now, Mr. Frysinger. A better place."

That's one version. One I *want* to believe, and, even as doubtful as I am, I sometimes do as I sit at that same intersection, engine idling and the light blinking yellow and no other cars about. The exact last place where my son was alive. Eliminate a single mutated gene gone berserk and he is a mere matter of seconds from continuing north, at dusk, the enduring emptiness of the sky suspended above rye fields the color of pewter. Those same fields that he always passed, slowing down for yet another look, on his way home from work. "An Ansel Adams in waiting," he would say, as if tempting me to confine my talents to memorializing local landscapes. The Walgreens wedged in there now among the commercial sprawl is where I also find myself, waiting alone for as long as it takes to have our prescriptions refilled—Mary-Helen's and mine.

And where I think, Tucker James Frysinger: high-school history teacher with a master's degree from my alma mater. Single but engaged to a long-term girlfriend whose face I remember downwind of that pile of burning leaves from which she slow-turned in a certain lovely motion. I have never said so, but I have imagined, at that instant and therefore ever since, dancing cheek to cheek with her at their wedding, her white satin gown cascading down from her bare shoulders.

At the very least she is old enough, presuming her longevity, to have grandchildren, but in my mind Tucker is eternally thirty-one. A number that causes each next breath of mine to flutter and go cold in my lungs. I see it on the day calendar and I immediately flip the page. Every year on the anniversary of his death, Mary-Helen sets the clocks ahead. Or behind—she is never sure anymore—but what does it matter, finally, she wants to know, an extra hour in one direction or the other?

I have ceased wearing a wristwatch, each invisible moment as timeless as the next shutter click that stops it cold. Stops the winds in Tiananmen Square and the fireballs of Molotov cocktails exploding in the early, unexpected hard frost outside the Budapest parliament. Stops the volleys of rifle fire and the stampede of wild horses across the Siberian steppes seconds before nightfall. Prematurely stops a heart.

Mine beats hard as I climb the stairs and ease open the door to Mary-Helen's new accommodations. She appears tiny under the sheet, and if her low moans speak the dream she is having, then I am merely the beneficiary of an ongoing grief. Which is why I tiptoe around to her side

74

of the bed, believing that my new knees might accept the full weight of my body, as they did when I first proposed to her, a ring squeezed tightly in my palm.

But I know better, of course, and so I lean down instead, and although I have not intended to wake her, her eyes in the blurry moonlight are open. She is staring directly at me, as if the stranger in each of us has simultaneously made that first intimate move toward whatever long and full life together we might have. I remember the first time her lips parted like this and what it felt like when I kissed them. Lips a man like me would have died for, and so I do not resist as she lifts her head a few inches from the pillow. Husband or prowler, I open my mouth just wide enough to feel the warm, wet tip of her tongue. The kiss is long; it is momentary, while just outside the stars continue to die out as they hurtle in their orbits.

And I don't know why, but suddenly I imagine the careful arrangement of bulbs that Mary-Helen plants each fall as tiny planetary bodies. Yes, an image of things long lost bursting back alive again and again into this earthly world.

PROWLERS

There's a ladder that leans against the back of the house, a sort of stairway to the roof where Marley-Anne and I sometimes sit after another donnybrook. You know the kind, that whump of words that leaves you dumbstruck and hurt and in the silent nightlong aftermath startled almost dead. Things that should never be spoken to a spouse you're crazy in love with—no matter what.

Yeah, that's us, Mr. and Mrs. Reilly Jack. It's not that the air is thin or pure up here, not in mid-August with all that heat locked in the shingles. It's just that we can't be inside after we've clarified in no uncertain terms the often fragile arrangement of our marriage. And right there's the irony, given that we fill up on each other morning, noon, and night— excepting during these glitches, of course, when we reassert our separateness, and all the more since we've started breaking into houses.

B&E artists, as Marley-Anne calls us, and that's fine with me, though never before in our history had we made off with somebody's horse. Tonight, though, a large mammal is grazing ten feet below us in our small, fenced-in backyard. This kind of incident quick-voids a lease, and we signed ours ten months ago with a sweet-deal option to buy. A simple three-bedroom starter ranch with a carport situated on an irregular quarter acre where in the light of day we present ourselves as your ordinary small-town underachievers. And that pretty much identifies the demographic hereabouts: white, blue-collar, Pet Planet employed. I'd feed their C-grade canned to my rescue mutt any day of the week if I could only sweet-talk Marley-Anne into someday getting one.

I drive a forklift, which may or may not be a lifelong job but, if so, I'm fine with that future, my ambitions being somewhat less than insistent. Marley-Anne, on the other hand, is a woman of magnum potential, tall and funny and smart as the dickens, and I buy her things so as not to leave her wanting. Last week, a blue moonstone commemorating our ten-year anniversary, paid for up front in full by yours truly.

Anything her heart desires, and I'll gladly work as much swing-shift or graveyard overtime as need be, though what excites Marley-Anne . . . well, let me put it this way: there's a river nearby and a bunch of fancy waterfront homes back in there, and those are the ones we stake out and prowl.

The first time was not by design. The declining late winter afternoon was almost gone, and Marley-Anne riding shotgun said, "Stop." She said, "Back up," and when I did she pointed at a Real Estate One sign advertising an open house, all angles and stone chimneys and windows that reflected the gray sky. "That's tomorrow," I said. "Sunday," and without another word she was outside, breaking trail up the unshoveled walkway, the snow lighter but still falling, and her ponytail swaying from side to side.

She's like that, impulsive and unpredictable, and I swear I looked away—a couple of seconds max—and next thing I know she's holding a key between her index finger and thumb, and waving for me to come on, hurry up, Reilly Jack. Hurry up, like she'd been authorized to provide me a private showing of this mansion listed at a million-two or a million-three—easy—and for sure not targeting the likes of us. I left the pickup running, heater on full blast, and when I reached Marley-Anne I said, "Where'd you find that?" Meaning the key, and she pointed to the fancy brass lock, and I said, "Whoever forgot it there is coming back. Count on it."

"We'll be long gone by then. A spot inspection and besides I have to pee," she said, her knees squeezed together. "You might as well come in out of the cold, don't you think?"

"Here's fine," I said. "This is as far as I go, Marley-Anne. No kidding, so how about you just pee and flush and let's get the fuck off Dream Street, okay?"

What's clear to me is that my mind's always at its worst in the waiting. Always, no matter what, and a full elapsing ten minutes is a long while to imagine your wife alone in somebody else's domicile. I didn't knock or ring the doorbell. I stepped inside and walked through the maze of more empty living space than I had ever seen or imagined. Rooms entirely absent of furniture and mirrors, and the walls and ceilings so white I squinted, the edges of my vision blurring like I was searching for someone lost in a storm or squall.

"Marley-Anne," I said, her name echoing down hallways and up staircases and around the crazy asymmetries of custom-built corners jutting out everywhere like a labyrinth. Then more firmly asserted until I was shouting, hands cupped around my mouth, "Marley-Anne, Marley-Anne, answer me. Please. It's me, Reilly Jack."

I found her in the farthest far reaches of the second floor, staring out a window at the sweep of snow across the river. She was shivering, and I picked up her jacket and scarf off the floor. "What are you doing?" I asked, and all she said back was, "Wow. Is that something or what?" and I thought, *Oh fuck, here we go, sweet Jesus*, and I wondered how long this time before she'd plummet again.

We're more careful now, and whenever we suit up it's all in black, though on nights like this with the sky so bright, we should always detour to the dump with a six-pack of cold ones and watch for the bears that never arrive. Maybe listen to Mickey Gilley or Johnny Cash and make out like when we first started dating back in high school, me a senior, and Marley-Anne a junior and each minute spent together defining everything I ever wanted in my life. Against the long-term odds we stuck. We're twenty-nine and twenty-eight, respectively, proving that young love isn't all about dick and daydreams and growing up unrenowned and lonesome. Just last month, in the adrenaline rush of being alone in some strangers' lavish master bedroom, we found ourselves going at it in full layout on their vibrating king-size. Satin sheets the color of new aluminum and a mirror on the ceiling, and I swear to God we left panting and breathless. Talk about making a score . . . that was it, our greatest sex ever. In and out like pros, and the empty bed still gyrating like a seizure.

Mostly we don't loot anything. We do it—ask Marley-Anne—for the sudden rush and flutter. Sure, the occasional bottle of sweet port to celebrate, and once—just the one time—I cribbed a padded-shoulder, double-breasted seersucker suit exactly my size. But I ended up wearing instead the deep shame of my action, so the second time we broke in there I hung the suit back up where I'd originally swiped it, like it was freshly back from the dry cleaners and hanging again in that huge walk-in closet. We're talking smack-dab on the same naked white plastic hanger.

Now and again Marley-Anne will cop a hardcover book if the title sounds intriguing. *The Lives of the Saints*, that's one that I remember held her full attention from beginning to end. Unlike me she's an avid reader; her degree of retention you would not believe. She literally burns through books, speed-reading sometimes two per night, so why *not* cut down on the cost? As she points out, these are filthy-rich people completely unaware of our immanence, and what's it to them anyway, these gobble-jobs with all their New World bucks?

I'd rather not, I sometimes tell her, that's all. It just feels wrong. Then I throw in the towel because the bottom line is whatever makes her happy. But grand theft? Jesus H., that sure never crossed my mind, not once in all the break-ins. (I'd say twenty by now, in case anyone's counting.) I'm the lightweight half in the mix, more an accessory along for the ride, though of my own free will I grant you, and without heavy pressure anymore, and so no less guilty. No gloves, either, and if anyone has ever dusted for fingerprints they've no doubt found ours everywhere.

Foolhardy, I know, and in a show of hands at this late juncture I'd still vote for probing our imaginations in more conventional, stay-at-home married ways. Like curling up together on the couch for Tigers baseball or possibly resuming that conversation about someday having kids. She says two would be satisfactory. I'd say that'd be great. I'd be riding high on numbers like that. But all I have to do is observe how Marley-Anne licks the salt rim of a margarita glass, and I comprehend all over again her arrested maternal development and why I've continued against my better judgment to follow her anywhere, body and soul, pregnant or not.

That doesn't mean I don't get pissed, but I do so infrequently and always in proportion to the moment or event that just might get us nailed or possibly even gut-shot. And how could I ever—a husband whose idealized version of the perfect wife is the woman he married and adores—live with that? I figure a successful crime life is all about minimizing the risks so nobody puts a price on your head or even looks at you crosswise. That's it in simple English, though try explaining "simple" to a mind with transmitters and beta waves like Marley- Anne's.

Not that she planned on heisting someone's goddamn paint, because forward-thinking she'll never be, and accusations to that effect only serve to aggravate an already tenuous situation. All I'm saying is that a bridle was hanging on the paddock post, and next thing I knew she was cantering bareback out the fucking gate and down the driveway. Those are the facts. Clop-clop-clack on the blacktop, and in no way is the heightened romance inherent in that image lost on me.

But within seconds she was no more than a vague outline and then altogether out of sight, and me just standing there, shifting from foot to foot, and the constellations strangely spaced and tilted in the dark immensity of so much sky. Good Christ, I thought. Get back here, Marley-Anne, before you get all turned around, which maybe she already had. Or maybe she got thrown or had simply panicked and ditched the horse and stuck to our standing strategy to always rendezvous at the pickup if anything ever fouled.

But she wasn't at the truck when I got back to it. I slow-drove the roads and two-tracks between the fields where the arms of oil wells pumped and wheezed, and where I stopped and climbed into the truck bed and called and called out to her. Nothing. No sign of her at all, at least not until after I'd been home for almost two hours, half-crazed and within minutes of calling 911.

And suddenly there she was, her hair blue-black and shiny as a raven's under that evanescent early-morning halo of the street lamp as she rode up to 127 Athens, the gold-plated numerals canted vertically just right of the mail slot. Two hours I'd been waiting, dead nuts out of my gourd with worry. I mean I could hardly even breathe, and all she says is, "Whoa," and smiles over at me like, Hey, where's the Instamatic, Reilly Jack? The house was pitch dark behind me, but not the sky afloat with millions of shimmering stars. I could see the sweating brown-and-white rump of the pinto go flat slick as Marley-Anne slid straight off backward and then tied the reins to the porch railing as if it were a hitching post. The mount just stood there swishing its long noisy tail back and forth, its neck outstretched on its oversized head and its oval eyes staring at me full on. And that thick corkscrew tangle of white mane, as if it had been in braids, and nostrils flared big and pink like two identical side-by-side conch shells.

I'd downed a couple of beers and didn't get up from the swing when she came and straddled my lap. Facing me she smelled like welcome to Dodge City in time warp. Oats and hay and horse sweat, a real turnoff and, as usual, zero awareness of what she'd done. Nonetheless, I lifted Marley-Anne's loose hair off her face so I could kiss her cheek in the waning moonlight, that gesture first and foremost to herald her safe arrival home no matter what else I was feeling, which was complex and

80

considerable. Her black jeans on my thighs were not merely damp but soaking wet, and the slow burn I felt up and down my spinal cord was electric.

But that's a moot point if there's a horse matter to broker, and there was, of course: Marley-Anne's fantasy of actually keeping it. Don't ask me where, because that's not how she thinks—never in a real-world context, never ever in black and white. She's all neurons and impulse. Factor in our ritual fast-snap and zipper disrobing of each other during or shortly after a successful caper, and you begin to understand my quandary. She does not cope well with incongruity, most particularly when I'm holding her wrists like I do sometimes, forcing her to concentrate and listen to me up close face-to-face as I attempt to argue reason.

Which is why I'd retreated to the roof, and when she followed maybe a half hour later, a glass of lemonade in hand, I said, "Please, just listen, okay? Don't flip out, just concentrate on what I'm saying and talk to me for a minute." Then I paused and said, "I'm dead serious, this is bad, Marley-Anne, you have no comprehension *how* bad but maybe it's solvable if we keep our heads." As in, knock-knock, is anybody fucking home?

She'd heard it all before, a version at least, and fired back just above a whisper, "I can take care of myself, thank you very much."

"No," I said, "you can't, and that's the point. You don't get it. We're in big trouble this time. Serious deep shit and our only ticket out—are you even listening to me?—is to get this horse back to the fucking Ponderosa, and you just might want to stop and think about that."

She said nothing, and the raised vein on my left temple started throbbing as Paint thudded his first engorged turd onto the lawn, which I'd only yesterday mowed and fertilized, and then on hands and knees had spread dark red lava stones under the azaleas and around the bougainvillea. All the while, Marley-Anne had stood hypnotized at the kitchen window, re-constellating what she sometimes refers to as this down-in-the-heels place where the two of us exist together on a next-to-nothing collateral line.

It's not the Pierce-Arrow of homes, I agree. Hollow-core doors and a bath and a half, but we're not yet even thirty, and for better or worse most days seem substantial enough and a vast improvement over my growing up in a six-kid household without our dad, who gambled and drank and abandoned us when I was five. I was the youngest, the son named after him, and trust me when I say that Marley-Anne's story—like mine—is pages and pages removed from a fully stocked in-home library and a polished black baby grand, and to tell it otherwise is pure unadulterated fiction. "Maybe in the next lifetime," I said once, and she reminded me how just two weeks prior we'd made love on top of a Steinway in a mansion off Riverview, murder on the knees and shoulder blades but the performance virtuoso. And Marley-Anne seventh-heaven euphoric in hyperflight back to where we'd hidden the pickup behind a dense red thicket of sumac.

Nothing in measured doses for Marley-Anne, whose penchant for drama is nearly cosmic. Because she's restless her mind goes zooming, then dead-ends double whammy with her job and the sameness of the days. Done in by week's end—that's why we do what we do, operating on the basis that there is no wresting from her the impulsive whirl of human desire and the possibility to dazzle time. Take that away, she's already in thermonuclear meltdown—and believe me, the aftereffects aren't pretty.

She works for Addiction Treatment Services as a nine-to-five receptionist filing forms and changing the stylus on the polygraph. Lazy-ass drunks and dopers, jerk-jobs, and diehard scammers—you know the kind—looking to lighten their sentences, and compared to them Marley-Anne in my book can do no wrong. Her code is to outlive the day terrors hellbent on killing her with boredom, and because I've so far come up with no other way to rescue her spirit I stand guard while she jimmies back doors and ground-level windows. Or sometimes I'll boost her barefoot from my shoulders onto a second-floor deck where the sliders are rarely locked. In a minute or two she comes downstairs and deactivates the state-of-the-art security system, inviting me in through the front door as though she lives there and residing in such splendor is her right God-given.

"Good evening," she'll say. "Welcome. What desserts do you suppose await us on this night, Reilly Jack?"—as if each unimagined delight has a cherry on top and is all ours for the eating. Then she'll motion me across the threshold and into the dark foyer where we'll stand locking elbows or holding hands like kids until our eyes adjust.

At first I felt grubby and little else, and that next hit was always the place where I didn't want to fall victim to her latest, greatest, heat-seeking version of our happiness. I didn't get it, and I told her so in mid-May after we'd tripped an alarm and the manicured estate grounds lit up like a ballpark or prison yard. I'd never taken flight through such lush bottomland underbrush before, crawling for long stretches, me breathing hard but Marley-Anne merely breath*taken* by the kick of it all, and the two of us muddy and salty with perspiration there in the river mist. No fear or doubts or any remorse, no second thoughts on her part for what we'd gotten ourselves into. It's like we were out-waltzing Matilda on the riverbank, and screw you, there's this legal trespass law called riparian rights, and we're well within ours—the attitude that nothing can touch brazen enough, and without another word she was bolt upright and laughing in full retreat. And what I saw there in front of me in each graceful stride was the likelihood of our marriage coming apart right before my eyes.

"That's it," I said to her on the drive home. "No more. Getting fixed like this and unable to stop, we're no better than those addicts, no different at all, and I don't care if it *is* why Eve ate the goddamn apple, Marley-Anne"—an explanation she'd foisted on me one time, to which I'd simply replied, "Baloney to that. I don't care. We'll launch some bottle rockets out the rear window of the pickup if that's what it takes." I meant it, too, as if I could bring the Dead Sea of the sky alive with particles of fiery light that would also get us busted, but at worst on a charge of reckless endangerment, and which in these parts we'd survive just fine and possibly be immortalized by in story at the local bars.

"We're going to end up twelve-stepping our way out of rehab," I said. "Plus fines and court costs. It's just a matter of time until somebody closes the distance." All she said back was, "Lowercase, Reilly Jack. Entirely lowercase."

She's tried everything over the years, from Valium to yoga, but gave up each thing for the relish of what it robbed from her. Not to her face, but in caps to my own way of thinking, I'd call our prowling CRAZY.

So far we'd been blessed with dumb luck the likes of which I wouldn't have believed and couldn't have imagined if I hadn't been kneeling next to Marley-Anne in the green aquatic light of a certain living room, our noses a literal inch away from a recessed wall tank of angelfish. Great big ones, or maybe it was just the way they were magnified, some of them yellow-striped around the gills, and the two of us mesmerized by the hum of the filter as if *we* were suspended underwater and none the wiser to the woman watching us—for how long I haven't the foggiest. But in my mind I sometimes hear that first note eerie and helium-high, though I could barely make out, beyond the banister, who was descending that curved staircase. Not until she'd come ghostlike all the way down and floated toward us, a pistol pointed into her mouth.

Jesus, I thought, shuddering, oh merciful Christ no, but when she squeezed the trigger and wheezed deeply it was only an inhaler, her other hand holding a bathrobe closed at the throat.

"Sylvia?" she said. "Is that you?" And Marley-Anne, without pause or panic, stood up slowly and assented to being whoever this white-haired woman wanted her to be. "Yes," she said. "Uh-huh, it's me," as if she'd just flown in from Bangor or Moscow or somewhere else so distant it might take a few days to get readjusted. "I didn't mean to wake you," Marley-Anne said, soft-sounding and genuinely apologetic. "I'm sorry." As cool and calm as cobalt while I'm squeezing handful-by-handful the humid air until my palms dripped rivulets onto the shiny, lacquered hardwood floor. The woman had to be ninety, no kidding, and had she wept in fear of us or even appeared startled I swear to God the lasting effects would have voided forever my enabling anymore the convolution of such madness.

"There's leftover eggplant parmesan in the fridge—you can heat that up," the woman said. "And beets. Oh, yes, there's beets there too," as if suddenly placing something that had gotten lost somewhere, not unlike Marley-Anne and me, whoever I was standing now beside her all part and parcel of the collective amnesia.

"And you are . . . who again?" the woman asked, and wheezed a second time, and when I shrugged as if I hadn't under these circumstances the slightest clue, she slowly nodded. "I understand," she said. "Really, I do," and she took another step closer and peered at me even harder, as if the proper angle of concentration might supply some vague recollection of this mute and disoriented young man attired in burglar black and suddenly present before her.

"Heaven-sent then?" she said, as if perhaps I was some angel, and then she pointed up at a skylight I hadn't noticed. No moon in sight, but the stars—I swear—aglitter like the flecks of mica I used to find and hold up to the sun when I was a kid, maybe six or seven. I remembered then how my mom sometimes cried my dad's name at night outside by the road for all her children's sakes, and for how certain people we love go missing, and how their eventual return is anything but certain. I remembered lying awake on the top bunk, waiting and waiting for that unmistakable sound of the spring hinge snapping and the screen door slapping shut. I never really knew whether to stay put or go to her. And I remembered this, too: how on the full moon, like clockwork, the midnight light through the window transformed that tiny bedroom into a diorama.

"Emphysema," the woman said. "And to think I never smoked. Not one day in my entire life."

"No, that's true," Marley-Anne said, "you never did. And look at you, all the more radiant because of it."

"But not getting any younger," the woman said, and wheezed again, her voice flutelike this time, her eyes suddenly adrift and staring at nothing. "And Lou, how can that be so soon? Gone ten years, isn't it ten years tomorrow? Oh, it seems like yesterday, just yesterday . . . ," But she couldn't quite recollect even that far, and Marley-Anne smiled and palm-cupped the woman's left elbow and escorted her back upstairs to bed. Recalling the run-down two-story of my boyhood, I noticed how not a single stair in this house moaned or creaked underfoot.

Standing alone in the present tense with that school of blank-eyed fish staring out at me, I whispered, "Un-fucking-believable." That's all I could think. As absurd as it sounds, these were the interludes and images Marley-Anne coveted, and in the stolen beauty of certain moments I had to admit that I did, too.

That's what frightens me now more than anything, even more than somebody's giant, high-ticket pinto in our illegal possession. But first things first, and because Marley-Anne's one quarter Cheyenne she's naturally gifted, or so she claimed when I asked her where she learned to bridle a horse and ride bareback like that. In profile silhouette, hugging her knees here next to me on the roof, she shows off the slight rise in her nose and those high chiseled cheekbones. She's long-limbed and lean and goes one-fifteen fully clothed, and I've already calculated that the two of us together underweigh John Wayne, who somehow always managed to boot-find the stirrup and haul his wide, white, and baggy Hollywood cowboy ass into the saddle. Every single film I felt bad for the horse, the "He-yuh," and spurs to the ribs, and my intolerance inflamed with each galloping frame.

Perhaps another quarter hour of silence has passed when Marley-Anne takes my hand. Already the faintest predawn trace of the darkness lifting leaves us no choice other than to mount up and vacate the premises before our neighbors the Bromwiches wake and catch us red-handed. They're friendly and easy enough to like but are also the type who'd sit heavy on the bell rope for something like this. I can almost make out the outline of their refurbished 1975 midnight-blue Chevy

Malibu parked in the driveway, a green glow-in-the-dark Saint Christopher poised on the dash and the whitewalls shining like haloes.

Not wanting to spew any epithet too terrible to retract, neither of us utters a word as we climb down in tandem, the horse whinnying for the very first time when my feet touch the ground. "Easy," I say, right out of some *High Noon*–type western. "Easy, Paint," but Marley- Anne's the one who nuzzles up and palm strokes its spotted throat and sweet-talks its nervousness away. I've ridden a merry-go-round, but that's about it, and I wouldn't mind a chrome pole or a pommel to hold onto. But Marley-Anne's in front on the reins, and with my arms snug around her waist I feel safe and strangely relaxed, Paint's back and flanks as soft as crushed velour. Except for our dangling legs and how high up we are, it's not unlike sitting on a love seat in some stranger's country estate. Marley-Anne heels us into a trot around the far side of the house and across the cracked concrete sidewalk slabs into the empty street. Paint's shod hooves don't spark, but they do reverberate even louder, the morning having cooled, and there's no traffic, this being Sunday and the whole town still asleep.

Marley-Anne's black jeans are not a fashion statement. They're slatted mid-thigh for ventilation, and I consider sliding my hands in there where her muscles are taut, and just the thought ignites my vapors on a grand scale, everything alive and buzzing—including the static crackle in the power lines we've just crossed under, and that must be Casey Banhammer's hound dream-jolted awake and suddenly howling at who knows what, maybe its own flea-bitten hind end, from two blocks over on Cathedral.

We're slow cantering in the opposite direction, toward the eastern horizon of those postcard-perfect houses and away from the land of the Pignatallis and Burchers and Bellavitas, whose double-wides we've never been inside without an invitation to stop by for a couple of Busch Lights and an evening of small talk and cards and pizza. Guys I work with, all plenty decent enough and not a whole lot of tiny print—meaning little or nothing to hide. Marley-Anne negotiates their backyards this way and that. A zigzag through the two or three feet of semi-darkness ahead of us, and the perfect placement of Paint's hoof-pounds thudding down. A weightless transport past gas grills and lawn furniture, and someone's tipped-over silver Schwinn hurtled with ease, the forward lift and thrust squeezing Marley-Anne and me even tighter together.

There are no sentry lights or fancy stone terraces or in-ground swimming pools, though the sheets on the Showalters' clothesline seem an iridescent white glow, and when Marley-Anne yells, "Duck," I can feel the breezy cotton blow across my back, that sweet smell of starch and hollyhocks, the only flower my mom could ever grow. Shiny black and blue ones the color of Marley-Anne's windswept hair, and I can smell *it* too when I press my nose against the back of her head.

There's a common-ground lot, a small park with a diamond and back-stop, and we're cantering Pony Express across the outfield grass. The field has no bleachers, though sometimes when I walk here at night I imag-ine my dad sitting alone in the top row. I'm at the plate, a kid again, a late rally on and my head full of banter and cheers and the tight red seams of the baseball rotating slow-motion toward me, waist-high right into my wheelhouse. It could, it just might be, my life re-imagined with a single swing, and the ball launched skyward, a streaking comet com-plete with a pure white rooster tail.

But if you've been deserted the way my dad deserted us, no such fantasies much matter after a while. And what could he say or brag about anyway? Truth told, I don't even remember his voice. It's my mom's crying I hear whenever I think of them together and apart. He might be dead for all I know, which isn't much except that he sure stayed gone both then and now. Marley-Anne and I have never men-tioned separation or divorce, an outcome that would surely break me for good. And the notion of her up and leaving unannounced some night is simply way too much for someone of my constitution to even postulate.

We slow to something between a trot and a walk, and Paint isn't froth-ing or even breathing hard, his ears up and forward like he wants more, wants to go and go and go, and maybe leap some gorge or ravine or canyon or, like Pegasus, sprout wings and soar above this unremark-able northern town. On Cabot Street, under those huge-domed and barely visible sycamores, Marley-Anne has to rein him in, and now he's all chest and high-stepping like a circus horse, his nostrils flared for dragon fire. He's so gorgeous that for a fleeting second I want someone to see us, a small audience we'd dazzle blind with an updated Wild Bill story for them to tell their kids.

We look left toward the Phillips 66 and right toward the all-night Laundromat where nobody's about. We keep to those darker stretches between the streetlights and, where Cass intersects with Columbus, there's the Dairy Queen with its neon sign a blurred crimson. The coast is clear, and we stop in the empty parking lot as if it were a relay station on the old overland route to Sioux Falls or San Francisco.

"So far so good," I say, and when Marley-Anne tips her head back I kiss her wine-smooth lips until she moans.

"Hey," she says, her mouth held open as if a tiny bird might fly out. "Hey," like a throaty chorus in a song. When I smile at her she half smiles back as if to say, We're managing in our way just fine, aren't we, Reilly Jack? You and me, we're going to be okay, aren't we? Isn't that how it all plays out in this latest, unrevised chapter of our lives?

I nod in case this *is* her question, and Paint pirouettes a perfect one-eighty so he's facing out toward East Main. Already one walleyed headlight wavers in the huge double plate-glass window of the Dairy Queen as that first car of the morning passes unaware of us. Otherwise the street is deserted, the yellow blinker by the Holiday Inn not quite done repeating itself. Above, up on I-75, a north-south route to nowhere, is that intermittent whine and roar of transport trailers zipping past. But there's an underpass being constructed not far from here, no traffic on it at all, and beyond that the sandpit and some woods with a switchback two-track that will bring us out to County Road 667.

Saint Jerome's Cemetery is no more than another half-mile distant from there, and I can almost smell the wild honeysuckle by the caretaker's shack, its galvanized roof painted green, and a spigot and hose and pail to give the horse a drink. The deceased are surrounded by a black wrought-iron fence, and there's a gate where we'll hang the bridle and turn Paint loose to graze between the crosses and headstones, and perhaps some flower wreathes mounding a freshly covered grave. Another somebody dead out of turn, as my mom used to say, no matter their age or circumstance, whenever she read the obituaries. Out of turn, out of sorts, just out and out senseless the way this world imposes no limits on our ruin—she'd say that too. She'd say how it grieved her that nothing lasts. "Nothing, Reilly Jack, if you love it, will ever, ever last." Then she'd turn away from me and on her way out glance back to where I was sitting alone in the airless kitchen.

And what are the chances that I'd end up here instead of in another life sleeping off the aftereffects of a late Saturday night at the Iron Stallion, where all the usual suspects were present and accounted for, and the jukebox so stuffed full of quarters that its jaws were about to unhinge and reimburse every drunken, lonely last one of us still humming along. But *here*, at 5:45 AM eastern standard, I kiss Marley-Anne again and our hearts clench and flutter, Marley-Anne shivering and her eyes wide open to meet my gaze. Paint is chomping at the bit to go, and so

Marley-Anne gives him his lead, his left front hoof on the sewer cover echoing down East Main like a bell.

Already somebody is peppering his scrambled eggs, somebody sipping her coffee, and what's left of this night is trailing away like a former life. The house we lived in is still there exactly the way we left it, the front door unlocked and the pickup's keys in the ignition. *That* life, before those cloud-swirl white splotches on a certain pinto's neck first quivered under Marley-Anne's touch.

AFTER EVERYONE HAS LEFT

Doyle Laidlaw has never attended an execution, has never, one way or another, asserted a conviction—pro or con—concerning capital punishment. He is an ex-husband and the father, still, of one daughter. That daughter, Ellie Laidlaw, is the reason, thirteen years after her disappearance, that he is, at this moment, sitting here behind the closed screen.

It seems another lifetime since he has accepted an invitation anywhere, and he has requested to be seated hours early, though he is not sure why. He is all alone, front row center, dressed casually, wearing sensible shoes and khaki slacks, no coat or tie, attired, perhaps, as he might be to see a Sunday matinee.

He is travel-weary and uncharacteristically unshaven, and, within seconds of closing his eyes, images begin to unreel slow-motion behind his eyelids: a receding tide, a tidal cove gone to mud, and a girl in a bright pink bathing suit and clamming boots crossing that hundred or so yards to the island where, as she's been told repeatedly, she must not go by herself.

"Nuh-uh," she says. "It's *not* dangerous," but Doyle and his wife Francine are adamant worriers, a condition, they concur, symptomatic of middle-aged, single-child parents whose absolution has come in what they refer to as their late-stage miracle of conception, this blond girl they worship and love. She is their consciousness, and they will escort her, they promise, across on tomorrow morning's outgoing tide, in search of starfish and horseshoe crabs and those translucent blue mussel shells she sometimes holds up to the sunlight and smiles. "Okay. Cross your hearts," she says, and in unison they do.

Ellie has, earlier this month, July, turned ten, the evening air warm and still, and Doyle Laidlaw has, with a dull pruning saw he found hanging in the unlocked tool shed, just finished butchering two two-by-fours into stubby blocks of kindling. He is yawning, coming, by degrees, fully awake. Francine has driven inland to the Burnt Cove grocery store for the hot dogs and buns and dill pickles he was supposed to have picked up earlier but forgot, and his counterargument of silence, his only defense, he knows now, here in the stark, whitewashed world of this observation room, is nothing less than an admission of guilt.

The rustic cottage he has rented on the coast for the week seems suddenly to tilt and spin again as he stands alone by the unlit fire pit, staring out at the shimmering horizon of panoramic ocean, those thousands and thousands of brightly-colored buoys nearly blinding him, and he listens, as always, to that distant, low-guttural echo of what he believes to be a single lobster boat motoring toward the Stonington harbor. It's all there in the police report, his brief nap in the hammock, twenty-five minutes truant is all, tops, a dreamless sleep, a mere doze, though he dreams nightly the opposite of every sworn statement he has ever made in his life, every whispered, guilt-ridden prayer of the non-believer, every angry, self-incriminating arrogation.

Sometimes half a day will go by, an elongated evening maybe, when Doyle Laidlaw quiets his thoughts and forgets that drive from northern Michigan to Maine. Maps and the *Rand McNally Road Atlas* and guidebooks, those spontaneous family sing-alongs and how, after arriving, the weather stayed indisputably perfect. Early afternoon breezes and cadmium-blue sky and stargazing nights so spectacular that Francine is, right now, holding her daughter's thin index finger and pointing into that immensity while enunciating clearly the syllables of stars, the mythic names of constellations. "Cassiopeia. Venus. Orion," she says, his bow full drawn into an arc of silver light.

And, in Doyle's mind, the lead detective jotting down every detail, his scratch pad filling in shorthand, laser-like, though he is alarmingly nonchalant, careful not to insinuate anything with his questions or momentary descents into wordlessness, his casual, faraway stares. He is young, late thirties, concentrated more than cold, and Doyle can see out the newly installed bay window behind him how the shallow-chop tide reversing itself has already risen. Half a dozen deputies are wading crotch deep in a semicircle toward him, silhouetted against the streaky sky, heads lowered as if searching for a body that might float by any second, mere inches below that purple-black surface.

The physical evidence is scant. Someone has found a dragonfly-blue barrette, someone a patch of moss torn up among the tiny scarlet hearts of reindeer lichen. But no weapon or blood-spotted leaves or fern stalks, no handwritten ransom note jackknifed to the trunk of a tree, no blond swatch or lock of angel hair. No semen. And of course no assailant, because in the multiple scenarios of murder and rape and abduction there is always a getaway boat involved, anchored or stashed on the backside of Pickberry Island, which is otherwise uninhabited and small, all thick growth and shadow, one of a hundred or more scattered across Penobscot Bay.

Never, over the ensuing years, a single suspect or even a distant lead. Until now, which is why Doyle has awakened early this morning in Texas, where he has never before been, to come finally face-to-face with one Clifford Lee Valentine who has been convicted in another similar crime. And who is scheduled to die at one minute past midnight, all appeals exhausted. He has confessed just one week ago not only to Ellie's murder but to two others, one in Rhode Island and the other in Connecticut. A plumber by trade, unemployed, a drifter at the time of his arrest in the spring of 1985, the only son of a father who, as the court records show, routinely branded him with cigarettes, the pocked scars cratered down the backs of his arms and legs.

Cruel, Doyle thinks, and yet without remorse—in at least a thousand versions of the same recurring dream—he inserts the lethal injection needle directly into this man's heart, this killer of kids who might even have paused, not side-eyed but straight on, to watch Doyle sleep. Who might, in fact, have nodded or smirked as he passed close enough to hear Doyle's open-mouthed breathing, head slightly cocked late on a quiet, laid-back Thursday afternoon. No cooler of beer beneath the hammock, and no radio playing. Doyle is a non-drinker, non-smoker, a careful planner, a grind-it-out advocate of small, sustainable desires, a lifelong disciple of modest ambitions, which are all he has ever coveted or claimed and then fled from into what has become the scattered jigsaw of his life.

He has, a second or two ago, imagined Ellie at twenty-three, another fleeting glimpse. All told it's all he ever sees of her, obscured by that same unaltered visage of Francine getting out of the car, a bag of groceries in her arms, purse strap slung over her shoulder. As always, and within a few steps of Doyle she's asking, "Where's Ellie?" and he's saying, "She went with you, didn't she?" and the screen door slapping hard behind them as they check her bedroom, the bathroom, and then the two of them back outside shouting her name, waiting a few panicked seconds, and shouting it again and again in every possible off-angle direction: behind them down the fire road, into the conifer woods on both sides, the fog horn sounding every thirty seconds in the distance.

"Where?" Francine says, her wide-set aquamarine eyes just inches from Doyle's and she's all bone and fascia and sobbing nonstop, arms upflung, "Where? Where did you see her last? Damn you, where, where, where?"

In the eternal time-lapse of those next frantic seconds he sees, in the tidal mud, two sets of footprints. Side-by-side, small and large tracks, leading only one way away from the cottage, and it is a furious run they make, Francine in flip-flops, he barefoot and out ahead, hands cupped around his mouth as he screams and screams his daughter's name. Erupting up the insides of his bare legs and thighs is something akin to squid ink, an expulsion of some dark and pulverized sea substance that stinks of decay, ashy and cold and wet. He is covered in it, black and doglike and wild with a terror he has never in his mortal being imagined or felt.

Doyle Laidlaw is a public school teacher, seventh-grade geography. A somewhat tragic figure for those familiar with his past, though most of his students pity more his thinning hair and fallen arches, and the way he shuffles stiff-jointed and takes off his glasses using both hands whenever he turns his back on the class to stare for a few minutes out the second-story window, snow coming down harder and harder like millions and millions of tiny moths. He seems then far gone, both lost and absorbed in some computation so oblique that even he can't factor in all the variables, the longitudes and latitudes of evil, the constantly shifting striations of ice-blue light out there in the godless, grotesque, subarctic fields of the Lord.

Midwinter and he has been granted temporary paid leave from his job in order to travel to Huntsville. A guest of the state and stated this way he believes his students might glimpse him differently in the collective quorum of their twelve-year-old imaginations. They who believe the whole world is theirs for the taking, the oversized classroom globe spinning and spinning first thing each morning beneath their fingertips. But he has said nothing to them, not one word, nor will he, not ever. He is who he is, narrow-chested, crowding sixty, though much, much older in the false dawns of 2:00 and 3:00 a.m. when he wakes shivering and alone, his face opaque and wavering like a jellyfish in the naked, glowering light of the bathroom mirror. He wonders if Francine, remarried, the stepmother of another daughter and a son, will show, and if she will still recognize him and perhaps sit down close by without any further need for hatefulness or blame.

He has not laid eyes on her in over a decade, her exact whereabouts unknown to him. No letters or phone calls, though sometimes in the deep, uncharted silence of her absence he believes he can hear the papery mouths of those Maine wasps in the eaves, chewing and chewing, their gray nests protected from the sun and the rain. Yes, the rain, he thinks, which bore down in sheets for a week straight, beginning the day after Ellie disappeared. Downpours flooded the streets and the abandoned granite quarries, the water rising and rising in the blueberry bogs, the steep embankments eroding as if the whole town might spill over into the sea. The number of hooded search party volunteers diminished hourly, without reinforcements arriving and without any clue or trace of Ellie. Even the bedsheets stayed sodden and clammy. And, in the cramped confines of that fishtank–sized room that Doyle and Francine rented short notice in the center of town, and over-stayed—a month in all—they said things too unhealable to ever mollify or retract.

"We've got each other," Doyle said, softly spoken and meant to buoy somehow but translated by Francine to mean as in "at least," and she said, "Don't you ever threaten me with that. Don't you dare," as if he'd already given up all hope of Ellie's reappearance.

"It's not a threat," he said. "No, please, that's not what I meant," and he says her name again to himself, here on this drizzly gray morning in the Lone Star State. In a whisper, "Francine," her arm extended full length, a shaky index finger pointed at him, and on the verge, he believes, of squeezing the trigger of the only handgun she has ever in her life imagined holding, and for no earthly purpose other than this.

There is a clock, Doyle assumes, in the execution room, the seconds ticking down. He listens with intense concentration but when he leans forward, elbows on his knees, it is another kind of time he recognizes, the automatic whir of the Kodak Instamatic rewinding. Is it he or Francine who extracts the film cartridge and hands it to the detective? Doyle cannot remember, though the overexposed front-page snapshot of Ellie—"the missing girl"—in the morning's newspaper appears to him again like a ghost child vanishing across those miles and miles of endless ocean, and gone again the instant he flinches and opens his eyes.

The room, he thinks, is warmer, sweat beading on his lower lip, his heavy breathing as thick and watery as a gag reflex each time he imagines reclaiming his daughter's remains. He has appealed by certified letter to Clifford Lee Valentine for a map, a place name, a single identifiable marker in the maze of this murderer's unreliable and, until now, recalcitrant recollections. The big sugar, as Clifford says, the final missing piece of the puzzle, and he has agreed to lead authorities to each grave site on the condition that his sentence be commuted to life without parole. Only then will he offer up the missing coordinates. But first a good-faith, up-front carton of Pall Malls, he says, which Doyle has actually packed in his suitcase but left, last minute, on the unmade motel bed where he slept fitfully, if at all. An hour perhaps, two at the most. Outside the prison vigils are already underway. Doyle knows this, having stepped carefully around those few handfuls of bruised, velvety rose petals scattered on the sidewalk by the main gate, the two Judas trees just beyond in full bloom.

Doyle has not yet met the warden, but has talked twice with him on the telephone, the conversations clipped, segmented, played and replayed in Doyle's mind because, off the record, "It's a no-brainer. Clifford Valentine is lying through his teeth. Out-and-out," as the warden insisted. "Just stalling for time and nothing more." He who will lead nobody anywhere except to his own overdue extermination on the killing table and, strapped in, whatever he has left to say, if anything, to Doyle or to the attendant priest, to the Almighty himself—not a slobbering sob word of it approximate to any truth beyond the tabloids. "Next thing he'll swear his abusive daddy told him to do it in a dream. Listen, we're beyond all that already, and on to God, Mr. Laidlaw."

What's left of Doyle's faith resides nowhere in God's making, though no doubt the veiled, blank-eyed mourners outside at midnight will sing hymns to Him, the Father, asking forgiveness while inside a choir of death-row inmates waits dead-silent in their cells.

He thinks not Valentine but Valentino, and that the warden is probably right that it's all an act, a predictable, last-gasp, dead-man-walking kind of con hastily cut and pasted from old news clippings of cases still unsolved. The warden has seen the spectacle played out a hundred times at least, and yet Doyle's hope—fortified against its own nonexistence—lies with this murderer who, in Doyle's blurred, closed-eyed image of him, has just tipped back his face, his pinched lips drawing hard on a cigarette in the holding cell not fifty yards from where Doyle presently sits. He can almost see him, no guards or handcuffs, no leg shackles,

95

because Doyle is *there*, too, blowing out the match he has just struck, Valentine nodding as they size each other up. There is a black plastic ashtray on the table between them, and Valentine is large or small, six feet perhaps. Or, in the ocular rush of this moment already fleeting, an oily five-three or five-four is likely the more accurate version: the timid, cornered predator last seen in Louisiana, and possibly staring out from a wanted poster Doyle might have passed without notice while checking his mail, as he does once each week, in his small hometown post office.

And here they both are, not quite strangers anymore, and Doyle says what he has imagined saying to this man forever: "I'm her father. Tell me," but what he really means is, 'Spare me.' Maybe even, 'Save me,' and Valentine in mock consideration saying, "Sure. Why not?" But just as abruptly, he shucks the routine and leans midway across the table, leering and flicking his ash. It is already late afternoon and Valentine, pointing at Doyle's wristwatch, says nothing else, not a single additional word as he slowly ticks the crystal with his fingernail.

What Doyle sees when he opens his eyes is a crew-cut guy in a green jumpsuit, a bottle of Windex hanging from his belt loop, and that exaggerated smile that Doyle's students might refer to in their cockiness as pea brain or retard. Is it for Doyle's amusement that he quick draws and squeezes the white plastic trigger, the plate glass dead-centered with a circle of misty liquid blue? Doyle has never seen a windowpane so clean, the white blind behind it still drawn, and the close-up scrutiny with which this fellow inspects his handiwork makes Doyle wonder if he inadvertently smudged it with his lips or forehead. He wonders if victims' families have pounded their fists or spat at or attacked the unbreakable glass with the heels of their shoes. He wonders if even a diamond could cut through it, and he can't help but visualize that next quick nozzle spritz as an expensive exploding jewel. No, not lapis but a blue pearl, and Doyle is momentarily delirious in remembrance of how Francine at their wedding wore a whole string of them, the small ceremony held outside and the clouds not only cumulus but speeding past as bride and groom delivered their vows.

Doyle says nothing and does not return this custodial inmate's maniacal grin if that, in fact, is what he is. Probably harmless enough but so task careful and slow that Doyle gets up. "Excuse me," he says, afraid the man might sit down on his lap.

96

He needs some air, something to eat, a normal late Saturday afternoon meal at a family diner, where the price of a spaghetti dinner is determined by the number of meatballs. That kind of place, a conduit home to the same rear booth at Grady's where he and Francine and Ellie used to go on Friday nights, idling John Deeres and Farmalls parked among the cars and pickups. He has not been back there a single time, and he avoids at all cost even driving by it, his mind terrified of trading places with who he was then in the calm, familiar middle years of *that* life.

Outside the sky is colorless, the taxis mustard-yellow, and more people—mostly women—have assembled in groups of *them* or *us*. They are interrogating one another with placards and whistles and catcalls, and those shiny black nightsticks the cops keep tapping to their palms remind Doyle, oddly, of fat holiday church candles, and altar boys, and in the dense fragrance of burning lavender he breaks into a fervent, stiff-jointed jog toward nowhere but away.

He sits alone on a stone bench in a park, evening coming on, and those two wing-clipped swans remanded to a pond so small they nearly blot it out with their size and whiteness. They could be happy anywhere together, Doyle believes, slender necked and their heads cocked and touching like mirror reflections of each other right there beyond the ferns and cattails.

He looks away, hands folded, unsure of exactly where he is in proximity to the prison. It could be a mile, two miles distant, a maze away, and he is not soaked completely through but the intermittent drizzle has left him cold and shaking and even hungrier in his present dislocation, though the very thought of food makes him nauseous. He wonders if Clifford Valentine is this instant eating his last meal and the taste in Doyle's mouth turns acrid. He wipes his lips. He's sure he's going to retch and bends over and dry heaves, his stomach muscles contracting tighter and tighter and he's on all fours on the uncut wet grass, his eyes squeezed tiny and black, and the corneas burning.

He cannot swallow. To steady himself he rocks slowly back and forth and each time he deep breathes he feels the heavy weight of his knees, as if a child were riding on his back, although every actual angle from which he might visualize such a moment has long since died. Sighted in this position by anyone passing is to observe Doyle Laidlaw for what he's become, sick and frightened and old, struck down by circumstances so obdurate and enduring that he might never again get up.

But he does finally. He rises to that logical next first step of facing toward and then walking in what must be the direction back to the prison, its chain-link, its glittering halo of razor wire. He wouldn't swear to it, but yes, he decides, that *is* after all where he's headed. Not by way of any acknowledged real hope for what passes as *closure,* a word he hates, but in lieu of there being an even darker place into which he'll plummet if he does not see this day through.

Not soccer but Kick-the-Can. That's what Doyle remembers from his childhood, outside at night in the driveway, waiting for his dad to get home, his mom having multiplied times two or three or four the hour he said he'd be away. Or the consecutive days, sometimes, that seemed to bend into or away from one another. There was the wind that flattened the grass, the rain, the undisclosed locations his dad ran off to again and again, the cowering home, and the weather always worsening. Like this, Doyle thinks. Just like this: the clouds gathering and the distant rolling thunder, and stronger and stronger gusts, and nothing but endless black above these in-the-ground floodlights shining upward. And downward and sideways, a groundswell of illumination so out of sync with those muted B-flat nothing-held-back blues riffs from a saxophone undulating from somewhere deep inside the prison.

Doyle enters through the main gate and is searched again, but this time wanded and patted down, legs spread, palms open, arms held out. He does not look the same, grass stains on his knees, and his gray hair matted flat to his head, his eyes wild and bloodshot. When asked for the letter of invitation, he slides it from his back pocket and holds it out, folded in half, and then in half again, the soggy creases on the verge of separating when the guard takes and carefully opens it. Then asks for some identification, and Doyle, nodding, hands him instead a wallet snapshot of Ellie. "Here," he says, his mouth twitching. "My daughter." And before he speaks her name he clears his throat and looks away. To the left and then right, as if posing for a mug shot profile, at which point the guard does recognize him and stands aside to let Doyle pass.

Into the men's room first, where he presses the button on the automatic hand dryer, and presses it again before it even stops, its coils blazing orange. Over and over until the forced hot air is swarming in a funnel around him. Doyle feels like a little kid. He's scared and chilled to the bone, and his nose is running. He's ten or eleven and yes, he misses his dad something terrible but not that unshakable image of him he suddenly conjures up: carcinogen cheeks, nose alcohol-pitted and purple, a brain choked stupid by booze. A loner to whom Doyle bore only the slightest physical resemblance growing up, so it is striking how much they look alike now in the wavering, shiny chrome reflection of the nozzle. It's as if in a human blink a switch has been made and it is not Doyle but his dad who is standing there sobbing, already more than thirty years dead.

"Excuse me, are you all right?" a man asks, his forehead so furrowed that his eyebrows almost touch.

Doyle has not heard him enter or step out from where one of the three beige stall doors hangs partway open. Nor has he heard a toilet or urinal flush, no water sloshing into the sink. It's as if he's appeared out of nowhere, dressed in a coat and tie, clean-cut, Caucasian, official looking but somehow non-penal. A lawyer for the state perhaps, the kind of attorney Doyle might have trusted had there ever been a trial, a jury, a guilty verdict handed down, and justice served not only for his daughter but for all the daughters gone lost and missing over time.

Yes, time, Doyle thinks. Remove just one minute and that terrible thing that just missed happening never does. They're a family again, he and Francine and Ellie. Maybe they return another summer, same Maine town and cottage, Ellie older and knee-deep in a tide pool, holding up two starfish like pentagrams, and the gulls screeching overhead.

"Please," Doyle says, "please," though only to himself, his voice tremulous and cracking, as if begging forgiveness in the pine-scented bathroom inside a Texas penitentiary is the reason he's traveled all this way. He breathes deeply. He sniffles and blows his nose and when this person touches Doyle's elbow, he glances away toward the ceiling lights that dim and then brighten again.

"It's that time," the man says, and, after he leaves, Doyle visualizes Valentine already en route, counting not the seconds anymore but the one one-hundredths of. It takes Doyle only a moment to calibrate just how close he is to watching a person die, put down, as the warden said, humanely like a dog or a cat gone suddenly feral in the household.

But even in the name of mercy Doyle hesitates to be seated among the aggrieved and considers returning to his motel instead and, in tomorrow's predawn, grab a shuttle to the airport, some breakfast there, and once airborne the great state of Texas receding forever away. Gone, and Doyle back in the classroom the very next day, his voice a mere drone in the chloroformed mindscape of his students still lost to their weekend.

He turns and walks to the mirror, close-up, and he can feel the dull pulse in his fingertips when he presses them to his cheekbones, which are puffy and bruised.

No, not a mirror but a window, and what he hears when he closes his eyes is the powdery thump of a snowball against the glass. He's in his study just off the kitchen, and he can see Ellie's red scarf and mittens as he looks up from his desk where he's been grading papers all evening, detailed map drawings of the world attached. Doyle tap-taps on the pane with his pen tip. Ellie's laughing and waving and Francine's face in the flood of sentry lights appears almost golden, her breath blue-white in the cold air and not even their shouts for him to come join them can break this silence.

Nothing can, except the amplified click of his shoes on the corridor tiles. He's late and half running, and by the time he steps inside, the blind has already been opened on the execution chamber. Clifford Lee Valentine is barefoot, strapped down, the cuffs of his green prison-issue pants rolled up just beyond his ankles, as if a major vein has been located down there by where the priest stands, clutching a Bible, head bowed so that Doyle cannot see his face.

But he can see Valentine's chest rise and fall, or fall and rise, the IV already in his forearm, fingers limp. He is clean-shaven, his hair dark and thick and parted neatly on the left side, and he does not appear panicked or pained, his eyes unblinking and almost opaque from where Doyle stands motionless at the back of the room. He is surprised by how few onlookers are present. Six, he counts, not including himself, the inmate witness side numbering exactly one, a small, white-haired woman who every few seconds offers Valentine another mute, confirming nod. He acknowledges in no way that Doyle can detect that she is even there, though he does not take his eyes off her.

Standing next to Doyle is the man from the lavatory, pad and pen in hand. Not a lawyer after all but rather a reporter poised to take down a convicted killer's last statement for a story on crime and dying. But it's the warden's voice coming through the ceiling speakers, flat and formal, mere words he's required by Texas law to recite, and without the slightest hank of pity or hate. The seat that Doyle occupied earlier is empty. He makes no move toward it down the narrow aisle as the warden pauses, then takes a few steps closer and addresses Valentine directly, hovering, staring down at the condemned before offering him in the pin-drop silence his unassailable right to speak.

The priest looks up, coaxes, but when Valentine shakes his head no everything stops, the moment on pause, except for the white-haired woman holding a rosary and pressing the backs of both bead-tangled thumbs to her lips. It takes only four or five quiet strides before Doyle slides in next to her. He can almost feel the fire in her hands, and the thin arc of Valentine's eyes shifting, locking on Doyle now, like two men lost and staring back at each other across an expanding field of snow. A silence so deep that the black wall phone doesn't ring, though the warden slowly lifts the receiver, not to his ear, but rather just picks it up and lowers it back into the cradle, and from somewhere someone starts the solution flowing through the clear plastic tube.

Doyle's lips are dry, his throat constricting and still he does not turn and flee the scene, Valentine's mouth opening and closing in quick small gasps, and the priest, face upturned, making the sign of the cross. The woman next to Doyle keeps praying, moans so low they remind him of distant trains or the wind through the stunted pines behind his house on those nights when he can't sleep.

He hadn't, before it opened, even noticed the door, but there it is, and a doctor has stepped through, the flat silver globe of his stethoscope already pressed to Valentine's chest, and Doyle's heart thrumming so hard he can feel it in his eardrums. *Ka-doom, ka-doom* as the sheet is drawn up over the entire length of Valentine's body, only the toes exposed, and that is the image Doyle holds onto after the viewing room blind is closed. Why he thinks of the slippers beside his bed he hasn't a clue, though maybe to remind himself how often he has sat in the dark, his knees drawn up under the covers, waiting for first light.

Everyone except this woman next to him has left, and when she takes his hand and squeezes tightly, he squeezes back. Not a single word is whispered. They stare straight ahead without expression, the two of them here alone, and more remote in their singleness than any truth he could have possibly, in this human life, ever believed or known.

SAINT OURS

Here's what the guy I *don't* live with anymore said: "Charlene, if you could only imagine yourself as a feral, teeth-bearing, timber wolf bitch in heat, then you and me—we'd be a whole lot better suited." His name is Paulie. And when, on our honeymoon, I refused to get down on all fours and snarl and snap and howl back at him, he grabbed and attempted to force me down onto the wall-to-wall pea-green shag, and I said, "This is grounds for divorce, you know?"

He'd been downing Kamikazes and doing bong hits—which excuses nothing—and I flashed that instant on how our vows had been so entirely misinterpreted, and in my mind already null and void for as long as we both shall live. And that at some undetermined future date I would sign and serve him with walking papers, and skip town well in advance of all the predictable fireworks.

The man whose bed I'm currently sleeping in has no clue that I'm still legally wed or, for that matter, that I ever was. Or that a fifty-fifty split of everything that Paulie and I own jointly might buy me a tank or two of midgrade. How I've even gotten this far mystifies, the rust-riddled GMC three-quarter-ton pickup in need of a ring job and a tread-bearing set of tires, and headlights that don't strobe or short out on the potholes and washboards and frost heaves. The truck is in Paulie's name alone and insofar as he is by nature ornery and vengeful, and because he always reverts to form, he has undoubtedly reported the vehicle stolen.

Vermont tags, and so when questioned I said, "Montpelier," when in fact the driveway I slowly backed out of almost two months ago is just outside of Bellows Falls. Lying is not habitual with me, though it is my theory that any potential love arrangement that can't bear a certain degree of deception was never in the first place meant to be. Not that love or longing or even a vague yearning was what was at stake. The plan was simply to hole up for as long as need be and attempt to reset and regain my bearings. No rush or panic and trust me when I say that any slue-footed P.I. who can track me here is worth his weight in minks and sables.

"Fair enough, but why Carp Lake of all places?" Grove asked, and my instinct was to lower the coffeepot onto the Formica tabletop, and slide right up tight to him on the midnight-blue vinyl of that back corner-booth seat where he used to sit near closing, and plant a kiss smack-dab on his lips and whisper, "You. You're the reason." Instead I said, "Why not?" and poured him another warm-up on the house, and look where I ended up, safely tucked under an elk hide that must weigh a full forty pounds, the fur thick and fist-deep and shiny.

Grove claims there are only three seasons in northern Michigan: July, August, and winter. Endless arctic wind chills and whiteouts, he says, and the county roads impassable for days on end. No mail, schools shut down, and no place to escape without snowshoes or a snowmobile, and I thought, Perfect.

A single February, he insists, can last a full year. For some people, half a lifetime, and even in the sack his wavy, dark hair appears wind-swept whenever I wake next to him, his head sometimes sideways on my lower abdomen. Other times in the drowse between sleeping and waking I'll reach into that empty space where, out of habit, I already expect him to be. Then I open my eyes to find him fully clothed and staring down like he's surprised to find me there, his cheeks as red as if he's just stepped inside from the cold outdoors after casting and casting his fly line into those blind, predawn hours of darkness.

Unlike me he's currently unemployed. But in three weeks, he says—on the trout opener—he'll resume guiding again. Just last week he got up and cracked the bedroom window an inch or two so that I could hear the water eddy and flow around that wide sweep in the horseshoe bend just upriver from us. He said, "Hey, Charlene, look," and in the slant of early morning light those two gigantic weeping willows that lean out over the far bank glowed iridescent, like lemons. Right, spring hopes eternal, and yesterday, like magic, the first of the dive-bombing kingfishers arrived.

I've only ever fished with night crawlers or miniature marshmallows on a bare hook, and a bell sinker to carry the bait down and out away from the shore. For bullheads or suckers, lazy, good-for-nothing pig-eyed bottom feeders as Darrell, my stepfather at the time, referred to them, and he sure never contemplated paying anyone to lead us any-where. He wouldn't even tell my mom where we were going. "Our secret spot," he'd say, and no, she couldn't tag along, and he'd quick-wink over at me. I was fourteen, my first bra front-hooked and lacy and shiny black. Sometimes on those hot, humid afternoons I'd say to him, "It's no different than a bikini top," and unbutton my shirt and sit there while he chain-smoked, his narrow eyes like a gar pike's or what I con-jured a barracuda's to be.

As part of our Just Say No education we'd previewed half a dozen perv films in homeroom, and which we referred to as C Block, gray concrete walls and those heavy, steamy, yeasty-smelling canvas green shades yanked tight to the sills. Although Darrell possessed certain tenden-cies, he never so much as copped a feel or moved on me in any overt physical way. Except for one time to tuck a loose strand of hair behind my ear, and eventually, like my birth father, he disappeared too, *his* current whereabouts unknown.

Grove is nothing like Darrell or Paulie. Everything neat and tidy, and when I first inquired as to his line of work, he said, "Dining on the fly. Strictly an under-the-table, word-of-mouth operation," and I thought, Okay, fine, but factor in his *Better Homes & Gardens* kitchen, and fancy-ass drift boat, and French wine by the case and it all points to some fatter scratch elsewhere.

Drugs. Reverse alimony. Insurance fraud that I'd heard Paulie and his Saturday afternoon chugalugging buddies gas on about while work-ing up their slow, predictable fury and daydreaming aloud about how just one fucking sweet-deal windfall of a scam would instantly trans-form them into blue bloods. Kings of the trailer park, as they said. But Grove's cover? "A moderate trust," he said, more question than state-ment, as if appealing to my imagination to buy into whatever he was selling, and I thought, Say again? As in, get screwed royally more than a time or two and a woman on the loose better damn well scrutinize the motives of any man. And that includes even a charmer as decent-seeming and soft-spoken as Grove.

As if reading my mind he said, "An inheritance." And to corroborate the claim he showed me the ornate, bowlegged cherrywood leather-top desk on which he ties flies in his shop out back. They're intricate and gorgeous and now and again he'll hold one out to me in the shallow pool of his palm and whisper its Latin name: *Isonychia*, he'll say. *Hexa-genia limbata. Ephemerella dorothea.*

In grade school I sat in the second row next to a boy from Brazil, whose name I can't anymore recall, and whose seat one day went unoccupied, and stayed that way for the remainder of the school year. Olive skin, eyes oval and dark brown like fresh roasted almonds, and I swear Grove could be that kid grown up, his teeth even straighter and whiter now, the moist-looking lips, the remote, wry smile. Quite possibly someone who, a few generations removed, might actually have been connected to the ruling class, and whose life out here in the boonies merely some oddball remnant of a more glamorous and pedigreed past.

Grove has a college degree in entomology, which explains why he examines so carefully the submerged stones he lifts from the riverbed, turning them over and over in his hands. He makes sketches and takes meticulous notes in his daybooks on what he sees. "Helgramites. Nymphs. Midges. Insect larvae," he says of the water samples he collects in tiny glass tubes teeming with invisible protozoa come to life under the intense magnification of his microscope. Incredible, and Holy Mary Mother if that constitutes scholarship, then maybe higher education is not, as my mom maintained, just another wide-eyed pipe dream. "Listen to me, Miss Cum Laude. Forget about the I.V. Leagues, okay?"

"*Ivy* Leagues," I corrected. "Like on vines and archways and court-yards." And she said back, "Beauty school, Charlene. Go there and call it college if need be. Think hair. Think manicures and blush and mascara," which struck me as unenlightened and small-minded and hopefully untrue.

My teachers all concurred I was plenty bright enough. A regular fucking brainiac, as Paulie used to say. A potential star pupil who loved to read, but nothing by the book, so to speak. Meaning nothing that was ever assigned, but I'd taken the SATs and scored nationally in the ninetieth percentile on the verbal. Somewhere in my old room at my mom's house I've still got that No. 2 pencil I used to blacken those oblong bubbles.

Grove, naturally, isn't privy to any of this. He never pushes or pries and neither do I and so, at least in the short term, our hidden private selves are therefore impossible to trace. All secrets aside, what's obvious to both of us is this: That I am all legs, disproportionate as a cricket, and that the hem of my tight-fitting waitress uniform quits a good six inches shy of my knees. I have witnessed men jolted back alive when I've slow-turned and walked away after taking their orders. It's a walk

I perfected in front of the full-length mirror behind my closet door, as if my career path had been determined when I was maybe ten or eleven, already a showgirl of sorts in my mom's lilac lipstick and three-inch heels. All prettied up and the mirror two-way, I imagined, and men of all ages huddled up and staring, and the sky above the house about to crack wide open, all thunder and rumble and hellfire.

Yes, me, Charlene St. Ours. That's my maiden name and as my dad used to say, a name as pure and precious as poured silver. St. Ours, as if a single patron was watching over us, the guardian saint of dreams, he said, except that hardly ever seemed the case, and no doubt goes a long way toward explaining how I hooked up with Paulie in the first place. That and dumb judgment and being eighteen and bone tired and emptied out by dead-end jobs and fewer and fewer prospects going forward.

My dad believed that the true worth of any life was how well you survived your own worst human share of it, and not how you warded it off, which he contended was impossible so why even try. Arguments I barely understood back then, but all things being equal, here I am, intact enough at thirty-three to believe, against the odds, that the happier outcome the human heart was meant to act on is still possible, maybe. If that includes toughing it out for tips at the Day-Runner for a while, so be it. I mean, could be it's as simple as this: We do what we do. We let down our hair, lips slightly parted, and undress like those goddesses men believe us to be in the early winter dusk, and sometimes we need to believe in that image, too.

So yes, I've consciously withheld from Grove any exacting, incriminating personal details: my hapless, head-on, rent-to-own wreck of a marriage, for starters, and Paulie either sucking down beers or passed out cold or gone off to the casino in some last ditch to resurrect our bankrupt fortunes.

It's sad but true that I've viewed more of this wide world than I'd like to admit from the tin-hootch roof of a house trailer with its cheap venetian blinds and russet-colored dollar-a-yard carpeting. During the summer months, Paulie stashes a grill and a Styrofoam cooler of Hamm's on the two wooden pallets and makeshift planking that he hauled up there, and refers to it—ready for this?—as our portico. Don't ask me from where in his limited vocabulary he exhumed *that* gem, but I quote: "Charlene. Go ahead and climb that ladder, Princess, and plant your deadfall of a fanny on our frigging, brand-new private portico, and for which we owe nobody not one red goddamn cent."

106

"Judas Frigging Priest" was my initial response as I ascended, and sat down on the ripped and battered Naugahyde recliner. And the sky blinding and peacock blue above as if Paulie had, in a sudden rush or brainstorm, positioned us that much closer to the Almighty himself, the arc of our lives suddenly all faith and mirth and sunshine and bells.

A eureka moment if ever there was one: this was my future, already rooted out and picked over, the reek of methane in the wrong wind direction wafting in continuous waves from the landfill that abutted us. So pungent sometimes, I wondered why, when Paulie torched a bone or a cigarette, the entire mobile home park didn't instantly incinerate in a single sonic-boom bomb burst of apocalyptic white light.

And so it felt magical when Grove cooked and served *me* that first dinner, an entrée of venison medallions, so tender I had to resist swallowing each bite whole. Followed by flaming creme de something or other for dessert. He's got a stand-up, double-door stainless steel freezer packed with wild game, each vacuum-sealed see-through packet labeled and dated. And a smokehouse out back and half a dozen stump seats arranged around a fire pit to entertain his wilderness-seeking fat-cat clients. He says that he offers them Cutty Sark or cognac. Coffee and sambuca. Hand-wrapped Cuban cigars, which accounts for the humidor, the first I'd ever laid eyes on, and perhaps, in context, a minor eccentricity after all.

There are enough books stacked on the living room shelves to rival my hometown library: *Thinking Like A Mountain*—that's a title that struck a nerve. So I started reading. And ever since, whenever a cloudbank in a particular shape rolls in, I imagine snowcapped peaks, and canyon passes where a train keeps wending through the switchbacks, a man and a woman meeting by chance for the first time late at night in the dining car. Not entirely unlike Grove and me, not if you blur your vision and ignore the smell of pork ribs, the spat and sizzle of the grill, and those distant, sad howls of coyotes late at night.

I suppose this merely confirms what my dad always said about me: "A dreamer is what you are. Never lose that, Charlene. Never, ever give it up. Make it too real, it's ruined. Remember—there's always a quiet place inside your mind somewhere. Find it and go there," he said, "no matter what."

He worked at the foundry—his face a deep copper color in all seasons. Except for around his eyes, the infernal lava-like boil and swirl of the forges impossible to look into without double-ply, black-lensed safety goggles. Often his lips got so badly blistered he'd press them ever so lightly to his boiler suit sleeve before kissing my mom. I don't know why but I intuited that moment of pain as true love, which it turned out over time not to be, and so I remain thankful that they never hazarded any other offspring. Ditto for me, at least so far. That, too, got to be an issue with Paulie, who, because we hadn't yet—his exact phrasing again—"made us a little monkey," accused me of secretly using birth control. For the record, I did, and do, distributed free at the county health clinic.

Grove and I have been together for exactly twenty-two days and nobody here is laying claim or talking long-term anything, and no mention whatsoever of where the potential holy mess that great sex between complete strangers sometimes leads. Ask my dad, who left with a woman half his age and whom my mom still refers to as "that little zip of a slut with the tight ass and the high-rise plastic tits." He promised support payments but nothing legally deeded and so you can figure in two seconds flat the upshot of that.

"Why?" Grove asked the first time he pulled up at the unnamed, slashed-rate four-unit hovel of a motel. Whitewashed plasterboard walls and ceiling, a stubby pull-chain and a forty-watt bare light bulb. One dinky window beside the hollow-core front door, where I'd been slumming, broke and depressed and convinced that I'd run through my life savings only to end up in a dive more dismal and claustrophobic than our faded pink coffin of a house trailer. No phone or TV, and someone's abandoned black slip still hanging on a single dowel in the tiniest closet I'd ever seen.

"Because it's all I can afford for now," I told him.

"No better than sheep sheds nailed together," he said. "That's all they are. And I don't mean to intrude on your personal space, but hey, listen. This is no place for a person to try and survive for more than a night or two."

That's when he offered to let me crash at his cabin until I got back on my feet, and to his invitation I all but broke down sobbing. No set timetable, he said, and rent-free, and best of all no questions asked. Plus all the high-ticket cuisine that my shrunken, growling, on-the-run stomach desired. Once every two months he drives south all the way to Traverse City to stock up, and when we sat down to that first candlelit dinner I could name maybe half of what I was lifting to my mouth.

"Y'know of course," Gina, the owner of the Day-Runner, says, and pauses, and I think, *No, I honest to God don't,* but it doesn't matter one way or the other because here we go again, round and round on another after-hours speed trap check-in of my misinformed emotions.

"Women end up alone and snowbound here's what happens first thing," she says. "They go stupid, and then downright loony. Get a glimpse of Grove a few days grizzled and it's no secret that he's been down and around that proverbial bend more than a time or two."

"Maybe I get the vapors for older boatmen," I say. "And who's snow-bound anymore? I can hightail it out of here anytime, if and when I choose." What I keep to myself is that the thought *has* seized hold more and more with every passing night, my few belongings stuffed in a pillowcase and already in the pickup.

Gina just nods and takes a deep, slow drag, the doors to both rest-rooms propped open and the undiluted smell of industrial-grade toilet bowl cleaner thicker than the smoke of her cigarette. Which, in the neon of the house lights dimmed down, turns a pale, murky, eerie green when she exhales slow motion through her nostrils and mouth.

It's almost the witching hour and we're the only ones in the restau-rant, having wiped down counters and tabletops, vacuumed, refilled the ketchups. Marking time, as Gina, the native martyr who's never in any hurry to leave, says. Yeah, just sit long enough and time gets earlier is her take, but I don't buy into a single disappearing second of it. She's got two out-of-the house kids, a daughter and a son, long goners, as she calls them, off and running from one mess to another. And, God forbid, "Uh-uh," no man onsite or lurking anywhere on the shadowy periph-ery. Precisely the way she prefers it, absent any hassles or obligations 'to love and cherish,' and which, as she says, is what all that commitment bullshit inevitably turns out to be.

Her feet are propped up on the opposite booth seat, right next to me, the soles of her shoes gum rubber, her ankles plumped-out and veiny. Her eyes, too, all glassy and half-lidded in their sockets, and I envision that if she were to close them she'd nod instantly off. And wake and rise minutes before first light to start the coffee brewing again, her sev-enth consecutive double shift this week. A menu that never changes and that I memorized in less than fifteen minutes so I could clock through the shifts with my mind leaping ahead toward other things. Like the new moon, and the next time it's full, Grove promises—weather permitting—that he'll slow-float me downriver so I can observe the swirls of monster brown trout turned carnivorous and rising for injured bats or mice or voles. He ties those, too, with deer hair and hackle, their eyes sad and oversized, and their tiny pointed ears so soft and real-looking I want to carry them into a field miles removed from any waterway and let them go.

"It's all illusion," Gina says, and points through the thick plate-glass window to the twenty-four-hour 7-Eleven across the street lighted up like a mackerel sky. "Even the First Lady at this hour is as ordinary and tragic as the rest of us. At this hour, Charlene, everybody's heart hurts. Present company no exception, and don't pretend otherwise or you wouldn't be sitting here in the first place."

The smoke rings she blows widen and break around me like the outlines of mottled, oval green mirrors, and for a few seconds I'm staring not at Gina but at my own face, ghostlike and reflected back in the sudden time warp of twenty years.

Gina says, "Excuse me, but I'm confused. Now tell me again what it is you're going to miss most on your way out? *If* and when you go."

Attitude aside, Gina's okay, but Venus flytrap all the way when it comes to late-night one-on-ones, where she's forever throwing down on me like this with questions and innuendo calculated pretty much to tick me off. Never one moment's tired silence to offset the running commentary. Like my mom at her nosiest sleuthing-around worst used to do. "Just wait, you'll see," but what I need is to get *gone* from here, where I've force-smiled and small-talked and balanced overloaded trays until my arms and jaw and brainwaves ached. Odds are that Grove will be awake, the woodstove aglow, like always, and the elk hide folded back on the king-size goose-down mattress. Feathers below, pelts above, but I don't want to confide or bitch-snipe another opening for Gina to crawl through and prolong the conversation.

"The way he washes and hand-dries and stacks the dishes. That's what I'll miss most," I say, as if Grove were the busboy I split tips with, the one who is nineteen and married and hitchhikes to work and back, a father already, and a second child on the way. A sweet, sweet-faced kid who, first thing after taking off his coat and hat, folds a white dish-towel lengthwise and drapes it over his left shoulder. Like he's about to back-step away from the scalding trough of the soak sink and instead burp and rock an infant right there, in the rising steam and clot of the kitchen.

His wife, who I've met one time only, bears a fair likeness to the baby-sitter my mom used to hire to watch me whenever my father stormed out, where to or for how long we never knew. In his absence my mom would sit alone, oftentimes for hours, in her Cutlass Supreme, parked in our driveway of spurge and flowering, impossible-to-kill, spiky yellow weeds. Always in that same sleeveless dress, open-backed and low cut with all the wrong kind of cleavage. Even her fake eyelashes and earrings drooped too low, as if her entire wardrobe was a fashion statement about gravity and early middle age and being suddenly single again and with nowhere to go. Only her teased dark strands spiraled upward from their roots into a hair-sprayed beehive of sticky platinum blonde.

She'd start the engine and a few seconds later shut it off. Take another belt of Bacardi straight from the pint bottle and chain smoke, the dome light on and then off and the tail fire of her cigarette butts arcing out into the blacked-up night like a spray of tiny meteors. I'd watch from the living room window, waving every ten or so minutes to try and summon her back inside, her entire body doing that shuddery thing that meant she was crying big time again. And my dad's cryptic parting words to us on his way out a couple months earlier? "She'll adapt," he'd said about me. "Both of you will, just give it time." But no place inside me ever came close to accommodating his absence, or my mom's chronic and forever deepening despair. "No, not a divorce, an annulment," she said. "Do you even understand what he's asking for, Charlene? What the word means? That *we* never happened. Never were. Not for one crummy, disappearing day of our lives together did any of this matter. So cruel," she said. "So goddamn godless and beyond belief pitiful and downright cruel. And what did we ever do to deserve this? What?" she said, as if I might on the spot hatch some fairy-tale scheme that would somehow make her lonely, self-loathing life a tad bit easier. No kidding, I should have taken a vow right then and there to never, ever marry or fall in love.

"Mm-hmm. Feature that," Gina says, and instead of stubbing out her Parliament in the black plastic ashtray, she stands the cigarette on end on the tabletop between us, like a fat blown-out birthday candle. "Knocks himself out on the domestic front, does he?"

"That's him all over," I say. "Times ten." And I flutter my eyelashes and without another word I grab my coat and scarf and long-stride out into the rear parking lot, the spare front door key to the cabin in my apron pocket. Along with my paycheck and a folded in half paper-clipped wad of maybe fifty tip bucks, not a single crisp, recently minted bill among them. Wages only livable under the ongoing arrangement, whereby I spring for pretty much nothing other than my own gasoline, and those few privacy items for 'the lady of the cabin,' as Gina has taken to calling me.

Never *to* her but in large measure, I admit she's not entirely mistaken. I am, for better or worse, a kept woman living for a change, free of re-possessors and delinquent bills and monthly phone threats to cut off the heat and electricity. Under those circumstances name me one woman who wouldn't have deferred a past that resembles in any way where I've come from? Grove's not only content with our arrangement, but determined not to amend a single thing. Some part of me wishes he would, although I guess the ban on heavy lifting those hidden mangles and menaces of our concealed histories still stands. Two nights ago I inadvertently mentioned x or y and Grove interrupted mid-sentence, silently pressing his index finger to his lips, and slow-shaking his head from side to side. Reminding me once again that we existed aware of each other not in the moment gone or about to be, but rather fixed in the continuous present only.

It's cold but no snow and glittering constellations galore, an intermittent flare pulsing beyond the trees. So far so good, I guess. After all, the engine turns over and catches on the first try. The idle's rough, plus a flaming acetylene-blue backfire or two, but when I hit the light switch even that row of orange operas on the top front of the cab blinks on. Grove has rewired the pickup from beezer to back end, a phrase I liked and hooted at when he first used it. He's also replaced the four baldies with retreads from the auto pound. Included in the emergency survival pack he assembled for me is a heavy black billy club of a flashlight that holds six batteries. Plus a couple of Mars bars and a thermal blanket in case of breakdowns, the roads to the cabin mostly two-track and sometimes snow-sealed or choked out by drifts or fallen limbs and no way to turn around. "Yes, by all means, in April. Nobody's home free yet," as Grove continues to tell me, the swollen eyes of winterkill deer the delicacy of ravens and crows and those bald, redheaded, hook-beaked, blood-faced turkey vultures, their wings stretched wide against wherever the barren white sky either ends or begins.

He reminds me that a snap freeze can claim your toes or fingertips. I take heed but wish on nights like this that *something* like love suddenly discovered superseded these routines of survival: Get safely back and get laid. Go to sleep. Morning coffee together while watching the purple ripples on the river so perfectly tuned but the music dialed down to zero.

Around the moon there's a halo of frost, but the windshield is clear and the gas tank nearly full. There's a sign for Good Hart pointing south, and what's left of the snow burns almost incandescent along the ditch line, the trees strung out in silhouette for as far as I can see. "You'll be

112

years getting there," my dad liked to say. "But that's okay." I'd nod like I understood as he walked straight away from me into the darkness. And where he'd stop finally and light those sparklers he always kept on hand in every season. A ritual he'd perform whenever I asked, and, from that same paced-off distance, he'd dazzle me with crazy-angled loops of fire.

Had Grove in a sudden turn of mind even halfway considered any part of my life worth telling, I might have mentioned that the looping, zigzag wing-light was so bright it turned that part of the field behind our house silver. Like an actual angel was out there dancing under the dome of the sky. I lean forward, and lost somewhere up there in the night swirl is the Lute-Bearer and the Fair Star of the Waters but in what direction I haven't a clue, and the pickup at such low speeds tends to stall out anyhow.

I hit the gas and the high beams and head in an unknown direction, and because the double thud of tires across the railroad tracks reminds me of a heartbeat, I grip the steering wheel hard against that chronic and violent shimmy as if to hold the pickup from shaking apart. Not until the speedometer's glow-green needle exceeds fifty-five does the world appear quiet and calm again. I crack the window barely an inch. And, for one brief disappearing second before that upcoming first sharp dip in the road, the power lines gleam in the rearview like harp strings.

WONDER

Their names: Mitchell and Michelle, and I couldn't help but wonder from what little he divulged if all similarities between them ended there.

She had been his colleague, young and bright and hired right out of grad school to teach French, but had bailed on academe for an American-speaking career in women's retail. The age gap between them, he joked, was a mere twelve years. He hadn't, as he put it, *quite* looted the cradle, and then he described her to me over the phone by quoting Melville's remark on the "rare virtue of interior spaciousness." I'd fallen pretty far away from phrases like that, but after being recently paroled, I thought virtue and spaciousness in a woman sounded like a plus.

I'd been married once myself, briefly, but since then those few women I believed I could have loved long-term always exited in a hurry, agreeing to meet me again only in dreams. That included Helen, my then-wife, who filed on the grounds that she wasn't ready for the early dark, the direction in which I'd been headed for a major portion of my life and, even against other more promising worldly designs, possibly still was.

But the bar with the payphone in back served cheap house drinks at midday, and Grand Forks happened along the way railroad towns did in my drifting and hiring on as a cutter and welder with every railroad from Union Pacific to Norfolk Southern. So I'd seen these States United and Grand Forks was a far cry from the most godforsaken place I'd ever been. But it was also where I finally ran out of options and ideas and laid out on the bar my last four twenties, and then tried to visualize if that was enough green for a one-way Greyhound bus ticket back home after almost two decades away.

114

Mitchell and I go all the way back to grade school, best buddies, and straight sober I might not have asked after all this time if I could put down at his place for a while. Just until I landed a job is what I said, though railroad country Petoskey was not, and I had at present no particular other line of work in mind. I'd gotten hold of Mitchell at his office through the college switchboard, and knowing something about how marriages misfire I figured he'd defer his answer at least until he checked things out with Michelle. Whom I'd never met, but the lead lines he threw me were high temperature, and outside the snow kept coming down, and all signs pointed toward northern Michigan.

"Alden," he said, "the spare bedroom is yours. For as long as you need it. You know that. No questions asked." Then he gave me his street address, a neighborhood I used to know, given that I'd grown up just a few blocks away in a household I'd done my best to forget. He said the backdoor key was hidden under a rock in the birdbath, in case I arrived while they were out or away. I told him, "I owe you one," and he said back, "Hey, who's counting, right?"

For sure I had been, an unending tabulation of regrets, as I'd stare sleepless into the void above my cell bunk, swearing to God and to myself a brand new life forthcoming once I was on the outside again. Ninety days, and the prospect of a positive outcome in spite of all those bad choices was my single, solitary focus and comfort. As a fellow jailbird said to me, "You make bottom, there's nowhere but up."

That part of my life Mitchell did not need to hear about, and I hoped never would. I'd sent him hokey, single-sentence, bumtown kinds of postcards just to let him know that I was alive. "And thriving," I'd write. "Thriving and still tossing them back." No return address—not ever— though I suppose the postmarks provided a scattered geographical jigsaw for him to piece together. Now and again a late-night catch-up phone call, which over time became less frequent, and then nonexistent. So there was a lot of silence to break when I decided finally to dial him up, and more guardedness on both our ends than I'd anticipated. But when I told him where I was calling from he said, "North Dakota?" and laughed a laugh I still recognized. And hearing it again like that, I smiled right through the lingering weariness that the booze hadn't even begun to touch.

Then he mentioned a beginning-level ethics class waiting on him in the next room. Which sounded right—a grownup version of that dreamy, oddball kid with the brushy hair who always took principled positions on complex moral matters that back then just felt stupid inside my head.

Like Nixon's lies. Like Chile and Pinochet, Vietnam and Cambodia, though the only war I cared about was the one that raged and raged inside our house after my dad died unexpectedly when I was thirteen, and my mother remarried badly and way too fast, and for which I'd never entirely forgiven her.

Whenever she took sides, it was always with him, a follow-orders kind of tyrant who had no job and no children of his own and boasted non-stop about his seventeen-inch neck and lethal forearms. And who, the day I refused to call him "sir," threatened in his new wife's absence to fill my mouth with the sharp, hooked, snapped-off ends of fence wire. He was forever stretching it around something—around his garden, the carport and doghouse, all around the property, so that the place resembled a compound by the time they sold it and moved away at the tail end of my senior year. Grown and gone, he said, meaning them, not me, and no discussion whatsoever about whether I planned to accompany them to New Hampshire, where he was from. None, and my dad, whom I loved and trusted and missed terribly, buried for what already seemed an eternity in Holy Cross Cemetery. And somewhere in the after-silence of all their sudden departures I landed a job at Olson's Auto Body, torching off mangled trunks and doors and fenders, the beautiful blue whistle of acetylene fire alive all day deep in my ears.

"Like pure music," I kept insisting to Mitchell one summer when he was home from Ann Arbor. He was about to head back to finish up his degree taking, and after maybe his fourth Rolling Rock he cocked his head in a kind of tin-ear grimace, as if the needle had just skipped sideways across whatever record album we'd been listening to. It was mid-July, blistering hot, and bare-chested he put on my welder's mask and slowly scanned the tiny, third-floor dive—my "high-ground," as he sarcastically called it—that I'd been renting by the week. In a certain odd angle of the lamplight, his pupils through the dark safety glass glowed red behind the reflection of my own pale and distorted face staring back.

"Oh, yeah, like pure music?" he said, and whistled into the throat of an empty beer bottle, his other hand torching the premises—floor and walls and ceiling—the whole homely place consumed in a magnificent imaginary whoosh of flames. Then he slid the mask up and said, "Let's get you the Christ out of here, Alden," as if the only way he could save me from myself was to set the whole damn place on fire.

The air was so thick and heavy it hurt to breathe, but a twelve-pack of ice cold ones—what we called green grenades—hit the spot and Mitchell insisted, "Sure you do. Just sign up for a couple of evening classes to start, and see how that goes." He said the cerebral world awaited conscientious minds like mine—"definitely"—and that I should take it slow to start. "Ease into it," he said. "Then decide if you're born to that kind of a life or not."

But game time for me meant all or nothing, and at twenty-two I figured to make up some distance by brain-busting my way through a full load and, as Mitchell predicted, to some pretty respectable grades. Except in Composition 101, where every interminable misspent minute dragged against my intended redemption. And where I watched the clouds or the swaying treetops of whatever excuse the window provided to daydream myself away from Professor Claybay's condescending double index-finger drumrolls against the edge of his scarred and ancient podium.

I'd taken an instant dislike to the guy, fortyish and doughy in the jowls like someone who'd never once imagined owning a souped-up shiny black Camaro or Chevelle and driving it hard and late into the night. I hated his whole act—the bored, half-stifled smirks, classic asshole all the way. The type you just wanted to smack in the face with a volley-ball. Once for every tongue-clucking pause he used to punctuate his contempt for each and every one of us. So I just assumed my same seat in back each day and concentrated on tuning out all the bullshit.

"Are we communicating?" he'd say at least once during each class hour, and then he'd call someone's name, which late on a certain Wednesday afternoon happened to be mine. Maybe I heard him and maybe not. I can't honestly remember. But when his tone turned from exasperated to downright mean-minded and he asked me point-blank if I was present—"In the here and now, yes, you, Mr. Grelling"—I nodded and said nothing back.

But I also did not look away. An ongoing problem I'd always had with petty authority. A problem that commenced immediately after my dad's death and never abated, and so I didn't take kindly to the way this guy's eyes stayed locked on mine. Still, had he moved on after making his point I might, in spite of the blood-rush in my ears, have let the incident pass. But instead he said, "Really? Then why don't you hold up your notebook and show us what competent note-taking looks like. What it is you found important enough to jot down during this hour so as not to waste my time."

The next day was Thanksgiving. A long weekend ahead, and all I had to do—the smart move—was to study the scuffed-up geography of my boot toe or duck away for a few seconds under the bill of my baseball cap. Anger, as my dad used to say, was always a mistake in retrospect, always a disappointment. He'd had big plans for me, big dreams for his one and only son to turn the world into a better place.

But right there, in the suddenness of all those undefined options disappearing, I slowly pushed myself into a standing position. And in a more or less grammatically correct declarative threat I said, "Push on it, pal, and I'm going to drop-kick an exclamation mark sideways right up your tight, compositional ass. All the way to the dead end of every one of your goddamn pretentious sentences."

He gaped and waited dumbfounded, almost hyperventilating, until I sat back down, and when he spoke again his voice cracked and wavered badly.

"Get out," he said. "Leave this classroom now, and don't you ever come back. Trash talk somewhere else because you're all done around here. You, Mr. Grelling, are history."

I raised my balled fist up under my chin, elbow hard on my thigh like I needed some serious time to mull over the implications of what he'd said, and how he'd finally inspired a little wrath with his not so compassionate fire.

Then he ordered me out again. "It's your last chance," he said, and I thought, *Come on, come at me.* But instead we all concentrated on his footfalls, heavy in the hallway as he left to go roust the campus feds.

"Hey, screw him," I said, addressing the entire class, tight-lipped and edgy in their seats. "Really, I mean screw this noise," and two or three students applauded, though only one young woman named Denise, who hadn't said a word all semester, picked up her books and followed me out to the parking lot. And then just stood there, high cheekbones and thick, shiny black hair to her shoulders. For a second I imagined her sliding into the passenger seat of my beat-up, last-leg Subaru and the two of us lighting out north all the way to Sault Ste. Marie under that dark and pressing late-November sky.

But I guess she had other plans for the night, a date maybe or dinner with her family, because all she said was, "Thanks. Best lecture of the semester."

I smiled and thought about shaking her hand, though what I really wanted was for her to reach up and brush my cheeks with her fingertips. But no such luck, and so I got into my car and watched her walk away, her outline already blurry beyond those first fat smacks of rain on the windshield. Then the wipers slapping hard all the way to the bank, where I closed out my savings account before stopping at my junk-cluttered single-bedroom while Mitchell's mantra about *corners, corners, corners* kept playing in my mind. I knew I'd just wrong-turned one toward somewhere I hadn't intended and might not easily get back from.

Corners and curves, and I thought about how the two of us had slow-dragged that jackknife's freshly honed steel blade in a crescent across our thumbs. And how, pressing them together, we'd pledged to each other, "Blood brothers forever." In a world of so many once-only-and-gones, we had suddenly grown wings. Or so it seemed as we crouched side by side over our handlebars and glided around and around those wide new slick-black cul-de-sacs, baseball cards clothespinned to the spokes of our silver Schwinns, our ascendance destined to continue on and on. Always in the late evenings under those gray-green streetlamps that eventually led back to our separate houses, mine with the TV on and the drawn blinds blinking a different hue with every single scene change.

This one was about to be major, and I considered giving Mitchell a call, a heads-up on my sudden change of plans. But I guzzled the last couple of cold beers from the fridge instead, and then just looked around. Just stood and looked at where I lived, the empty ravioli cans, the unwashed dishes piled in the sink. And without even shutting the front door, I turned and descended the stairs two and three at a time. Like a burglar, though I sure could never have imagined that years later I'd be accused of exactly that. A thief held at gunpoint by the whimpering, drivel-lipped husband of a woman who swore first to him and then under oath that she had not invited me in.

Caught red-handed, the prosecution argued, and I agreed, by hubby himself, home unexpectedly. And me with my pants down and my dick in the cookie jar. But no ski mask—"I mean, God bless the crazies, but how about we return for a second to planet earth?"—and no stolen jewelry, and to hear her tell it that night in the bar, she wasn't close to being fucking married. Which I made clear to the judge and suggested from the stand that maybe the cops should have dusted the Trojan for fingerprints, given that she was the one who'd rolled it on and then rolled back the bedcovers. That's when the court-appointed lawyer threw up his hands, and I exited the courtroom innocent of all felony charges but nonetheless in handcuffs to serve two consecutive counts of aggravated contempt.

All part of the bar mirror's dark and smoky past, I thought, my face staring back from behind those tiers of coppery silver bottles as I reclaimed my stool. I was the only customer in the joint, and current circumstances seemed suddenly promising enough to order one last round for myself.

"To you," I said, lifting my glass. A simple toast to maybe being on the brink of something better, and for the first time in a long while I felt grateful to be alive. I toasted Mitchell, and then I toasted my dad. Already I was older than he was when he died. "A bad heart, or enough bad luck," he used to say, "will lead to an early grave," but when I shut my eyes, I could almost feel the old neighborhood's steady beat before things had even the slightest chance to play out wrong. That's what I wanted again: a world scaled back to fit the innocence of that skinny kid's body I used to live inside. At least until the school of hard knocks did its masterful job of teaching all hope and happiness right out of me, summa cum laude all the way.

The snow continued falling but only lightly into the purple twilight when I stepped outside and followed the bartender's simple directions to the bus depot. A left and then a right across the intersection two blocks up. The massacred Samsonite I carried was the same one my wife Helen had fast-packed in a rare tirade before finally throwing me out and filing for divorce.

Up ahead the bus to Escanaba was already boarding, and those last three twenties and change got me a seat and a neatly folded navy-blue blanket. A good-looking single woman to sit beside and cover at the knees and let sleep against my shoulder while the frigid world outside slid by was a long shot indeed. Nevertheless, I figured this was my chance to dream up some better stories to tell for when I arrived.

I stood alone for a moment in the dimly lighted aisle, checking both sides, and then I passed slowly all the way to the back without a whispered word to anyone. And without anyone making eye contact or leaning out, or signaling in any way for me to stop.

Nothing big-city about Escanaba, a 1950's throwback kind of town I liked a lot, and hitchhiking out of the Upper Peninsula I almost crossed over to the other side of Route 2 and stuck out my thumb going north. But the southbound rides came fast, and a hundred plus feet above the Straits on the Mackinac Bridge in those gusts of dwindling light made reversing course seem like a lousy idea once I touched down on the other side.

I hadn't only been all day on the road but more like lost in a continual time warp. And suddenly there I was standing hungry and lightheaded under the streetlamp in front of Mitchell and Michelle's aluminum-sided two-story, 1228 Keefe Avenue. No lights were on, no car in the driveway and I considered simply sitting on the front porch stairs until someone arrived.

120

But it was clear-skied, and an all-too-familiar chill already filling my bones. Nothing like Fargo or Grand Forks, of course, where one February it got so badass arctic I could hear the railroad spikes contract in their ties. Too cold even to snow, and those full eight-hour shifts I'd worked outside in the freight yards had taken their toll.

I rang the doorbell just to be sure, and when nobody answered I tried turning the knob. There was a heavy brass knocker, but I didn't want to make that kind of racket so late and listened instead to the few faint disappearing notes of the wind chimes hanging in the next-door neighbor's tree.

Around back I could see the harvest moon reflected and swirling in the birdbath as I fished out the key and unlocked and opened the backdoor. The wall switch was right there, but before I could even flick it on I heard whispering. I was certain of it. Two voices back and forth, and I stopped dead in my tracks. I don't remember for how long—well beyond those interminable few seconds it took for my eyes to start to adjust. And when a woman's voice said, "Who's there?" I stayed absolutely still, except for the speeded-up motor of my own deep breathing. I thought I smelled marijuana, but maybe not, and then a woman's voice asking, "Mitchell, is that you?"

I hesitated, and then I cleared my throat and said, "No. No it's not. It's not Mitchell."

Then the sound of pants sliding on, a zipper riding shut. Followed by another run of rapid whispering and what sounded like a slider rolling open, and footsteps slapping across a terrace. Possibly only one set, I wasn't sure, and the slider closing and clicking shut.

"Are you still there?" the voice asked, as if it were me, the intruder, who'd turned tail and fled unseen back into the night. It crossed my mind to do just that, half a dozen crouched strides out of there and forever gone.

But right then music from a clock radio started playing, Frankie Valli and the Four Seasons, and if the adrenaline weirdness hadn't already hit an all-time high, it sure did when the music stopped abruptly and the woman walking into the room straight at me said, "You're Mitchell's friend, aren't you?"

I didn't like being the one on the defensive, fielding all the questions, and so I said, "Whoa," and before she got any closer I spoke my name at her in the semi-dark.

"That's right. Alden," she said softly, the words measured and gentle-like, as if I'd sleepwalked into the wrong house, a kid again, and here was this lady quietly reassuring me that I'd entered a safe place and everything was all right.

"I rang the doorbell," I said.

"Doesn't work," she said, "and anyway that's not what I'm asking. Why don't you turn on the light?"

The distance between us was maybe four feet, and yet her words seemed to be coming at me from some other dimension, more like a dream, and in it she was doing something with her hand. Something relaxed and slow and silent, though the harder I concentrated, the more her outline wavered and blurred.

"Watch your eyes," I said. Then I hit the switch, and in the sudden flood of the overhead as she stepped forward, I believed the lip balm on her pinky fingertip was intended for me, her full lips already glossed and blowsy and sore looking. Like what happens after long, hard-friction kissing, and we were standing almost close enough for that to have occurred. Not that my mind was processing the possibility, though to have claimed it as an entirely unattractive thought would, I was certain even then, prove false and perhaps, given enough time and distance, even cowardly.

"You're letting in the cold," she said, giving me the quick once-over as she closed the tiny round tin and slid it into the back pocket of her beltless low-rider jeans. Her white T-shirt read, MAKING IT HAPPEN—no bra underneath and her breasts sizable—and I tried not to make that the moment's focus either, the door still ajar behind me.

"Probably I should just leave," I said. "Before Mitchell gets home."

"In precisely forty-five minutes," she said. "He never lets his classes out early. He never surprises me like that. Like you did. Ten-thirty he'll be here. Upbeat and on the dot, so I should go upstairs now to take a shower and dry my hair."

It was shoulder length, a shiny shade of brown I liked, styled I could tell, but falling over one eye until she pushed it back behind her ear. She looked like a woman who, unlike me, had never spent any time standing blank-eyed in unemployment lines, and never would. Her toenails were polished red, and what Mitchell had identified as a twelve-year age discrepancy seemed way out of whack. Without turning a blind eye to numbers, mid-twenties was as high as I was going to get.

She wasn't model-stopping-you-in-your-tracks-to-gawk-at beautiful, but attractive in a healthier, less body-abused sort of way. Dark eyes. Wide mouth turned down, even when she forced a smile and said, "We'll have to work on the timing, but as long as you're here, I'm Michelle. Mitchell's wife. He's been looking forward to seeing you."

We shook hands and I closed the door, and right up front I said, "Listen, this is none of my affair," and she said back, "No, it's not. It's mine."

"It's none of my business is what I meant. And since I didn't really see anything anyway, I guess I'm good with that," I said, though I wasn't, not entirely.

She folded her arms and stared wide-eyed at me, a slight flex in her hip that I liked. Then that slow, expressionless, continuous nod as if we'd sealed some secret deal or understanding, and which maybe we had.

"I'll show you the guest room," she said. "Then you can just make yourself at home."

That entailed walking through a combination library/entertainment area, where she snapped on a stand-up lamp, weakest power, then picked up two throw pillows from the carpeted floor and tossed them onto a love seat. On the wall, behind glass, a movie poster of King Kong chest-pounding out his primordial rage as death planes squalled into the frame behind him. My all-time, bar none, favorite flick, and I wondered if Mitchell and Michelle owned the video, but I didn't ask.

Instead, I watched her slide a wooden dowel into the slider track and pull the draw chain, and I imagined for a disoriented couple of seconds that she was going to start the VCR playing, and maybe project the beam onto the wide, slightly wavering screen of the blinds. But she didn't move. She continued standing there facing away from me, and said, though barely audible, "He means nothing. Nothing to me at all."

I didn't know the truth of that, one way or the other. Or whom she was even referencing, though I assumed it to be the phantom caller who'd momentarily slipped out of the scene. But who in my mind I watched get into his parked car a few blocks distant and sneak farther away into the night, worried I figured, or even terrified, of whoever might show up later swinging a baseball bat against the flat, bruised face of his front door.

"No need for an explanation," I said.

"Why would you?" she asked. "Men never do."

A theory advanced by other women I'd known on their slow or fast track out of flings or marriages. Helen, for one, and every failed attempt to argue her back ended in that same dead silence love always leaves in its vanishing.

I can't recall what I said then, but Michelle turned and sat down hard on the floor, hands pressed between her thighs, head lowered. Spent, I thought, desperate and scared and why not?

Beside her the numerals on the radio alarm slapped over, four times. A stretch between 9:59 and 10:03 PM in which no cars drove by, the silence seeming to widen and settle in around us, until she half-gulped back what sounded like a moan that subsided only slightly after I knelt and held both her shoulders, and resisted only minimally when she leaned in against me.

She could not have been more exposed if she'd been stark naked, and after she pulled away I gathered up her underthings—bra and panties—from the black leather swivel recliner and said, "Here. You might want these out of the way."

It was 10:28 when she left for the soft whispering of the showerhead. And I imagined not Mitchell's headlights bending around the corner, but rather the twin beams on our identical silver three-speeds. That was the summer we'd sneak out our bedroom windows at a designated time and cruise through the cold air eddies and swirls that always drifted in from the cemetery and the surrounding fields a few hours before midnight. I could almost hear the intricate reverse click-clicking of our pedals as we'd enter those mysterious, isolated thermal pockets left by the sun. And where we'd sometimes stop, straddling our bikes and naming the few identifiable constellations we knew by their animal names: Swan and Bear and Fox. Then we'd be off again, covering what distance we could up and down that next adjacent street as the whole town dreamed around us.

I retraced my short path back out of the room, my stomach growling, and listened to the drain water swirl down through the pipes. What would Mitchell think? His wife in the shower and some strange, weatherworn drifter in a faded Carhartt and hooded sweatshirt sitting all alone, hands folded on the kitchen table. Like someone waiting to be interrogated. Like someone guilty of pressing with his tingly fingertips along the spinal ridge of a distraught woman as she wept.

The only reason why a guy like me ever took a job, or ever would, is money. I'd started young, full-time blue-collar at seventeen, determined to abide by my dad's edict never to freeload, never to be beholden in that way to anyone. The price, he said, was a guaranteed loss of will and self-respect. He was a man driven by optimism and fairness in all things and, because I was his flesh and blood, it felt good to cash my first paycheck and stock Mitchell and Michelle's home deli with Kaiser buns, honey ham, cheese and olives and limes, and a month's supply of freshly ground, high-grade Columbian. Coffee, not weed, though one night Michelle tapped on my door, a joint in tow, and in the home of the other most moral man I'd ever known and looked up to, I invited her in.

"Merci," I said, before I took my first serious toke in over a year and sat down next to her at the foot of the unmade double bed. She was still wearing the dress she'd worn to work, and the way she crossed and uncrossed her legs, I could see the soft white skin on the backs of her knees. Nothing happened except that we got good and stoned. Got quiet and loud, and I was asleep by the time Mitchell arrived back from teaching his three-hour honors seminar called Situational Ethics. About the fourth time I woke that night, sweaty and dry-mouthed and sitting bolt upright in the predawn darkness, I resolved—just to be on the safe side—to steer clear of the dope and the bourbon whenever Michelle and I were together alone.

She never mentioned her lover, if that was ever even the proper determination. Never once rounded on him or on the subject of her infidelity, acting as if I'd discovered her three weeks earlier locked instead in the arms of her husband as they watched a film together. One night each week, Mitchell would make a ritual stop at Blockbuster on his way home from work. Always Michelle's selection, though I never once heard him gripe about her picks, and so assumed their tastes to be one and the same. Never anything Hollywood, and I came close on a couple of occasions to recommending *King Kong* or *Star Trek* or *Bride of Frankenstein* just for a change of pace.

Mitchell's French was, as he put it, passable. So I alone sat reading the subtitles, and reminding myself all over again why I had never been a serious watcher of foreign films. Not even Sin City stuff, though I admit to pressing the pause and replay button on a particular frame or two in my day. But never anything that charged me in the way Fay Wray's dress hem always did, sliding thighward as she reclined in the fleshy black cave of King Kong's muscled palm.

Which is simply to say that *Un homme et une femme* was doing nothing to keep me awake or entertained. It was Saturday night, I'd put in a long week cutting Christmas trees, and I figured Jean-Louis somebody or other could unzip the leading lady's sleeveless dress without me being there to cheer them on. Yet I stayed right to the end, as I always did, not so much to be polite as to see Michelle lean her head back and to the side and kiss Mitchell on the lips while the credits rolled. A kiss orchestrated, I thought, for my benefit and mine alone.

That's the image that continued to loop around and around inside my head as I toppled blue spruce and Fraser firs at Londrico's tree farm.

Mitchell would drop me off each morning, driving several miles out of his way, my lunch box and his briefcase between us on the seat. He a tenured professor dressed to a T; me in Pac boots, Carhartt jacket, and matching bibs. In the glaring clash of our separate work-world attire, we looked our age, the years, as he said, dating us by everything youthful that they'd stolen away.

He talked like that, softly, in metaphor, and read poetry and philosophy and listened to books on tape. Except when I was along, and he'd crank up Springsteen just like old times minus the new Ford Taurus and the gray invading our hair. Mutt and Jeff dullards we might have scorned two decades before, has-beens attempting to sing those booze-whipped lyrics we loved all the way back into prime time.

It felt good, though, cruising and hand-tapping the beat against our thighs, Mitchell's raspy, out-of-range, single-note falsetto just bad enough to excite in me that same old road desire to light out half in the bag, never to return home again.

In my absence, the area had changed so dramatically I hardly recognized entire parts of it, the gated lakeshore communities and the upscale downtown with its gas lanterns and cobblestone sidewalks and espresso bars. A whole lot of what I imagined before I arrived back had, from my perspective, been bargained away, and reasons to stick around much beyond the holidays were hard to come by. I'd be unemployed again by then anyway, and that did not cause me to lose even one second's sleep.

Still, I liked looking down the empty tree rows, flatbeds from Georgia and the Carolinas being loaded at the snowy field's edge. It was the kind of work that Mitchell and I might have teamed on together as high school kids but never did.

"Pick you up around five," he said. It was Monday, the engine running and the car in park, and the two of us staring out the windshield, the sky salmon-colored above the wave of green- and white-tipped spires. Another day, I thought, of sunshine and stretches of snow, weather unable to make up its mind.

I got paid by the stump, but I was in no hurry that morning to hit it hard, and might well have gone into the shed to turn on the beat-up space heater, and slow-sip another cup of coffee before pulling on my gloves and safety goggles and starting the chainsaw. I had the padlock key in my possession since I was the only cutter working that particular eighty all week, which I liked.

126

"You bet. Five sounds perfect. I'll meet you right here," I said, and got out of the car and leaned back in as I always did and told him, "Teach 'em up, Doc." But this time he didn't smile, didn't register in any manner at all. Just nodded, the music off, and I said, "Mitchell, you okay?"

Which he appeared to be at breakfast, and on the ride over as well but for sure not anymore. He seemed lost somewhere in thought, and I figured that thought's subject might be female, and that I had not in my silence adequately covered his back as I'd always done before, no matter the circumstances.

"He was there at the house, wasn't he?" Mitchell asked, not looking at me, and I said, "Who?"

"It's a straightforward question," he said, without raising his voice. "Either you know what I'm talking about, Alden, or you don't."

He leaned back, arms out straight and his knuckles bone white on the steering wheel, like he intended to crush the accelerator and fishtail up the double-stump row and come barreling out on the far side of the plantation. He stayed right there, saying nothing else, patient in a way I'd always envied and had long ago identified as the complete opposite of me.

It wasn't difficult to figure what he inferred when I hesitated for a few long seconds, then shut the car door and turned away and unlocked the shed and stepped back out a few minutes later, chainsaw in hand. The car was still there idling, but I did not acknowledge Mitchell's presence, or gesture in any way in his direction. I simply opened the choke full until the spark plug fired on the fourth or fifth pull, and I squeezed the trigger hard. The two-stroke screamed until I backed off and inserted my earplugs to muffle that awful high-decibel whine, and then I slowly walked out into the trees.

With every tank of gas I'd stop and file and tighten the chain, and at one point, cutting my way back down the spruce row, I did glance between the trimmed boughs to see that Mitchell had driven away.

The morning had turned to flurries, the temperature falling fast, and my knees had started to lock, my fingers blistered and going numb in my gloves. The bite of the wind out of the north went right through me. But I stayed at it until late afternoon with only a short lunch break, determined to finish strong on my last day. I hadn't planned on cashing out on such short notice, though in my mind hitching a ride south with the last of the haulers didn't sound so bad. Free transportation in exchange for helping them unload, wherever that might be. Savannah, Charleston, somewhere out of the cold.

If I concentrated I could just barely hear their diesels idling on the far side of the much larger adjacent tract, and I might even have started in that direction when Mitchell pulled up by the shed. It wasn't close to full dark yet, but his headlights were on, and the snow slanting through that muted double tunnel of the low beams took on a whiteness that was almost blue. Like the thin frozen rim of the moon some nights, I thought. I could see his silhouette as he stood, and the tiny clouds of his breath rising.

It was one of those intervals when any number of outcomes appeared possible, none of them happy. And I wouldn't have faulted Mitchell if he'd opened the trunk, heaved my bulky suitcase in my direction, and driven away. Almost nothing would have surprised me.

Except, of course, the thing he did, which was to nod and breathe in deeply the sweet, thick scent of all those freshly cut evergreens, and then walk, still dressed in tie and coat and wingtips, right by me without uttering a word. He took his time but not a long time before hauling one of the bigger blue spruces back to the car and, without him asking, I helped tie it to the roof. Just that morning I'd offered Mitchell and Michelle a free tree; she, more than he, appeared eager to get out the ornaments and put it up early for once.

Mitchell's family always had a Lionel train circling under the base of theirs, and bubbler lights and lots of tinsel hanging down, and after my dad died I spent every Christmas Eve and Christmas over there—a second son, as Mitchell's dad used to call me. I even had my own stocking, with "Alden" scripted down its candy-striped length, hanging from their mantel.

That's what I remembered as we drove to Meadowbrook, the nursing home and assisted care facility where Mitchell's parents, both in their mid-eighties, now resided. He said that their lives there were not unpleasant: a conscientious staff, round-the-clock care. That he stopped by afternoons on his free hours, at least every other day. He said, and without rebuke, that Michelle refused to visit, retreating as far as possible from what lurked just beyond the lightfall. He made even that sound poetic, as if such an admission were in no way incompatible with his ability to love and be protective of the person she was. I wondered if his parents asked about her and, if they did, what he said to them.

I didn't know the nursing home, but the landscape of certain streets along the way there seemed familiar. A few wreaths already on the doors of houses, and one giant Santa attached to somebody's chimney, like he was trying to keep warm, huddled under the huge emptiness of the sky.

No stars anywhere and not one word from either of us about what he'd asked me earlier, though had it come up again I would have answered yes. I would have told him that I was sorry.

But it was Mitchell who apologized. "I should have told you," he said. "It wasn't fair to let you walk blind right into the middle of all this."

"The marriage, you mean?"

"It's been on the rocks for a long time," he said, "and there's nothing left to do but give it up. Just let it go. We thought early on," he said, but he didn't finish. Instead he looked over at me, and his face in the head-lights of the oncoming car seemed both old and young at the same time, and very tired. "And my parents. Jesus Christ, Alden. Celebrating their sixtieth on New Year's Eve. Imagine," he said. "Sixty years with the same person."

He'd been married fewer than five, and wedlock for me had been a brief six months. I'd been close to no one for so long that sometimes I'd delude myself into believing it a privacy I'd come to by choice.

"Your Mom?" Mitchell asked.

"Nope," I said, and shrugged. "Don't know." And that seemed like explanation enough as we pulled up in front of a large, well-lighted three-story brick building, the walkway shoveled and someone standing by the double doors, smoking a cigarette. Clearly there was a festive event taking place inside, and that event, as we entered, included a piano player whose rendition of "Mack the Knife" wasn't half-bad. A tune my dad had liked and sometimes hummed. Had he been among those gathered, he would have gotten up off the couch to welcome us and assist in the tree's alignment in its stand.

But it was Mitchell's folks who came over. They were all dressed up in formal evening attire, and he shook his dad's hand and kissed his mom on her cheek. She seemed not to notice, concentrating instead on me on my back as I reached under the bottom branches to adjust the three screw-in braces. Even upside down I recognized her immediately, silver-haired and eyes as wide as portals, dark and smart like Mitchell's.

"You remember Alden, Mom," Mitchell said. "From over on Sycamore? He's back visiting. He's been away a long time."

I waved up at her from out of that past, a dislocation far too removed for such on-the-spot recall. I wanted to tell her that I had trouble some nights, too, my own face in the bathroom mirror only vaguely familiar.

But Mr. Yates stepped forward and tapped my boot sole with his cane, his shoulders stooped as he studied me for maybe a full thirty seconds. "Yes," he said. "Yes indeed. You were always such a nice, polite kid. You always liked to help us out. I remember. Look at that," he said to a much younger woman who was suddenly there by his elbow, "he hasn't changed a bit."

"I see that," she said, and smiled at me as she handed him a clear plastic glass half-filled with something bubbly and golden like champagne.

"*Salud*," he said, and took a sip, and the woman turned toward Mitchell's mom, who was still standing there tightly clutching her purse.

"Las Vegas," Mitchell's mom said. "The Sands."

The woman nodded and pointed over at the piano player, as if to interpret for me, and then she put her arm around Mrs. Yates's shoulder and sang along: "*Danke schoen*, darling, *danke schoen* / Thank you for walks down Lover's Lane."

And right there in the shadow of the newly erected tree, in the angle of the light as I stood up, in the slight shifts of sorrow brought on by the kindness of their voices in flight, I stepped toward that woman, and when the song ended I addressed her by name.

"Denise?" I said, the dimmest glimmer of recognition slowly taking hold in her eyes. I remember swallowing hard, nervously wetting my lips, and Mrs. Yates pointing toward the small ceiling speaker and saying, "Wayne Newton. He's a real heartbreaker," and Mitchell asking, "You two know each other?"

"During our college days of arrested development," I said, and Denise smiled at that, her eyes still on me.

"More like martial arts class," she said. "You were great, though. You said the right things. You were the brilliant one, Mr. Grelling. On that day anyway. How could I ever forget that?"

For a second the room went quiet, and I thought about how that brief tirade had changed my life forever and not necessarily in the finest ways. I wanted to tell her she should have come with me. That I would have taught her how to open and close that passenger-side window with a pair of rusted vice grips, and that we might have ended on a beach somewhere in the warm sun of Mexico. An unlikely but not impossible summary of what might have been us for a while.

The piano player started in again, Andy Williams this time, "Sail Along, Silvery Moon." I looked his way and I could see, beyond the white lace curtains framing the window, snow falling again. Against that backdrop a single elderly couple danced cheek-to-cheek, holding each other close, lost somewhere deep inside their own private radiance.

Mitchell had already palmed his mom's elbow and was leading her out there, her hair shining under the cut-glass chandelier.

"May I?" Mr. Yates asked, his hand held out to Denise, who grinned and curtsied and did not glance back at me. And which was, I suppose, at least in part why I ushered myself outside, my jacket zipped against the late-evening swirls and gusts. From where I positioned myself, just beyond the rim the light cast out, the music was no more than a distant thrum.

Another town, another time, I might have been a complete stranger stopping to watch for a moment those diaphanous human shapes floating slowly by like ghosts. Sons and mothers, husbands and wives, and one still dark-haired caregiver who'd followed me just far enough one day to link me to her past. Not that I knew a single intimate thing about her, or ever would. But she was dancing with my best friend's father, and that was the way the world looked. A lot like the snow globe that my dad used to shake and put down in front of me when I was a little kid in love with the silent watching of the objects gone white. A tiny, trance-like galaxy into which I'd stare, and stare, until whatever had perished, magically reappeared. A few rabbits, and a Christmas bear feeding bright red apples to a spotted deer.

Outside the nursing home the snow fell faster. Fell thick until all I could see were my own hands reaching up to pull the sweatshirt hood over my head. Like my dad used to do for me from behind, tying the drawstrings before we'd start downhill on the sled, the runners waxed, and Mitchell with his arms around me, and my dad on the far back leaning hard and steering us with the taut muscles of his thighs, as though the wind were trying to strip the moment away.

But there it was, my dad dead almost thirty years, now back, and my one and only friend dancing with his mom, and who might not even have known his name. Or the name of that handsome older man with his arm around a slender, smiling woman half his age.

Some bemused God with an odd flair for the holy, I thought, the window amber-lit, and me with my head bowed against a sudden gust, my breathing even and slow. No traffic. And when I closed my eyes I felt, if not anointed, then content. That for sure. And yes, perhaps even grateful for whatever next thing might begin.

131

FROM
THE GOAT FISH
AND THE LOVER'S KNOT

THE GOAT FISH AND THE LOVER'S KNOT

I told my dad, "As far as I know," when he asked if the entire clan would be there. Meaning my best friend Darwin and both his parents, Mr. and Mrs. LaVann, who owned a cabin on a lake about an hour's drive north of Cadillac in decent weather. And, although we couldn't have known it then, that was where the sheriff's department deputies would search first thing after Mrs. LaVann went missing. Went renegade, was how Darwin would amend it after she finally did call from somewhere far out of state, but only to let them know that she was alive and not to worry and that she'd come back home when she could. When she was ready. Though of course she never did.

Secretive and distant, and with a foreign sounding name, which was how, a year earlier, she'd introduced herself to me the first time I stopped at their house after school: Marenza Czarny. I imagined some war-torn country, like maybe she'd been a refugee or something, but when I later asked Darwin where she was originally from he said, "Bay City. Born and raised." She'd *dreamed* the name and legally changed hers *to* it the day she turned eighteen. "A conversion," he said, and rolled his eyes, but offered up no details, and I left it at that.

My dad would not have liked her. Tall and thin, high cheekbones and long, shiny-dark hair with red highlights that showed through in the sun. Not a line in her face. The kind of beauty that rarely—if ever—was available to men such as my dad, men who knew it, and so maligned its very existence.

I calculated her to be mid-thirties, max. A good ten years younger than her husband, and to see them together constituted the most perplexing

135

mismatch I'd ever seen. Not that Mr. LaVann wasn't upbeat and good-natured enough. And occasionally even fun to be around, and way less strict than most other dads. But he had one of those fat, flat faces, like he might have played tuba in junior high band. How he and his wife had gotten together defied in my imagination what a certain woman's attraction to a man might be. Other than money. He'd spend his afternoons drinking coffee and poring over spreadsheets fanned out across their dining room table.

Darwin and I had both turned fourteen that summer our lives changed, and then changed back, though possibly not for the better.

Anyway, it was Mrs. LaVann—that's what I called her to be polite, and she never corrected me—who said at the lake one day, "Here," and handed us half a dozen perfectly good pie tins. "See if you boys can find a suitable use for these."

True, I'd yet to see her bake anything. Or cook for that matter, unless sliding a bagel into the toaster oven qualified. We bypassed panning for gold and Darwin grabbed a hammer instead, punching a hole through each tin with a single swing and a ten-penny nail. Then we hung them from a gnarly apple tree branch with different lengths of fifteen-pound monofilament: giant wind chimes that we took aim at and made dance and spin with at least a thousand high-pitched BB dings.

Their cabin was rustic—"weather distressed," as Mr. LaVann put it. "Authentic. It's a look people pay for," he said, and shrugged, and I wondered if that held true for the slightly cockeyed windows and the skull plate and antlers anchored above the front door. There were exposed beams and a shallow-pitched corrugated metal roof that sounded, whenever it rained, like snare drums. "Vintage 1950s," he said. "Someone's change-jar, one-board-at-a-time dream getaway." And that he'd picked up for a song, he said.

When I later mentioned this to my dad, like maybe we could swing it too, own *our* own vacation place, he just nodded, the canned laugh track from some TV sitcom filling up our living room, my mom silently clapping her hands. Pandering *shit*coms, as my dad called them, came as close as my mom, withdrawn and prone to depression, was apt to get to making it through each day.

It can happen—it *does* happen—the doctors concurred, with a bad enough scare. That scare turned out to be having kids, having me.

136

She never offered advice one way or another on much of anything. Mostly she'd go silent and look away. It was my dad who ragged on me to canvas the neighborhood. "Go door to door," he said, "and lock in a few contracts weeding, and edging, and mowing lawns. A paper route— it's not too late. Hell's bells, sell some damn crickets and night crawlers to the local bait shops if that's what it takes. Anything to get you centered. To do right by what's expected of you around here."

I didn't really know what that was. Better grades, a tidier bedroom. Community college looming somewhere in my future? Or possibly enlist in the army, which would at least lock on to one thing we'd have in common. He'd spent two tours in Vietnam, just before the war ended.

"That's the problem with your generation," he said. "With all you kids. Everyone's lost and mouthy and muddle-minded. Can't think straight or tell fake from real, the goddamn Hope Diamond from a glass doorknob up the ass."

He said something about pursuit—what he called "pressing ahead, no matter what"—as opposed to selfishness and extravagance and greed. Suckering up to the almighty dollar. This was epitomized, though he didn't name names, by Mr. LaVann, his money clip, and his Oldsmobile '88 convertible with a front seat so deep and soft it was more like driving a couch.

I'd never openly contradict anything my dad said. But sometimes, to secretly get back at him, I'd sit on *our* couch, and imagine a steering wheel and a tinted windshield, and then fantasize running the back roads after I got my driver's license in another couple of years. Top down and the radio blasting and, hopefully by then, a girlfriend crowding right up tight to my shoulder and hip, and throwing her arm around me.

By contrast my dad pointed out that he'd never one time in his entire life owned a new car, a fancy redesigned model straight off the showroom floor. He bought used, and hadn't missed a day of work in twenty years, "And why do you suppose we buy butter and cheese by the brick?" he'd ask. "Any idea, Wayne? Any clue whatsoever?"

He sold life insurance, his sales pitch being that if the dead could speak, who was the person they'd be thanking? "That is correct . . . yours truly," he'd say. "All those grieving wives and daughters and sons of the deceased."

Mr. LaVann, on the other hand, had made a killing manufacturing deep fryers, a business he'd started, and which now afforded him as much time off as he wanted. Weeks and weeks, and like Darwin and me, he had the entire summer to just screw around and be a kid again. Raise some innocent hell, he said, that you could later translate into stories to joke and laugh about. He claimed Dunkin' Donuts and Burger King as clients, but I'd never once gotten any freebies when I'd bike over to either establishment and drop his name, as if I were his heir and only living son.

At his angriest, my dad actually had trembling hands when he talked to me, his face turning crimson, as if the very air I breathed was bankrupting our household.

"Okay?" he'd say, pointing close up as if he meant to poke my chest, and I'd nod and nod like, yes, I understand. "Do you?" he'd say, like deep down he knew that a narrow, insistent certainty such as his could never dictate where I was headed in my life. I hated how every conversation took on the urgency of a hurricane or tornado drill, and all I really wanted was to get as far away from the dangers of that house as quickly as I could. So when the LaVanns invited me—their treat, they said—to spend an entire month with them, I jumped at the chance. Against all odds I appealed to my mom—who, for once, when the subject came up that night at dinner, turned to my dad and said, "Harold. It's too late. I've already told him he can."

The cabin had only two bedrooms, so I slept alone on a cot in the loft. Back then I was not a sound sleeper. Almost any noise and I'd be wide awake, listening, as I was that night, already halfway through my stay, to those same low-grade whimpers and moans, which I anticipated but still hadn't grown accustomed to.

Why I opened my eyes and stared out at the lake, its shimmery pewter-colored surface, I'm not sure. Maybe to concentrate my attention away from what was going on right below me. It never lasted very long, and afterward the cabin always quieted, and eventually I'd doze off. But when I heard footsteps, and then the screen door slowly open and close with a slight wheeze of the hinges, Mrs. LaVann appeared on the lawn: not ghostlike, exactly, though the moon was bright, and ground mist lifted and resettled in thin vaporous clouds around her.

I had no trouble seeing that she was naked, and how she took hold of the hand pump's heavy red arm. She lifted and depressed it three or four times until the water gurgled and then surged full force. On a rope around her neck hung a bar of soap that glistened, white as snow—and no doubt felt just as cold when she spread her legs and washed herself down there, and then rinsed off, which seemed, even for her, an odd and unusual way to shower, given that there was always plenty of hot water inside.

I wondered if she was okay. If maybe she was feverish, or tipsy, or possibly sleepwalking. She did not look up to where I was spying down on her, if that's what it constituted, and by the time I got outside she'd already wrapped a towel around herself, and she didn't appear all that startled or surprised to see me.

I pretended I hadn't known that she was out there. I said, "Oh, sorry. I was just about to head out fishing," which on a lot of nights would have been true. With one hand she held on to the spot where she'd tucked in the towel flap below her breastbone, and she smiled and—as if I'd asked—said, "I just needed a little fresh air is all."

I nodded as though I understood, and she nodded too, as if standing there together was the most ordinary occurrence in the world. A complete non-event like almost everything else that summer, meaning that we could pretty much come and go as we pleased—me and Darwin, together or alone—and so I'd tiptoe out with my spinning rod and tackle box and row to the north end of the lake, into a certain cove of stumps and sunken deadfall where the fishing was always way better. Walleyes, mostly, which I'd catch with glow-in-the-dark split-tail jigs, and when I'd get back I'd tie the stringer to a dock cleat and wait until first light to gut and clean them. Usually everyone else slept in, and like magic there'd be a batch of fresh fillets in the refrigerator, the flesh as orange as spawning steelhead or salmon. Sometimes I'd leave a fish whole if it was big enough, head and all, and Mr. LaVann would stuff it with breadcrumbs, and olive oil and garlic, and then wrap it in tinfoil and grill it for dinner. And, as if it were part of a ritual, he'd salute me and wink.

One morning a week or so before the pump incident, Mrs. LaVann, always the earliest riser after me, pushed her chair back a little ways from the table and slung one long leg over the other when I entered the kitchen from outside. She was barefoot and wearing a sleeveless, loose-fitting cotton sundress, the neckline not so low, but plenty low enough. I'd recently undergone a growth spurt, and, at almost 5' 8", just looking down to meet her eyes made me plenty nervous enough.

"Are you having a decent time here, Wayne?" she said.

"Yes. Thank you. I like there not being any neighbors, and that this time we're not just up for the weekend." I said, "And I like hearing the loons, too," and mentioned that even though my dad rarely took me, fishing was my number-one favorite thing to do.

"Come over here," she said, and I did. "Now give me your hand," and with her polished red thumbnail she carefully lifted maybe half a dozen scales from my palm that I had no idea were there.

I liked how that felt kind of tickly, and I said, "Yeah, I was out again last night."

"Yes, I know. All by yourself on the water. I wonder, what would your parents say about that?"

"I'd never tell them, uh-uh. And Darwin, he's sworn to secrecy. He'd never say otherwise, and in return I don't bug *him* to go with me. He gets antsy if the action's slow, and he hates changing baits. He says we ought to chum them with a few blasting caps and every closed-mouthed lunker down there would turn belly-up, and all we'd need is a long-handled net to heft them into the boat."

"He takes after his dad in a lot of ways," she said. "He'll do well in a man's world." She smiled at that, and when she let go I took a few tentative reverse steps and stopped.

"I'm always careful, Mrs. LaVann. And I'm a strong swimmer," and then right out of nowhere she said something about train miles. Like they were somehow differently calculated, and that there was a whole other universe out there, which she believed, over time, I'd see my share of. "I hope you do. It's in you," she said, and I thanked her for that, too.

That was as close as we'd come to a quiet, private conversation, prior to finding myself with her standing nude behind a quarter inch of towel. And her saying, "Maybe one of these nights you'll take me with you. I don't fish but I could swim close behind in your wake. I'd like that. Something to break the monotony. Something different to look forward to."

I said, "Sure. If I see you out here," and I imagined muscling the oars in a way I'd never done before, and how I'd help her into the boat if she got chilled or exhausted, or simply felt like shooting the breeze on a laid-back midnight boat ride.

This wasn't a lake that accommodated pleasure crafts, pontoons, or ski boats. Or even those low-horsepower outboard putt-putts you sometimes saw on jonboats or on the flat backs of canoes on other lakes. As Mr. LaVann pointed out, not a single public launch site anywhere. And the cedar shoreline was so dense and tangled and spongy that if you somehow shimmied through and took half a dozen steps in any direction you might never, even with a compass, find your way back. Thousands and thousands of wilderness acres were forever decomposing, so when the air got muggy some afternoons and lightning struck high up in the sky, that bitter taste of sulfur intensified tenfold on your tongue.

Darwin and I explored only as far as we could pole into the inlets and feeder creeks, which were crystal clear, and shallow, and where one time we found the bone-white spine and ribcage of what had to be a black bear.

"Or some flipping Sasquatch," Darwin said, and we reversed as fast as we could to get out of there and back into the lake. "Come on, let's just haul ass out of here," he said, but I was sweaty and hot and mosquito bitten and so I stripped to my Jockeys. And when I dove in I stroked hard for the silty bottom, where there were water pockets so frigid you could feel, in a matter of seconds, your lips turning purple and your nuts contracting to the size of twin pearls.

I stayed under for as long as I could, close to a full minute and a half, and when I surfaced Darwin was just sitting there motionless and smoking a cigarette. Each day he'd pilfer a few from his mom as she floated on her back out front of the cabin. I wasn't sure if Mr. LaVann even owned a swimsuit, and ankle-deep was as far into the lake as I'd seen him wade—his pants rolled up, his shin bones pale and hairless—to yell to his wife that he was headed into town. That he had a shopping list, and errands to run, and was there anything else that she needed? "Hey, do you hear me? I'm talking to you."

One time he actually broke open a roll of quarters and skimmed maybe two or three bucks' worth, one after the other, across the calm flat surface right at her before he turned and walked away. I imagined her wincing, as I'd seen her do on occasion when she heard him pull off the two-track and into their driveway. She didn't quilt, or play solitaire, or read paperback novels, and so I figured maybe *this* was her hobby: drowning out her husband's voice, her head tilted back and her ears submerged. But maybe whatever understanding they'd reached as a couple was solid enough to survive these momentary standoffs.

"How does she stay in so long?" I once asked Darwin. She was way thin, her one-piece tight and shiny black like sealskin, and he said, straight-faced and matter-of-fact, "She's part reptile."

"Right," I said. "And the sun's her heat lamp." He just stared at me like, *Wait long enough and you'll find out.*

And that's exactly what I did, with only one week left before I'd have to go back home, and two weeks before I'd have to go back to school. To Ms. Cosgrove's English class. She was one of those teachers who believed that not only would we smarten up by incorporating into our limited vocabularies the Word of the Day, but that we'd become more worldly for it. I'd managed just fine thus far, and without any heavy-duty studying, to maintain a straight B average. I hated school, so above all else I did not want the summer to end. I even considered, as a protest, sneaking into the classroom early on the very first day and erasing whatever exotic, impossible-to-remember word she'd written on the blackboard and substituting *DAREDEVIL*, or *JITTERBUG*, or *HULA POPPER*.

I'd been thinking a lot about Mrs. LaVann. How she'd do this lotus thing out on the far end of the dock. Just hunker motionless out there for an hour or more, nothing moving except for her arms held out like she might rise and silently fly away without ever once looking back.

It was strange sometimes to think of her as Darwin's mom. Or anyone's mom. As foolish and misguided as I might have been, I'd wait for her outside for up to half an hour before I'd give up and push off on my own. Not to fish, which in itself should have been a sign, but rather to lie back on those two life preservers that neither Darwin nor I ever wore. Not even that time an early evening thunderstorm blew up out of nowhere, and he, on his knees, grabbed hold of the gunnels while I navigated the wind-driven swells until we beached just a few feet from where his mom was standing, soaked to the bone and sipping a glass of wine, her sunglasses pushed back on her head.

"Good thing your father wasn't here to witness that," she said, and I noticed the corked bottle in the sand by her feet. She always drank more in her husband's absence, and he'd been away this time for three straight days and nights. I wondered, if Darwin had ever asked to go home with him, if I'd be given the choice to stay, and which is what I would have done. Then maybe I'd lie to Mrs. LaVann about how, for special occasions, like Thanksgiving or Christmas at our house, I'd get to sip some wine, though in truth I'd yet to experience the effects of even a single drop. And, until that summer at the lake, the urge hadn't culminated in anything more than an invitation from Joanna Pliss, a girl I liked okay, to someday steal a couple of my dad's Miller Lites, and then together we'd figure out the right time and place—which we never did.

It wasn't until the night before we were supposed to leave the lake that Mrs. LaVann materialized out of nowhere. I don't think I ever really believed—just hoped—that she would show up to swim behind me, but when I'd bent to untie the bowline and stood back up, I found her there. The water was warmer than the air, but still I'd put on a sweatshirt and long pants and a Tigers baseball cap. But there *she* was wearing a bikini, one I hadn't seen before. My eyes had already adjusted to the dark, but the bright yellow iridescence half blinded me like a flashbulb.

She leaned toward me and whispered, "All set?" and before I could even answer she stepped to the edge of the dock and shallow-dove, and when she surfaced she was already stroking toward the middle of the lake.

Have I mentioned the lake's name? It's Half Moon. Or that my mom is 5' 2", and overweight and afraid most days to leave the house? That my dad is my dad, but everything in this life is conditional, like it or not? He wouldn't have liked me standing upright late at night in a tippy fourteen-foot aluminum rowboat so I could keep a watch on my best friend's mom. I fastened on her and did not for one second look away. Not up or sideways, and especially not back toward the cabin where a light, at any moment, might come on.

For a few seconds I *would* lose her, but each time she'd reappear when the clouds separated and those star clusters cast just enough illumination for me to spot her yellow backside, like a trapline buoy being towed by some monster pike or muskie.

I'd taken one oar out of its lock to use like a paddle, wishing that Mr. LaVann had equipped the boat with one of those high-intensity sealed-beam searchlights powerful enough to cut through mist or fog, and reaching out a hundred feet or more.

"Slow down," I wanted to call out, but even soft talking carried across the water, and the last thing I needed was for Darwin or his dad to hear me and discover the two of us missing. The plan, or so I *thought*, was for Mrs. LaVann to breaststroke directly behind the boat as I rowed. A slow, relaxed pace. I wondered if she had any idea where she was, or where she was headed, like possibly to some sunken island I hadn't discovered—where suddenly, from out of the deep heart of the lake, there she'd be, standing up to her knees and waving me in, the other hand planted on her hip.

That, however, did not, and still doesn't, approximate what transpired. Had things gone differently, gone badly, and had I been called to testify, I would have sworn to nothing more than a summer about to end, a final boat ride, and a woman I suspected had already entered the final days of her marriage and, for some reason, wanted me to know that.

But no one asked. No one was up waiting for us, to hear how my chest had already tightened and, fearing the worst *and* having lapsed into panic, I'd cupped my hands around my mouth as I quietly called her name. I don't remember how many times. Over and over, and in every possible direction. "Answer me, please. Answer me wherever you are."

When finally she did, she said, "Wayne, I'm right here." Exactly where she was supposed to be, just a few feet behind the boat, which sat in a still drift while she treaded water right there below me.

I said, "Jesus, Mrs. LaVann," though I was hyperventilating so badly I almost couldn't get the words out, and my teeth were chattering. "I thought you'd drowned."

"No, no," she said. "I'm sorry. I was on my back, just thinking about things. You've seen me do that every day. And how distant and muted the world becomes underwater. And besides, I'm a floater. I couldn't sink if I wanted to. I'd have to jump overboard hugging an anchor."

"I couldn't see you anywhere," I said. "And nothing else mattered. It didn't make sense something so awful could happen."

"Here, help me," she said, and I reached over and held both her hands, and she all but walked out of the lake and into the boat.

She said, "Look at you. You're shaking. I've frightened you something terrible." And the next thing I knew we were sitting side by side on the center seat, as if rowing together we could make better time getting back, and maybe build a fire in the fireplace, and sip some wine or even better some brandy, a blanket draped across my shoulders and back.

And the truth is that I have, in fact, done exactly that, though certainly not in the LaVanns' cabin, but rather in my own, on another lake in another state, and with a woman my age who became my wife for a time. A good twenty years after Mrs. LaVann said, "Shall we stay then for a few more minutes while you calm down?"

I had no idea how late it was, or how long until we'd be packing the car to head home, me and Darwin in the back seat, the two of us silent and staring out at whatever zoomed by on the other side of the road, while Mr. LaVann glanced back at me in the rearview.

"Look, Wayne," she said. "There's the Goat Fish." And then she pointed above the lake's south end and said, "And there's the Double Ship," as if the sky were a sea, and we were mariners charting a

144

course to who knows where. "There—the Wreath of Flowers," she said. "The Lover's Knot . . . the Dragon's Tail."

Our heads were touching, and her wet hair stuck to my right cheek. The sky was clear. Back then I couldn't differentiate one star from another, though I understood them to be millions and millions of light-years away.

I saw Darwin just one time after he and his dad moved downstate. As I did, too. First for college, where I earned a degree in fisheries from the University of Michigan, and then to work for the Minnesota Department of Natural Resources, where I am still employed. I'm single again and have two children, a daughter and a son. They're nine and eleven. We—my ex and I—share joint custody, and, most weekends during July and late into August, they spend time with me at the cottage I bought a few years back. It's a fairly short drive from where they live with their mother, and with whom I'm cordial. For a while we even considered getting back together, a second go-around, but the outcome seemed so clearly forgone—and no one, especially the children, needed to go through that again. We care for and trust each other, and that's another kind of love.

If anything, she believes me to be overly protective. Our kids, Delaney and Gregory, are not named after my parents, and who against the odds are still together—my mom wrestling with her demons and my dad has finally grown tired of railing against the world's inability to measure up.

Again this year, before I drained the pipes and closed up the cottage for winter, the kids and I rowed out, as we always do, to a spot we know, and I slowly let down the anchor. The kids, wearing wetsuit vests and snorkel masks, slid quietly, one after the other, into the lake to float motionless above a massive trunk, its branches alive with snagged plugs and lures, a few of them mine. The tackle tree is what we call it, and the water there is ten or twelve feet deep and clear as a well.

I made a show of drawing into my lungs all the air they can hold. "I'll be right back," I said. "Don't you guys go anywhere," and they both smiled and nodded.

When finally I kicked my fins and dove, baitfish flashed and scattered everywhere around me, as though we were on a reef, the hovering sun

145

weightless on my children's backs. Instead of a knife strapped to my leg, I carried a pair of miniature sewing scissors to snip the tangled leaders at the swivels, and collected what I could: a Johnson Silver Minnow, a Rooster Tail, a shiny chartreuse Krocodile. A Berkley Power Worm that twisted and wiggled as if it's alive.

Then came my favorite part of all: looking up and watching the slowmotion rise of my air bubbles toward those two sets of wide-open eyes, magnified behind their masks. They've got their mother's eyes—bright blue—and my dark hair, and the way they breathed so easily through their snorkels made them sound as if they were dreaming, arms outflung in freefall.

After they're in bed and asleep I'll sometimes turn off all the lights and stand just outside the front door to stare across to the far end of the lake. Maybe sip a cold beer and be alert for shooting stars, feeding fish, voices that just might trail back on a certain current or breeze. Women and boys and time gone missing, gone elsewhere, gone lost.

And this: I have listened to migrating snow geese fly toward a moon as thin and silver as a hook. I'm forty-two. I band blackbirds whose molten gold irises glow with the fury of fanned embers, and I get paid to stay watchful and record how many return. The miles and the months, and whatever that passage might tell us.

ALL THE TIME
IN THE WORLD

My father's name is Bradley Chicky. He who fanned fifteen consecutive batters to win the 1989 Division II high school state championship. A spider-arm southpaw submariner whose full-ride scholarships mark this town's first ever big league prospect.

Except that it's the new millennium, the year 2004, and so long gone are those glory days that just this morning he gripped the baseball's tight red seams in the double hook of his prosthetic to demonstrate how to throw "No, not a downer, a sinker," as he said. "And here, like this for a heater, like this for a splitter, okay? Got that?" As if right out of left field, the blue, mid-November twilight snow falling, I'd decided to try out for some latter-day version of *A League of Their Own*.

No matter the weather he'll sometimes play catch in the backyard with his girlfriend Lyndel, who stops by certain evenings after work. If I decide to hike those couple miles instead of riding the school bus, there they are when I get home, two silhouettes in the semi-dark. She hasn't spent the night, nor he at her place, and I assume it's for my sake that they're taking things slow. We're up to twice each week that the three of us sit down to dinner, the extra leaf just recently reinserted into the dining room table. She might, as he maintains, *be* a dynamite Chef Boyardee, but bite-wise I take maybe one or two and, blank-faced, lower my fork to the plate, and excuse myself without a single word. They haven't yet, but if either of them attempts to coerce me back I swear I'll yank that new linen tablecloth from underneath the serving platters and silverware, the ceramic gravy boat and those oversize glasses of ice water, like some irate and vengeful magician.

He says to give her a chance, she's a good sport, spirited. A real gamechanger is how he puts it, a welcome addition. Plus she's plenty smart, he says, reads a ton, and has a two-year degree in health and fitness from the local community college. "In time you'll grow to like her, Sam," he says.

"Right," I say.

But nothing deters his enthusiasm, her painted fingernails flashing signs and my father bent over at the waist and staring in as she squats and rocks back on her heels, her ass mere inches from the half-frozen ground, a Detroit Tigers ball cap worn backward, as if that's cool. Sometimes she takes off the catcher's mitt and warms both hands in her armpits. Shrugs and shivers and yet acts as if this is the most fun she's had in decades. Home plate is maybe fifteen yards from where, in full windup, he releases the ball, every pitch a slow looping change-up though he claims that some scout's speed gun once clocked him at 101 mph. Other times he'll practice his pick-off move, his sneaky slide step. All of it, under our current circumstances, about a bazillion light years removed from the majors.

Anyway, Lyndel teaches Pilates and yoga at Go Figure, so *hers* is pretty much perfect in that camouflage sports bra and short-shorts getup she occasionally wears, a shiny silver bracelet on either wrist like handcuffs. Standing straight-legged she can touch both elbows to the floor, fingers folded like she's praying, and then hold that pose before tucking under herself as if she might push all the way up past her own backside, like something out of a Chinese circus. She's twenty-six. Seven years younger than my father and a full eight years older than my mom was when she had me—Samantha Ann. Or, as that sheriff's department deputy I hand my urine sample to every other Saturday afternoon always singsongs, "Sam Chicky, Sam Chicky," like he's propositioning some teenage junkie slut, which so isn't me.

I mean, against the odds I'm holding it together, doing my best, resisting every temptation, and avoiding lockup by side-sailing as fast and far away from the local pot and meth heads as possible. Staying clean. And stripped naked not a single body piercing or the fancy needlework of some butt-crack tattoo. No hickeys either, ditto the eyeliner, and the sad fact is that foreplay thus far pretty much constitutes locking fingers with a guy.

But just one time, when Deputy Dildo orders me to empty my pockets and sweatshirt pouch, I imagine, among my personal and lawful contents, that I had nerve enough to plant a couple of Trojan Ultra Thins.

Packets I could flip right onto the counter. Free samples from the Journey Church for safe, underage sex is what I'd offer up, an inside joke with me and my best friend Allison. Maybe bat my eyes and nod toward the empty holding cell, the stripped-down cot, but like my father reminds me, "Zip it. Keep your motor mouth shut and your thoughts to yourself." To ensure that I arrive there on time he's the one who chaperones me, and then waits outside in his pickup, where he rolls down the window. Leans his head against the seat rest, his hook visoring above his already closed eyes, and says, as I exit, "Remember, no attitude, right? Do you hear me? No bullshit this time."

My official guilty-as-charged? Random theft and alcohol. As in every morning before school, my father in the shower, I'd refill the same juice box with straight Bombay Sapphire from the secret survival stash in my closet. And from which, during third-hour phys ed, I'd sip between sets of stomach crunches and jumping jacks, and the one time I puked the gym teacher thought it was food poisoning or the flu and called my father at work to come pick me up.

I haven't lapsed in almost three months and counting, and the NO ENTRY sign on my bedroom door I removed voluntarily. Not that he'd walk in unannounced one way or the other. It's the tone, as my father says, the negative message it sends. Sort of like how I used to gnaw on ballpoint after ballpoint until the spring and the ink erupted inside my mouth. Now I take notes instead, and my grades, as of just last week, they're back up again above average. Nothing *Quiz Bowl* or *Odyssey of the Mind*. Nothing, as my teachers make clear, that even approximates my full potential, though so far no backslide either, and so no more hassles and scare tactics from the principal and guidance counselor about having to repeat the school year.

But three sheets flapping I'll shoplift almost anything spur of the moment. A silk blouse, more booze, Elmer's and Magic Markers to uncap and sniff all day. Rubber cement. Model airplane glue. Bottles of syrupy Robitussin as chasers. Once, a chew toy and a couple packs of liver chips, plus a Basenji pup to feed them to. Scooped up in broad daylight from Spoiled Brats, our Front Street pet shop that's likely, like so many of the town's landmark mom and pops, to turn belly up, the census here being in perpetual long-term free fall.

I named the pooch Ty Cobb, for my father's all-time favorite ballplayer. An innocent, warm-blooded addition to the household that we could love and care for together and spoil rotten in my mom's absence. We'd never had a pet. Not so much as a goldfish or gerbil, and when my

149

father, bleary-eyed, home finally at the tail-end of another fifty-hour work week at the foundry, offered his dead hand to be licked and sniffed, the puppy peed right there on the living room carpet. "I'll clean it up," I said, and the first words out his mouth, "Why didn't you just leave our names and phone number and address? And hand over a note saying, *BEWARE: KLEPTOMANIAC ON THE PREMISES.*"

"Maybe I bought him," I said. "Did you ever consider that?" And he said back, "Tell it to the judge," and then he threatened to press charges himself and wave bye-bye as the juvenile-delinquent facility van pulled away. He'd had it, he said. "Enough is enough, Sam. The dog's got papers, a high-dollar price tag, and there's no buying you out of this. Not after the fact, and I don't even want to. Listen: this isn't kid's stuff anymore, an impoundment or rescue mutt; we're talking a felony offense. Do you understand what that means, the possible consequences? Trust me, you've just taken on way more than you ever bargained for. And God forbid that I lose you, too."

He sat me down at the kitchen table and coached me, sentence by sentence, as I composed what sounded to my ears like a heartfelt letter of apology and remorse. Still woozy and half hungover, I took a while to get the words "appealing for clemency" unslurred, but the cops, they'd already been summoned anyway, a good hour in advance of that written admission of guilt. The final period, the sincerely yours, the scribbled, almost illegible, back-slanting left-handed signature I'd sometimes practice in the back row of every class to annihilate another wasted few seconds of mandatory school time—all of it made little difference.

"She does it for attention." That's what the first Family Services social worker—young and nervous and strictly by the numbers—concluded. A rookie, as my father insists. Limited. Right or wrong she attributed such aberrant behavior to my mom's midnight departure eight months earlier, and my on-the-rebound father still somewhat tilty in *his* thinking. Like I told her, he and I, we do our best to tune each other out, and, whenever possible, communicate telepathically, or in single-word sentences. *Sorry* is not among them, except, I guess, whenever I attempt to decipher the Morse code of his hook tap-tapping on the Naugahyde couch cushion as he watches the History Channel or *60 Minutes* with the sound turned off. Around Lyndel I'm occasionally more forthcoming, and way less inclined to play the victim, the angry, uppity, unstable, at-risk, insolent, wayward, and all-mixed-up crazy child—

150

"the offending minor," as the juvenile court judge referred to me. I'm also less inclined to lay the blame so directly on my parents, or on anyone else for that matter. And for sure not Lyndel, who I first off figured for a ditz I could easily despise, my every silent glare announcing, "I can wait you out. This is not your house. There is no later on, no better tomorrows here. This is who we are. Leave now."

Truth told she's okay, with no grubbing up or big-sister stupid stuff. No offers of a free radical Jazzercise class or any personal trainer tips to improve my bust line or ease the pain of those killer premenstrual cramps and spasms. And her laugh . . . it's eerie-weird in the extreme, like a fun gene long dormant from this dysfunctional family. Zero rug rats and never married. When I finally asked her what's the deal here anyway—my father chasing after the young stuff—she said, her jeans low-slung, her hair blue-black and shiny, "Lyndel, not Lolita." Which I didn't get, but I winced when she added, "Your dad is a good man at a bad time and half out of his mind with worry over you."

I'm fifteen, and by far the tallest girl in the entire school. At twelve I stood an even six feet in my mom's high heels and magenta lipstick and had a premonition of myself as Miss Michigan turned runway supermodel and swinging five-hundred-dollar handbags. Leggy and gray-eyed like my father and, reformed or not, I don't for one second assume that I'm the only guilty party here whenever he asks, all pissed off and judgmental, "How brainless can you be?"—and I, too, lose all composure and fire right back. Exactly like my mom used to do, the same zinger about how he'd forfeited a life of fame and fortune—and, as she said, for what . . . one goddamn dark night of the soul's idea of a joke?

"Beyond belief" is how she'd phrase it, and my standing comeback was, "Yeah, remember that?"

"Every day," he says. "Every last painful detail." He means the homemade guillotine, and that forged steel doorframe he hauled out of the county dump. Pulleys and half a dozen oblong window weights, and the side-by-side outhouse shitter holes sawed crosswise and hinged like a double yoke to fit those frail, pale, aristocratic necks of Louis XVI and Marie Antoinette. A last-ditch, hands-on world history show-and-tell he brainstormed to salvage a final passing grade so he could graduate and they could flee to Florida or Arizona or Texas: no-hitters, perfect games, a College World Series MVP ring, and trophies enough to fill a hallway of polished glass cases. Jerseys and scorecards and pennant flags to autograph. And so my mom, already pregnant with me, could follow the team bus in that white Mustang convertible she imagined was already theirs, and think about the sprawling brick ranch or split-level they'd buy, the backyard in-ground swimming pool with its rainbow of underwater lights, and a trampoline. And eggs any style.

All of which sure beat, she said, slow-dying here in this squatty, spawned-out, northern Michigan toss-pot of a town where they married anyhow, for better or for worse, and honeymooned in a cheap rustic cabin just a few miles south. And where some twisted turn of fate determined that I, too, would be born and raised.

"Let it rest," my father would say, his name stitched in red cursive above his work-shirt pocket. "Good God Almighty, do we always have to end up at the same damn crash site?" My mom, each and every time she'd wig out or fly into overwind—didn't really matter anymore what for—insisted that the moment was forever fixed in her memory. The bedroom walls, they're so tin-can thin that I've awakened nights to screams unlike anything you've ever heard unless, as she'd say, you've witnessed close up a human arm lopped clean off below the elbow in a public school classroom.

You couldn't make it up, that's what the local newscasts reported as far across the Big Lake as La Crosse and Fargo. Freak of freaks. Grimmer than grim, and referring to him, all six-foot-six, as the next Big Unit but with his career closed out just like that. "You don't want to hear this," they said, as if it might incite or traumatize young athletes everywhere, and then they provided a graphic play-by-play anyway. The teacher present—"My God, the magnitude," the news anchors intoned in hushed voices—his teammates and his teenage fiancée all gathered for the execution, laughing and hooting and slapping him on the back, and then, as if in stop-time, looking on in horror.

They mentioned how he'd done his homework. His stand-up easel and flip chart and a dean's list gabble of gruesome facts about the French Revolution: how king and queen were beheaded separately in 1793, His Majesty in January and she in October, a child bride, barely fourteen when they tied the royal knot.

"Jailbait," my mom—her baby bump already showing—interrupted. "Cradle robber." And my father explaining, to her and to everyone, that if he could have he'd have spared the queen's life and maybe changed the violent course of history. But this was now or never and all that mattered was to pass the class, a measly C-minus their gateway to the future, and what was theirs right there for the taking.

"And Jesus Christ from there the hell on," my mom said, and wherever he'd found the mannequins, the padded church kneeler, was beyond hers or anyone's comprehension. Not to mention those flowing indigo robes. Coconuts for heads, faces sandpapered smooth and spray-painted white and pasty like a geisha's, and which, on this day two centuries later, would tumble and roll together—their carved pink lips barely parted, blindfolds refused and their doomed eyes neither closed nor staring downward in disgrace but rather looking straight ahead.

By all accounts they were still crazy about each other, my father ad-libbed, as if the case for true love at any age might invalidate all those trumped-up and treasonous charges. They admitted to nothing, he said, and right to the bitter end remained poised and silent, resilient and un-afraid.

Then came a drum roll, and that honed and weighted industrial paper-cutter blade way too heavy for a single release lever and a make-shift shear pin. But even at that, as my mom calculates, what were the odds, the prospects of such an ungodly, unforgiving physics, that it would snap full force exactly as my father reached in to straighten those two wavy white wigs borrowed from the drama club.

Family Services social worker number two—older, seasoned, the pack's dominant jackal with the focused determination of breaking through to me alive in her eyes. A veteran, according to my father, a prime time, no-nonsense professional. They've talked, and a few times all three of us together. He says for me to pay close attention, that this one knows her stuff—a warning that she's seen it all, every defiant, cocky-young screw-up like yours truly. Her square, Army-green coffee mug says SPEAK YOUR MIND, but whenever I offer an opinion she wide-eyes me with the emptiest, most remote and dismissive stare in creation. Glowers like she can see right through me from the onset to the absolute end of my socially impaired and substandard existence. Nods. Clenches up. Says stuff like, "So." Says, "Uh-huh. Fair enough, though the victims of much greater calamities cope and move on, don't they?" Always slams on the brakes with some loaded, instant override question like that. Then says, "Go on, please." As in, "'Sing it again, Sam,' and let's see where *this* next burnout version of reality leads us, shall we?"

And against which we somehow forge our slow way hourward. It's all part of the guilty plea, and of me being perceived not as some danger-ous criminal but rather as not really giving a shit. Even wanting to get caught red-handed, making a desperate appeal for help—denials and anger issues and the like. So mostly I just tuck in, nod and grimace and gut-roll through every session. I close my eyes. With my finest fakery I stammer and bite my lip and sometimes cry because it's a thin ledge I'm walking—that's the message loud and clear—and the falloff rate for girls my age is nothing to frigging underestimate. I'm good at this: hand tremors and hyperventilating on demand. Within seconds I can double my pulse rate and begin to run a fever. Wicked sweats and hiccups, and the whole act so convincing that I once said "Hollywood" when she asked about potential career tracks, and she didn't for one dense second even catch the irony. Talk about a movie set on Venus or Mars.

Her name's Ms. Foisie. Early forty-something, springy strawberry-blond locks drawn back into a ponytail. Perfume so thick that you enter the room and boom, a giant blast of Chocolate Daisy or Autumn Snakeroot explodes straight up through your nostrils, and those eyes, I swear, wide-spaced and lobelia blue, and the pupils black as dahlias. Feather earrings to top it off. I've never admitted as much, but it's enough to get a person high. For that initial full hour of her "getting to know me," I kept scanning the room for bumblebees and hummingbirds. A praying mantis, maybe and the featured talk that day all about my parents and the recklessness of teenage sex and marriage. "You do," she said, "understand what I'm telling you, correct?"

I nodded. "The basic thrust," I said, and she said, "Which is?" and I said, "Things happen. Things buzz"—but hey, not to worry, no lick and stick from where I rest my weary bones and noggin. And look, no engagement rock, and I was *still* patiently waiting to go all wild and wet in my dreams. It's why my father reams me out about the wise-cracking. A curse or spell, he says, but pure reflex is what it actually is, totally spontaneous and, come on, only meant as a joke. All in good fun, woman to woman to possibly lighten the psychic load just a little, and her husband and two sons smiling sideways at me from out of that fancy, gold-leafed photo on her desk.

Allison says no sweat. Says, "Remember, we're good." Says, "Hey, guess what?" and we simultaneously flip each other off. This goes back to the carnival fortune-teller two summers ago, who held my hand and explained the length of a woman's middle finger predicts her future. Me? I'd be some modern-day Egyptian queen, all satin clad, dripping rubies and sapphires, ruddering down the Nile at twilight while dining with sheiks or whatever, instead of serving breakfast for minimum wage at our local Denny's.

I whirled around in a full circle on my tiptoes right outside the gypsy tent with its heavy canvas flaps and burning candles and Mason jars of giant scorpions and smiling horseshoe bats in formaldehyde. I said, "Holy rip-shit," confirming that wherever in the hemispheres the spirit took us was where *we* were headed, nonstop into the slipstream of epic romance and greatness and maybe even a blockbuster feature-length film or two, with Oscars and Golden Globes. And so we made that pact to go and go as we sashayed arm in arm in our skintight miniskirts and flip-flops through the slowly rising mist of the midway—what my mom called the land of stuffed lions and lambs, and that prized oversize panda she insisted nobody ever won: "Nobody, Sam. Remember that. Above all else remember that when the fairyland dream smoke clears, women like us, like you and me, we always, every single solitary time, wake up elsewhere. And that other life we wanted so badly? The one back *there?* It's nothing more than a mirage, the simple-sad story of our botched and misguided lives."

What I now believe is that the price of my father trying and trying to prove my mother wrong about him actually made her love him less. The ring toss, that pyramid of milk bottles that never wobbled or fell and, in her eyes rendered him a mere figment of his former self.

The postmark on her last few letters is from Kenosha. They're addressed to me and me alone, and to my knowledge she's made no other human contact hereabouts. I could lie, tell my father, "Mom asked about you. How you were doing." But what she's conveyed thus far is this: That in her new job she individually hand-wraps brandy-soaked chocolates in a warehouse where they pipe in *Peter and the Wolf*, and musicals like *The Sound of Music*, and Judy Garland's "Over the Rainbow."

I've thought for the millionth time, "Just hop a Trailways Sam," and it would have long ago been a done deal had she ever once offered to take me with her. Or had she, after the fact, dropped the slightest hint that the choice was mine, legal or otherwise. Or that of course she wants me to move out there or, bare minimum, come visit for an extended stay—though yes, it's too late for this Thanksgiving, but consider Christmas as a possibility, okay?

She says the Salvation Army ringers are already at it with their handbells and hanging red coin kettles. And the tree on top of the water tower is decorated with ten thousand translucent stars, a galaxy of tiny blue spires aglow in the night sky. If only she had a balcony or fire escape, she thinks, she could see the display from her single-occupancy efficiency apartment. It's small, of course, but has a TV and microwave and mini-fridge.

She says, "Can you imagine it, a town with prehistoric sturgeon in the rivers? Caviar!" she says. And a brand-new Grand Union that hires the blind as greeters, as well as to stand at the head of every other aisle to offer toothpicks and so much free sample food that it's impossible for anyone to go hungry. So far not word one about another man in her life, though that's how she's ended up where she has, morose and alone, lost to us. That's the part I hate her for, and refuse to forgive. Except that I haven't, against my father's will and certainty, ruled out entirely that she still might rally like someone suddenly waking from a decade-long coma and remembering her husband's name, the address and phone number where she used to live. Or like the mute who picks up a smoky cat's-eye marble or piece of mica, and holds it to the sun, and begins to lip-sync some long-forgotten serenade about leaving and love—and then just dodges the holy, haphazard hell right out of there and straight for home.

Instead, she claims that the haloed prison lights she drives by some nights remind her how lucky she is to be so free and alive. Though possibly it's a lunatic asylum, she can't be positive—the grilled windows and the like—but either way it's just another case in point, as my father would argue, to fortify his position against her return.

That's true. It's like she's writing from a land so foreign and far-flung I had to locate it on our Rand McNally atlas just to remind myself that she's only in Wisconsin: a straight shot north through the UP and then, at any given junction or crossroads, just hang a louie and hold that sightline all the way to the horizon.

What's clear to everyone is that if she hadn't in fits and flashes beat it out of here so often, we'd *already* be on our way to rescue her, whispering, "Where are you, where are you?" and then begging her back. First time she fled was on foot, and my father found her shivering in the predawn just blocks away, silent and shamefaced, her eyes closed like she'd been slapped. And then him leading her by the hand slowly past the neighbors' houses, up our porch stairs with the dying potted spider plants, and back inside. Once a regular homebody, she began disappearing, no telling when or where to, a half mile or so beyond the town's outskirts to begin with, and later got stranded out by the I-75 motor

156

lodge where that grid of high-tension wires crackles and hums. And that was followed not long after by collect calls from Menominee and Battle Creek, though never before had she crossed state lines or stayed gone for more than a day or two, a week at most. But this time, come spring, it'll mark a calendar year—and by then, according to my father, she'll have forfeited all rights, including visitation privileges.

He says about having filed for divorce, "How wrong you are. We've done everything we can. Everything humanly possible, Sam. There's no turning back, not anymore, and your mother and me, we've *already* gone our separate ways. No other alternative exists, and for sure no coping or compromising away what she *imagined* and believed back then should've been our lives going forward."

What *I* imagine is her vanishing, not for months or even years, but forever. And the only photograph in my possession is a grainy, 8 × 10 black and white my father secretly snapped of her—like some private eye, while she stood staring skyward into the storm light as it massed and rumbled tidal-like directly toward her: the air electrified and a giant monochrome shadow eclipsing those endless windswept alfalfa fields—the entire silvery span of them and her head flung back and her arms outstretched as if, as he reported it back then, she was waiting to be abducted by aliens.

"It's who she is," he said. "A human lost and found and lost, and, for good measure, gone, and gone lost yet again. Elsewhere—that's the direction she's always been headed in. The sequel to the sequel to the sequel, Sam. Look," he said, as he handed the photo to me. "Look at this. Look closely and tell me honestly that you or anyone can conceive for her a happier outcome."

Ms. Foisie agrees. As she's said repeatedly, "Let's let the credits roll, shall we?" Her take is that my mom suffers from a chronic case of arrested development, the defections so numerous that even I had to admit that I'd lost count. But hope, nonetheless, springs eternal, right? "And she is, after all," I've continued to argue, "still my mom. Is she not?" And Ms. Foisie's standard comeback is, "Yes, she who has self-destructively turned your lives into a charade," and implying furthermore that she'd turned me into my own worst enemy.

I suppose I could have revealed, but wouldn't ever to the likes of her, how some nights my mom would sit on the end of my bed and patiently cast whichever hand shadows I requested, animal or reptile or insect. Rabbits, dragonflies, camels and storks and pelicans. Sometimes that scary profile of a crocodile, her index and middle fingers slowly scissoring up and down, while that raised knuckle of an eye socket floated across the calm, imaginary white water of my bedroom wall. How it was me who held the flashlight, who aimed the beam as if it were a magic lantern. How it took two hands and all *ten* fluttery fingers for her to simulate the erratic nose-diving flights of those swallows that nested in the rafters of our unused woodshed. And how one time my mom said, right out of the blue, "No, your father *can't* do this." Which was exactly what I'd been wondering. And then, turning to look at me, she speculated that if his double hook were diamond-tipped he'd score each windowpane and tap out a thousand perfect pinpoints to let in the moon and the starlight.

My father calls it the best Christmas present ever, that I've been taken off probation for good behavior. Or possibly, as Allison speculates, the judge was doubling down on my redemption in this, the season of miracles. Either way, as of this weekend, this very Friday night, I've been rewarded with an eleven PM curfew. "On the dot and not a second later," my father said, and if the roads start to get bad I'm to head home immediately. They already almost are, though suddenly it seems like we've got all the time in the world.

Because Allison has graduated from learner's permit to driver's license, we're sitting on the front bumper of her parents' second car, a dented, high-mileage Oldsmobile Custom Cruiser, recently tuned-up, and with four new snow tires. Plus a first-aid kit, and emergency roadside flares—all fizz without the firecracker—stashed in the trunk.

The early pardon calls for a celebration. As Allison says, "Out the door and on the loose like old times. Only better," and I agree wholeheartedly now that we're much older, wiser, and wily, and have wrangled a set of wheels and a full tank of gas, notwithstanding that there's absolutely nowhere to go in weather like this. It's why we're bundled up against the freezing cold, scarves and hats and a Hudson Bay blanket around our skinny shoulders like a double cape, and the snow slow but steady-falling in giant feathery flakes—a scrim half-obscuring the lights of the town below us, the abandoned gravel pits with the rusted-out derricks and the limestone quarry beyond. The only color is the blurry, rectangular, neon-red Dairy Queen sign. Otherwise, everything's white, the pines and Doug firs on the steep downward slant ghosting over, and the foundry smokestack—though we can't see it—like a vertical ice tunnel into the sky. Months. That's how much winter's ahead. And yet there's not a single county plow taking notice. And no wind at all, and even when we strain to hear that unmistakable shrill whine of transport trailers out on the interstate, we can't. Everything's quiet, the loudest sound anywhere the tips of our two cigarettes burning back with every inhale.

We've been parked for maybe half an hour at this scenic, no-name lovers' lane overlook, but of course no one other than us is about. No jocks on the prowl, but girls like us, we take it on faith that some night hence we will draw them out of their small-town, shit-box lives in droves and teach them how to love us. How to kiss and kiss us all over until their lips and tongues go numb. How to follow the sway of our hips gliding us like phantoms across dream fields so vast that even a search party of thousands couldn't detect a single trace.

Instead, here we are, waylaid in the panorama of so much emptiness that Allison tilts her head heavenward. She says, "Hey, Sam, we gotta go," but even so she leans back against the hood and closes her eyes and remains silent. The snow sticks to her long lashes like tiny white wings; her face is almost luminous. We are beautiful is what I think, travelers momentarily stranded inside the closed-off borderlands beyond which lie our future lives. I imagine my father standing and staring out the living room window, conjuring a blizzard, and how the winter roads will begin to narrow, and the Black Creek Bridge we have to cross to get back, always the first to ice over. He'll switch the porch light on, and the TV weather station. He'll call Allison's house to see if we're there, the car's colossal ass-end fishtailed safely up the gradual incline of their driveway.

And I imagine my mom, listening to that din of voices inside her head, the fade-ins and fade-outs, the New Year almost upon us, and my overdue trip to visit her never taken, the intervals apart growing longer by the day.

"Look," I say: the moon is almost full, and for those delayed few seconds before the snow falls harder into the dark, the disappearing landscape turns purplish blue. "Like a dying spotlight," I say, and this is a pageant, a dance we do while opening the car doors and sliding in. The engine catches on the very first try, the wipers clearing the windshield with one wide swoop. We're ready to launch, and the Olds is no longer a car, as Allison says. It's a catamaran, and the roads are rivers. You can see in the low beams how slowly we're drifting over the snow, leaving no wake. No stars to follow home, though for now, for this night, it is where we're headed.

A WOMAN GONE MISSING

Her age is thirty-three. Already twice divorced, though neither is the father of her teenage daughter, Trinity, who has opted to spend her junior year living with her biological dad four hours south in Kalamazoo. Getting to know him better is what she says.

His name is Bernard Sawyer. B-Saw back then, Vanessa's first serious high school boyfriend. Unlike her, he's a college graduate. A meteorologist. He sends up weather balloons to gather data and describes his failed marriage as a category-four. His vocation is his passion. Has been since grade school, and because he comes from money, and because he continues to take home a living wage, he's the one who paid for Trinity's braces—and the day they came off, to have her model-perfect teeth bleached white as frostbite. Not to buy her off, because he's not like that. He's generous with Vanessa, too. Meaning that he has never one time, as far as she knows, slighted or maligned her in any way. To Trinity least of all. And yet, a metal-mouth no longer, this girl wants suddenly to shame the world with her beauty. Devour her mom's dour cautions about the thunderous, unrequited fantasies of love.

Knocked up on the high dive is how Vanessa might describe the night, the blatting slap of the pickup's tires as she and B-Saw crossed the narrow bridge, ignored the distant, intermittent heat lightning and the No Trespassing signs. Then fishtailed up the steep two-track in four-wheel, no AC and the windows open. Hair blowing across her face and the humidity at 100 percent. Hotter than Hades, and the forecast going forward that called for more of the same. Tornado weather was what B-Saw said, and the drive seemed to her like forever, a sweaty six-pack of Rolling Rock between them on the shiny vinyl bench seat. Which, of course, is where they could have gotten laid a hundred times over. But didn't, and, come hell or high water, they would never violate their commitment to each other to wait. No regrettable weak moments, though sixteen and horny they did everything but. A few times on the oversize living room couch in his parents' vacation cottage. Summer people who'd motor away in their pontoon, highballs in hand, as if to reward such responsible kids with a little space and privacy.

And still Vanessa and B-Saw stayed faithful to the plan. Had for the second summer in a row since they'd first met, and the planning became part of the foreplay. She, with the fairy-tale imagination, said, "In a tub of jasmine and white roses," though he opted for something less flowery, someplace dangerous and forbidden—and so, yes, *this* is where Vanessa goes, is exactly where she stood high up on that same embankment while B-Saw peeled off her soaked-through tank top and cargo shorts, her bikini underpants, and hung them on a branch as if to dry in the nonexistent breeze, like laundry on a clothesline. Then *he* stripped, and together they descended, and waded naked into the subarctic spring-fed lake at midnight.

Great Hollow, it's called, and in the science of inexplicable natural phenomena, and against the base laws of latitude and longitude, and in the absence of any known thermal vein or current, the lake, even in deepest winter, refuses to freeze over.

Notwithstanding that neither Vanessa nor B-Saw could see it, he swore the abandoned tower rig lay straight ahead, across the surface shadowless and flat-calm and silvery, trout colored. Whatever had been mined down there he didn't know. Possibly diamonds, he said, a lie she liked, and she pointed at the sky alive with millions and millions of glittering stars. He'd memorized their names, which ones formed which constellations—Swan, Bear, the Three Guides and the Three Hunters. A sixty-minute swimmer, she'd already started to shiver as they breaststroked side by side through pockets of water so frigid she could feel her calves and thighs tighten and throb, her lungs collapsing like a bellows, teeth chattering. It was too cold even to pee, and she almost said, "Help me." She almost said, "We can't, we've got to turn back," but then there it was, like something out of *War of the Worlds* looming above them in the moonlight.

They treaded water, craned their necks heavenward, with the safe and commonplace queen-size truck seat, or couch, suddenly drifting away like images from another galaxy. She'd begun to lose her coordination when she grabbed hold of the ladder, and as she climbed slowly upward her knuckles appeared blue on the corroded wrought-iron rungs. She wondered if it was mist or smoke or the steam from their bodies rising all around them, rising above the gold-tipped tops of the shoreline trees the higher she got, and with B-Saw so close she could feel his breath warm on her backside.

At some point he'd let go of the sealed condom, and no, she'd never exactly committed to the pill. Not that she meant to get pregnant, but like the last two survivors on a sinking ocean liner they did it anyway, in a crow's nest seventy-five feet in the sky. They did it quickly, standing, cheek to cheek, her legs barely apart, and each vertebra in her back pressing hard against what must have been a mast or a flagpole. A bride and groom, she later thought, slow-dancing nude on a wedding cake, though already long vanished was any happily-ever-after, the marriage that never was.

And gone, too, is Vanessa's daughter, who packed up her entire room, closet, and bureau drawers. Everything but the full-length bedroom mirror, in front of which, before exiting, she paused, cocked her hip, and said, "There," as if imagining herself in fishnet and high heels, the starlet of some banned bootleg music video.

Clinton Styles—the man Vanessa did marry. And although he kept the volume low, the videos he owned and watched were violent: *Full Metal Jacket, A Clockwork Orange, Reservoir Dogs.* "All four and five stars," he argued. "Classic flicks"—which meant nothing to her, and she asked him to please not set that mousetrap under the heating grate by the TV anymore. It frightened her whenever it snapped and rattled and ruined whatever show she was watching. Romantic comedies mostly, where people not so unlike her almost always turned out okay.

But one evening during dinner, barely four months after they'd tied the knot, Clinton said, "No, it's a lot of different things." He'd *wanted* to give the marriage his all. Believed against the odds that it could work its magic, but "What," he said, "in hell's name was I thinking?"

Meaning their difference in age and how little they knew each other, the whirlwind of it all. Meaning stepfather-hood. Meaning diapers and diaper bags that no amount of Tide ever seemed to get completely white and clean-smelling. The baby colicky and wailing, and him being relegated to smoking his Lucky Strikes outside no matter the time or the weather, as if she and Trinity had taken up sides against him. Without asking, Vanessa had emptied the cigarette butts and sponged clean the ashtrays and stored them away, out of sight. As for the oval burn scars on the Formica countertop, there was precious little she could do, other than to point each one out as a house fire waiting to happen, and their security deposit already gone up in flames.

"Go ahead. Keep this up," he said. He said, "Fuck it," maybe he'd just as soon trade in the whole goddamn loused-up deal for a bottle of muscatel, a Motel 6, and a screamer to pile-drive and pay for and be done with. The occasional fist through a plasterboard wall.

But that wasn't Clinton at all; it was pure frustration talking, and she'd whisper in bed, "Shh, you'll wake the baby," and she'd slip out to the sleeping porch the instant he rolled off her and started to snore. Better this, she thought, than to quit the marriage cold and go live with her mother, the worst of the worst of all possible options. And there were, after all, nights on the porch when it smelled like rain, and moths pinged like moist cotton balls against the screens. Her complexion was perfect then, and her breasts still twice their normal size, her stretch marks beginning to disappear. To mention nothing of her lips, and those long upcurled eyelashes, the natural dance of her waist and hips when she walked.

Her long-term goal was to home-school herself, develop study skills like B-Saw had, and get her GED, perhaps at some point take night classes and graduate with a nursing or pharmacy degree from the community college in Traverse City. After all, how difficult could it be to count pills into those opaque orange containers, like the ones her mother lined up on the shelves of their medicine cabinet? But first things first, she thought, and promised herself that starting the very next day she'd stop eating peanut butter and raspberry preserves straight from the jars with a spoon. That didn't happen, and Clinton joked, "Tamper-proof lids. That's the ticket." They didn't yet own a bathroom scale, but it wasn't easy to miss that she'd already started to put on weight. He smiled. "Baby fat," he said.

Before she'd ever met Clinton she'd concluded, "Why not?" to a start-up, rebound romance, after B-Saw, who drove up three different times to see her, said, "Please, Vanessa. Listen to me," but she wouldn't, her decision as decisive and final and as contrary as his. A test of wills. "And, in case you're interested," she said, "the baby's due date is May. Possibly even on Mother's Day."

She acknowledged *his* position, said Yes, they'd screwed up, a mess of their own making. "I admit it, okay?" she said. His parents had blamed

163

her as if she'd set out to trap their son, this wild and headstrong girl who refused to come to her senses. But B-Saw never encouraged that, never poor-mouthed or backstabbed. It was always *we*, always *us*. And never any tirades or taunts, and not one time during her early term did he mention the A-word. It was her mother who said, "There *are* no free abortion clinics, not here in Mancelona there aren't. But somewhere. Believe me, you have it and you'll never, for as long as you live, feel young like this again. Never."

As if for one single solitary second Vanessa had conceived of such a cowardly, unthinkable act. She'd relocate, but not for that, to Frankfort, a tourist town where maybe a young pregnant girl waiting tables could pull down decent tips. She'd been there once and liked it, the beach and the break-wall, the public park. But no matter where or what, she'd have the baby. And not only wouldn't she put it up for adoption, she'd do a way better job of raising her child than her mother ever did, which wasn't saying a whole lot.

And Clinton Styles, hadn't he recently completed a stint in the navy, his ambition to someday become a merchant marine? That's what he claimed, on Lake Michigan or Lake Superior, and his favorite song Gordon Lightfoot's *The Wreck of the Edmund Fitzgerald*, a few verses of which he sang to her. He'd recently moved from Bad Axe to Frankfort to be closer to a maritime academy, though he hadn't yet gotten around to submitting his application.

He was 6' 2", eyes blue-gray like a husky's, his car a bright-red, high-mileage Chevy Nova, insured by State Farm. Plus he'd handed her a bank passbook with more deposits than withdrawals. Collateral, she thought, and his voice just disarming enough to convince her that a life together need not be—and as he promised it wouldn't be—all mongoose and cobra.

As for his gig back then, rotating a two-sided octagonal sign on a pole—STOP and SLOW—and the diesel and tar fumes so strong he'd arrive back home to the motor court with fewer and fewer brain cells under his yellow hard hat? "Mindless," he said. "One-armed," and he'd swivel his wrist one way and then back the other. "Totally rinky-dink and so boring," but not to lose heart, it was only temporary. True or not it constituted for Vanessa the closest thing available to a protected and halfway stable life, a decent enough paycheck every two weeks, a roof over her infant daughter's head, bread on the table, a Frigidaire that stayed cold. And, admittedly, a life with someone she maybe didn't entirely know and love, but someday she might, and who she at least trusted to watch Trinity when vanessa showered and shaved her underarms and legs, a towel twirled around her head like a turban.

In his defense, Clinton was *not* a wife-beater, a thief or a cheat, or an ugly drunk who'd say, "What the fuck are *you* looking at?" and then hurl himself across the dinner table to scream in her face. And no window curtains blown back from a thrown boot or a gunshot blast. She'd seen enough of that in her growing up, before her father was arrested and convicted of crimes both petty and serious, and eventually sentenced away.

And there were, in fact, for as long as the marriage lasted, calm and companionable quiet stretches, TV shows they agreed on and Trinity asleep in her crib, most likely dreaming good dreams. It's fair to say that on certain days, whatever their future held seemed no more and no less haunted for them than it did for anyone else.

They'd met, for God's sake, she and Clinton, at the public library, where Vanessa was shelving books from a cart. One of her two part-time jobs and Trinity like a papoose on her mother's back, the best-behaved baby ever. Poster child. Fat cheeks, and her hair shiny-black and spiked like a Mohawk. A magnet for lonely men, who stopped and whispered, "She's so beautiful. Is she yours?" Sometimes they'd take her tiny pink hand between their thumb and index finger, and one time an older guy with a misshapen smile and overbite tucked a smudgy phone number into Trinity's squeezed palm. Whenever Vanessa turned around, these strangers always seemed stunned that she wasn't Ottawa or Chippewa, wasn't from the reservation. And by how young she was, like someone they might have seen not all that long ago playing hopscotch or jumping rope on a sidewalk.

What Clinton Styles asked about when he said, "Excuse me" was a reading recommendation. "Science fiction, I guess?" he said. "Or a good Western? Nothing too heavy." Back then she hadn't been much of a reader, so she simply shrugged and, using both hands, offered him the book she'd just lifted from her stack and was about to shelve. Its title, *The Elegant Universe.*

And so, no, for her it wasn't love at first sight, but he was polite, not unattractive. A mask, her mother said. "Don't kid yourself, they've all got issues and needs. Go slow, he's been around, unlike you," she cautioned. Vanessa agreed, even under such desperate circumstances, that

165

what she really needed was a live-in, a roommate, not a husband, and what she *should* have said when he proposed was, "Okay, yes, I will. I accept, but remember, no sex after marriage."

They kept the wedding simple, with a justice of the peace and the ceremony absent any frills or pageantry. No best man, no maid of honor, and the ring sized, she thought, to fit her pinkie or to wear on a chain around her neck. Not so much as a walk-through rehearsal. They simply showed up at the courthouse casually dressed. (A bridal registry, Vanessa concluded, must be where couples like them paid for the service.) And her mother, weeks after the fact, when Vanessa described it, said, "What'd you expect on a mercy rescue? Complete strangers throwing rice? A reception of lobster ravioli and corked champagne? A honeymoon at the Mall of America?"

And the bigger question, "Do you, Vanessa, take this man?"—who one year later to the day, on the eve of their first wedding anniversary, left her the Nova, the key and the title, and the remaining twelve payments. Either that or sell the car for whatever she could get. Plus he'd signed a check for the next two months' rent. Then he hitchhiked downstate and took a ferry from Ludington to Milwaukee, Wisconsin. The note he left also said, "From there, wherever it leads." It said, "No regrets. It's simply where we left off." It said, "And remember, never spoil the ending." Just like that. Broosh. Gone, and never a single postcard to follow.

That night the trees out back whipsawed, and although there was no damage from the falling limbs, gale force winds ripped shingles from the roof. It was already a week after Thanksgiving and she needed to baste and cook that thawed, bruised-looking tom in the tinfoil turkey tray before he spoiled. One hundred-and-eighty degrees for the breast, one-twenty for the thighs is what that gourmet TV chef had recommended. Sure. But her days were still hand to mouth, and she hadn't budgeted for a cookbook or a meat thermometer or even an inexpensive apron, so how, with an oven she'd barely used, and a husband who'd ditched out on her, did someone manage that?

"A Mexican divorce in goddamn Michigan," her mother would have said. "A blessing that the power went out during the storm—that turkey's just one less thing to fail at and beat yourself up about. And for what?" Another lost someone to feel sorry enough to bail her out? Serves her right. After all, Vanessa could have gone home for the holiday. Hadn't she gotten her driver's license? She had a car, a safety seat for the baby, and so why *hadn't* she simply picked up the phone and dialed?

Every now and again she does. She closes her eyes, and breathes deeply, and summons the nerve. Her mother's fifty-two. She lives alone in that same house, where Vanessa was raised, and sometimes, like now, while sipping a glass of Diet Rite and vodka at twilight, Vanessa will close her eyes and, against her will and better judgment, she'll go there again.

1050 Willow Road, and there *he* is, her father, facedown in the backyard, his fists balled, and Vanessa's mother strangle-voiced and saying, "Christ on a bike." Her throat is rubbed red as rhubarb, her left eye half-closed and swollen, her brutal dye job grown out a full inch at the roots. It's not the first time he's done this, but she says, "Accidents happen, you'll see. Just leave him alone, leave him be. He'll make his way inside on his own." She says, "Sweet Jesus," as she lights a cigarette, her red fingernails chipped and her hands trembling. "Just another goddamn day in Paradise." She says it in gulps, like she should be deep breathing into a paper bag.

But by morning he's nowhere in the house or on the property. Not that they can detect, though it's all junked up out there, a regular dump, and could be he's asleep in the back seat on any one of those half-dozen beaters. Wrecks he's towed in over time, hoods popped, and the smashed windshields infused with what look to Vanessa in the early light like giant, silvery-blue spider webs. Convex and oval-shaped, what she understands in retrospect to be the perfect head-on impressions of anonymous human skulls and faces.

She has just turned eight, and she wonders why the prior evening's brightest star has survived so long into the daylight. Her mother hasn't a clue, and "Margie—Baby Doll" is what he calls her when he finally *does* reappear after two days, hangdog and hungover as usual, and although his hands stay shaky on her hipbones, he says, "Truce." Says, "We're good. You'll see. I promise we'll figure this out."

But that summer nobody's good with much of anything. Delinquent mortgage payments, a rust-ravaged car that even he can't start anymore. A single offhand, mistimed remark and tempers flare like hay fires, so much meanness and shouting that Vanessa has to cover her ears and hum while the ground shifts and tilts around her. Because he's been fired and laid off and fired again, he's recruited her to assist him in his new job so that he can spoil her rotten, buy her everything she wants. Root beer floats and a Cabbage Patch doll, a bicycle pump so he can inflate her flat rear tire.

"How?" she asks. "And when?" and he brushes her bangs back from her forehead and says, "Come on, I'll show you. Hop in."

She's not supposed to ride in the truck, a flatbed with no passenger-side seat belt, but her mother, like always after a drag-down, is napping. She's swallowed those pills again. She's dead to the world and she'll be conked for a long while and groggy and silent when she wakes, her eye already turned a sallow yellow and green.

And yes, that loose front tooth Vanessa pushes on with her tongue tip both hurts and soothes, and her father says, "Now remember, you just stand there. Right next to me, and act like you're about to cry." She hardly ever cries anymore, and, in that 7-Eleven, the E-Z-Mart, and the Tastee Freez a couple of towns over, she listens to him as he harangues each confused and apologetic cashier. "And the purchase price was how much? All right then. Here, go ahead, count it yourself," he says, and hands back the bills. "That's correct, you shortchanged me," and even Vanessa, an eyewitness to his every sleight of hand, cannot detect how he does it, like a card shark or magician.

"Bingo," he says on the ride home, "easy as that." He says, "Now we're getting somewhere," but the money's mostly lost to the booze and ciga-rettes, and a week later he strips a house, foreclosed and standing empty, of its fancy crown molding and mahogany doors. What he calls salvage and scrap, serious profit, but his quick resale estimates are so far under that he needs another beer and a shot, another Pall Mall, something to dull the great dismay that is theirs ongoing.

Needs, on yet another caper, for Vanessa to scale a drainpipe or trel-lis to a second-story balcony or porch. And sneak inside, and down the stairs, and unlock the rear slider. "That's it," he says, "good work," be-fore the more serious looting ensues in bedrooms and dens. Eventually this ends, first with his arrest, then the guilty-as-charged and, as a multiple repeat offender, no less than fifteen years in a federal peniten-tiary. Before he is led away in handcuffs and asked by the judge if he has anything to say to the court, he nods, shrugs. He is already stand-ing. He says, as if it were a last request, "Just wondering if anyone here's got a smoke they can spare for the dead?"

Sometimes Vanessa can hear her mother's noisy inhale, the cigarette pa-per crackling through the phone lines like distant radio static. It's been two and a half decades since Vanessa last saw or spoke to her father.

Trinity knows next to nothing about him. "I was eight when he left," Vanessa tells her. "I hardly remember him at all."

"Eight?" Trinity thinks, knowing *she* remembers plenty from when she was that age, which instantly invalidates the amnesia of her mother's past. Aloud she says, "Maybe someday . . ." but she doesn't finish, as if to solve the mystery or cover up might distance the two of them even further. Trinity just offers her an icy, unblinking stare and adds, "Dad, he tells me everything."

She favors him in looks too, same thick dark hair, same straight nose, and that sudden slow-motion chewing whenever a dinner conversation stalls or loses its bearings. It's no wonder she opts for the Sawyer side of the family.

"They're educated. They're nice," Trinity says. "They don't play Risk or Go Fish all night to kill time, they talk to me. And they travel everywhere. They go on cruises and have their leaves blown and they don't live a million miles out in the boonies."

To hear Trinity talk, obviously it means nothing that her maternal grandmother squeezed Vanessa's hand throughout the entire eight hours of that interminable labor. Nor all those picture books Vanessa had saved, and that mobile of black and white sandhill cranes she made that danced in the air currents above Trinity's crib. The girl has threatened to legally change her name from Lavanway to Sawyer when she turns eighteen. She says that her *other* grandparents have two Siamese cats that sleep right on the bed with her and purr and purr whenever she visits.

The closest thing to a pet that Vanessa ever had were nasty, beady-eyed minks that her father bred and raised in cages behind their house. They frightened her, captive wild creatures with their fang-like incisors and high-shrieking midnight wails into the snow or the wind. Into whatever disease and neglect finally killed every last one of them, their pelts ratty and dull and worthless. Vanessa has never admitted as much, but despite her banishment, she'd always hoped that after their grandchild was born the Sawyers would relinquish such a selfish, and superior, and unreasonable stance against her.

They never did, as if the score they needed to settle was with time itself, and what Vanessa has wanted to tell them is no one lives long enough for that. Although she's got nothing to answer for anymore, she'll be forever unwelcome there, and so instead she diets down a few pounds and feels better. Almost like herself again, she laces up her cross-trainers and runs at night whenever Trinity's away, and when sleep, that sweet and distant rain, falls so rarely.

It's why Vanessa is wide-awake and out the back door, down the steps, the neighborhood quiet, the windows dark everywhere. Ready, set, go. And in her rush to get away, she doesn't even bother to stretch, her legs churning as she veers across backyard lawns, the freshly mown grass lush and oddly fragrant. She knows this route so well she can do it with her eyes closed, and sometimes for almost half a minute she does, blind to all those security spots snapping on, one after the other, and lighting up the distance behind her as she goes.

Why? Because this is the hour of the wolf, and so even when she stops she continues to run in place. Like now, under a full moon, where the slide and the jungle gym and the bars of the swing set shine like platinum, and her heart racing and racing as if she's been chased. But there's no one around. Just a lazy waterspout, and a fountain where lonely day-timers toss nickels and dimes and quarters. What *she* wishes for is a body better shaped to carry the weight of her drooping ass—bringing up the rear, as her second husband, half-drunk in the sack, liked to say. But he's long gone too, so X the ex and, if need be, she'll hump it until dawn in every conceivable roundabout, zigzagging direction home just to be rid of him in her mind.

Since divorce number two she's allowed only a handful of men to follow her inside, though almost never beyond the kitchen or living room. Ironically, and in Trinity's absence, she's decided to quit them, too, their come-ons and promises, which, calculated in time and regret, have cost her plenty.

The prenup as well—but at least, and without a court battle, she's ended up with the house. Not rented, owned. *Her* place and everything up to code, wiring and plumbing, with the driveway recently resurfaced. A safe neighborhood and a manageable mortgage, and just last month she took that second pillow off the bed, a symbolic act, and invoked the mercy rule on dating.

"I'm done," she said to Trinity on the phone. Trinity, who refused to be introduced to any and all future men of the house, but nonetheless hurried downstairs whenever the doorbell rang, and stood there stone-faced. Said nothing. Gave them long dark looks, a silent sendoff to wherever her mother was headed: to a movie or dinner or the bar at the bowling alley. At worst, and depending on whether she'd had a second Bloody Mary or screwdriver, a make-out session in the guy's car parked

170

a block or two away. But even then Vanessa was always back before ten, her self-imposed, romance-killing curfew.

All she really wants in the end is for her daughter to come back home. Re-enroll at her old school and visit her father every other weekend, like she'd been doing for the past couple of years. Only once a month before that, and before that hardly ever.

Factor in Vanessa's recent raise as floor manager at Old World Gifts & Furnishings, and she's finally had a satellite dish installed. With the remote Trinity could now flip through hundreds of channels and watch whatever she wants. Watch B-Saw, in fact, on that all-weather station as he arcs his arms like a god. As if *he's* compelling those speeded-up incandescent radar blobs that swirl across the new flat-screen, west to east, across the vastness of all those places Vanessa has never been.

And worse, she tunes in and way more often than she probably should. She's learned the language: temperature bands, snow thunder, wind-chill factors, jet streams and supercells, the weekly almanac. Sunset and sunrise. But the segment she likes best by far is called *Show Me a Glory*. It's where viewers send in photographs of sundogs or the Belt of Venus, or that rare moonbow captured last week in the sky above Sweet Lips, Tennessee. All these from people who, unlike Vanessa, own telescopes and fancy-ass cameras and keep a careful watch on the world.

Moreover, she actually fantasizes sending in that blurry Polaroid she's saved of her and B-Saw from their junior year. They're standing on the abandoned soccer field of her old high school, and he's hugging her from behind. He'd set the camera on a tripod, on a five-second de-lay. They're in love. They're facing into the afternoon light, and they're almost glowing, radiant against that background of random, ordinary clouds on an ordinary late summer afternoon in 1985. If she were to follow through she halfway believes, for old time's sake—for that mo-ment when the shutter clicked and that already developing snapshot slid toward them—that he might reach out like he did then, and show it, along with those sprites and elves and blue jets: the tiny, bright, emerald-colored auroras trapped inside raindrops that illuminate the nighttime ground as they spiral and fall.

Everything, Vanessa concludes, is, more or less, what it seems. And more so all the time, year in and year out. The mercury rises, the mercury falls. Like the seasons, and already it's February again, the snowbanks

171

piled high, and the county plows tearing by all growl and sparks and flashing orange beacons. She's invested in quality snow tires. Emergency provisions such as road flares and extra matches, Mars bars and a Hudson Bay blanket stored in the trunk. Jumper cables. But on a night like this, and the storm predicted to worsen, who's going anywhere?

What she hears from Trinity is need-to-know only. Thinly coded signals and dispatches. The girl is pulling down good grades for the first time ever, a straight A in chemistry, a B+ in AP English. She's on a mission of merit and discovery, her father all over again. She's got a sun lamp by her desk, she says, and recommends that Vanessa get one, too. "Especially up where you are," she says, as if it's the cure for all her mother's longings and moods.

About Trinity's bedroom being repainted a lighter blue, and the new TV and satellite dish, her daughter says, "Maybe over spring break, okay?" But that followed immediately with something about a getaway vacation to the Grand Canyon. "The Southwest," she says, as if Vanessa had never opened a Rand McNally or spun a globe in grade school. As if she has never imagined anyplace other than the great white nothingness of winter on the forty-fifth parallel.

Maybe now is the perfect time, Vanessa thinks, for a mother-daughter road trip. Or possibly all three of them could travel together. Rent an RV, chart a course, and end each day in a different state park campsite along the rims of famous canyons and rivers and lakes, before it's too late.

But it's B-Saw talking first once he gets on the phone. He's all business, friendly as always—but distant, and so mostly Vanessa only half-listens and drifts. Her feet are tucked under her on the couch, and she's poured a shot of whiskey into her coffee. Taster's Choice. It's become a ritual—the aroma, the sheen of the steaming crystals. She knows, by the time she finishes her second cup, she'll be good to go. She'll close her eyes, lean back, navigate by dogsled if need be, across a landscape so white and flat that she might in fact be dreaming.

"Mush," she says after she hangs up. She almost laughs, and yet, within minutes, in the pre-predawn cold outside her window, she can almost hear the dogs huffing and howling under the invisible, icy-blue crescent of the moon. But no, she does not walk out onto the porch and down the steps into the yard in her nightgown. Instead, and because she makes this slow trek down the hallway to her bed, and sets her alarm clock for work, there will be no freezing to death, no lost fingers or toes in this story. It's hers. It's ongoing, and so she'll go there, too, and it goes like this.

ON THIS DAY YOU ARE ALL YOUR AGES

And the longevity genes are on your side. Your mother, at eighty-one, still owns that same outdated two-bedroom, bath-and-a-half red brick ranch where you grew up, a valid driver's license, and a Buick Skylark that, as she says, was built to last.

And your father, former Special Forces, had *already* lived a dozen lifetimes before he died of unnatural causes. Not a shotgun or a noose or a hose attached to the exhaust pipe, because nowhere in your family history is there any evidence of that. And even you, Marjorie Breitweiser, a casualty of late-stage divorce and addiction to loneliness, will not be the first.

And most certainly not midmorning on a Saturday in April such as this—clear skies and the forecast going forward calling for temperatures in the upper sixties. If you could, you'd bury the past and live each day as if it were your last. But the truth is you want her back, that feisty, quirky kid who, in recollection, keeps kissing her own wrist and calls it practice.

Remember that? The eleven-year-old who harangues against any elective surgery to correct those severely crossed and oversize eyes? It's a fact, especially when you're tired or upset, that they're apt to wander off on their own, and almost touch. But why tizz out about it is what you'd like to know. After all, your vision is 20/20, and, as you insist, in the end that's all that really matters, isn't it? No floaters. No migraines or blackouts or seeing double. No dizziness or trances, and the world, as far as you can tell, in perfect focus. So what's the big hurry anyway? You're already wearing braces and how many correctable features can there be in a single face? Besides, there must have been back then, and may be even now, someone out there somewhere determined to love you exactly as you are.

"Don't hold your breath," your mother says. It's no big deal, an upgrade. "A routine realignment is all," and you imagine two tiny, silvery blue wheels spinning silently behind your closed lids.

She reads you the riot act, calls you selfish, belligerent, and naïve. She says, "I don't need this." Says, "Snap out of it, Marjorie, before it's too late, or believe you me you'll forever regret this." She refers to you in moments of frustration as Miss High and Holy who can't see past her own stubbornness, a first-class drama queen.

Could be she's right, but screw the attitude adjustment. You like who you are, and when she holds up a hand mirror and says, "Honest to God," it's she who's rattled and shamefaced, not you. Still she offers as evidence before and after photos of women and girls, and guarantees—one hundred percent—that the outcome will turn you gorgeous. Best in show, she jokes when she's in a better mood, as though you're some poodle or Shih Tzu or Pekingese. Talk about freaks of nature.

"Maybe," you say, but she says, "No, not if, when." She says, "Argument over. Now look at me," but your stare-downs of late have become so intense that sightlessness might seem a mercy.

And then out of nowhere it's 1977 and you've just turned fourteen. An only child of a single mother, and still a minor when Clifton Zelony unlatches and holds open the door to the toolshed behind his parents' house, as he will again and again over the next few weeks with bribes of cigarettes and ice-cold cans of his old man's Miller High Life.

He lives just down the street, around the corner, and it's impossible to determine anymore whether hormones or a simple case of the late summer doldrums brings you there. Either way there you are, a little tipsy. Beyond that? Well, he's not much to look at: gangly, a blond peach-fuzz mustache. Hardly ever smiles. Quiet for the most part, low-key, and, at least thus far, he appears harmless enough. Unlike the boys your mother repeatedly warns you about—those wild and wayward shaggy-headed creatures of excess needs and desires. The way-too-easy-to-fall-in-love-with heartbreak types, who, in the end, constitute nothing more than a giant waste of time and energy. She says, "Just remember to keep your damn legs crossed."

Which is less and less a problem, given that your interest in Clifton grows old in a hurry. The making out, the convoluted trails he charts across your body with his fingertips, then dinners down your tight, flat stomach with his tongue, the two of you curled up on the plywood floor among the rakes and spades and bulb planters, your breasts barely button knobs.

He's the first guy you've let touch you like this, and although he's unzipped your cut-offs and lifted the elastic of your underpants with his thumb, you haven't gone all the way. Nor will you—not yet and for sure not with him—and when you break it off a week before school begins he simply nods at first, as if being ditched is just one more cruel and fucked-up initiation into adulthood. Except, of course, that he's gone tight-jawed and doesn't even blink. He leers, hate-faced. As if from out of a mug shot, though that's still years away and since when is it a crime to sight down the length of one arm and squeeze an imaginary trigger?

"Ka-boom," he says. And sure enough he unleashes the cruelest litany of epithets and taunts you've so far endured: Inbred. Mongrel bitch. Lemur. Spider monkey. "A rescue mission," he says. A tease and a scag he wouldn't be caught dead with in public, though he hangs around to watch you put your T-shirt back on, and untangle an earring from your hair, which is long and auburn and wavy. He's two years older, about to be a junior, but suddenly spooked silent when you look up and lock eyes, like you can see right through him into the godforsaken future of *both* your lives.

Soon after all that, you do give into the procedure. You say to your mother, "All right, I've changed my mind," and for a full week following you wear a blindfold, crisscrossing pirate patches. All day, all night, and you swear to Clementine Pugh, your gullible best friend and confidante, that rather than straightforward corrective surgery, the doctors went ahead and ordered two transplant pupils and corneas flown in nonstop from Brazil. Carefully packed in an urn of smoking dry ice. Like something better suited to a mausoleum shelf for safekeeping.

And no, you tell her, you have *not* yet seen what you look like. Everything is pitch black, but on whatever day you finally do open your eyes, and turn on even the dimmest light, it will feel like fire, like touching a lit match to a tablespoon of magnesium. It will burn and burn, but for now in the shower you're like Helen Keller, your body braille, and the bar of almond-scented soap that washes over you holds images and secrets too terrible to ever disclose. "Things *he* sees and dreams," you say. "Close up, in 3-D."

"Like what?" Clementine says, and you lean toward her and whisper that the deceased donor was a boy exactly your age. "Exactly *our* age," you say. "A dead boy's eyes," and she squints and backs away.

"I don't believe you," she says, but of course she does, and when you singsong, "One, Mississippi, two, Mississippi," she shakes her head and starts to cry. Glances this way and that before she flees into the ordinary, everyday visible world that has suddenly begun changing shape all around her.

When you actually do take off the patches what strikes you, from dawn to dusk, season after season, is that half a millennium is apt to elapse without notice. And that someone, perhaps Mr. DeWitt, your elderly next-door neighbor, is destined in the next half second to stop dead in his tracks and abandon his push mower on the uncut front lawn. He's already mowed and raked the entire backyard, bagged the cuttings, smiled over and waved to you like always. It's a day like any other: disappearing vapor trails overhead, and that ravenous and relentless shrill cawing of crows.

Except that going forward you don't see him anywhere for many days. Then a full month passes, and your mother explains in her matter-of-fact way that he's housebound now, and rides a slow motorized lift to the second floor, and then back down. A walker, a wheelchair, a subscription to retirement radio piped in from who knows where. He's suffered a stroke. His daughter is there to care for him, and in anticipation of what comes next she's added his name to the convalescent home's endless waiting list. A room thick with wintergreen and a view of either the road or the parking lot. *That* future or something like it, and no possible way by then to circle back and begin again.

"But *we* can," you declare decades later, and you halfway imagine, in spite of your husband Ward's long protracted response, a salvageable outcome. "Marjorie," he says. "For starters, how about we give it a rest, okay?"

The sun's not even up, and because you've gone off again on that same tangent about how life begins at fifty he's already folded the morning paper, and put it down beside his pancakes and scrambled eggs and bacon. He folds his arms and leans slowly back. It's pretty much the only exercise he gets anymore, this former college scholarship swimmer who railed and railed from the outset against ever having kids, and confused good sex with doing the butterfly. If he'd had a better sense of humor

176

you'd have bought him a stopwatch by now, along with a free sample-pack of Viagra.

But it's been a while since any of that, the romps and moans and breathlessness, your hair in sweaty tangles. In fact, during the past few years you can count on one hand the number of times he's gotten into bed before you've drifted into deepest sleep, curled up on your left side, facing away, your diaphragm long ago stored in the bottom drawer of the nightstand, like a relic from another era.

Still, you share certain interests. Politics, old black-and-white films, auctions and estate sales, the garden out back with its night-blooming flowers: raised beds of dragon fruit and evening primrose and Casablanca lilies. You've even taken a foreign-language class together in preparation for that promised and already-twice-postponed second honeymoon to Mexico, though even about this you rarely argue. You eat out every Tuesday and Saturday, and, more often than not, converse in ways that make you feel present and necessary. For these reasons you've managed to remain optimistic and married for almost fifteen years and counting.

"I'm sorry," he finally says. "But why put off until tomorrow . . ." and once again it's Friday, but you can tell this one is unlike all the others, and you want more than anything in this life for him to take back what he's about to say. It's been coming, later than sooner as it turns out, but here it is, and by early evening he'll be packed and gone, a note on the kitchen table when you get home from the pharmacy, where you count capsules and pills and work the drive-thru window.

Prescription after prescription placed inside those thin white paper bags and stapled shut. Vicodin, Adapin, Zoloft, Lunesta. Methadone. Drops for earwigs, for cataracts, ointments for ringworm and canker sores, for boils the size of raw oysters—and, worst of all, for those scars and fourth-degree body burns and skin grafts. You've seen the small children in profile, pale faces unlined and unblemished, flawless until they turn to see who's talking over the scratchy intercom to their mom or dad: that nosy woman asking for addresses, birth dates, verification of who they are. You can't help imagining their lives, what happened and how, the deep grief and remorse of such misfortune. Sometimes, when that hand reaches toward you with the clipboard and credit card for the co-pay, you almost toss the starched white smock you're wearing to the floor and walk out of there for good.

You've explained this to your husband, but there's a timetable, an ongoing countdown. As he points out, gone are the days of decent salaries and health benefits, any lasting loyalty to even the long tenured like you. "And who, by the way, is hiring people our age?" he'd like to know. "So just hang in there, Marjorie. Hang on," and you do.

He's a CPA, a numbers guy, strait-laced, nose to the grindstone, a man born to balance the accounts of others. Orderly and measured and responsible. Kind. A good soul. And yet somehow, out of the blue, he works up the nerve to explain these last few years as the longest and most debilitating of his life. He calculates, on a scale of one to ten, a negative three, the days interchangeable and leading nowhere, except deeper into the dead zone of married life. And so why drag it out any longer? He's met a man. He's in love and so there it is, out in the open. He says, "At last. Did you really not see this coming?"

"No," you tell him after maybe a full minute, as if his words have traveled an enormous distance to find you. You've intuited nothing, not a single slipup affirming even the slightest suspicion or disputed claim. Not a clue, and no matter how often or far you reverse the dots, you simply cannot connect them. Where you end up is where you always end up after thousands and thousands of hours on your feet, and the lunches you pack and unwrap so slowly that more than half your lifetime passes.

You put in for all the vacation days you've saved up, the leaves already red and gold, and the tight multicolored mum clusters glowing under the new moon. Along with the uncarved pumpkins on the front porch stairs, they help to dress up the emptiness of fall.

You stay busy by painting the ceilings, the interior walls of every room and hallway, and you remain indoors as if quarantined. Your husband has not come home, and won't. And, in advance of the divorce, you agree over the telephone to a fifty-fifty split of all assets. Right down the middle. Or, as he puts it, fifty cents on the dollar. Plus you get the house, with its new energy efficient furnace and A/C, and the mortgage paid down by half.

It's more than fair is what he argues, but at any cost he's the one flying high; you can hear it in his voice as clear as a cowbell. You might even in the ensuing months or years wish him well but definitely not yet. Forgiveness is a test against anger and loss; these take a while to get over, as they did with your father, a DOA at the ripe old age of twenty-nine.

It's your mother's story to tell. And she has, countless times, how he returned all screwed up to the Upper Midwest after back-to-back tours in those godforsaken jungles most people couldn't locate on a world map. Violent mood swings, and his only job offer was loading bull balls and hog cheeks and giant blood clots into idling semis at the rendering plant: part time, graveyard shift, and to which he'd said, "For fuck-sake," and went AWOL halfway through his fourth week.

He started pounding down what your mother called widow-makers. And cranked up the Beach Boys and, in the predawn two thousand miles from the California coast, he caught a wave and for almost three full downtown blocks hung ten on the roof of a war buddy's speeding van in 1964. Like two barhopping frat-boy daredevils in fatigues and combat boots, when *he* should have been slow dancing in nervous circles around the hospital bed that night you were born. Five weeks premature: three pounds, eight ounces, and no wonder the truth comes to you again and again so long after the fact: that this, after all, is what men do.

Last night another snowstorm and the schools are closed. The only gaff is that you're not a teacher, and with each sidesplitting shovelful you curse the delinquent plow guy to whom you've made clear what time you're expected, each and every weekday morning, to be at work. That's the thing, it's getting on toward 9:30 and the drugs in their plastic bins are waiting. Pills powerful enough to induce a coma, to slow down or speed up a heart.

It's minus fifteen degrees, and you're wearing an ankle-length goose-down parka, lightweight and black as a shroud. A scarf and a ski mask, too, your eyes bright blue in their dark sockets. You haven't even brushed your hair or put on any makeup, and because your mittens are already wet you shake them off and lift your half-frozen fingers to the oval mouth hole and breathe.

Every few seconds the wind kicks up, and you face away. Toward the picture window soaped last Halloween after you turned off all the lights and went to bed: *OGRE, WENCH, GHOUL.* But on this morning in midwinter disguise, you concede that the reflection staring back at you is none other than the grim reaper herself, your shovel a scythe, and that this first February, divorced and alone, has taken, minute by minute, a merciless toll.

You could lose your job, which you need more than ever. It wouldn't surprise you if the call came right now, as you stand hunched over, knee-deep, stock-still and shivering. You can hear the low-hanging power lines hum, and the thermostat is set at eighty-five just in case the electricity *does* go out. No fireplace or backup generator, and the snow falling even harder—a total whiteout.

Like a dream, you think, and just like that it's All Hallows Eve, 1972, and your mother, from as far back as you can remember, has designed and sewn every one of your costumes. As always, this one fits perfectly, like a second skin. This year you go as Joan of Arc, a young martyr your mother has read books to you about. And shown you reproductions of ancient paintings, and fashioned you a helmet, and ballpeen-hammered an aluminum vest. A sword with an open-mouthed trick-or-treat sack dangling from the tip. You tap on the neighborhood doors with it, and grownups hand over the spoils: candy and coins, apples as round and shiny as blown-glass orbs.

"Who are you supposed to be, dear?" Mrs. McElvoy from down the street asks. She's old and wears one of those pointy bras under her sweater. Perfume so strong it makes your eyes sting.

"Guess," you say, and she says back, "Well, can you give me a few hints?" and you tell her, "Okay." That you're a saint, nicknamed the Maid of Orleans, a protector of the French people during the Hundred Years' War. The year is 1431.

Then you straighten your shoulders and say, like you're the lead in a school play, "Yet must I go and must I do this thing."

Mrs. McElvoy smiles and shrugs, her hair the color of smoke, and backlit by a hallway light so bright you imagine flames rising around *all* the magnificent, sacrificial witches throughout history who have been bound and burned alive at the stake.

Now, as always, on those occasions when you visit your mother forty-five minutes away in Manistee, the last thing you do before you leave is lift and stare at the glassed, grainy black-and-white portrait of your father in that standup frame on the mantel. He's a handsome man, shiny thick hair combed back, and the bones of his face a mirror image of yours. Two Purple Hearts. A dead ringer, your mother says, but she always stops short of naming names anymore of film stars long deceased. She says instead, "If only he'd lost his trigger finger to a chipper or cherry bomb when he was a boy. Anything to have kept him home, for all the goddamn good his military service did for anyone." She used to say, "Tell me, Marjorie, what sin did we commit to deserve this?"

"Nothing," you'd tell her, and she'd answer, "And for future reference, no. I'll never remarry," though you can't remember a single instance of ever having asked.

Today she goes silent after a verbal skirmish. She closes her eyes, and then, out of nowhere, asks, "When did you last hear from Parish?" Like *he's* your ex, and therefore grandkids must, in some unfathomable permutation, figure into the equation. She means Parish Mackey, a college sweetheart who, whenever he kisses you in memory or in dreams, still makes your nipples harden and ache.

Gordon Swogger, Billy Payne, Leo Shea—a roll call of the missing, men you've dated, one or two you might even have loved had they not stood you up in such hurtful ways. Your mother never forgets or confuses them, but you remember best by far Johnny Zale. It's 1989 and he's driven you home for spring break on his Harley, detouring almost two hundred miles west from East Lansing on his trek farther north into the Upper Peninsula.

You're both road-weary, chilled to the bone. Plus there's a hazy half moon, and the temperature falling, your one and only opening to invite him to spend the night, as he has a few times in your dorm room. There's little your mother can argue and not appear insensitive and rude.

He's met her before and so he says to you, "Thanks, but hey, three's a crowd, right? No worries. I've got some speed, I'm sure I can make it okay."

Maybe, but Marquette is still another six hours, not to mention those vast, low-lying stretches of dense fog along Route 2, and nothing but a broken, hypnotic yellow two-lane centerline to follow.

And so you bring out clean sheets, a blanket and pillow. The two of you sit shoulder to shoulder on the pullout couch, talking even later into the night than usual. Your mother is asleep, her door closed. He touches the backs of your knees, your lips.

"Not here," you say. "Uh-uh." You say, "Sweet dreams" when he leans in yet again, and they are. But what you remember best, after he sneaks into your bedroom and gently shakes you awake at first light to whisper, "I'm checking out, gotta go," is that shiny chrome chain snaked through his belt loops. And the billfold it attaches to in the back pocket of his jeans as he throttles away, bent over the handlebars, the ass cut out of his leather chaps, and the sky endless and silver-rimmed like a mirror.

"To hell and gone," you remember your mother said at breakfast. "All of them"—meaning those wild and beautiful boys. "Let them go. Even if they plead on hands and knees, don't you ever give in and follow." How is it, you wonder, that she can remember them even now?

You change your major last minute, from nursing to pharmacy. Three extra semesters to finally get your degree. But it fits you, and you land a hugely better-than-expected job right out of college, which affords the freedom of your own place: a bare-bones, reasonably priced, clean, and quiet efficiency in Traverse City. As well as your first car, a low-mileage Mercury Sable. In addition, you manage to pay back every loan ahead of schedule. And *still* you sock some savings away, and promise yourself to someday travel both far and wide. New Zealand, maybe. Caracas or Acapulco in February or March. You like the sound of Swissair and imagine whispering to the pilot, "Doesn't matter. Wherever you're headed."

You grow used to your independence, to being alone, though friends worry and Glenda from work comes up with an unasked-for prospect: "From all reports he's a nice guy. Good job, never been married. No red flags. Hey, it's worth a try."

"Another gift from the gods," you say, and she says, "Fine. But if you change your mind . . ." and the blind date who knocks that Friday evening on your front door arrives holding flowers, his khakis creased and pleated, spit-shined loafers, a monogrammed white Oxford shirt.

His name is Ward Beal and he takes you out half a dozen times before inviting you up to his place. Dinner, movies, sometimes a drink afterwards. He's pushing forty. Just overweight enough that it doesn't surprise you when he forgoes the stairs and waits for the freight elevator door to open. An empty, humid, dark, and airless square box of a space, like something a small missile might rocket out of. It's fusty smelling and claustrophobic, *and what*, you ask yourself, *was I thinking?* But only until the elevator stops and you step out into a century-old studio apartment above a bookstore on the town's main street. Paintings and track lighting, exposed brick walls, and floor-to-ceiling windows with a distant view of the bay—and the place is immaculate.

Ward never raises his voice or cuts you off midsentence, and he apologizes profusely the one time he bears down so hard on a letter he's drafting to the editor about traffic and the lack of parking, that the pencil lead explodes in a thousand different directions. "He's passionate," you tell Glenda. "And smart, too," but leave out that he's still a work in progress when it comes to the bedroom.

"There's no option in the rental agreement to renew the lease," Ward says, and you see it as an omen. The timing feels right for the two of you to make a commitment. You keep it simple, and elope on foot a few blocks south to the justice of the peace. And sign papers later that afternoon on a newly constructed split-level on a cul-de-sac with asphalt so smooth and black it looks at night like a deep, slow bend in a river you can float down forever.

You've been orphaned five weeks in ICU, and now, whenever you cry, your mother is there to lift you out of your crib. It's not advised and yet she carries you from room to room, nursing you through these first nights home with song. The motion is dirge-like, minor key, and frightens you so much you learn to stay quiet, to lie still. The crib is not in her bedroom, but the walls are thin and you can hear her ragged breathing, the way she suppresses and chokes down the air.

But listen to this: in the daylight she hums. She inserts the pacifier into your mouth, and bends even lower and whispers, "Hi, Marjorie," and carefully opens your eyes even wider with her index fingers and thumbs. You watch her pupils dilate into two perfectly synchronized gold dots. You follow them wherever she looks: out the windows, at the TV with the sound turned off, at those government checks that arrive each month and her childlike scribble that endorses them.

Other times she stares transfixed at nothing, her eyes blank, glazed over, and she whispers to herself in tongues. Or plays solitaire at the kitchen table, where you sit strapped into a baby carrier, the kings and jacks the same bright red as her lips and nails.

Your favorite game is hide-and-peek, the way her fingers splay and then her hidden face appears like a vision. Furthermore, that's also when she confers with you: "Are you a happy girl?" she says, a dozen times over just to be certain. But she worries, too, and when she hunts up the different doctors' telephone numbers, you send silent signals pleading, "No, no, no."

She pencils in every appointment, and with a Magic Marker crosses each day off the calendar with a fat black X. You like the smell, like the cool scent of rubbing alcohol, and the way her fingertips play different tunes on your belly and back.

If the stroller tires were cast in brass, they'd carve deep grooves in that quarter-mile square of sidewalk that surrounds your block—a couples-only-with-kids kind of neighborhood, though you don't see the fathers often, and when you do, your face pinches at the sound of their coarse, open-throated voices. Sometimes they call your mother's name, but it's a furious, concentrated gait she maintains until you're out of earshot. That's when she slows down and you watch the illuminated undersides of the clouds as they ferry giant pools of sunlight across the endless sky. It's this pace you like, and how you can magically hold your own bottle with your own two hands now.

Your mother's thin, back in shape already, and sleepless some nights she carries you outside, wrapped in a blanket. She stands in the center of the small fenced-in backyard. "Look, Marjorie," she says, and you point, too, at the Weaving Sister, the Polish Bull, the Outer Kitchen. "The Wreath of Flowers," she says. "And there's the She-Goat, the Sea Stone, the Calf of the Lion."

Later in the summer comes the aurora borealis, those meteor streams that glitter and disappear in showers of pink and gold. Even after they vanish the grass is speckled silver. And the dark interior of the house also brightens, and you can see into your bedroom, to the mobile that orbits back and forth like a mirage in the air currents above your crib.

She lowers you, barefoot, to the ground. You wobble on your fat knees—you of the future slim waist and dancer's legs. Your mother, backing away, gets down on *her* knees, arms outstretched, and says, "Okay. Come to me, Marjorie."

You do not cry or sit down. You open your clenched fists and take that first impossible bowlegged step on your way to her. The distance covers approximately seven feet. It's easier than you imagined, moving like this through the shadows cast by that same moon, almost full again and rising.

THAT STORY

Wherever my mom finds these articles I haven't a clue. All I know is that she clips them out and hands them to me to read. "Look, Fritzi, another miracle," she says, the most recent having occurred somewhere outside San Francisco.

For a good laugh I pass them along to Dieter and Brinks while we smoke in my dad's Plymouth Fury, the odometer frozen at 172,605 miles. The car is up on blocks, transmission shot and hubs painted purple. Rear risers but no tires, and snow up to both doors so we have to crawl inside, like it's an igloo or a fort, and always with some half-wrapped notion of someday firing it alive and driving hellbent away from Bethlehem. Not the one in Pennsylvania, but a town so remote you can't even locate its position on a USGS map.

And therein resides both the irony and the farthest far-flung implausibility that somebody hereabouts discovers a visage of Christ in a lint screen at the local Laundromat, and that then, along with our name, we got ourselves a shrine and a destination to boot. "Imagine it," my mom says, but a million pilgrims desperate to put a knee down in this nothing town suddenly adjacent to God and heaven confounds even the dreamer in me. And yet, as misguided as such an influx sounds, it's what she's apparently banking on. Which might explain why she's hand-painting all those Baby Jesus Christmas ornaments, preparing to make a fortune off the endless caravans of sinners soon to arrive here in the provinces. But she says, "Nope. Uh-uh." They're nothing more than another scheme designed to fill and quiet time. Besides, she says, each month at the diner she always manages to sell at least a few to the truckers to take home to their wives.

I hate to admit it, but a miracle is precisely what it'll take to hire a lawyer high-profile enough to enter an appeal and get my dad's sentence overturned from first-degree manslaughter to self-defense. Guilty or not, my mom maintains, when a married man slurps bar vodka from some strange woman's navel, he's going to pay a heavy price somewhere along the line. I remember how, right after the trial, she sat me down at the kitchen table and held both my hands and said, "Fritzi, listen to me. All premature deaths are wrongful deaths. But some, like this one, they're so senseless it makes them more wrong than the others. It makes them," she said, "eternally unforgivable."

Their divorce, final come May, has for a long while now been inevitable and therefore okay, I guess. Except for Bobby Bigalow, my mom's new boyfriend. Every word that falls from his loud mouth is either a rule or a sermon, and whenever he mentions my dad I can feel him present in my balled-up right fist. I know all too well that a single punch placed perfectly to the temple can kill a man, and so I afford Bobby Bigalow a wide berth. I'm only five-foot-six, but place a bet that I can't hoist a frozen hay bale over my head and you'll lose. Not that I'm prone to feats of strength or violence, but if he ever touches me or mistreats my mom I swear I'll take that first swing and at least rearrange his dentistry, that sneer of a smile, those tight snake lips. Maybe send him packing with a jaw wired shut and eating through a straw—though of course there's my mom to contend with, and thus the quandary.

Dieter and Brinks and me can't see him, but we know he's standing not ten yards in front of us, eyeballs straining, and so in unison we drag all the harder on our Lucky Strikes, imagining ourselves magnified behind the windshield. Tough guys you come at with a length of pipe and who leave teeth marks in the metal.

A fit father or not, my dad taught me to never take one backward step, no matter what, and for starters there's that tradition to honor and uphold. Besides, I've never been fingerprinted or booked on even a single juvenile misdemeanor charge.

Flat-out lucky is Bobby Bigalow's take, and I'd second that—but never face to face the way he'd like. He's the type, you confess anything and he dangles it in front of you like a noose. What he wants is for me to shape up, to shit-ditch what he refers to as my attitude and lack of focus, and commit to a new start before it's too late. Beginning

186

with my friends, "those ones," as he calls them. He means tribal kids. (I'm one-quarter Ottawa on my dad's side, my hair shiny blue-black just like his. The resemblance in our facial features, however, is not all that close except in the eyes—"like night minus the moon," as my mom in happier days used to proclaim.) We've grown up together, all three blood brothers, and when Dieter's snowmobile is up and running we like to shoot the glass insulators from the tops of the telephone poles with our pellet rifles. Or ding the silver dining cars mere inches below those lighted windows where couples leaning forward keep toasting their lives, the train whistle within minutes fading into the invisible distance.

Right now, we blow slow-motion smoke rings above the head of the Day-Glo dashboard Saint Christopher, perpetually open-fingered and palms up, who seems to say, "Okay, fine. But you're fifteen years old for chrissakes, and so just what, pray tell, is the goddamn battle plan going forward?"

It's late February and the ashtray is packed with a fat stack of Trojans, like it's a free customized in-car dispenser. We've got a bottle of Thunderbird, which Dieter scored on the reservation. Like my dad I've got no alcohol tolerance, so just a few quick hits and I envision a fig bush flowering inside Gloria Masterson's skin-tight Levi's. She's never afforded me the time of day, but there's a buffalo robe on the backseat just in case, and even the thought of it warming those impossible contours of her body accelerates my heart rate by plenty.

I can see my mom peeking out through the living room window, her hands cupped to her face like blinders. Everybody staring at everybody else, and no one advancing or uttering a single sound. A virtual stand-off. Our prefab is a repo, two bedrooms and the wall so thin between them that some nights I can hear the static of my mom's nylon stockings as she undresses for bed after a double shift at the Honcho out on old Route 668, just north of the four-way stop. Out on the void, as she says, where idling, slat-sided transport trailers shake the entire parking lot like some low-grade version of the San Andreas Fault. I've seen it firsthand, the plates and silverware rattling on the Formica tables and countertops. My mom gets long hours and low pay, but jobs are tough to come by, and because we're barely hanging on she's locked in there against her long-term wishes. She's first on the seniority list, and I can't recollect when she last called in sick. Or when her credit card wasn't maxed to the hilt.

In one of the articles she gave me, a waterspout somewhere in South America spewed up coins of solid silver and gold. Not a thing you'd think to hope or wait around for, but there it is to consider, as opposed to the cash register she tends day after day, all sticky with pitted nickels and dimes and quarters. Her dream is to someday see the Himalayas, though she's never even one time in her entire life left the state. Mark my words: Bobby Bigalow is not her ticket to anywhere you'd read about in a guidebook or travel brochure.

He's from Texas, an ex-rodeo cowboy out of Amarillo—or so he claims. He's got a slightly stooped back, so I calculate it's possible some pissed-off Brahman bull whiplashed him into early retirement a few lifetimes ago. Dieter's verdict is pisswilly on that, and Brinks agrees: Bobby Bigalow's just a self-glorified blowhard. He's got hair like General George A. Custer, wavy and blond, and I don't blame my mom for wanting company, but when the metal storm door opens and he steps back inside, I say, "Fuck him."

"And the horse he rode in on," Brinks says, though it's a Chevy Silverado he drives, and sometimes he'll rev it up real loud before he leaves, glass-packs growling, always the near side of midnight. Always after a few beers on the couch with my mom, arm around her neck or waist, and as she closes the blinds now I can see the vibrating blue waves cast by our secondhand, widescreen Sony Trinitron.

At least for the time being the arrangement isn't live-in, and so I suppress any impulse to tell my dad about what's transpired on the courtship front. I will, however, as a last resort if at some point I need his counsel. On the final Sunday of every other month is when we talk, 7:00 PM sharp. And it's only because he inquires that I betray my mom's whereabouts. Battalion II bingo, I tell him. Same exact routine replayed in every single solitary conversation. "Yes, she drives herself," I say, but what I withhold is that it's also where Bobby Bigalow calls out the numbers that have sent my mom home a winner these last few times in a row. It's where they met. An omen, she says, that against all odds she and I are fated for a life of lesser burdens.

During those allotted fifteen contact minutes, my dad says her name a lot, Laila, in ways that turn each next sentence lonelier than the last. He's never denied that trouble feeds the passions of bad men, and on the witness stand he said simply, in his own defense, that he did not, first off, consider himself to be among them, leastwise not by intention. Just some nobody, he said, with a pint in the glove box and a drinker's lack of judgment—and, no, he conceded, he was not ignorant of a rec-

188

ord of arrests too long to overlook after a Sunday night bar fight turned deadly.

"Then you're spared now to contemplate a different life going forward," the judge said. "But for the one you've mangled thus far, Mr. Boyd, you've run your quota of last chances. For which I hereby sentence you to eighteen years in a maximum-security prison without the possibility of parole." Bars and razor wire and turrets and armed guards—that's how my dad describes the joint. The big hole, he calls it. He says piss in the chili long enough and right here's where you end up, all dulled out and dead to the entire world.

"Bum rap," Brinks says. "I ask you, where's the justice?" He means that another weekend's shot, and we're out of cigarettes, the smoke so thick inside the car that I crack the window. There's a ladder that leans against the house, and a path I keep shoveled up to the roof peak for when the motor on the rotating TV antenna seizes. Mostly all it takes is half a dozen cupped breaths and a single knuckle rap to get it started again, but I refuse to watch the tube in Bobby Bigalow's presence. Dieter, as if he's reading my mind, says, "Well, you want this waste out of the picture or what?"

The honest answer's as dumb as trying to stare down the sun. The night air is frigid and still, and as my dad sober used to say, a man's mind in winter isn't meant to be enlightened, or sought after, and any attempt then at decision making only invites grim and sorry thinking. I'm eye level with the snowdrifts that the wind has sculpted, the temperature's single digit at best, and it's beyond me why I say what I say, but I do, inviting trouble of a magnitude that we don't need and yet sometimes covet. I say, "Yeah, big-time," both hands locked on the Fury's steering wheel, and envision running Bobby Bigalow off the road and deep into the frozen turnip fields stretching away in all directions.

"It'd at least break the boredom," Dieter says. "There's that." He's got a deep voice and braids that sway when he walks, and every single paper he writes for English class is about the vanished nations rising up again. At school we stick close together, and if anyone wisecracks about the amulets he wears, we're a small war party to deal with. The same goes for Bobby Bigalow, who's a grown-up version of that same small-minded, small-town bully. He potshots us and takes cover behind my mom's loneliness, never smiling or offering to drive Brinks and Dieter home so they don't have to snowshoe those five miles each way just to sit in a backyard beater in the bitter cold.

"Why would anyone in his right mind do that?" Bobby Bigalow asked a few weeks back, and in my best attempt at a nasally Texas drawl, I said, "'Cause we ain't got a rowboat. That's why."

"Ha, ha, ha," he said. "Talk that bullshit and you and me, pal, we real plain and simple got us a problem to reconcile."

He leaned so close to me then that I could see the pockmarks on both his cheeks flare crimson. A grown man's glare I'd never seen fastened on a kid before, but I thought, "Hate-stare somebody else, you Lone Star loser." The only scare tactic that had ever worked on me was when my mom threatened to leave. And sometimes she did go off for a day or two, with my dad stammering in her absence, "Honest to God, Fritz. Honest to God," like it was a double vow to fix everything that had, for years, spun further and further out of control. Speeding tickets and DWIs and racking up points enough to have his license revoked ten times over. Resisting arrest, disorderly conduct, urges that over the long haul define, as my mom insists, a weak man's feverish nature.

Brinks says, "The Quonsets. Let's blindfold him and escort him there."

That's where the turnips are temporarily stored after harvest, on dirt floors cut deep like bunkers. No windows, and even in summer it's always cool, the perfect place to build our ritual fires. Shavings and sticks and just enough flame to get our knife tips glowing. Check out our inner arms and you'll witness remnants of an ancient art, the raised scars long and blade-thin and climbing almost up to our elbows.

Bobby Bigalow's got matching spur tattoos on his biceps and a silver belt buckle big as a shield. And those gaudy western shirts with fake pearl cuff and button snaps. He's a sorry-looking stand-in for anyone I might consider habitable company for my mom. She's thirty-eight, strawberry-blond and narrow-hipped, and still pretty enough for men to get the fidgets when she walks by. So, sweet-talking Bobby Bigalow into relocating somewhere else won't be an easy sell. He's already acting like a stay-around, helping himself to beers and snacks from the fridge, and sometimes shuffling the mail as if searching for something that's his.

He complains that if he doesn't time it perfectly he gets caught at the crossing gate, warning lights and bells and those freight cars throwing up sparks, and I'm halfway thinking right there's our optimum ambush spot: on the far side of the rails, so that after the sleepers and the caboose get past, there *we'd* be, the single high-beam of our snowmobile bearing down like a phantom train about to pancake his sorry ass.

Dieter's waiting on parts so he can rebuild the carburetor in auto shop. He figures by midweek. But for right now, before he and Brinks trek home, he mimics the man in Spokane whose reattached left arm at nightfall points involuntarily at the Northern Cross, according to one of my mom's articles. Not that we buy any of it, that's for sure, but it nonetheless provides us some hilarity. Holy Mary Mother of God, you lose a limb and sew it back on and all you can think to do out there under the heavens each night is reach up and thank your lucky stars?

Brinks says, "Man, if it's me I hit the casino and honk down on the lever of a thousand-dollar slot and watch the place light up like a munitions factory."

Dieter's all over that and I am, too. A little revenge for the years our dads lost to the gambling and the booze, for those declarations to change everything that ever hurt or harmed us if only they could. One summer, our faces streaked with war paint, we sent up smoke signals to the gods on our dads' behalf. If certain girls happened by, we'd turn to them and tom-tom the drums of our flat naked stomachs, hoping they'd stop and maybe dance for us.

That failed to happen, then or ever, and here we are, me and Dieter and Brinks. When we bother to attend, we each maintain a steady C-minus average in a much-lower-than-average school district so far north that the cloudlight hovering some nights turns the landscape a bluish-gray shade either gorgeous or violent, depending on your state of mind. Ours hasn't been that great of late, and to make matters worse my mom appears more and more dazed by bogus notions about Bobby Bigalow.

"He lies," I tell her. "He's a bully and a sneak." But her standard comeback is that he treats her well and that I shouldn't begrudge her another chance with a man.

"Those flank steaks," she said. "He's the one who bought them, not me. Please, don't judge him so harshly, Fritzi, inasmuch as you can't possibly know in advance how a thing might turn out in the end."

I figured she'd interject my dad as a negative example, but she didn't. Which in its own cruel way made him appear even more expendable in our lives going forward. It's as if Bobby Bigalow's got her under some spell. I've seen her turning this way and that in front of the full-length mirror, her hair down, wearing nothing but red lipstick and a slip, and making silent-still music with her hands on her hips.

Dieter says that you can crush dry gumroot and swamp irises into a fine yellowish-blue powder and boil it into a tea that forces the fork-tongued to speak the truth or else their skin pusses up and peels away. But he can't recall the exact mixture or the other herbs, and the tribe's last medicine man died long before we came into this life. And anyhow, if we wait for late spring all might be forsaken.

"We'll figure something," Brinks says as he crawls out the window, and half a dozen snowshoe-lengths later he and Dieter are out of sight. They come and go in silence, leaving no tracks or drag marks, because a few weeks back we attached a horsehair tail to the ass end of the snowmobile. The two five-tined pike spears we carry with us are spoils from a raid over on Lake Tonawanda, where we war-whooped and circled the shanties to make certain nobody was inside when we finally kicked open the door. Nobody other than those nude centerfold pinups, of course, tacked to the wall and staring back at us, with their slightly parted lips all glossy and blistered in the blue flames of my dad's brush-chromed Zippo, and Brinks and Dieter's pilfered Bics. And so go ahead and try following them across the stark windswept pastures and fields of white moose and deer and coyote, and just see how long before you're completely turned around out there where the spirit world is everywhere alive.

Here's my mom's best one yet: a capstone gets jimmied from a long-abandoned well in the Ozarks and blind lungfish cry out in the voices of angels.

"Poetic," Dieter said.

"Downright inspiring," Brinks chimed in, all crocodile with a case of the weepies. Wet-vac all the way and, right, real funny, but maybe all miracles are a matter of need and deceit—all honest-Injun horseshit, as Bobby Bigalow says about Dieter and Brinks, and sometimes about me, though never when my mom's within earshot. I've seen him fingering her Christmas ornaments and eye rolling and shaking his head. I've seen him drink milk straight from the carton and then stare at those missing children in a way that blames everyone but himself, my mom's personal savior. And mine as well, if only I'd offer up some measure of contrition and a commitment to believing in forces other than myself and my two pull-trap friends. Yeah, we've got a few illegal beaver and muskrat sets, but so what? Not that Bobby Bigalow'd know a thing about where they're at. If he did he'd turn us in first thing to Church Stoner, the CO who's been itching to bust us for years, but even he—who's grown up in these parts—can't track us.

192

But a week or so after that night in the Fury, we tracked Bobby Bigalow, and it's possible that he and my mom went dancing like she said this past Friday night, but Dieter hit seventy-five miles per hour on the snowmobile to position us at our outpost on Summit Hill. We could see the lights of town. The crisscrossing of the streets, the dull red pulse of the Grand Union sign, and Bobby Bigalow hooking a right toward that strip of drive-ins and cut-rate, off-season motels. Which merely reinforced that nothing is sacred or safe with him around. I suppose I could have waited up to interrogate my mom, but to what end other than to start my own blood throbbing? And I backed off on the attack front anyway, so as not to arouse or inflame suspicion.

Until this morning when, before boarding the school bus, I said, "It's my house, too," and she did not say back, "Of course it is," or, "It always will be," like I'd anticipated. She said, "Yes, within reason," but anyone reasons this out and they've identified the source of all our impending anguish and grief. She doesn't see it and no doubt won't if I don't intervene on her behalf.

"It's not an open subject, Fritzi, and I'm tired of feeling so disenchanted and god-awful all the time. I've been too long at my wit's end, but I'm dating someone now, and it's not as if they've arrived in twos and threes. Have they? I know how resentful you are, but I don't want us to face off like this all the time. And whatever happens going forward, I want you to promise not to hold it against me."

I remained silent and stone-faced. We both did, and then she said a thing I knew might someday prove to be accurate, though to hear it spoken conjured in me a consideration I hadn't until that moment ever fathomed, and hoped I'd never in a different situation have to again. She said, "If you want to blame someone, blame your father. And if he asks, you tell him the truth. That he, and he alone, is the one who led us to where we find ourselves on this very day. As crazy convoluted as it sounds, he's the one who introduced us to Bobby. Tell him that, Fritzi. And tell him that except for a man being dead, I'm glad in the end that he did."

Dieter met me as I stepped off the bus, and said, "Everything's still a go?" and I said back, "Full bore," and we both nodded. We've stashed two sickles and a roll of electrician's tape in the Fury, and the wolf headdress that he signed out from the tribe for next week's history class show-and-tell, plus a peace pipe that we've been sucking without success for residual effects.

The forecast is for a blow out of Canada. A foot or more of snow, and you watch—that'll be Bobby Bigalow's ruse to finally spend the night.

And I don't mean on the couch, and I don't care to wake to that next morning, and breakfast, and the final rubble of my dad's last possessions boxed and banished to Goodwill without me even getting to go through them.

I ditched early, right after civics class, and by late morning I'd already stopped obsessing about what our civics teacher, Mr. DeSclafani, called a God-spot, this bay in the brain that functioned to dial back the onset of anger and treachery and revenge. I didn't raise my hand, but if I had I would have mentioned the afghan that Bobby Bigalow unfolds and drapes around my mom's shoulders just to tick me off. And how sometimes he even winks at me from right there behind the couch. In my head I hear my dad's old rant: "Give ground one time to that, and you'll be doing it on a daily basis," and so it only makes sense to "bring 'em on, all comers. Every last Fo, Fuck, and Fum."

And tonight as Dieter and Brinks and I see it, we're going to right some wrongs is all. If things foul up maybe we'll move on Dieter's backup plan to screw a spigot into one of those giant wine casks we've seen stacked on the boxcars and drink our way west on the rails to the Columbia River Gorge. Out where his dad lived for a short while after a stint in the service. And where he fished for king salmon that danced on their silver tails in the froth and the sunshine, right there below what he called the great nonstop booming of the falls. Last we heard he was living outside Montreal, and I suppose someday that might be a destination for us, too. I can't legally visit *my* dad until I turn eighteen, but like Dieter says, at least there's no guesswork concerning his whereabouts.

My mom's scheduled to work a double shift, and she left wearing a polished, silver-veined quartz stone around her neck. I've never seen it before. A gift from Bobby Bigalow no doubt, who just last night complained about the lousy water pressure like somehow he owns that right. The pipes not being buried deep enough under the frost line's the problem, and so we have to let the faucet slow-drip whenever the mercury dips below fifteen degrees. Sometimes I'll place an empty, upside-down ice-cube tray directly under the tap in the kitchen sink just to drive him batshit. I spare him not one reminder that in my eyes he and my mom are maybe hot-wired for the short run but are destined for an abrupt chill-down.

He's clueless that Dieter and Brinks tracked him home to some double-wide off Tapico. Off Arrowhead. Off a no-name two-track that backs up to state land where the proposed hydraulic dumpster was supposed to go. All that's there is a giant hole half filled with the dead weight of ruptured appliances and bedsprings and bald tires. TVs with bullet holes through the picture tubes. Plus a few metal shopping carts that we hauled out for the caster wheels we used to build ourselves three suicide skateboards.

We've re-mapped our attack-and-capture strategy in favor of just happening to be in Bobby Bigalow's neck of the woods later tonight. You know, to search the clearings and snow fields for a high-stepper who might teach us how to make our squaws go dumb between the bedsheets, a phrase he let slip that caused the first time I'd seen my mom flinch in his presence, her mouth muscles going taut. I wanted to say, "There. That's who he is outright. A croaker always running his lily-livered mouth and why parlay the likes of him into heartbreak? Why him?" But they're a twosome plain and simple. And, like Brinks says, all love's a fluke either temporary or lifelong, and without incentive Bobby Bigalow ain't about to scare or bugger off anytime in our immediate future.

But, as I wait for Dieter and Brinks to pick me up, I'm *all* Indian, and the sickles are razor sharp and already taped to the insides of my wrists for a better grip. Like curved tomahawks or talons. And the wolf's skull plate a perfect fit, my face smeared with lampblack from the inside glass of the kerosene lantern my dad always used whenever we dipped smelt in Otter Creek.

There's a full moon and the air's frostbite cold, and I remember how he said years ago, when I inquired, that he'd proposed to my mom under a meteor shower, the tracer tails so intense they turned the skyways platinum. There's Orion, the hunter. And this is the car in which my parents first dated, first kissed, and only since Bobby Bigalow does my mom, without a second's hesitation or any apparent regret, say straight-faced that it was all a colossal mistake, "a marriage so doomed and misguided." Think on that awhile like I do: I pull up short of calling her a liar, but she's nonetheless knocking a lot of careless and hurtful wrong words about.

That's a fact, and rather than let her pawn her wedding ring, last month I zinged it with my slingshot as far into the constellations as I could. And is that not, when I hear the muted roostertailing of Dieter's snowmobile up a certain draw still half a mile distant, why I roll down the car window and crawl outside without a second thought? Yes, on all fours, dressed in furs and wolf fangs and ready, finally, to move out across the frozen tundra, under the miracle of these winter stars.

"No mercy," Brinks says. He's holding a ball-and-claw table leg, and Dieter's brandishing one of the pike spears. There's no barking dog to quiet, but there is a second vehicle in Bobby's driveway. It's definitely not my mom's Cherokee, and it's parked directly in front of the pickup, which appears to be sniffing the Jeep's hind end like it's got in mind to hump it.

We're standing back a short ways from the slider. No blinds and the kitchen lit up, but nobody's stepped into view yet. I've never seen wallpaper like this before. A jungle-clot of jonquils—all summery and yellow—and flocked here and there amid them are a few oversize roses the dark blood color of mulberries.

"Some weird shit here," Dieter whispers, and it's true that the icicles hanging halfway down in front of the glass distort this woman who appears out of nowhere like a ghost among the vines and tangles. She's stark naked, and she stops at the stove and leans over and turns her head sideways to light a cigarette from one of the front burners. Then she leans against the counter and folds her arms over her breasts like she's shy or cold, or maybe even afraid and cowering.

No one says so, but we despise Bobby Bigalow all the more when he swaggers in zipping up his pants. What I notice most, though, is the ceiling, textured and flecked like ours with fake chips of mika. And how this woman is knock-kneed and shivering as the moon disappears and more snow starts to fall. It's the exact same posture I've seen my mom assume too many times—though bundled up of course. I imagine all four gas jets open full, and the oven turned on the way we always have it to survive the night whenever our furnace conks.

"It ain't his place," Brinks says. "He don't live here, Fritz. It's hers, and *now* how the fuck may I direct your call?"

The only one I'm certain owns a cell phone among us is Bobby Bigalow—some new fancy-ass gadget that takes snapshots and that he keeps holstered on his hip. I've heard it ring, though never have I seen him use or answer it. What I flash on instead is one of those old-fashioned cameras, a bellows and a black hood and that slow, hand-held explosion of gun-powdery light. This would make a one-in-a-million portrait, a classic: three armed and angry young chieftains standing side by side, the single threat of each of us tripled in the camera's eye.

"Let's dial this up or duck out of here," Dieter says, ice forming on the black buzzard and eagle feathers in his hair.

"Your call," Brinks says. "Either way." But when he passes me the wineskin it's my dad I imagine, half-drunk and fury-fisted and cleaving through the snow toward whatever door that Bobby Bigalow is about to exit.

Like father, like son, and it takes only a matter of seconds for me to calculate that weeks or months or years from now I might own up that, "Here, overtaken by rage and revenge, is where I pummeled and perhaps maimed or even killed a man." Or, "Here's where I stood with my only two friends on earth one February night. The snow suddenly coming down so hard that a man my mom believed mattered passed unaware within ten feet of us after being with another woman. We could smell her perfume, her nakedness, his beery breath, could hear him hiss between his teeth as we watched him disappear."

Neither is a confession whose details can redeem a thing. But have I mentioned the jukebox at the Honcho? Merle Haggard and Mickey Gilley, and truckers who change dollar bills into quarters, and my mom who's destined to start humming those heart-drain tunes again real soon, one way or another, no matter what goes down here.

When I give the word we sneak away. Dieter starts the snowmobile. "Hang tight," he says, and it's as if nothing can touch us as we tear-ass into all that whiteness, flying blind and the trees coming at us out of nowhere. There's an abandoned cellar hole we somehow avoid, and then we're airborne over the not-so-high rock-face outcropping we've survived at least a hundred times. The snow's coming in waves like wings, and we rise, I swear it. Three lost-cause kids in crazy getups, straddling not the wide seat of a Polaris sled, but rather a bareback horse, its black tail combed shiny by the wind.

That story. The one riddled with God-spots and paybacks and love full-blown for women we might someday make giddy and, despite our best intentions, betray. Thunderbird and muscatel. Dads who've gone missing, and a mom who, against all the evidence, believes in miracles she's determined to pass along to her son.

NEW STORIES

THE NEW WORLD MERGING

(for Pete Fromm)

Beatrice Blanc. Or as my dad sometimes mispronounces her name and then rolls his eyes like he and I are in cahoots, Beatrice Blank, though by all accounts she's got a ton more going on these days than he does. Meaning a new job for starters as a paid trainee at the hospital two towns over, in Ishpeming. On the pediatric ward, no less, and her favorite part is form-fitting miniature body braces to correct infant spinal curvatures and deformities. Future gymnasts and ballerinas, as my mom contends. But when, after forty-nine straight days without a cigarette she lights up and French inhales, there's no missing that she's anticipating a lesser outcome on the home front.

Who can blame her? After all, my parents, they're still unmarried, except by common law—just this side of sixteen years living together, and counting. It's either never the right time or place. Especially not in mid-February, the temperature at minus nineteen degrees, and the kitchen's drop ceiling hung so low that from my tiptoes I could reach right up and bury a newly sharpened number two pencil halfway to the eraser. It's only been since this past June that she's earned her community college degree, and, like her I've always been a decent student. A's and B's, even if currently I'm borderline-failing algebra II because of so many absences. And my dad who's good with numbers and solving word problems, but not so much when it comes to patience, and conspiracy theories, is out on the lake in his ice fishing shanty, clueless that the underpowered furnace he just last week repaired, has given up the ghost again.

We'll most likely survive until he drifts back home after midnight with his six-pack of empties and bucketful of smelt, his cloudy bloodshot eyes. That's how he winters through, his downtime before orders kick in again and the foundry reopens and orders kick in again and he's back to seventy-hour workweeks. We'll get there, he says, and that inside of three months things should start to get better, though for sure not to my mom's way of thinking.

She calculates that at this rate we're destined to live on the brink from here on out, smack-dab in the silent snarl of so much cold and gray. Not to mention the stink, as she says, and the way certain foul odors gather and linger until late spring. Like sewer sludge that no amount of ammonia or Clorox or all-out scouring can entirely eradicate.

And why would it when for almost half the year the windows remain double-sealed with plastic, and so even in broad daylight the world's a blur. It's like this under-furnished 1950s house trailer has been tented over in order to fumigate some vile and incurable infestation. It's depressing all right. Akin to looking through cataracts is how she puts it, not withstanding that she's got 20/20 vision, and takes clear and careful stock of the day to day. What I'm saying is that she's thirty-six, even-keeled, and has until recently taken most of our setbacks in stride. But this time she's beyond miffed that on top of everything else, come bedtime we've had to put on our boots and coats as if preparing to flee.

"Maybe we should," she says. "When if not now, for God's sake."

A part of her is serious, but lucky for everyone my dad's got the pickup. Besides, how practical would it be in the dead of night to just pack up and swing a one-eighty away from here like a couple of runaways? First off, where's there to go? And how far could we get on roads like these? Last week's blizzard has increased the total snowfall to within an inch or two of the top rope on our clothesline. Conditions and circumstances beyond our control, as my dad says, except that it seems like every other minute I'm questioning whether to believe him or not. What's true is that we've been forced to downsize from our deluxe doublewide with five acres and circular driveway, to this—a wish jug of dimes and quarters. At her worst my mom refers to the place as a grave, and who can refute that we're still in a state of shock and mourning?

We know the drill, my mom and me, and without a single word we slide our chairs up tight to the stove, and open the oven door, and turn it on, along with all four burners, to high. Then she checks the wall clock as if to remind us that the plan is simple and straightforward. And that even against the odds maybe all is not forsaken if we just stay calm, and hunker down, and annihilate another winter-weary chunk of eternity.

"Mom?" I ask, but she just closes her eyes, an unlit Pall Mall between her index and middle fingers, an ashtray and Bic lighter balanced on her thigh. The calm before the storm, and which is why I go quiet and concentrate instead on how the coils glow orange, then crimson, and how eventually they appear to bloat and subside, as if exhaling thin, invisible ribbons of vaporous fire. I can feel it when I press my fingertips against the skin of my reconstructed upper lip and nose, a momentary confirmation that the long-term prognosis might not be a total fabrication after all.

And yet sometimes, like right now, I still involuntarily sound the alert: "Shhhhhh. Listen. They've broken loose again," and my mom, always to the rescue, gently shakes my shoulder, and says, "No, they've been put down over a year ago, you know that. Both of them. Good grief it's just the wind, Ridge. Hey, wake up. Snap out of it," like I've dozed off or accidently hypnotized myself. But either way, on certain nights I swear I can hear their nails clicking against the aluminum siding, as if they're standing on their hind legs, wild-eyed and ravenous, and staring in at me.

The majority of my classmates, they're considerate; they nod, and hang back and leave me be. But not Lugo Burton. He calls me Dog Bite. Calls me Cujo. Whispers, "Sick 'em," and snaps and growls, and bears those pointed, oversized yellow incisors whenever Mrs. Mulholland, our 4th-period English teacher, turns her back on us, and diagrams sentences on the blackboard, the chalk's insistent click, click, click like some batty, stuttering skeleton.

Even though Lugo's been held back twice, I'm almost his size, and, if he keeps it up I swear I'll face-plant him on that flat, square tombstone of his desk. And warn him in no uncertain terms to "Shut your idiot yap." The only problem is that barely two months have elapsed since this latest surgery, and so I'm doing my best to steer clear of any and all confrontations.

Especially with Betty-Ann Vanmeter, my first serious flame, and for whom I'd give anything if we could just pick up where we left off. We'd been going gangbusters, bumping hips in the hallway, and making out behind her locker door, and where I wished each time we'd shimmy even lower, all the way down onto our heels, and kiss and kiss until the classroom doors started closing around us. But fast-forward to the faded scent of her perfume on a certain shirt I keep hidden in my bureau drawer, and you get the picture, the rejection, the lovesick goose bumps. Whenever we make eye contact now she stiffens and winces, and, when she looks away, I'm positive it's because she feels partly to blame. And which might explain why she refuses to sit next to me on the school bus, where the frozen windswept turnip and beet fields appear vast and white as we pass by them day after endless day.

But that's the thing; whatever anger and confusion I might harbor's got zero to do with her, and never has. Unlike the way I've seen my dad double down by mock-hugging my mom and pressing his fishy palm across her mouth like a gag. "Whatever you're selling we can't afford right now, so how 'bout you give it a rest, okay? Not another word," he'll say, though of course at that point she's already been muzzled and restrained.

He's merely pleading his case, I get that, but still, it's not the least bit funny anymore, not after how many replays? Possibly back in the day, but the teasing has gotten edgier, meaner-seeming lately. And especially when he addresses her as Miss Hoity-Toity, Miss High-Maintenance minus the pedigree. Fact is, she never, ever puts on airs, or wears designer anything, and rarely fancies up with any lipstick or eye shadow. Furthermore, I've never once seen her in high heels, or pin up her hair and pirouette this way and that on the balls of her feet in front of the full-length mirror.

I remember one time how my dad whipped open a paper bag, and handed it to her, and said, "Here, try breathing into this." And then sucked in his cheeks and went silent, went hangdog—kind of folded back a few steps and massaged his temples, like maybe a migraine was coming on.

"Sonofabitch," he said, and, righting himself, broke the seal on a pint of Old Museum, while I secretly tallied on my fingers how many hits I estimated he'd need this time to take the edge off. He refuses to budge on his conviction that around here we pay as we go. We eke it out, scrimp and salvage and file away whatever we can, and hope for the best. "But for now this here's all we got. Home sweet frigging home, like it or not."

In his defense, it's rare that he unleashes his full frustration, even if deep down this time of year he's wound awful tight, and apt at any second to let loose about how maybe, for old times' sake, we *ought* to swap out what my mom calls the dreary, godforsaken mangy green shag for some high-ticket hardwood, their bedroom for a boudoir. The goddamn drainboard for a dishwasher, items we not all that long ago possessed free and clear.

During these face-offs he's careful never to directly mention the mauling, the mounting medical costs, those IOUs on the bank loan, the bogus, bullshit hypotheticals and disclaimers. Nor how we'd been suckered, stolen from outright, and how he'd been doing some accounting of his own. From day one, payback is where this has always been headed, and the way I figure it's only a question of when. And how, as I overheard him one time say to my mom, if only he'd been there with me he would've bludgeoned their skulls to smithereens with his bare hands.

As to why our lives are such a wreck, and who it was set these events in motion, whose dark soul deserved to follow those two hellhounds— his words—into the underworld? That falls to me, I guess, given that it was yours truly who swiped the padlock key, my dad home asleep, and my mom working OT.

I'd drawn Betty-Anne a map, and sketched a picture of a shanty all by itself, like the last checkpoint into Siberia. She balked, scrunched her eyebrows, shook her head, and said, "You're not serious, right?" but then agreed, although mid-morning on a Saturday was asking a lot. But okay, for me she'd set her radio alarm if I promised to trundle out early, and crank up the kerosene heater. "Hot enough to make me sweat all over," she said. And, as an added bonus, that she'd bring a blanket, and I envisioned the two of us spreading it out over sixty feet of solid blue ice and water. Then slowly peeling away layers of goose down and polar fleece, piece by piece as the glow from the Coleman lantern sealed the windowless walls with gold.

I waited for her until almost noon, but she never showed. For whatever reason, I never heard. The weather most likely, or an argument at home, and then grounded for the weekend, phone privileges revoked. Who knows? Just another impossible daydream gone bust, but otherwise no permanent damage done, and, when finally I opened the door, the snow was falling so fast and thick that my tracks had completely covered over. I figured either wait awhile longer, or take it on faith that forging blindly ahead I'd eventually hit shore, and from there, another half hour max until I arrived home, nothing too out of the ordinary. I'd sneak the key back where it belonged, and whiff the air, thick with fresh pan-fried smelt and crushed corn chips, my dad's money-saving lunchtime staple.

But what I smelled, seconds before I saw them, was manky and rank, like a decomposing carcass. I'd broken trail for maybe a hundred or so yards and when I stopped, bent over and gripping my knees, two black snouts appeared out of nowhere, steam rising from their slavering tongues and jowls. Wolves, I thought, thick coats, yellow-eyed, and panting like they'd been circling, and circling, and there I was, sucking wind, and staring them down, a weird, faraway roaring in my ears.

I'd heard from my dad how they'd migrated from Canada, a small pack, narrow in the flanks, half-starved and nearly poached out of existence. And that you could verify the species by their tracking collars, but these two were wearing choke chains with silver tags. And at their feet, what appeared to be the leg bone of an elk or whitetail.

I stayed perfectly still, fingers tingling inside my gloves, and suddenly unable to swallow or gulp any air. "Good dogs," I said. "Good boys," and they slowly wagged their tails, large mixed breeds, possibly husky and German shepherd. I was almost close enough to pet them, snow gathering on their backs and hackles, their muzzles wet and blood-smattered.

"What'd you guys get into?" I said. "Whew," and sniffed into my coat sleeve. "Where's your owner?" and they cocked their heads, ears up. I said, "Sit," and they did, tense and suddenly quivering, as if waiting for me to toss them the last T-bone on earth. Or wing a Frisbee and watch them vanish into the whiteout within seconds, like phantoms or ghosts, an optical illusion I could later craft into a whopper to lord over Betty-Anne.

Instead I said, "You stay," and backed away, one shaky, hesitant slow-motion step, and then another, and then a whistle not far off, and a muffled voice calling, and, by the time I cupped my hands around my mouth and shouted, "They're over here," the dogs were already on me.

I'd forfeited most of sophomore year, and maybe should have ditched out entirely. But so as not to have to repeat, the doctors agreed to my return just one week after the feeding tube had been removed, and the million maggots my mouth infections had become, finally cured. Ditto for the chills and high fevers, the blood blisters that my mom drained into sterilized squares of gauze. And during which time I spoke almost not at all. Whenever I tried, vowels sounded like nasally moans and squeals, *p* and *b* words components of an alien tongue. And my mom, patient as God turned speech therapist, imploring from me one unpronounceable syllable at a time, her face muscles coordinating in slow motion the movements mine attempted, but refused to make.

"You'll be okay," she assured, and reassured me. "You'll get it back. Not all at once but slowly it'll happen. You'll see. Some scar tissue, that's what the doctors say, and worst case a hint of a lisp, but that eventually you'll adjust, you'll be fine."

Because I wasn't by the time I reenrolled, I decided, if called on in class, I'd simply shake my head. Sit mute and pay attention as best I could, take notes like always, but as far as class participation I couldn't reconcile any upside in that, half my words still stringy and slurred.

It worked for a while. No serious kickback from anywhere until my Supreme Court teacher, Mr. Dopke, said, "Uh-uh. No more," and detained me after class, and then again after school. I knocked on his classroom door, and when he opened it, he was decked out in his Perry Mason robe, and clip-on tie with its perfect Windsor—his typical quiz and test day getup, and which already felt like overkill.

"Have a seat," he said, and motioned towards his oversized, lacquered oak desk, the blotter bordered with color portraits of all forty presidents. The year 1984, and Ronald Reagan—whom my dad despised—gazing up from the center with that shoe-polish black hair, and pasted-on simpleton grin.

The perch, that's what we'd dubbed it, or the throne, the whole stupid caboodle situated on a raised platform. On the blackboard Mr. Dopke had printed my full legal name—Ridge Cade Jr.—along with some made up case number, and the official verdict, I assumed, resting in his hands.

I'd tried early on to like him, but why lie about it? Those tossed in Latin phrases. And the way he presided, his arms folded like some bored, exasperated magistrate. Day after day, that same sneering, concentrated disdain for us, five crowded rows worth of homegrown dunces and dimwits, a collection of future nobodies staring blankly back at him.

To be fair, during a parent-teacher conference (my mom told me this) he'd referred to me as potential college material. Mentioned scholarships, perhaps someday a year abroad, but which I translated straightaway as a ruse. Me who'd yet to cross state lines, and suddenly headed toward the far-distant corners of the earth? A dream spin that even my mom deemed flattering, though perhaps a touch unrealistic, and for sure nothing I even remotely aspired to anyway. A different life fine, but not *that* different, my ambition being to maybe someday attend Michigan Tech, a few hours farther north into the U.P. And my dad, an advocate of practical, sensible skills, all nose to the grindstone, said simply, "Priceless. Talk about a snow job." He said, "Look around," meaning, *Ridge, come on—get your egghead out of the goddamn clouds.*

Justice Dopke—though no one ever dared address him as such—cleared his throat, and drummed his fingers, as if to say, "I can wait you out. We're on no deadline. What's more, I own what's left of this day, and you've got a bus to catch. And your boots, Mr. Cade, I noticed, are unlaced, and the weather's nasty and getting worse, and it's a considerable hike home from here, isn't that the sensible and obvious takeaway?"

I unzipped my dad's army surplus jacket, sat up in the chair, and, when I fisted my hands, they disappeared knuckle-deep into the frayed sleeves, wind ripping overhead through the ancient ductwork. He said, "What's the matter, cat got your tongue?" like he was talking to an eight-year-old, or hadn't heard or read about the attack in the newspapers, the gory details, although it had been written up from as far downstate as East Lansing.

He said, "I ask only because it's unlike you to hold back, isn't it? And here I am, simply doing my job and calling you out for your own good. A few words to the wise, that's all, and for which you can thank me later. Go ahead, Mr. Cade, and exercise your First Amendment right, I'm all ears."

I almost said, "Take it up with my dad, why don't you?" But one word about any of this getting back to him and there'd be another headline in the making. So I nodded and primed myself to *just sit tight, wait him out*, although the last thing I needed was any pity, or a pep talk from the likes of him.

He said, "Don't shut down, Mr. Cade. That's for cowards, and you don't strike me that way. So how about it, a trial run, a simple declarative sentence or two, just you and me. What do you say? Take a knee, or come to the table?"

The final bell had already rung, the busses gone, and when I stood, he said, "Approach the bench," and I did. "All right then," he said. "Good," and, without a second's panic or premeditation, I reached out as if to shake his hand, and seized his gavel—and which he always pounded down to adjourn each class—and wielded it like a tomahawk as I war-whooped my way out of the room, and down the empty, half-dark hallway, and out the emergency exit into the elements.

The owners' names? Luther and Meeky Hoig, and although thirteen months have elapsed, for the time being they remain front and center, and possibly slated in some way I don't fully comprehend, to endure either my dad's wrath or his weariness. Just biding our time, I figure, keeping track, the two of us silent on the slow approach to their house, a modest split-level. No garage, same as us, but bunkered even farther back off the beaten track. And take it from me, the fact that my dad ever even sleuthed out the place tells you plenty.

On clear nights he'll kill the headlights, and, parked in the middle of the road—as if so they'll feel our eyes on them—we'll watch the Hoigs float back and forth like shadows behind the blinds. Everything's in black and white, except for a violet hue, and what I imagine are thin, ultraviolet tubes, as if someone's already potted seeds for a garden.

My dad has never said, "Now pay close attention," or, "Mark my words," or, "So long as we've come this far," like he'd worked out the details to advance some failsafe jackpot of a plan. Never once asked me if I wanted to weigh in, and help collect on a certain unpaid debt, or at least a long overdue interrogation. The answer? No, I do not, and, whether it helps or it doesn't, I pray nonstop every single time that we never leave the cab, and make our slow approach to the house, and knock on their front door. And my dad, who goes a burly six foot four, beginning the conversation by dangling a couple of makeshift leashes, something to tie the Hoigs up with so that we can do some looking around.

They're the type all right. Cooters, hoodoos he calls them, tightwads who clutch their wallets in daylight and in dreams. Who save and save, and squander not one slim goddamn dime, and then check out with a million bucks stashed between their box spring and mattress. He hasn't actually said so, but I know what he's thinking, that right or wrong, there's one sure-fire way to find out, and collect what he's already referred to a couple of times as shares held in trust.

He's yet to meet them face-to-face, but I have. Him anyway, Luther Hoig, the one who found me. "Sweet Mary, Mother of God," he said, hovering, and grimacing, and then helped me into a sitting position. "No," he said. "No, no, this can't be," and folded his scarf in half, and then in half again, and handed it to me to staunch the blood flow.

"Can you walk?" he said, and when I nodded he bear-hugged me up from behind as best he could. He said, "We'll get you out. We'll get help," and then led me staggering slowly across the lake to the abandoned railroad tracks, and out to the road, both dogs heeling directly behind him, perfectly behaved, their tags jingling.

"How could this happen?" he said, and only then did he let go of my arm in order to hail a county snowplow, its lights flashing orange and red. And the driver raising his steel blades and transporting me, his hand on the horn while bugling through squalls like a giant thundering ambulance, and pulling up right outside the automatic sliding glass doors of the emergency room entrance.

Punctures, open tears and gashes. "Sweet dogs," as Meeky Hoig later described them to the sheriff's department deputies. "Frolickers. Big babies, obedient and well trained." Had never bolted before, never snapped, or nipped at, or bit anyone, and not a soul willing to come forward and refute those claims. And yes, they'd had all their shots, and records to prove it, and blame aside, might it be a credible assumption that the boy spooked them with his terror, lost like he was? A kid who'd never had a pet and, given the conditions, might *already* have panicked, and possibly even grabbed hold of the dogs, as if they'd been dispatched for the sole purpose of his rescue.

The empty, fenced-in enclosure from which they'd escaped is attached to the side of the house. No BEWARE OF DOG sign, or PROCEED AT YOUR OWN RISK, no yellow crime-scene tape bannering across the chain-link. Meaning, the trail's gone cold, case closed. At least that's what my mom says. But my dad, he swears, not on your life, and so here we are, at the ready, yet again.

Thus far he's refrained from sipping even a single beer during these surveillances, and which I translate as a good omen, a positive sign. And no handgun stowed in the glove box, no rebar or table leg hidden behind the seat. No ski masks either, nothing like that, and not a shred of evidence to the contrary. Plus my dad with no priors except for one DWI so long ago it hardly warrants even wishing away. The whole thing, it's beyond crazy, and, off the record, what cooked up alibi could two late night snoops broker for being here anyway?

And there's this: how he always hangs his pocket watch from the rearview mirror, the numerals glowing green in the dark. That's so he knows the exact moment we need to vacate in order to pick up my mom as scheduled, the geriatrics and the newborns separated by a single floor. My mom thinks it's beautiful, a metaphor, a rush of happiness, she says, the new world merging with the old.

Whenever my dad and I spy on the Hoigs, they move so slow and bent over, you'd swear they're on hands and knees, attempting to sneak on by us. "The walking wounded," as my dad says, but that it justified in no way the pittance they'd offered, not to mention they'd never so much as sent an apology or a get well card. And the lawyer, shaking his head and explaining to my parents, "That's all well and good, but you can't draw blood from a stone. What's done is done. My advice? Pull the stopper. Just go ahead and settle. Move on."

Maybe that's what my dad's attempting to do, one way or another, and if anything in this life is certain, it's that sooner or later something has to give. Still, I'm hoping nothing disastrous transpires, and if it doesn't, then possibly, come summer, I can land a job at the bowling alley, working the shoe rental, or setting pins, or buffing the lanes after hours. Minimum wage, but nonetheless a third income to help make ends meet, my dad by that time already back stoking the blast furnace at the foundry, and casting fire hydrants, and sewer grates for cul-de-sacs and boulevards in cities and towns unlike ours.

I agree there's more than enough blame to go around, but mostly it's mine. I ought to know, though my dad has never once asked me, "Why, why?" You want to know why? It's simple: because he's lived his whole life up here in the boonies, too. And me at fifteen years old, bored and plagued by an unrestrained desire to slip my fingertips under the elastic waistband of my now ex-girlfriend's long johns, and seeing where that might lead.

To right here as it turns out, a sad attraction, my dad's head on the headrest, and his arms folded across his chest, eyes closed, as if he's fallen asleep. It's like we've settled in, and I've drawn the first watch. I'm underdressed and already beginning to shiver, but afraid to wake him quite yet. Not while there's still time enough for him to lift his hands to his mouth, and warm them with his breath, and, in an abrupt rush of adrenaline, twirl his index finger clockwise, signaling that on this night it's finally a go, and then swinging open the driver's-side door, and stepping out.

My mom's got no clue what we've been up to. If she did she'd pack a suitcase, and, without a single word, hightail it as far away from the two of us as humanly possible. She assumes I'm right this minute doing my homework, slowly catching up, while my dad drifts deeper and deeper into the nonstop hiss and static of our ancient Sylvania console T.V. no matter which way he angles the rabbit ears, or sculpts them in aluminum foil.

Above the Hoig's roof there's a quarter moon, and smoke lifting from the chimney toward that intermittent parachuting of stars. But without light enough to illuminate a whole lot down here, other than that silver BB circle glimmering like a single gemstone embedded in the windshield. I can make out the Dragon's Head, and the moons of Jupiter, and, brightest by far, the Row of Pearls. My mom's the astronomer in

211

the family, and I haven't forgotten how she used to wake me at all hours, and lead me outside into our backyard, and point skyward, naming for me the constellations, one after the other as I repeated them back.

But on these stakeouts I'm merely a tagalong, an accomplice to my old man's grief and bewilderment. And come what may, should I be called on someday to testify, I'll swear under oath that we're no more or less law-abiding than anyone else struck dumb by lousy luck and winters such as these. And where, when I gaze back at the house, the blinds are slowly scrolling upward like one of those standup home movie screens, and I can see the Hoig's side-by-side silhouettes framed in the picture window, hands like blinders around their eyes, foreheads pressed to the glass.

My dad doesn't see them as I nudge him awake, and point at the time, and say nothing as he turns the ignition, and shifts into drive. As to what will become of us, whatever we do next, or don't do, your guess is as good as mine.

Other than at this moment to go pick up my mom who always sits between us on the drive home, her arms outstretched across our shoulders like wings. Like we're at the local drive-in except that it's still winter, heat blasting up from under the dashboard. What's for certain is that she'll describe for us, detail by detail, the almost silent murmurs of those sleeping infants. How they sing, and sing, as she says, like invisible angels who tend to each other in the night.

AT ANY GIVEN TIME

"No, not Rome," my mother said. "Romeo. *That's* where all roads lead, at least for the likes of us." She said it often, daring me—a bored and distracted high school senior with a solid B- average—to prove her wrong. "For the love of God just do it," she said. "Enlist. Get the holy hell gone, and the sooner the better, Doc, because no matter what, staying here will only hurt you worse. Go," she said, as if a curse had been cast on this Michigan town where she was born and raised—and, at barely seventeen, forfeited what might otherwise have constituted (my interpretation) a happier life by having me, Dennis Dean Holliday.

She did hair at Goldi-locks and dyed her own pure platinum. Sometimes between appointments, and feeling weak in the knees, she'd turn off all the lights and collapse under the giant hood drier, eyes closed, and cry. She, my mother, whose first name was Marceleen, was herself an only child, and *her* parents suddenly more than half a century deceased.

And about *him*, my estranged old man? A figment, a ghost who drifted in from time to time but only ever in dreams, and always with a different face, one grotesque configuration after another of my own. There were extended stretches when I'd wake screaming, spells when sleep seemed a self-inflicted punishment for being born.

"No, not true, not even close. He was a lot of things but never a monster. Young and scared, I guess. Smart, for sure, like you," she insisted, whenever I described how he'd chase me, irate, red-eyed, and furious like some demon possessed and, each time I looked back, gaining ground. Although I pleaded with her, she never once elaborated further,

213

or produced so much as a single grainy black and white Polaroid for me to memorize and then secretly file away.

As for yours truly, I'm all grown up, and then some: a lifer, a career navy man as it turned out, a master chief petty officer two decades retired. Not high brass but medals enough—the Navy Cross, a Silver Star—and a man who, while on leave a couple lifetimes ago, said "I do" in full dress uniform instead of a tuxedo, and when we kissed I held my new bride by her hips, among in-laws and guests I'd never before met, and would never lay eyes on again. Then a hurry-up two-day hotel honeymoon in San Francisco before I shipped out, and came back, and then packed off again. AWOL is how she described it, from a marriage that survived an official three years, four months, and thirteen days. Had it lasted, we'd now be celebrating our fifty-fourth.

I did not contest or ask for a thing in the divorce. And, as far as I know, I fostered no children, though I believed back then, 1965, in fatherhood, and imagined a small troop of our own. Mine and Irene's, and I confess there was one night, alone in the pitch dark on the flight deck of the USS *Ticonderoga*, when I climbed to the top bridge and contemplated taking the plunge. Toes over the edge, and ready to end it all, I let go of the handrail and might even have crossed myself, but like a last-second sign from above, an aurora of stars dive-bombed the ship, and I hauled ass back to my bunk. Forehead pressed against the portal, I prayed and prayed, and by first light I felt blessed, and less hopeless— and have, more often than not, remained so en route to that last stop or stand before finally crossing over . . .

I turn seventy-nine on April Fools', four days after the new moon—that moon I have watched in all its phases while sailing the South China seas, or rounding Cape Horn, or, one time, spying close-up into a lunar extravaganza through a periscope from beneath the Straits of Gibraltar, the crosshairs glowing gold and nearly blinding me. My ongoing fear is that someday eons from now the stars and the planets, in all likelihood, will, like us, perish. I tell you this even though it is top secret, and spoken about only *below*-deck, in low whispers and in tongues.

Because I have grown partial to cold, desolate climates, I currently reside in Whitefish Point, an outpost as far north in Michigan as one can be without fleeing the country, the shipwreck coast of Superior. Last count, over three hundred wrecks, though fewer than thirty remain intact: ore carriers, bulk freighters, a steamer tug that went down in

1875, a lumber hooker with a wood propeller—and every inch of every sunken craft preserved and protected from vandals and salvage divers. The world is three-quarters water, and I've sailed most all of it and can't anymore imagine living on a coast anywhere other than right here.

The Whitefish population this time of year is 588, according to the latest census, and you can count me among those permanent residents who live alone and will do so, no doubt, from here on out.

There's a post office, where I rent a mailbox one year at a time. Also a volunteer fire department, and, as recently as ten years ago, you'd have marveled at the speed and agility with which I exited my vehicle, sometimes while still chewing my dinner, and pulled on those heavy, fire-resistant-rubber yellow gloves with my teeth.

July through August the gift shops stay open until just before nightfall. As does the funeral home if there's a need. Tourists oftentimes mistake it for a B & B, and if they inquire about the nightly or weekend rates, Maxine Easterday nods and opens the door to one of the two viewing rooms and points at the casket. "Will this do?" she says, smiling as they turn and walk away.

Tomorrow will mark day ten since we've seen the sun, and the current temperature says nine degrees—cold enough for those downstate weekend warriors who arrive with their ropes and crampons, and attempt to climb the frozen waterfalls. The few who make it plant flags of their alma maters on the translucent, acetylene-blue summits, like amateur Admiral Byrd's.

It's early February, and in the open air a hundred yards offshore snow swirls and funnels up like waterspouts, and lately the effort it takes to spud the hole leaves me lightheaded. I say, "No worries—vertigo, inner ear," if anyone asks, and if need be I can self-medicate with a pull from my flask and then follow my own footprints back. But so far so good if I simply sit on the upturned bucket, put my head in my gloved hands, and begin counting down from my current age until the Bay tips back flat and stationary, and the nausea passes.

After all, I've seen sailors heave for weeks straight, swells breaking across bows and sterns, the pitch and hammer of the massive hulls depth-charged and listing portside, and the bilge filling fast—a life, my friends, at sea.

My all-time favorite book is *Moby Dick*, although the hat I wear is right out of *Doctor Zhivago*. And this: some evenings, before the sky darkens, silver-lined snow clouds cast shadows in the shape of horse-drawn sleighs.

In a parallel world, *you'd* take the reins, too, and, exiting a whiteout or squall, fall crazy in love all over again, your ex-wife beside you, a blanket covering her lap, and her lips crimson. Yes, I have regrets; my God, we're only human, and yet I'm here to confirm that occasionally entire days elapse when nothing seems impossible or out of reach, and the miracle—it's this simple—is that, like me, you're still here and, against impossible odds, grateful to be alive . . .

"Ship to shore. Hey, ship to shore, come in. Do you copy? Over."

It's the Shananaguot boy, Danny, squinting down at me, as if through the eyehole of a treble hook. He always stops to check see if I'm still breathing. He's young, tall and slope-shouldered. He's half Ojibwa. Smart, a good heart, and by far the best fisherman around. Every weekend night, from inside his shanty, he jigs for whitefish that he then donates to the few diehard off-season cafes and bars for their all-you-can-eat deep-fries. As he says, "A nation fed . . . ," like we're some long-lost tribe unto ourselves.

Danny hightails it straight from work at Hiawatha Telephone to the bay and a six-pack of Labatt Blue kept ice cold under the snow. He's not even close to borderline alcoholic, though the season after awhile can bring that on, and I've been known to sip my own slow way through the gaps and blanks to try and dispatch those lonely, seemingly bottomless hours. (Vernors and Beefeater, thank you.)

I own my house free and clear: a split-log exterior with a stone fireplace, a wraparound screened-in three-season porch on a double lot, and an ancient roll-top where I sit stooped over once a month writing checks to pay my bills. A phonograph with a diamond-tipped needle, and—say what you will, but this I know—vinyl is the voice of angels, scratches and all. Sarah Vaughn, Nina Simone, Nat King Cole.

Plus there's a smoker out back, a sundial, and a gas generator in case the power conks. Sometimes during ice storms the electric lines sag so low between the utility poles that the entire town buzzes and hums. My place is the last one on the dead end. It's called Lake Shore, and I keep a telescope with an infrared lens positioned by the upstairs, east-facing guest bedroom window. Sleepless I'll pour a nightcap and focus for as long as it takes until Danny Shananaguot steps outside for another brew, or to pee, the light from his gas lantern exploding silently from the doorway behind him, like a single, faraway bomb burst.

216

He's the father of one breathtakingly beautiful daughter—enormous cobalt eyes, olive skin—and his girlfriend's name is Rose-Ellen De-Groot. He says they're going to tie the knot, come summer or fall, and that of course I'm invited. "The guest of honor," he says, like I'm his long-lost old man finally come home. He shows me images on his smartphone: winter rainbows, sundogs. And, just last week, a video of himself and his family, building a snowman in their backyard played at ten times normal speed.

"Hilarious," he said, and ran it forward and back.

It made me dizzy, and I said, "Danny, for God's sake slow it down, what's the hurry?" I said, "Presley's pills, Kennedy in Dallas, the DMZ," but like *he* said, the words crystallizing on his eyelids, "Where the hell *that* come from?"

Another place, another time, and trust me, not all that long ago. "Just a friendly reminder," I said, "that we're all here on loan, and the call date's approaching at light-speed."

He nodded, wiped his nose with his knuckles, and said, "Good deal then. Long as you remember to leave me the front door key in your will."

"Just might," I said. "You never know." But I withheld that before my ashes even cooled some state probate gravedigger would already have motored up from Lansing and changed all the locks. They know where I live, but not that I suffer night sweats if I kick the thermostat up past sixty-five, my cholesterol sky-high, and my hair gone white but still thick and cut in a flattop. My off-again, on-again addiction to strong black coffee and sleeping pills. And most importantly, no living relatives, no emergency contact list Scotch-taped next to the wall phone.

I'm still here and rolling the dice, rattling the ice cubes. I drive a 2003 Toyota Land Cruiser, bought used a few years back with 210,922 miles, a winch and towrope, decent tread, and a set of tire chains. Like I told the guy, "Hell, *some* miles left? It's barely broken in."

As long as I'm able to climb the ladder two stories to shovel my own roof, and beat free the ice buildup along both gables with a shingle hatchet, I'll hold on to what's mine. Minus those annual donations I make to the library. And to the Great Lakes Shipwreck Museum, located out by the light tower. Right through Labor Day, visitors rent headphones and take audio tours. Mammoth anchors and anchor chains, plus thousands of artifacts under glass. And, the main attraction: the bell from the *Edmond Fitzgerald*. They ring it starting at 8:00 AM and every half hour thereafter.

My watch most mornings ends at approximately twenty-two hundred hours, another half day come and gone. It's Saturday, the wind gusting to ten or twelve knots, and the temperature dropping. Farther out the ice tightens and fractures like gunfire, followed by a time delay—usually only a matter of minutes—until the water laps up inside the hole, as if something huge has cruised by right under me.

Tinsel-sided torpedoes. Heat seekers. That's what Danny calls them. He says, "Oh, yeah, they're down there all right," and just last week my rod bent double, and I held on with both hands until the reel spooled and the leader snapped. The North American freshwater record for whitefish is fourteen pounds, six ounces, and Danny swears that's only the tip of the iceberg.

"Here you go," he says this time, and kneels on one knee, shakes off his polar mittens, and clips a small blue Swedish Pimple onto my swivel. "Try this, a foot or two off the bottom," and I pantomime, at six-second intervals, the soft, limp-wrist, up-and-down technique he taught me this time last year.

He leans closer, stares into my face and says, "Remember, no cat-naps." Says, "Stay out here much longer you'll start to grow gills," and he peels back his coat collar to show me the two identical oblong hick-eys on both sides of his neck. "And scales," he says, and points to his boot, the black rubber toecap speckled silver, like sequins. "Just say-ing," he says. "Be careful, yeah?"

When he lifts the frozen rope, the toboggan with all his gear and his cooler full of fresh fillets seems to float over the snow behind him as he goes . . .

My mother's cancer comes on fast. Lungs first, but now it's everywhere—throat, pancreas, and spleen. She's fifty-two years old, her mouth belled-out and hanging partway open, showing her back molars riddled with gold. Her chances of surviving the night are zero, first light at the absolute latest. That's what I'm told, in whispers, and how hearing is the last sense to go. "I'm sorry you're so late," the nurse says. "But it can't hurt to talk to her, especially now."

Right—after the last call, after closing, after having traveled nonstop for three full days and nights through half a dozen time zones, a blur of arrivals and departures and delays. Passport control, and finally an off-duty taxi driver I hailed who, when I said, "Please, it's an emergency," exceeded the speed limit by double in order that I arrive in Romeo, where all roads lead and converge, before my mother was already dead and buried.

"There's no pain." That's what the nurse tells me, fidgety, matter-of-fact, and checks the IV, and then the bladder bag of clear liquid, hanging bedside from its aluminum pole. As she leaves, she swishes the floor-to-ceiling curtain around us, like a matador.

A veteran of foreign wars, I have witnessed soldiers airlifted from jungles, deltas, and deserts, mega-doses of morphine shot into their veins. Double amputees, men missing their faces, convulsing and squeezing their own throats closed, an entire ocean igniting all around us. I have sat with them, zipped up body bags, gut-heaved bitterness into immeasurable and permanent grief.

There's a glass of water on the tray table, and my mother's fingers are splayed wide on the sheet top, as if she's about to push up into a sitting position to assist with her own dying. Someone has clipped her nails, and combed her hair. She cannot weigh eighty pounds, the circumference of her wrist smaller than a cane or a pool cue. She is barely recognizable, and after I take her hand and read the name on the plastic bracelet, I press my thumb to her pulse. *Keep a calm heart* is how she signed off in every letter, though mine pounds nonstop until I take off my glasses, and close and massage my bleary, burning eyes.

All night, I'm in and out of dreams. In one I'm nineteen, back home after twelve weeks at the Recruit Training Command outside Chicago. A hero's welcome, the way we're celebrating, my mother and me, with pizza, vodka shots, and beer chasers. First time for me drinking in front of her, and she says, "Hell's bells, Doc, you're old enough to die for your damn country, go nuts." She says, "Duty calls," and we clink bottles. We've been at it for a couple of hours, and she can't stop laughing as I rise from the couch, snap to attention, and salute the TV.

"At ease," she says, doubled over, cracking up, trying to catch her breath, and "Sweet Jesus," but I've already turned up the volume on the National Anthem. It's midnight, Eastern Standard Time, and every station in our part of the world is signing off, and the picture tube is already black, except for what looks like a final radar blip disappearing dead center.

She leans back and draws on the cigarette between her fingers, the smoke curling in thin, vaporous blue ribbons above the dark screen and between the skewed V of the rabbit ears. Piled next to her, the half dozen cartons of Viceroys I purchased tax-free from the PX. The heavy glass ashtray on the floor is a nest of lip-stained butts, pale pink to blood red.

From as far back as I can remember she's burned through a pack and a half a day.

Her hair's no longer teased out, and it's half back to her natural brown, and grown past her shoulders. When she's relaxed and sitting down she twists it around her index finger, like a schoolgirl, and, minus the makeup, her face is so pale you might mistake her for someone who's sick or allergic to the sun. But tonight she's all dolled up, and each time she inhales her fingernails glint like oval pearls, even though there's no new boyfriend, as far as I can tell.

Stationed on the mantel there's a photograph of me, in my white hat and jumper, my arms around the shoulders of Frankie Defer and Gerald Beal, all three of us deep-tanned and smiling, front and center, from the standup frame. We've made it through with flying colors. We're shipping out soon, though where to we haven't a clue, and, "No sir, never in our lives have we heard the names of so many foreign countries."

All we know is that we've spun classroom globes in junior high to annihilate a few more wasted minutes until lunch. Or until that final bell before we rushed the exits like storm troopers, past the flagpole, where we fanned out in groups of twos and threes, as if on patrol. Past the armory with its World War II tank out front, and its gigantic, slightly raised barrel aimed above the fairgrounds, and feedlots, and railroad tracks, as if homing in on that impossible, way-out-of-range vanishing point beyond the horizon. Nearer to us are the narrow streets of our neighborhood, the dinky houses and carports stamped out identically and located, as my mother maintained, smack dab in the goddamn middle of nowhere.

It's a simple matter—that's what we've been told—to wire money from anywhere in the world to anywhere else in the world—and so I've already designated that a portion of every paycheck be wired home to her. I figure what, maybe ten grand over her lifetime if I don't bail or get my ass blown off?

She takes it all wrong, says, "Come again?" Says, "Doc, since when did I become a rescue mission? What's that even say about a mom, mooching off her own son? My clients, they tip just fine, and, as far as I can tell, it's still a far cry from camping out around here."

"Okay," I say. "But you never know, and so just in case, that's all." It won't be a lot, not right off, just something to supplement her take-home, a hedge against the shortfalls so that she need not worry about things quite as much . . .

My shoe-tops glow white in the submerged, greenish light, and when I sit upright in the chair, my mother's eyes are wide-open, pewter, pale blue, birdlike. She does not blink: one for yes, two for no. Instead, she stares right at me, present and accounted for. It's like we're caught in a time warp, and every wished-back memory, every upbeat detail and question I have imagined asking her, scrolls right past.

It's as if we're calling to one another across vast, unfathomable distances, and I imagine that out there somewhere US Navy jets are breaking the speed of sound. That trees bend and tremble, and buildings shake. That the wooden crossties of abandoned trestles splinter, and, from out of those deep holes behind the pilings, schools of fish pack in under log jambs and cutbanks—the world out there, as my mother so often remarked, all noise and panic, chaos, and confusion with a capital C.

But here it's so quiet and still that when I lean in close enough I can hear her slow, almost imperceptible, intermittent breathing as her pupils dilate and glaze, and her lips go slack. The backs of my fingers keep brushing her cheeks and forehead.

"Yes, rest," I whisper, though all night we've been speaking beyond words about the long and the short of it, the beginning and the end and everything in between, intersecting and reforming and compressing into this one pure distillation of *all* our time, together and alone, infinitesimal and everlasting . . .

The Gulf of Tonkin, 1968, and the USS *Coral Sea* has been decorated up like a fifteen-block Fourth of July bash: banners and streamers, flags flying. Red-white-and-blue Frisbees riding the high air currents and boomeranging back, and a makeshift stage midships, loudspeakers cranked as if to live-broadcast the concert stateside.

We're hearing the song of the summer after the Summer of Love, Nancy Sinatra's "These Boots Are Made For Walking," and hers come up over her knees—and from there, bare thighs and short-shorts.

A Sunday matinee for which she's been flown in, and she's marching in place, hips thrust forward, high-stepping like a majorette, and blowing kisses to the entire fleet: color guard, the fry cooks and SEALS, flyboys wearing their aviator shades. High Command. Officers and grunts, mechanics and medics, welders and mail clerks. Helmeted MPs. Even the radio rats have been invited up into the daylight.

A perimeter of gunships surrounds us, anchored half a mile offshore, and everyone's clicking away. Snapshots to mail eight thousand miles across the pond: to old torches, new flames, wives, and fiancées—moms, some of them, or about to be. And a special note for those former high school classmates who have deserted us to link arms in protest of our being here—us, the oppressors, the baby killers.

"Turncoats," that's how Tripp Flees dials them in.

"Ignorant motherfuckers," Dale Gilbro says. "Our good names gone to shit. Man, talk about getting your nuts snipped."

"Roger that," Tripp says, "and in your case before they've even dropped."

Since my divorce I haven't received so much as a *Dear John*, a token *stay well, stay safe*, from Irene. Not one word, and every letter I've sent to her returned, sometimes months later, unopened. I keep a trimmed-back color snapshot of the two of us in my wallet, and even through the blurred plastic you can make out the San Francisco Bay behind us, and Alcatraz farther off in the watery distance, our heads pressed against each other, all smiles up there on the seawall. But like Johnny Paladino says, in times as rude and nasty as these, who touches gloves anymore?

For sure not him, a recruit from Nebraska, a cornhusker who shouts into my ear, "How'd you like to scratch up the backs of those?" He's twenty-two and so gung-ho he maintains a regimen of three hundred push-ups per day while wearing a head-strap to which he attaches a ten-pound weight, veins bulging in his neck. Sometimes, as if to exhaust his own fury, he refuses to quit until his nose bleeds.

There's a boxing ring onboard, but no one dares step in with him. Fast hands: a combination of hooks and uppercuts, straight rights. Skips rope and pummels the big bag. Search-and-destroy, that's his attack plan—simple, straight-ahead, and like he says, why *not* for someone who dreams, night in and night out, of incinerating villages? He carries a brush-chromed Zippo, which he flips open and closed, his fingertips dancing above the wavering blue flame as if he's tickling the ivories, practicing scales. Says, "Big mistake not joining the marines," and, first thing each morning, he slashes another day from the face of his calendar with a fat black X.

He says, "How 'bout you sweethearts stand down while I escort the entertainment to my private quarters, white shit-kickers and all? Talk about making *my* top forty." He says, "Mercy me." Says, "Shama lama fucking dingdong" . . .

I've got a ruck that's already packed, and a solo, three-day shore leave commencing mid-afternoon, a morale boost of my own, meaning a little

222

R&R in the Hotel Something-Or-Other named after American walk-ups like me. The whore hootch, Tripp says, where temptation reins and human depravity's the name of the game. He says, "Who knows, this first time tests out okay, maybe you and me, we ought to go MIA until this damn war ends."

Rank, bottom-end rooms. No fan or A/C, no electricity period, and an indoor shithouse located at the far end of the hallway. That's how it's been put to me. Narrow, high-ceilinged rooms, beds with headboards that look like mortared truck grills.

"So live it up, Doc. A faceful of whatever you can afford for the weekend. Here's to muff and moonshine enough to set your Michigan throat on fire."

I've folded American dollars inside my shoes. No dog tags or wristwatch, nothing in my pockets, and a fully loaded 9mm handgun to wedge between the squeaky bedsprings. All standard issue to combat the ambush of inertia that's landed me here in the first place.

But like my bunkmate, Cardell Opie says, "Hey, Doc, case closed." Says that the future is now, and I am merely a replacement for the last maggot, baptized in the name of hate and outrage and mayhem, sin and despair, the rocket's red goddamn glare.

It's approaching nightfall, and when the desk clerk in his busted English offers me an upgrade on the room, I say, "Negative on that" and pay just for some booze and the prostitute, then head up the stairs he's pointed to and go into the appointed room.

She spots *me* first, sitting on the edge of the bed, having waited for what seems like forever while mixing down the hundred-plus proof with nothing more than my own spit. No glass, no water or food, and someone's piss jar in the corner like an abandoned urine specimen.

She says, "Hello," and then whispers her name, which I can't make out, and I shake my head no. I've been standing guard, with the door cracked only a few inches. Already I'm seeing double, squinting one eye and then the other, and still I can't determine in the shadows if she's fifteen or fifty. She's dressed in a skin-tight mini-skirt and a blouse embroidered with brightly plumaged birds. Plus clear backless see-through high heels, her toenails painted magenta. Legs as skinny as a heron's, and when she takes that tentative first tiptoe in my direction she spreads her arms, like wings, and pushes the door just wide enough to sidle through.

Behind me, framed by the only window, mountains rise up white in the moonlight, so bright it illuminates her face and arms and neck. But I'm thinking, *dark, anonymous love*, and I stagger up to draw the curtain.

Instead, I steady myself and watch her slide and lock the deadbolt. And, with a single shake, unpin her hair, which falls halfway down her back. As she turns towards me, she says, "Mess around now, yes?"

"No. Uh-uh. Dance," I say, and she rolls her shoulders, shimmies downward until her ass touches the floor, where she pauses to unbutton her blouse. She's flat chested, her strapless bra silky and lacy and pink, and in between the fade-ins and fade-outs, I see she's missing two fingers on her right hand.

"No, with me," I say, and tap my chest. "Dance with me," and when she kicks off her shoes she can't be five feet tall, and the room is beginning to warp and distort around her. Then it's whirling in circles, the rainbow of birds blazing up like frenzied bats, and her face is everywhere, lips bitten back, teeth bared. And *my* face is forced deep into the pillow, and the handgun misfiring a thousand different times at point-blank range, the muzzle pressed against the base of my skull.

Or, maybe she *never* shows. Maybe it's all hallucinated, the jug sucked dry, and the door still slightly ajar in that last brain flash before blacking out. And, for whatever actually happened or didn't, here's how it ends going forward: I'm dressed only in my navy briefs, fevered and shivering myself barely alive enough to roll sweat-drenched onto my back, and my hands shaking uncontrollably. Teeth chattering and my eyes two slits closing like a violent blind purge against the demons of first light, the air humid, putrid and congealed, and stinging my lungs like tear gas. Like I've been chloroformed, interrogated and savaged, beaten black and blue.

Please, which is all I can offer up. *No more*, but not ten solid seconds in and I'm tripping again, and someone's bent over me with a horse needle, a final blood draw to sell black-market to the marauders and vampires of the night . . .

In the predawn of what must be my evacuation, I'm back from the dead, bunkered in the selfsame bed, same room, no brains blown out, no clots or globs dripping from the walls or ceiling. No entry or exit wounds, my money confiscated, along with shoes and socks and shirt, plus my only change of underwear, rucksack, and firearm. Everything picked clean.

And then I hear it, the slapping of rotors somewhere above me, and I'm down the back stairs, out the door, and into the rain. Another drunken sailor lost and humping it half naked across the empty street and into the field, toward the LZ. I'm ankle-deep in mud, a mist so thick that it veils the mountains, and the chopper hovering for a few interminable minutes before nosing through.

I stare up, waving my arms, but my insides cramping so bad that I drop, and, on all fours, I'm dry heaving again, coughing up another lung. Through the roar of the megaphone I can barely make out a voice calling my name and followed by the glare of the landing lights descending.

"Yes, it's me," I whisper. "The one and only. The legendary Doc Holliday," and I lean back on my haunches, and un-holster and extend both index fingers, and blow smoke from the barrels of twin six-shooters— my signature move among the endless jests we deploy to fortify ourselves against such brutal and incurable loneliness. Just blink it back and never budge. Whoop it up. Laugh it off, and "Fuck if I know, a skull and a tongue's the last damn thing I remember."

Close enough, bro, 'cause there ain't no explaining it anyhow. It ain't meant to be understood. That's the key. Abracadabra, the ultimate sideshow, and that's it, more or less, a warm-up to the Apocalypse. Unclassified, and so fuck the formalities and trust that nobody, not in this life, ever figures it right . . .

Just think it and it'll play. It'll be there even after fifty-some years and how many heart attacks? So far, just the one, right there on the bay-front, laid out flat on the ice, the sky cloudless, slate-colored, and Danny Shananaguot's on one knee, calling for backup on his smartphone, and telling me, "Don't talk, the helicopter's on it's way." Telling me, "I don't care," and he crosses my arms over my chest and covers my upper body with his coat. I can't formulate the words, can't for the life of me make myself understood, or lift a finger to point up at the crows that keep flying, one after the other, directly above us with fish heads in their mouths . . .

The first sound I hear is that unmistakable faint dinging of cleats against the hollow metal flagpole. Like I'm back in elementary school, daydreaming as always, and staring out the window, where the light shimmers and dulls, starbursts erupting behind those slow, flat, dark clouds, like it's already twilight. I've drifted so far away that Mrs. Lumbrezer makes no attempt to call me back, and not one time does she tap me on the shoulder with her pointer, her footfalls up and down the aisles so quiet it's as if everything's underwater, the whole world slipping away.

The first familiar voice is Danny's, and my release will be into his care. Yes, he's the closest to family, and has already jumpstarted the VA paperwork, and installed handrails in the shower. A ramp to the front door, which I don't want or need, and I make a show of it by sliding my legs over the side of the bed and standing, feet apart, no shortness of breath, hands at my sides.

A triple bypass, though it's not the ticker so much as the incapacity of sufficient motor skills to coordinate the movement of my right arm, the hand dangling like a locked claw, and my lips numb.

About the recovery, the cardiologist says, "We don't know for sure. Only time will tell." He's young and cheerful and all tanned up, like he's just back from Miami or Malibu, a white coat, and a stethoscope around his neck. He says, "But either way, your days of shoveling snow are a thing of the past, Mr. Holliday. Hire it done, and, come spring, welcome it by getting outside for leisurely, easy jaunts to begin. Seems to me there must be an entire frontier of walking to be done up there. I'll see you back here then." He pats me on the shoulder, shakes Danny's hand, and leaves.

The snow is falling so fast and thick that three stories down there's no making out the ground. "Spring?" Danny says. "Oh, yeah, that's right, when we all bend over and fart wildflower seeds into the wind. All that love and color." He says, "But hey, one day at a time, so for right now let's just get you the hell out of here and back home."

By his calculations, we should pull in just before dark. He's placed a pillow behind my head, and reclined the seat partway, like a portable hospital bed.

His rental rig, courtesy of my insurance, is as big as a hearse. "Signed, sealed, and delivered right to my front door," he says, "and sporting every whistle and bell. Everything but dancing girls and a minibar." An upgrade from his Scout International with a windshield that ices over, a busted gas gauge, and the hood tied down with bungee cords.

The dashboard's lit up like a cockpit, and, according to the display, the roads are bad enough to have forced school closings: windswept, patches of black ice, an accident on Rt. 31, outside Petoskey.

"Let me know if you need to stop," he says. "Anything else before we push off? You good?"

I can barely feel the speed bumps out of the parking lot, or the warm air through the vents—everything muted, and every next thought a jumble of slurred, unpronounceable words I don't even attempt. The windows are tinted, and, shoulder-to-shoulder, some stranger, unshaven and hollow-eyed, leans so close that our foreheads touch. He's not so much staring at me as through me, off into space, as the town gives way to pine forest and fields, a collapsed barn roof, the tops of the fence posts barely visible. And there, in the hypnotic drift and doze, it's like we're floating, riding a tidal pull across the wavy tundra, its dips and swells always true north, and the only color in the pervasive, formless white sky is a blue water tower, the obscured letters like giant runes: Oden, maybe, or Carp Lake, the Straits after that, and then across the bridge into the U.P.

Except for my name on the speakerphone I can barely decipher Rose-Ellen's voice, the conversation fading in and out. I want to tell her, *Stay with us. We're almost there,* as if we've been following the signal of a single heartbeat, buried under an avalanche. Or lost in a snowstorm, in a memory you can almost call back, across both distance and time. We're on our way. We always have been, the ghosts of our pasts, spread out and making wide sweeps into the emptiness, holding on tightly to each other's hands.

GRACIE AND DEVERE

The twins' combined age is twenty—two years older than their mom when she had them, born healthy on New Year's, a few minutes after midnight. Small-town celebrity babies, though strike the birth father sticking around for the local newspaper photographer, and ducking out instead into the hospital parking lot for a cigarette, and some cold air to clear his head.

Except for the bell-shaped birthmark high up on Devere's left thigh, the girls are identical, their wobbly, bow-legged first steps having occurred almost simultaneously. Ditto their discernible first spoken words: "Bye-bye." And how they waved to him, their about-to-be absentee daddy who, on that morning, did not, as he'd promised, go outside only long enough to install his daughters' safety seats in the decade-old, high-mileage family Ford Falcon. He backed it slowly out of the driveway instead, and cranked up the radio, and hightailed it for parts unknown. Currently, the safety seats hang side by side from the garage rafters like tiny abandoned swings.

And, seemingly out of nowhere, and absent any encouragement from anyone, the twins have long since ceased straddling the heat register after taking their baths—big girls now, who used to laugh and lindy like showgirls as their nightgowns filled and lifted.

They're ten and a half, and still only their mom, whose name is Lydia Pantalea, can tell them apart. Occasionally a new boyfriend—she's had only a few, plenty nice enough but none serious, all short term—will get down on one knee and swear he detects the subtlest difference

228

in their eyes, which are silver-blue, like Siberian huskies—sled dogs. But come on, it's late June already, and school's out, and the girls on their fire-engine red Schwinns with polished chrome fenders could give a rip about winter: those sub-zero wind chills, and the nearly-impossible-to-negotiate snow-swept roads, with whiteouts so dense and ghostly that even the looming water tower sometimes vanishes from sight.

The girls have never climbed it and they never will, unlike those older wild boys who scratch their initials and dates with jackknives under the gigantic numbers: POPULATION 3,972. They're bright, these girls who already read at a tenth-grade level. Dreambirds, their mom calls them, future co-valedictorians—whatever that means—and a whole new world out there to set on fire.

As Lydia's parents, their hopes sky high, had wanted to believe that someday *she* might, and offered, if she agreed to defer—a gap year, she remembers, that's what it's called—and work fulltime instead, they'd match whatever amount she contributed toward her tuition down at Michigan State. A sacrifice well worth the investment, they said, a huge deal, storybook, she being the first of the extended Pantalea clan to apply and be accepted to college. She could continue to live at home, and yes, all right, with fewer restrictions, a later curfew, though getting knocked up had hardly figured in as part of the plan. And, God forbid, and certainly not right out of the chute, but over time—morning sickness and her belly enlarging—she worked up the courage to tell them, half-trembling, and anticipating the worst.

"Well, talk about a game-changer," said her father, a quiet-spoken, inward man, his face blank and unreadable. "So much for a higher calling." And, without another word, he exited the room, while her mother, in tears and with fist pounding the kitchen table, referred to her as reckless, selfish and mouthy, edgy, impossible to please. *Or* believe. Said, "Always on your high horse, but now you've really gone and done it." Asked, "Why?"' Asked, "How in this world?"

"What's it matter now?" Lydia said, defiant as always. "Half a six-pack. A lovers' lane, a darkened back seat. Who cares?" And, true to form, her mother enumerated from that ever-growing checklist every-thing Lydia had ever in her life done wrong. Second, and third, and fourth chances squandered, like some headstrong, lost-cause teenager who might better, for everyone's sake, have been hauled off and placed in a halfway house.

They've since moved, not to Naples or Corpus Christi, but rather to Wheeling, Illinois, a place for which neither of her parents, separately or together, had ever expressed to her the slightest interest. Here and gone, and no forwarding address, like two distant and recalcitrant relatives.

"No, not early retirement. Who can afford that? Just starting over from the ground up is all," they said, as if Lydia had single-handedly dragged them through the wringer, squeezed them dry, sent them packing. "Imagine, in our fifties. And not getting any younger," they said, and, as the final measure of their intractable dismay and disappointment, shook their heads and looked away. Offered her no assistance whatsoever.

Estranged already for nearly a decade, they never write or call, but in the clearest dream she's ever had, Lydia, lost and holding a single quarter in a strange city somewhere, late at night, lifted the payphone receiver and dialed the operator, reversing the charges. Both her mother and father on the line, she inquired if they might consider renewing the offer now that she'd reformed, a responsible, single, twenty-nine-year-old working mom of two. Never married, doing her best, her tubes tied, and so no need whatsoever to wig-out again on that front.

Her life. And a salaried job at last, as a fulltime tollbooth attendant on the U.P. side of the Mackinac Bridge. The commute is less than half an hour in good weather, and along with decent benefits the work affords a living wage. Enough to catch up on the rent, more than a full month past due, and, hopefully, pay down some debts after the dead-end of working produce at Kroger, where she arranged pyramids of oranges and grapefruits, and shucked the wilted, exterior leaves from those crates of lettuce and purple cabbage heads. Snipped thorny rose stems and wrapped them in green tissue paper for Mother's Day bouquets.

Finally a one-time employee of the month, but minutes afterward she stared blank-eyed at her misspelled name under that smiling 8 × 10 glossy black-and-white photograph of her, thumbtacked to the corkboard above the shopping carts and gumball machines. Three years, rarely late and all day on her feet, she managed not a single pay raise. No bonus or promotion, her only perk sneaking trash from home into the company dumpster.

And then *poof*, she opens the Sunday newspaper and, instead of clipping discount coupons and perusing insert flyers, she skips right on past even the funnies to the classifieds. Makes a phone call early the next day, fills out an application, and two weeks later gets an interview and an offer, her take-home exceeding by more than double any other job she's ever held.

A *once in a blue moon*, she thinks, *a crossing over*. And, closing her eyes, she sight-maps a whole new route into her family's future.

"We're on the verge," she's assured the girls. "We're on our way, but *only* if we're careful. And if you'll agree to help me around here, because I can't do it alone anymore."

They will—with a serious gut check. They'll take the lead, in fact, but lobby first thing for a moratorium on that watery, vein-blue nonfat milk she brings home. As well as the bargain items demoted from the store shelves to those bloated wire-mesh bins clogging all twelve numbered aisles. But the twins' biggest gripe by far, which has bugged and embarrassed them, is their mom's longstanding justification for not factoring in a weekly allowance, for always crying poor.

"It can't be helped. Not just yet," she's told them. "I'm trying, I'm doing my best, and when things get better, when the time is right . . ."

"Like now with your new job?" they say. "It's not fair."

They feel cheated, stiffed, the only two kids they know who still don't get one.

Oh, *Ple-e-e*-ase, Lydia thinks, *what is this, another arbitration hearing?* She draws in a long, deep breath and says, "All right, we'll try it and see," as if in observance of whatever other good fortune might lie ahead, and only then do the twins brainstorm about how best to cost-cut whenever and however they can. If their mom, who's promised to quit smoking for as long as they can remember, attempts to light a cigarette, they blow out the match. If need be, they'll pilfer her pack of Parliaments, and cup their ears when she demands it back, as if they can't hear a single frantic word of what she's saying. Sometimes they run out of the room, doubled over with laughter.

Their father, Ward Lee Lendakis, has failed to provide a plug nickel's worth of court-ordered child support—and worse, he has at least twice violated the long-standing restraining order against him.

"Try stopping me," he's threatened. "They're my daughters, too"— which has led to warrants, and arrests, and even some cooling-down time in the local lockup. Lydia still believes deep down that he is not an insensitive or dangerous person, and that he might *still* turn his life around and start plunking down whatever he can.

"Listen," he says, "I'm good for it. A bit strapped at the moment, but I've got a few feelers out, some decent leads. I swear I'm a different person now. Back more to my old self."

But within days, weeks at most, the wake-up is followed by crossing that dark line back into the blackouts, the trademark drinking and then sobering up. Like a lizard growing a new tail, Lydia thinks, but refrains from using such snarky, vindictive language around the kids. She's done her best to stay even-keeled as she carefully steers and cautions them clear of him. And yet, what she believed back then—before and for a short while after the twins were born, as farfetched a fantasy as it seems now—was that he *would* reform, accept responsibility. This boy, her high school sweetheart, who'd always made decent grades without even trying, and ran varsity track, excelling in the long jump—though none as far as the flier he took on his way out of *their* lives.

Over time, the years and miles have widened, and his last known whereabouts was over on the Port Huron side, Jeddo or Roseburg. The twins don't inquire all that much anymore, but when they do, their mom, as a matter of course, simply refers to that part of her life as "the crash site": last rites, bygones, end of story.

She neither denies nor tries to justify anything. The less said the better, and the girls on the comeback say, "Never mind. Forget it," but behind her back, out of earshot, they imagine him differently, as if all along he'd been secretly sending them gifts, letters and snapshots to spread across their hand-smoothed beds. They draw various artist sketches of him and plead his case to one another. Unlike their mom, they'd never, ever press charges, or testify against him, no matter what. Tomboys, daddy's girls, and although they'll gladly throw the book at him for leaving them like he did, they nonetheless dismiss their mom's claims that it's for their own safety and well-being.

"Yes, we understand," they say, and yet the verdict is always the same: that everyone, just as the nuns taught them, deserves one last chance, don't they?

Rather than hire a sitter, Lydia's invested in the instillation of heavy-duty, tamper-proof cylindrical locks. "One for you, Devere," she says, "and the other for Gracie." The girls nod in unison, and, in spite of the fact it's always been a safe, and quiet, and friendly enough neighborhood—a rare and lucky find—they love the intrigue, and the intricate sound the metal makes sliding into the doorplate.

"We'll be fine, Mom," Gracie says. "Don't worry."

"Yep, we'll behave. We'll be good," Devere concurs. "You'll see," and, when she snaps off the overhead light, both girls giggle and point at the blinds they've just minutes ago drawn tightly to the windowsills, the room in semi-darkness, like a tablecloth draped over a birdcage.

They've crossed their hearts, and promised not to inquire 'Who is it?' should anyone knock, or pound, or ring the bell. "Whoever, and whatever their needs, is entirely beside the point," their mom says, and she's made clear that no one they know has asked, or been invited, to drop by. Nor should the twins leave the house after dusk for any reason. Period.

"Remember, no hopscotch, or jumping rope in the driveway. Even the front porch steps are off-limits," she reminds them. "You stay put. You hold the fort until I get home. And don't wait up for me. Understood?"

Just yesterday the girls picked out half a dozen videos at the Blockbuster in Pellston. *Dirty Dancing* is slated for night number one, plus a tube of Pringles and peanut brittle. They share the same tastes, and neither girl feels the least bit nervous, deprived, or betrayed in any way. Furthermore, they've never suffered nightmares—no goblins, or ghouls, or giant spiders. Never cried out in their sleep. They are the antithesis of needy, clingy, fawned-over kids. In fact, they're euphoric, and a resounding *hurray-hurray, hallelujah* presides as their latest mantra.

It's not the graveyard shift, though certainly not the one Lydia had hoped for, either—3:00 PM to 11:00. But beggars can't be, she reminds herself, and besides it still puts her home before midnight. She's baked lasagna, the girls' favorite, and, microwave-ready, wrapped it in tinfoil and placed it in the fridge, along with a two-liter bottle of Dr Pepper. As a final safeguard, she's written Betty Amaltifano's number in bright red Magic Marker numerals on a white paper plate and Scotch-taped it right beside the wall phone. "Doesn't need to be an emergency. If for any reason you feel the least bit anxious or uncomfortable, or if the house seems too empty without me, you call her and she'll come right over."

Then she plants a kiss on the top of each of their heads, and steps outside onto the frayed black welcome mat. She'd hoped to savor this long-awaited moment, their future, but here it is, and she's crippled instead by a debilitating case of the jitters. Second thoughts times a thousand, and yet, against her better judgment, and with all the willpower she can muster, she closes the front door. A decision, she's

233

told herself over and over, borne of circumstance and necessity: the wiper blades peeling away, and those dreary, energy-saving low-wattage light bulbs nearly impossible to read by. Yes, they're good girls, fast learners who'd never go anywhere without first asking.

"Okay, lock it," she says, her voice muffled, and they do, in perfect sync, as if from inside a secret chamber. They watch the knob turn slowly back and forth.

"Good. Now, look at me," and the twins, on their tiptoes and taking turns, barely recognize her, the glass concave and Coke-bottle thick, her features a dozen different configurations of puzzled. The face of a total stranger, older and disoriented in her Smokey the Bear uniform minus the hat, and the sky beyond as it brightens seeming wider-spread and even farther away.

"Okay, I guess. It's now or never. So here goes," she says, and unzips the side pouch of her purse, and drops in her two house keys.

The twins wear theirs around their necks, like newly minted charms, or scapulars. They squeeze them, and silently pray that she'll get on with it: stop fiddle-farting around, calm down, do an about-face, and walk to the car for heaven's sake. Stop beating herself to a pulp and scram. They understand—they get that she can't help it—but enough already with the mother hen. They're perfectly capable of fending for themselves, and really, is it so difficult for her to grasp that they're on vacation, and already stir-crazy, and have lives and plans of their own, too?

She leans toward them again, mere inches away, and squints into the not-so-inconspicuous recess at what looks like a tiny bauble, or a hidden mirror. As if the peephole were invented not so much to identify potential home invaders, but rather for her to concentrate a final, bitter self-scrutiny on this trial run that she's plotted and is compelled, for all their sakes, on this otherwise nondescript day of their new lives, to undertake.

"Any last minute requests?" she asks, and met only with silence she says, for the umpteenth time, "I love you. You're all I've got, so stay close to home. I'll tell you tomorrow at breakfast how it goes up there on the bridge, whether I still suffer vertigo like I used to." She smiles at that, then says, "I can't, but if I could I'd check in on the two of you with my walkie-talkie"—which she's clipped to her waistband, like a meter maid's. "So while I'm gone you take care of each other," she says, and breathes deeply. And again, and then one final time, to try and steady her nerves before finally stealing away.

"Nine, eight, seven, six . . ." Gracie says, and, after their mom drives off, out of sight, "Okay. Coast clear."

But when Devere takes a peek through the blinds, there's an unfamiliar pickup directly in front of the house, and so slow-moving it's almost stopped, with a thin wavering cobweb of exhaust rising from its tailpipe. She can't make out the driver, someone lost most likely, and looking for a certain marker or address. Theirs is 1602 Orchard: a boxy three-bedroom, bath and a half, fenced-in backyard, and the mature maples almost fully leafed-out. An absolute miracle of an upgrade—a real *house* house, as their mom says.

"What's the holdup?" Gracie wants to know, and Devere shrugs, says, "Nothing. False alarm."

"Let's go then," and within minutes, changed into their matching swimsuits, the twins are on their bikes, pedaling side-by-side, zigzagging around mailboxes, and the occasional hydrant, and those hazardous after-winter potholes.

Then, veering left and right through the narrow hodgepodge of one-ways, where they used to live, adjacent to the trailer park's rear entrance. Right there in that dinky, unoccupied pale green singlewide with salmon-colored skirting, and those warped, water-stained ceiling tiles, and no basement in which to hide from the hail and the lightening of those murderous thunder boomers that one night shattered half the windows. And, worst of all, that snake-like tangle of extension cords plugged into a single five-outlet power strip. A firetrap. Everything out of code, and fuses blowing should either girl, bundled in sweaters and two pairs of socks, knees pressed to her skinny chest, dare to get out of bed in the pitch dark, and sneak into the kitchen, and crank the space heater to high.

But it's the route they take. A shortcut, and, detouring wide of the downtown with its stoplights and intersections, the twins head north along the old access road to the abandoned depot and, no ghost trains barreling by, cross the tracks and duck under the loading dock, sneakers swinging by their laces from the handlebars.

Both girls have painted their toenails red, to match their bikes. If there are no barking or charging dogs with which to contend, Gracie and Devere always ride barefoot after it rains, as it did all night and late into the morning—downpours that rinsed the sidewalk clean, but the air hot and clammy now, their bangs sweated to their foreheads, and their pale shoulders greasy with sunblock.

The girls' intended destination? The bankrupt Glory Ridge subdivision project their mom read about in the newspaper, and then drove over with the girls, who wanted to see it too. The giant flop, as Lydia called it. "All that spongy, slanting pastureland, and look, no sewers or culverts, and what'd they think would happen? A waterslide's what it is. I bet on the right day you could float an apple from up here all the way down," and she yanked on the emergency brake, and watched off over the marsh as if staring out onto another world.

"Look," she said, the sky reflecting like pewter off the still surface, and where a great blue heron lifted straight up on its enormous, outstretched wings. "So lush and tranquil," she said, "isn't it? Look at all those lily pads. They should leave the place alone, a sanctuary for watercolorists or birdwatchers."

Glory Ridge is located just beyond the junior high the twins will attend after another year. Beyond that, on the town's outskirts, is Go-Go Squeeze, the cavernous fruit processing plant, against whose bitter tang of fermentation both girls squint and press their lips together as they pass.

But most annoying by far is that white wooden cross their mom's pointed out a hundred times at least—where the unsolved hit-and-run occurred a few years back. A shocker—"Struck dead" is how she puts it, "just like that." A local kid not a whole lot older than the twins, and hitchhiking alone in the late evening to who knows where?

From there the destination is not far, at most another half mile on Route 81, the main two-lane artery in and out of town, and where the twins are forced to ride single file along the narrow shoulder. If their mom had any clue as to what they're up to, she'd ground them, and possibly register them for summer classes. Or enforce even darker consequences, like catechism with the Sisters in the basement of the sweltering Holy Cross rectory—the ultimate, unthinkable damnation.

But for now, here they are, free and thumb-ringing their chrome bells as they fork away from the traffic, the angry honking horns, and continue past the half-finished, boarded-up model home, and surveying stakes, and FOR SALE signs galore, most of them all-the-way fallen over. Lot after sodden, grassless vacant lot, but the winding blacktop still new and smooth enough that the twins, spread-eagled on the long gradual downhill toward the flooded cul-de-sac in front of the marsh, let go of the silver-tasseled handgrips. A few daredevil seconds is all, straight-backed and balancing on their backsides.

Which is what those boys, befuddled, and huddled-up halfway out on the raised weathered marsh planks, and glaring back, see: two ditzy, screaming look-alikes, and the runoff chain-guard deep at least as they enter the spring-fed spill full-tilt, the water fountaining up all around them, like thousands of shiny, translucent liquid pearls.

The weirdness merits a closer look, so all three boys close in, their body language anything but friendly. *Shit fish* is what they call the carp, but here at their favorite kill site nothing's rising close enough to the surface, at least not yet, so already the day's adding up to a total dud, a turd in a sock, a complete and goddamn bust with a cherry on top. They've got mouths on them, these boys, especially when they're angry or bored, and attitudes to match. Fourteen-year-olds cut loose for the summer, their only mission to search and destroy, stir up a little mayhem before calling it quits and heading home for dinner.

The twins, soaked and still squealing like banshees, have not yet seen them approaching: the one with a cast on his left wrist; the taller, gangly dark-haired one who's shirtless, a cigarette dangling from his lips and a black tee shirt hanging like a beaver's tail from the hollow, baggy ass of his low-riding jeans; and, pulling up the rear, the sharpshooter—stocky, cocksure, and dressed head to toe in camouflage, with a crude homemade long-handled gaff in one hand and a pellet gun slung over his shoulder.

"Uh-oh," Gracie says. "Don't look now,"—though for all she knows these boys who stare, and glare as they approach, might be harmless enough. Maybe. But it's a mute point anyway, given that there's not nearly time enough to reverse direction, and flee.

The twins' one-piece swimsuits are golden orange, the color of carp, but why would *they* be the target of anyone's taunts or torments? They never have been before, not really. Jokes and jibes about them being clones, about being Siamese whenever they sit hip to hip on the back seat of the school bus—goofy nonsense stuff like that, about how, if the twins swapped first names, or assumed each other's school desk for the day, who'd be the wiser? Even their future boyfriends could be unwitting two-timers should the twins someday coordinate a secret switcheroo.

But all of this in good fun, harmless enough, so how come Devere, who's just spotted them too, flinches when the smoker finger-flings his butt above the pointed, spiked heads of the cattails?

All three stop a few feet away, positioned in a loose semicircle, and the one with the cast points at Gracie, and then at Devere, back and forth, as if his index finger is a ballpoint pen he's offering the girls to sign the cast with.

"Check it out. Dead ringers," he says. "Carbon copies."

He adjusts his mirrored sunglasses, maybe worried he's seeing double. "That weird or what? Two for the price of one."

"Cheap dates," sharpshooter says, and leers, like *he's* got them clearly in his sights, and then asks, "So what's up? You girls lost or something?"

They shake their heads no.

"Then whaddaya doing here?" he asks as he glances back at the marsh, spreading almost out of sight like a tidal plain.

"Cooling off," Devere says. "Having fun."

"Uh-uh. Wrong again. No girls allowed," the tall one says, and drums his flat, bare stomach. "This here's our private hunting grounds. But hey, as long as you're here . . ."

He slides a Swiss Army knife from his back pocket, and extracts not the blade, but rather the corkscrew. "We're not going to hurt you," he says. "There's nothing to be afraid of. We're just having us a little fun too."

"Cap it, dildo. Spare us the sweet talk and just do it," sharpshooter says, and the tall kid steps closer, shrugs, as if to say *Like yeah, sure, no big deal,* as if whatever's about to happen, it's a far cry from their first time.

"If you don't mind," tall kid says as he seizes Gracie's bike, yanks it from her hands, tips it sideways, and then shouts, "Think fast." He lets it crash so that, other than the right pedal and half a handlebar, the frame is completely submerged.

"Yowza," he says. "Whoo-ee"—and, wearing heavy rubber boots that come up to his kneecaps, he bends over, bares down and twists and twists clockwise until the rear tire pops, and the air hisses and pisses up from a good foot and a half underwater.

"Now ain't that a bitch?" he says. "Major bummer. I mean, of all the places to get a frigging flat? Talk about shitty luck. And by the way, how far did you say you two runaways are from home?" When neither girl answers, he says, "Batten the hatches," and clicks the corkscrew back into the handle. Then he slides the knife into his pocket, sloshes slowly behind the twins, and tugs loose both bows at the napes of their necks.

"Peep show," cast boy says, but what's to see other than these frightened, and shivering flat-chested girls holding the stretchy fabric tight to their collarbones? From somewhere the girls hear the water perk and burgle as they stand rigid, statue-still, and gaze away as if touched in some creepy, weirdo version of freeze-tag.

"Now, don't go anywhere," the tall one says, and toes the kickstand up on Devere's bike. Mounts it, blows them a kiss, and says, "Be right back," and, weaving side to side, heads partway up the incline, all knees and flapping elbows, and where he swings wide into a figure eight, pulls a couple of wheelies, and then careens straight downhill, dead-out pumping for all he's worth, a thin wet rooster tail arcing up, and the bike dwarfed beneath him.

"Fucking insane," cast boy shouts, and sharpshooter's dancing, and war whooping, and swinging the gaff as if gouging the fat, blue underbelly of the sky.

The planks are laid end-to-end, the makeshift dock a few feet max in width, and, halfway out, tall boy yells, "Geronimo," and lets go of the handlebars, the bike seeming to accelerate from between his legs, and vaulting heavenward before nose-diving into the drink and out of sight.

They're all three out there now, torqued, and hooting, and trading high-fives because nothing on this day of their lives could be funnier.

Although the twins have backed up a few tentative steps, and turned, they do not start running and calling for help—because there it is, its hood nosed over the crest of the hill, that same pickup Devere spied earlier right outside their house. She's sure of it, as if materializing out of thin air.

Someone they know, or their mom knows? One of her former boyfriends, who saw them headed this way and, calculating the worst, thought, *They ought to know better, the traffic, the sometimes dangerous ways of the world*, and followed? They'd be easy enough to track, even at a distance, their rear lights pulsing like panicked, speeded-up double hearts.

Whoever it is raises the visor and bends forward over the steering wheel, his elbow poking out the driver-side window. And then he's out of the truck and pitching forward on his approach, as if he might break into a trot, and then bull rush them with bad intentions. Instead, he maintains a quiet, easy pace, the pavement steamy, and this figure like an apparition floating through a mirage, hair shoulder-length, and shiny black like that of the twins. He glances over at them, presses his index finger to his lips, and they both nod.

Could it be him who vanished before they turned two, and whom they've since seen only twice in their entire lives? Surprise visits, and both not seeming so awful at first, but inside of five minutes their mom was seething, stabbing the air with her forefinger, raising her voice and reading him the riot act: "How did you find us? Have you lost your mind, showing up here like this? I've warned you how many times to stay away? Nothing's changed and nothing will. They don't *want* to see you. Not now, not ever, and goddamn you for doing this to them. And to me."

And the twins were shielded, half-hidden behind her, transfixed and staring, and staring, as if to memorize him during those combustible but nonviolent few minutes before she said, "Is that what you want? Is that what it'll take to get you to leave and stay gone, for them to say it to you themselves? Then fine. Have at it"—at which point he looked at them, from one to the other, and whispered their names: "Gracie . . . Devere" and then averted his eyes and, straightaway without another word, backed out the front door, easing it shut behind him and, as he'd do again the one other time that they know about, that they can re-member, drove away.

"Maybe we should just go," Gracie says, as though by bearing down on those dodos he's opened a passageway for the twins to bolt. Except they've got no shoes, no summer calluses on the heels or balls of their feet, and the highway berms are like parallel fairways of busted beer bottles, cigarette butts, and blown-out retreads. Plus how far could they get before the cops stopped and picked them up as if they'd just escaped from some serial kidnapper?

No, nothing that bad, they'd say, nothing like that—though, offering the state trooper or sheriff's department deputy no plausible explana-tion for being there, wouldn't he turn on his blue lights, and order them into the cruiser's backseat, and interrogate them, question after ques-tion? Check the Amber alert? Maybe play one girl against the other? Write down on his notepad their names and ages, ask, *Where do you hurt? Where do you live?* Inquire about the keys around their necks, ask for a telephone number no one would answer, and eventually drive the twins home to an empty house? *Is your mom around, your dad?* And the twins by this time bawling, shaking their heads, and refusing to answer or to confess that in their minds there's no crime more seri-ous than summoning her from the bridge on her very first day on the job. Maybe arrest their mother for negligence. Fingerprint and photograph her. Even take her children away.

But if they can get to the pickup—a hundred feet or so is all—and lock themselves inside, they'll have a perfect sightline to witness the outcome. A stern lecture, they hope, an important lesson learned before the issuing of a final warning for those bullies to stay away, to stay gone and never show their cowardly, predatory mugs around here again. It'd serve them right.

"Okay, quick," Gracie says, but before they make a run for it, Devere says back, "No, wait, it's not fair, three against one. What if he gets hurt, or someone drowns or something? Then what?"

But it's no contest, and the girls know that as he closes in without the slightest hesitation, eyes dead ahead, and cast boy, as if the ghost of his *own* irate father has suddenly appeared, says, "Holy shit," and he and the tall one sideslip off the shallow end of the dock, then wade waist-deep into the eelgrass, and out of reach. They circle wide, hands raised above their heads, while sharpshooter, still stretched out on his stomach, unguarded, chin resting on his forearms, stares down at Devere's bike, as if hypnotized by the glinting rear spokes rotating backward in ultra-slow motion, as though time might stop altogether in the suddenness of what's about to rain down.

The three-minute egg, Ward thinks. The four-minute mile—and, although he's never run one of those, he's thankful for those five-minute snoozes he caught while staking out the house in the predawn, and throughout the morning. A virtual eternity, but he's clocked in now, on automatic pilot.

"Boo," he says, and sharpshooter turns, slowly stands, and first thing attempts to straight-arm this dude who's stalked right up on him in broad daylight, his hambone buddies already in full retreat, slopping across the empty lots, every mad-scramble footfall sucking down and kicking up fat clods of mud.

"Afternoon," Ward says, bats the hand away, cuffs the kid's hat into the marsh, and coils his shirtfront so tight against his windpipe that within seconds sharpshooter begins to plead and wheeze, his fingers clawing at his throat to try to loosen the pressure.

Face-to-face, their foreheads almost touching, what activates Ward's fury most is the image he sees of himself, though five or six years older, in the kid's eyes. All manner of smashups flash back: the confusion, the dereliction and deceit. Evade and escape, as he saw it back then, and that ever-growing stockpile of fuckups forever locked deep inside of his skull. And his old man, long divorced from Ward's mom, and living alone, and serenading himself with half-baked monologues supposing this and supposing that, and how if only he'd joined the army and retired after twenty years he'd be sitting pretty this very minute, living like a king off the government tit.

"Shit in a ditch," Ward's dad would say. "Shit in a goddamn ditch." His eyes were bloodshot, and that bruised, fat-veined hand was wedded to yet another pint of Jim Beam or Old Museum. "Cheers," he'd say, whenever Ward stopped by, AWOL from his mom's place only a few miles distant. She, the salt of the earth, though sometimes the rules felt unreasonable, even demeaning, the way she tried to rein him in with needless conditions and rebukes. That's when he'd split, crash on the couch at his dad's, when he just needed a breather, stay a day or two. And that's where, underage, he learned to drive, and choked down his first beakful of cheap booze. Like father, like son, living with the high-dollar risks, Ward admits now, of being bad seed born. Of being caught so unaware on the wrong side of some terrible, fitful wind.

And there was Lydia, already four months pregnant and still prattling on about college downstate. No declared major, not yet, she'd say, but maybe sociology, given how she liked the sound of a career with so many syllables, like something they might magically translate into their future.

Jesus. East Lansing? Thing is, it was crazy what happened, at light speed, as if they'd orbited into some distant, alternative universe, while all Ward wanted was to stay put; he was already a decent mechanic with a steady part-time income, and with the good sense to sock away whatever he could. At sixteen, for God's sake, he'd rebuilt the entire engine in one of his dad's old Ford clunkers—in which, a year later, on his way to school, rain or shine, he'd pick up Lydia a couple blocks from her parents' house, where he'd never been welcome, just another uncouth local loser headed nowhere, though right along he begrudged them nothing. He'd prove them wrong, and some nights now, unable to sleep, he still imagines himself part of a NASCAR pit crew.

"I can't breathe," the kid says, his face turning crimson, and those pupils black and slick as leeches, rolling back up into his forehead.

242

"Don't talk. Don't say a word. Just listen to me." But the kid, how could he? Whatever Ward says is a guaranteed waste of words, and yet, for what it's worth, he whip-kicks the kid's feet out from under him, and only then eases the pressure and finally lets go as he bends and lifts the pellet gun by the barrel and, in a single motion, hammer-throws it so far out over the marsh that he barely hears the splash. Years later, what the kid will no doubt remember most is how, right there on his knees, he pissed his pants while holding his hands palms up like some stunned and speechless supplicant.

Behind Ward a sudden hatch of white moths rises—millions, it seems, thick, and slow, and silent. Like snow, Ward thinks, almost holy. The kid, head bent forward, a sudden tremor worsening in his fingers, shivers.

"Low odds you'll ever buy in, but hey, who knows? Could be that someday you'll even thank me," Ward says. "I'm off duty now, but I see you anywhere near here again, I'll fast-track your ass in front of a judge and jury. We got the victims. Got a witness, that's me. Got our perp, that's you, caught red-handed. Got the whole shmeer. Case closed. As for your pals, pass it along: save yourselves some serious grief, and maybe spare your parents some high-ticket legal fees. Or work it off yourself into your old age. And most important, keep in mind all you get's this one warning. I'll be watching. Here. Elsewhere. You'll never know. Exactly like today, like this, except next time no mercy. Nod if you understand."

The kid does, and Ward says, "Get outta here, and leave the meat hook. I'll see if we get a match on the fingerprints. But either way, we got you dead to right on this one, and so before I change my mind . . ." and he turns sideways to let the kid pass.

The encounter has left Ward shaken, even breathless, as he walks off the dock and into the spill, retrieves Gracie's bike, and carries it up to the truck. Not sure they're even there, he squints into the sharp glare off the windshield, shades his eyes, and only after he yanks open the tailgate and slides the bike in backwards does he see their faces—both girls watching him through the closed rear window. He hasn't been this near to them in years, and yet they've never looked more familiar. He unties the sneakers from the handlebars, goes around to the driver's side, discovers the door locked and the key in the ignition.

Good, he thinks. *Smart girls.* One way or another he'll salvage the other bike, and then get these kids home, safe and sound.

He taps on the glass. "Want to help?" he says. "I best not walk out there, not on that bottom, and likely get myself swallowed up. I sure don't see the attraction in that."

The girls remain stone-faced, and he says, "Roll down the window a crack so I can hear you," though they haven't yet made a peep. "It sticks a little," he says, and so Gracie reverse-cranks with both hands.

"There. How's that?" she says.

"Do you two know who I am?"

Devere says, "We think maybe."

"We're pretty sure," Gracie says.

"Okay. That's good. Everything's all right. You're safe now."

"It's really sweltering in here," Devere says. "Can we come out?"

"Pull up on the lock," he says, and then steps back away from the door as both girls exit.

"Those are my sneakers," Gracie says.

"Uh-huh. Here you go." She unknots and slips them on, says, "How deep's Devere's bike, can we get it?"

"Let's take a look," Ward says. "We'll figure something," and, within minutes all three of them stare down from the end of the dock. "Any volunteers?"

Devere takes that to mean her, and she's the better swimmer anyway, the better diver—not that it makes any difference because that's not the plan, though she can't help imagining those boys holding her upside down by the ankles, dunking her, forcing her to hold her breath for longer and longer. But this man is nice. This man is their father, and it's got to be ninety degrees out here at least, and he says, "Okay. Hold the handle way down here. Real tight. Yep, with both hands, and see if you can loop the hook through the spokes. Everything weighs less underwater, so it should be easy, a piece of cake. Don't worry, I won't let go. I promise."

She wishes she had a mask, a snorkel, but as Ward lowers her to within inches of the surface, she can see the weeds waver and part, and the water as clear as a streambed. Stumps everywhere. Minnows flash here and there, and the reflector on the rear fender winks and glitters like a single round red eye.

"Got it, got it," she says. "First try," and Ward, sitting back on his heels, slowly stands, his legs spread wide enough for Gracie to crawl through and grab hold of the tire. The girls can't stop giggling, as if they've just dredged up the find of a lifetime.

Ward wonders if all of life is a series of failed attempts to manage loneliness. Wonders—not so much in this moment, but will soon, in another hour or two, after he drops them off a block or two away from their house—if he deserves even a passing nod in the direction of for-

244

giveness. He won't ask his daughters. He won't do that to them, though they hug him now, like two young girls he happened upon in a bad situation, and one that is not, for once, of his own making.

A flat tire, he thinks. Such a minor repair, a simple fix, a patch and some glue. He could do it blindfolded. And he won't rule out something approximate to that. Not today, of course, but possibly down the road apiece? There's a law against him being here, so close to his kids. Even on this day when they most needed him. But who knows? If a few things could only break right for him . . .

Ward, Gracie, and Devere squeeze into the cab, and just before he starts the engine he says, "Not a word about any of this to your mom."

They lift the keys from around their necks, and make-believe lock their lips. They owe him that at least, grateful for having wiggled out of so, so much trouble.

IF MY FATHER HAD EVER HUGGED ME, EVEN ONCE, I WOULD HAVE BECOME AN ACCOUNTANT

(Ray Ramano)

Against the odds I did anyway, a certified CPA, and who, at forty-three, has already outlived my old man by almost a decade, a fact I accept and do my best not to dwell on.

As my wife Lizzie, an incurable optimist seven months pregnant with our first child, reminds me, "Live in the moment, Lloyd. Eat while the food's still hot." And yet just this morning she read aloud an article asserting, that somewhere in the blur of those first whispers or lullabies resides that one remembered something that every newborn stores away, and is later either formed or broken by. She's bright, curious and open-minded, but likewise vulnerable to such far-flung, New Age confabulations. I half listened, sipped my coffee, and, without annoyance or protest, opened our local newspaper, its contents unremarkable though grounded nonetheless in issues both relevant and commensurate to our middle-class life here in the suburbs.

A practitioner of common-sense goals and agendas, it's not a reach to believe that I was born to this: systems, scales and statistics, and, long-suffering and badly in need of companionship some years back, I adopted on a trial basis from the SPCA, an aging, half-deaf schnauzer. Trimmed his snout, and the shaggy tangle half covering his eyes, removed the choke-chain collar, and, on the spot, and befitting his sweet but nervous and finicky disposition, changed his name from Wonder to Reality.

Lucky for us—Lizzie and me—that apparently opposites do attract, and then run parallel. Take our recent marriage, for instance, her third, my first, her exuberant, carefree laugh juxtaposed to my earnest but tentative thin-lipped smile. And whereas most nights it's lights out for me by nine-thirty, she stays up reading Jane Austin and George Elliot.

She's four years younger. She looks it too, and, without exception during our courtship, remained rigid and intractable on no front *other* than to have a baby before she aged out, her every desire directed and streamlined to that end. Me? Not so much, the buzz of paternal longing a myth, I assumed, in my genetic profile. At best a passing twinge or two, and so when finally I acquiesced and popped the question, ring in hand, she said, "Well, hello there family man."

Prior to my arrival she'd partied hard, circling the drain, as she said—a longstanding history of getting messed up all over again: three speeding tickets, a DUI, and suspended driver's license. Not to mention a twenty-four hour hold in lockup, and what she deems currently to be the rockiest, most reckless interludes of her life. But here's the better news: that's over, and on the day we closed on the mortgage, I mounted the stairs two at a time, and carried her across the threshold of our modest split-level into what she now refers to as this safe, good light.

Already a percentage of every paycheck is portioned to accrue in total an Ivy League education—or, more likely, its Midwestern equivalent—by the year 2014. We've listened to the baby's heartbeat, our daughter, and some nights I imagine following that sound out beyond the star-mist, and into a dimension where the inventory of all human peril collapses around us like a parachute of silver and gold.

For my birthday joke gift last May Lizzie gave me a T-shirt that said FORWARD on the front, and THINKING across the back. That's me, measured, reliable, steady as he goes, a grown-up, the S-curve into our cul-de-sac, as Lizzie says, my nerdy homespun version of the autobahn. It's true. I drive a low-mileage, pre-owned Oldsmobile Cutlass with an extended bumper-to-bumper warranty, and four brand new all-season Goodyear radials. Unlike my old man, I schedule tune-ups and oil changes weeks in advance. I blaze no trails. I honor guardrails, and rumble strips, steer hard right, and pass only those vehicles stranded in the breakdown lane. Certain late Friday afternoons during rush hour men twice my age stare over from low in their seats, and flip me the bird.

Lizzie's 5" 5' and wears tight-fitting threadbare cut-off jeans, and flip-flops, and that same, oversized maze and blue University of Michigan sweatshirt. And where, lately, among the flowerbeds of peonies and delphiniums, she'll sit back on her haunches, eyes closed, and lift her face to the sun, in this, the month *before* the month when everything's in full bloom, and a July 4th due date is not, I assure you, a matter of dumb luck or sudden good fortune.

We're responsible latecomer parents to be, our house mold and lead and radon free. I've already installed childproof safety gates at the top and bottom of the staircase. And last month sealed the hairline cracks and fractures, then repainted the baby's bedroom, the color scheme a combination Kiss of Butter and Touch of Sky, and *on* the ceiling—Lizzie's bidding—a swirl of animal clouds: sheep and ponies and trumpeting Baby Dumbos. She's talented that way too, and holds a degree in literature, with a minor in arts education, and not all that far down the road I calculate our combined incomes will justify an upgrade to marble-top and stainless, a microwave with a rotating center, Lizzie's future dream kitchen. But first things first, and, safe conservative-leaning neighborhood or not, there's the more immediate and practical consideration of this family's security.

For now, it's vapor spots and double locks, and, until recently, a nickel-plated .45-caliber Ruger Single-Six, one of a dozen models I'd researched, its ballistics, the statistical hedge or risk of domestic gun ownership. A mission contrived in defiance of common sense, me being a lifelong non-hunter who knows virtually nothing about firearms. Standing at the counter I studied the graph I was handed, the intersecting red and green lines that indicated a slight upward rise for the average armed family's collective longevity.

Off-camera, and, with few exceptions no lies or secrets between us, I came clean, admitted to Lizzie what I'd done, an insane impulse purchase to say the least, and even crazier was that I then followed through by walking into the police department to be fingerprinted and licensed. "I'm sorry," I said, "I should've asked for your input, for you to weigh in on this too."

"Yes," she said. "You should have. What in the world were you thinking? It's so—I don't know—tilted, and cynical, and so entirely unlike you. But just take it back and it never happened, Lloyd, simple as that."

"If that's what you want, okay, but I should point out it's paid for in full, and that we stand to forfeit more than half its value. Plus the added benefit that in certain states insurance rates decrease by as much as fifteen percent times however long we live here, year after year, an ongoing investment in our future."

"Really? I've never heard of such a thing. Which states exactly are you talking about?" she asked, and I said, "Texas, for starters," but as she pointed out we currently reside thirteen miles east of Grand Rapids, and this city with a population just shy of 200,000 is nowhere demarcated on the national crime map.

She'd been lazing barefoot on the couch, resting, and, down on one knee, the A/C humming for the first time all spring, and the double-paned windows closed, I said, "I get it. But hang on, I just want you to listen," and she did, without another word, to that perfect clicking whirl of the pistol's spun cylinder.

Against her hesitations and better instincts, we've rented time at the indoor shooting range, and where we've learned to load, and, legs spread wide apart, arms extended, taken careful aim at those stationary, faceless paper targets of intruders, madmen and child abductors I imagine mugging for women unsuspecting enough to unlatch and swing open the screen door. The muted canned background laughter of TV sitcoms, and the newborn sound asleep in its bassinet or crib.

Lizzie's the better marksman by far. Fiercely concentrated she never flinches, a natural as the instructor contends, the groupings tight and chest-centered, the velocity of impact equivalent to that of a speeding freight train.

"Hell's bells I'd say your firstborn's got no worries," the instructor said. "A pregnant mom packing some serious thunder. My advice, live on," a tone I didn't much like, and Lizzie shooting me a look, and shaking her head at this bloodless bulls-eye of a charade, at *me* with my temples throbbing, and hands thrust deep in my dress pants pockets.

"Enough?" she said. "We're good? If so, let's go home to our actual life, and put this damn thing away."

Within easy reach but out of sight I slid it into the top drawer of the nightstand. Don't ask me why but last thing before I knock off, if Lizzie's out of the room, I check, and there it is, directly below the Princess telephone that she reaches for whenever I'm working late, that manic last-minute rush around tax time. Tired more easily these days she hates that I wake her, sometimes in rapid succession.

"Please, Lloyd," she says, "for heaven's sake, this constant worry and paranoia: forced entries, crazies on the loose. You're going to make

249

yourself sick. We're perfectly safe here except that you're scaring the wits out of me," and which, first off, was exactly what I'd intended to dispel with a hedge against the unforeseen.

Remote, so improbable, as Lizzie argued, and I agree, except that the panic's real, and talk about worse fears realized, this past Friday I discovered the back door not pry-barred open but visibly ajar, the porch light extinguished, and the bulb almost loose enough to plunge from its copper socket.

Heart hammering, my throat constricted and gasping for air, I tiptoed up the dimly lit stairs, lifting each shed item of clothing: nightgown, flip-flops and panties, and that new padded, large-cup bra with elastic crisscross-in-the-back straps. And, for what it's worth, the doorknob, for that interminable half-second before I turned it, felt like my old man's fist, and another restraining order balled up in his palm.

Just business as usual growing up, the place booby-trapped, and the going rate for propane like a knee to the nuts, as he'd say, his face tinged blue in the light of those Bunsen burners he sometimes used to quiet the nearly frozen water pipes in the kitchen. Accident prone, my mom would say about her bruises and black eyes after he'd skipped out again. And, hopefully gone this time forever, I swore if need be I'd make it my life's mission once I got old enough to intervene, and go ahead, let him try picking on someone his own size for a change, and see who cowers first, freezes or folds.

But there in our bedroom where Lizzie'd conceived, her body was propped motionless against the headboard and foam-filled pillows, and the sheets turned back like someone had painstakingly smoothed the folds down low on her thighs. And, stopping me in my tracks, her naked stomach seemed another world under her pressed palms, as if she'd felt for the first time the baby kicking. And, on my side of the bed, the pistol, along with a fistful of bullets scattered like jacks. "Take it," she said, her eyes closed. "Sell it back at whatever cost. Or better yet, throw it off the Sixth Street Bridge on your way to work. Just get it out of our life, Lloyd. Get it once and for all out of here before one of us snaps. It's such bad karma, all this negative energy. My God, just look at us."

Start with me, who's been employed for eighteen years by the downtown firm of Sidewall and Slime, as a wisecracking ex-coworker of mine used to say. The malign was neither accurate nor amusing; in fact, it struck me dumb, given the opportunities for advancement, a possible partnership in trust down the road. Add to that the benefits and perks, and which include a box seat at Fifth Third Bank Field, home of the West Michigan Whitecaps. Triple A. An office, I suppose, away from the office, and located exactly midway between third and home plate, and where committed and loyal middle-aged lifers like yours truly are encouraged to entertain perspective clients.

Already on my ledger, the Yankee Air Museum, and Bellitoc Bottling, and, among others too numerous to mention, the Maids of Marriage, a nonprofit legal-council in support of women screwed royally in divorce settlements. Do I donate to it? No more or less than I do to all worthy causes—with an honest, and thorough down-to-the-last dime quarterly statement indicating either their solvency or debt, who's benefited, who's lost. Otherwise, I remain uninvolved, administer no council, and concentrate instead on managing and taking care of what I can.

Between you and me, I've only ever attended baseball games alone, my collar up, cap pulled low on my brow. And only when Lizzie is out of town visiting her sister, Ginger, in Ypsilanti. I decline all such invitations and can estimate to within minutes her time of arrival there. She has, needless to say, no clue as to *my* whereabouts. If I'm at the ballpark her calls go to the answering machine, and, otherwise on my person at all times, and immediately after I park the car, I stash my business cards in the glove box.

I'm no kind of athlete; I never was, and for sure no fan of cheering crowds, and loud-talking hawkers hauling shoulder trays of chilidogs, pretzels, peanuts and cold beer. It could be that I attend solely to watch the miracle of small children career the base paths between innings. Their shouts are like songs whenever I'm able to silence those tremulous organ notes exploding from the stadium speakers, the outfielders orphaned in that endless green sea of outgoing tide. I'd never admit it outright, but I don't give a rat's patootie whether the home team loses or wins. Or, as my old man would no doubt translate from the grave, "Who gives a fiddler's fuck anymore about baseball? Or about any other goddamn thing."

He who either purchased or pilfered for me my first mitt and then paced thirty feet across our backyard absent any turf and side-armed pitches so hard and fast they caused my right palm to blister and bleed. Lizzie would have a field day speculating about why it calms me to fill

251

out the scorecard: the logic of its digits and codes, the early season attendance so slight that foul balls thwack and rattle against the seat backs in row after empty row. She'd prod and encourage me to open up, get out in front of whatever it is, be more forthcoming.

About what, I'd like to know. That I've witnessed games called not because of rain or fog or lousy franchising, but rather because some nights the neon scoreboard looms like a square pink and yellow moon that freezes the batters in mid-swing? Freezes something in me, my old man demonstrating not a headfirst slide beside the foul-smelling diamond-cut square of old carpeting, and the junked-out television set, but there he is, passed out and it's not even noon. And my mom, running towards us from the house, fingers flicking as if to shoo me away, and shouting, "Leave him alone, Lloyd. He's just short on sleep is all, you know how he gets, no harm done," always the automatic reset to these same lies, and cover-ups, and guaranteeing us no chance whatsoever to believe, then or ever, in a safe and happier outcome.

Beyond belief is what I'd think, but correct her under the circumstances you're as bad as your old man with his unshaved mug half-buried in the dust, his mouth wide open, eyes rolled back into his brain. And yet, on the last day of peewee league tryouts he's there. He's reemerged from somewhere, maybe to bargain his way into my good graces and finally set things right? He calls me sport, tousles my hair because I've made the cut; I'm on the team, though later that same week I whiff three consecutive times, and when I boot an easy two-hopper back to the mound, his face behind the chain-link backstop incandesces like fire in the early twilight already fading away.

Explain even that much, and every potential hazard, every fear casting back to your deepest childhood gets set in motion all over again. How we lose the opener on my error, and then drive those few interminable miles home alone, just him and me. No pep talk about how everyone, even Senior Smoke, occasionally flubs one, but hey, it's only the first game of the season, nerves and whatnot, and besides, the radio's broadcasting a Tigers twin bill. Depending on the score, he works the dial hard, cranking the volume, shutting it down, like an argument that rages and fades because they, too, he says, "for rat-shit sake," are goddamn bums, losers headed nowhere but into the cellar yet again. He says, "Good Christ Almighty in America."

He's flush with lies, tampers with the truth, an imposter of a father, a traitor though I don't dare contradict his whopper about how he's

252

worked damn hard to teach me to throw a cutter, a slow curve. When in fact all he ever actually managed was to describe one time how a serious submariner's knuckles are supposed to come within a single millimeter of scraping the mound with every pitch, and the ball's red seams rising right up under the batter's chin. A warning. A brush-back.

"You hear me?" he said. "You make the batter's box a nightmare, like a trap door straight to hell, and through which every batter passes. Do that you'll mow 'em down one after the other, and maybe even throw a no-hitter. You got the genes, the big hands, long fingers, but you gotta want it worse, Lloyd. Fundamentals first and then some gut and gravel, some fire," and he'd take another pull from the half-gone pint bottle stashed under the seat of our Econoline, and which on certain swaybacked roads listed from side to side like a waterlogged boat, unmoored and drifting, and the high beams so walleyed they made me cross-eyed and dizzy.

But even more so once he parked in our driveway, killed the headlights, but not the engine, and slow-drank himself further into the darkness until Detroit's bullpen blew a cushy four-run ninth inning lead. "Wha'd'ya figure those wheezes get paid to play like that?" he said, while the dashboard clock tick-tick-ticked like a time bomb.

At eleven years old I hadn't a clue what else to do other than follow him silently into the kitchen, where he opened and slammed the drawers, and then, in his messy scrawl, tallied on a paper bag a scattershot of zeroes but no decimals or dollar signs, a spreadsheet for my mom and me, my first hard lesson in simple economics.

"This," he said, "is where we're at. A dipsy-fucking doodle of nothing," and slapped down a couple of worthless scratch tickets on the table. "Go ahead, add 'em up," but of course we made no move, and he said, "That is correct. On a sliding scale, we're ass flat and coming home hard. Spikes high," he said, his eyes unblinking and bloodshot, and leveled on me. "But thrown out once again by a goddamn mile."

Place me at a hit-and-run crime scene and a mere glimpse of those disappearing license plate numerals in my mind's eye will remain forever indelible. Or better yet, scramble numbers from one through one hundred, and, in that exact and random new sequence, I'll recite them back verbatim, given a mere fifteen minutes' lead time.

Lizzie's standing joke, her favorite, is that she fell in love with a supermarket scanner minus the beeps and bar codes. "The price of admission," I say, because it's all in good fun, and no one in this family is

253

ever going to go to bed bruised or hungry, and no church key on a string adorning the rearview like a graduation tassel or rosary. If it's me who loads and unloads the shopping cart I'll tell her to the penny what we owe before the conveyor belt moves a single item along.

"Bet?" I sometimes say straight-faced to the silent, expressionless checkout clerk and bag boys, but they've either witnessed firsthand or heard about this guy already, and by turns they just stare at me like I'm some genius numbers freak or cyborg. Lizzie predicts that as soon as they see our cart loaded up with Gerber's and Huggies there's no limit to how human and ordinary I'll suddenly seem. Just some poor kid's oddball, addle-minded dad, the crow's feet, and hair already gone gray beyond the temples, his necktie loosened for the first time that anyone at Food-Star can recollect.

It's what Lizzie's banking on, a more relaxed, less uptight version of me. She claims that at thirteen months a child can mimic, weeks after the fact, the identical actions it observes. "You should smile more," she says. "You should hug and kiss me, and croon the deep secrets of song, the imprint of a daddy whose heart is tender, and merciful, and calm." She bats her eyelids. "And you should begin by taking out that flipbook of yours and burning every last snapshot of *you* as a kid. Cheese," she says, as if in response to what she occasionally calls my silent, lockjaw version of Munch's *The Scream*.

She has her first contractions three weeks early. We're assured that this is normal, merely tremors of the breasts. It's Saturday, and while she naps, I test the stroller, as I've done at least half a dozen times already, up and down the driveway. I've assembled it step by careful step according to the instruction manual. Fancy silver-spoke wheels; they're more like bicycle tires, lightweight, finely calibrated and balanced for less resistance, and, given that Lizzie's a runner—check out her calves— she says that our child will know the world early on by that rhythmic beat of her mother's feet on the pavement.

I exercise on a treadmill, each tenth of each digital mile accumulating to maintain a desired weight of 168 pounds. That's where I'm holding at this exact moment, down in our basement, listening to the steady sound of my own breathing. Lizzie argues that hyper-walking at 3:00 AM has less to do with staying in shape than driving myself ragged and loony. A liability, as she says, and that I'm making ready for a stroke, or heart attack, a nervous breakdown, but as far as sleep aids and will-

254

power, I've priced them out weeks ago as worthless, and so here I am again, navigating by the odometer's dim red glow.

In inverse ratio to the baby's due date my legs and lungs are marathon tested. In fact, just last night I closed my eyes and envisioned passing through town after small town on the outskirts of nowhere in particular, but always ending up at the exact same playground, benches abandoned, swing seats hanging low and stationary. And where I continued to run in place, the northern lights so bright that the monkey bars, and the slide, and the chrome arms of the seesaw nearly blinded me. Nobody else, naturally, is ever around at this hour, just me stripped to my boxers and sweat-soaked tee shirt, a soon-to-be-father who has never fed, or burped, or even turned on a sprinkler for the neighborhood kids. Anxiety attacks is Lizzie's take, the result, she speculates, of following that same long out-of-date mental map back into my past, refusing to ignore or let it go, a hypothesis with which I do not disagree, and why I always end up right here, smack-dab in our own house, frightened and disoriented, and so entirely alone.

Yes, I've opened that door, owned up to her that as a kid I believed Chicago was a *state* close by, not a city, and where my old man promised we'd someday visit but of course never did. "No worries. No hurry," he'd say, and that he'd make it up to me. "Sooner or later we'll get even, mark my words," though it sounded more like a threat or vendetta than a plan. Like maybe he'd lost a couple quarters to the cigarette vending machine and figured to bust the whole damn thing wide open with a tire iron or Louisville Slugger. Make off with a little silver, but either way, "We'll get there, you'll see," he said, "all in good time," though each next day arrived and left without us ever once climbing into the van and going anywhere the slightest bit fun as a threesome.

One night after he'd vanished again, I heard what I took to be a long-delayed oncoming train's distant whistle, and, on all fours, made my slow way to the open, upstairs bedroom window, and where I waited and waited, chin on the sill until the low clouds parted, and the rain stopped, and there, standing directly below me in that sudden glint of moonlight, was my mom, soaked and stoop-shouldered, and hugging herself, her silhouette stock-still, and those unmistakable notes of someone crying, and crying, not unlike me, the last two stranded passengers of the night.

"Lloyd," Lizzie says, sounding winded, and far away. "Do you have any idea what time it is? How long you've been down here? Please, stop beating yourself up and come to bed."

I nod, and slow the pace but when I squint in her direction, she's merely a blur in her white nightgown, a disembodied voice, a ghost or vision lifted by the breeze through the slider screen, and carried away.

She's born Catherine Carroll Quigley, middle-named for her grandparents on Lizzie's side, and who live in Milwaukee. I've met them only one time. Likeable souls if first impressions hold, cheery, Old World Irish minus the accent. Although they've yet to see the baby, Lizzie's provided them with snapshots, along with all the pertinent information: Weight: 7 pounds, 2 ounces. Length: 20.28 inches. Time of birth: the dusk low-hanging and turning to night. I watched her arrival, and when I whispered her name I was the first to speak it, our daughter with her father's dark hair, her mother's puffed-out cheeks, as if already huffing her own slow and determined way into the universe.

I'm just minutes home after a seemingly endless workday, and have entered the house quietly, on tiptoes, past the swivel lounger where Lizzie often cradles, and hums, and nurses our daughter. I continue into her bedroom, and turn on no lights, the full moon through the window so enormous and bright that I gather her, wide awake, from her crib and carry her outside to the back deck. We sit on the top step, her back on my lap, head resting in the slight depression between my knees, her face illuminated, eyes open and staring right at me. She turns seven weeks old tomorrow, and this typical, ordinary late August shows no signs of fall except for the sudden briefness of the days, and the tips of the spruce trees glossed silver, as if with frost.

Soon enough the leaves will go, later the snow, her first winter, her first few steps sometime next spring? But for right now she raises both tiny hands, fingers dancing in all directions, as if evenly divided on where to wave, or to whom, though other than the crickets and the fireflies, and the quickly disappearing arc of those few shooting stars, it's just the two us, and I whisper, "Hi." And touch my index fingertip to thumb, and fit it around my eye like a monocle, or viewfinder, and lean in close, and wink. She smiles, kicks her booted feet, and then tips her head, ever so slightly, toward the continuous whirl of the sky, this night, this imprint, this longing that is ours.

SQUALLS

"We're just plain bad for each other, Archie," Z says, cutting, character-istically, straight to the point. Still, she *has* consented to this drive—"One hour," she says. "Tops." After all, what's left to say that can possibly take any longer than that? Probably nothing. Nonetheless the Caddy is full of high test, the minutes already fleeting and, by her own reluctant admission, she concedes again to that unmistakable, deep-seated some-thing we just can't resist about each other.

I've owned this land yacht, a ruby-red 1975 convertible, for longer than I've known Z. Power seats and electric eye on the dashboard, and a trunk the size of a pickup bed. A take-charge Coupe DeVille that I lucked into with a ridiculously lowball estate sale bid.

We're here on good tread, the snow slashing so hard into the head-lights that we're momentarily blinded and staring dizzy-eyed into the tunnel between these fields of last year's standing corn. But this is not a storm we're cruising through; these are Michigan lake-effect squalls that slow us, sometimes to a crawl. But once they open up, the road is slick-black and entirely inviting, my arm around Z like old times, the world wildly alive again, and the radio loud.

"Archie," she says, turning the volume down a few decibels. "We've been down this road how many times before? And to what end?" When I don't respond she says, "You do realize, don't you, how hopeless this is? How completely insane?"

I can tell she's softening, making this the most delicate moment of the drive so far—one wrong utterance and it's over, and no doubt for good. Still, I launch into this spiel about real caring and trust over the long haul. I argue that on a sliding scale maybe we've slid as far as we're going to into that marital dead zone all couples fear, and from now on the momentum's thrust will be up, up and away. It's the kind of testimonial you can only ever deliver straight-faced to someone you honest to God love, and actually mean it. Impassioned assertions that do not, however, as I've discovered firsthand, bear up well against the lessons of either logic or experience.

Z's an artist, a master glassblower with a degree from RISD, and I remind her how often she's argued her theory that anything can be transformed by art and love. Absolutely anything.

"This marriage?" I ask, flicking the wipers off again as we finally exit another squall. But this one's different, dissolving so slowly at the thin, opalescent blue rim of first light that it feels mystic. And I get serious chills when a swan emerges from that same dense snow behind us, with its wings outspread not three feet above the wet and shiny hood. It's that close, and Z whispers, "Archie," and I hit the brakes hard. On black ice as it turns out, and we're spinning now into a series of 360s, the top-heavy front end of the Caddy hesitating just long enough at the apex of each wide swoop for us to glimpse the torture of that enormous white bird's interminable somersaulting on the pavement.

We come to a stop in an empty field, the engine stalled. Z is holding my hand, squeezing it, and the radio is suddenly all static, like the snow, and Z is humming some made-up song. Just staring out the tinted windshield and humming, like she's been stunned. I can tell already that one of the swan's wings is broken, and one eye is completely shut, and the wind keeps lifting its neck feathers.

I don't want to move a muscle, but the gasoline fumes are strong and I'm afraid the car might blow, so I switch the ignition off. And maybe it's the tinkling of the keys on the key ring—I'm not sure—but Z lets go of my hand and leans forward and takes off her navy peacoat and says, "Here." She says, "Please, Archie. You've got to go help it. You've got to."

What's most humane in this situation would be to put the swan out of its misery as quickly as possible, and by whatever available means. But try explaining that to the woman you've loved and are losing and so desperately want back in your life.

"Look, there's an inch of ice on its wings," I say, though I'm not sure how that matters exactly, except perhaps to solve the mystery of this terrible accident we've just witnessed.

"Go get it, Archie," she pleads, and she starts to cry because the swan is staring back at us with its one good eye, from me to Z, back and forth like that.

"You don't just walk up on wounded things," I say with absolute certainty. "Not on wild things, Z. Listen, I don't even have any gloves with me," which sounds like the chintziest and most insensitive and cowardly excuse in all God's creation. "Listen to me," I say, but she doesn't. Instead she lowers her face deeper into her hands and I notice, really for the first time when I touch her hair, the first hints of gray, and how, unlike me, she's not wearing her wedding band. Which frightens me so much I get out of the car and breathe deeply into the cold air to try and clear my aching head.

And it begins to snow again. Enormous feathery flakes floating down slow motion and so thick that when I wrap Z's coat around the swan and pick it up against my chest, I know she can only imagine in what direction I've gone, where it is I've bolted to under pressure this time. The only reason I don't call out to her, like someone lost and panicked, is that this bird has actually leaned its face against mine, and seems to be asleep.

Even more so when I lay the swan in the back seat, collar up, those black anchor buttons fastened like a line of poker chips down the center of its breast. It would be comical if it weren't so damn sad.

Z says, "Archie, look," and I do, this time in the rearview mirror, and what I see is that orange bill opening and closing as though it were trying to speak. Because I can't get the car started there is nothing we can do. The plumes of pink sulfur from the emergency flare I've already lit are visible on the road's shoulder. But no one is driving this far outside of town on a Sunday morning. I imagine parishioners attending early Mass, and lighting candles at the feet of St. Francis, birds perched on his fingers in the Church of the Sacred Heart where Z and I were married in a tiny private ceremony.

Z, now huddled under the blanket I stash in case of winter breakdowns, asks, "Is it really true that swans mate for life?"

I nod, close my eyes, and wonder if the other is up there circling and circling, and then crack the window and listen for that unmistakable slow whistle of its wings. I hear nothing, and I realize that it's not in me right now to confront the loss that sound would mean.

Z says she needs to say a couple of things, which she worries might seems foolish, but I tell her no, that nothing could with such a beautiful creature dying so close to us. She has no idea how soothing the music of her voice is. No earthly idea.

"We go way back, don't we, Archie? she says, and I nod, her head on my shoulder, her right arm draped over the seat back where I know her fingers are fluttering slow, final dances for the swan. Then Z asks if I remember *Swan Lake*, which of course I do, the only ballet I ever attended.

"Yes," I say, "every last detail," the tight black strapless satin dress she wore and the way the camera shutter seemed to stop in mid-click, and that handful of white rose petals she threw toward me, laughing on those mammoth granite stairs outside the theater. And how she flapped her arms as though *she* might rise and fly, a raven, I thought back then, or a crow, or yes, a rare and elegant black swan.

"Archie," she says again, "don't you wish sometimes that we could retrieve the best parts of our past—just those—and hold onto them forever?" I swear to her that we can, which I know is a lie. "No," she says. "It's over. This time it has to end. This time for good."

"I know that," I tell her, and although true or not true, I want to believe that nothing ever really dies. But Z is already reaching for the swan, and crying again, as there must always be a first to cry out among the great flocks that take off by the thousands to migrate home. And then pair off, and because the world is sometimes like this, one must go on alone.